P9-BJK-589

BOOKS BY BRIGID BROPHY

FICTION:

PALACE WITHOUT CHAIRS   (1978)
THE ADVENTURES OF GOD IN HIS SEARCH FOR THE BLACK GIRL   (1974)
IN TRANSIT   (1970)
THE FINISHING TOUCH *AND* THE SNOW BALL   (1964)
FLESH   (1963)
THE KING OF A RAINY COUNTRY   (1957)
HACKENFELLER'S APE   (1953)

DRAMA:

THE BURGLAR   (1968)

NON-FICTION:

BEARDSLEY AND HIS WORLD   (1976)
PRANCING NOVELIST   (1973)
BLACK AND WHITE: A PORTRAIT OF AUBREY BEARDSLEY   (1970)
LITERATURE WE COULD DO WITHOUT   (1968)
DON'T NEVER FORGET   (1967)
MOZART THE DRAMATIST   (1964)
BLACK SHIP TO HELL   (1962)

PALACE
WITHOUT CHAIRS

Brigid Brophy

———

PALACE

WITHOUT

CHAIRS

Atheneum

NEW YORK

1978

Library of Congress Cataloging in Publication Data

Brophy, Brigid, 1929-
    Palace without chairs.
    I. Title.
PZ4.B8735Pl   1978   [PR6052.R583]   823'.9'14   77-18387
ISBN 0-689-10883-4

Copyright © 1978 by Brigid Brophy
All rights reserved
Manufactured by Halliday Lithograph Corporation
West Hanover and Plympton, Massachusetts
First American Edition

TO MICHAEL FOOT

Indeed, although chairs do appear in
Velazquez's pictures, one gets a sense
of a palace rather short of chairs, even
if protocol had allowed sitting in them.
Michael Levey: Painting at
Court, p. 140

Thus, regardless of real rank, all the
children he painted became princes and
princesses.
Michael Levey (of Van Dyck)
in essay on Gainsborough's
The Painter's Daughters
Chasing a Butterfly

Winter Palace

Chapter One

His Royal and Religious Highness Crown Prince Ulrich of
Evarchia returned to the Winter Palace unrepentant.

He was following the route by which, according to tradition
and topographical probability, his great-uncle by several gen-
erations removed, Archduke Rupert 'the Blue', had brought
home the news of the victory of Burgos. Thanks to a failure of
twentieth-century machines, he was also using his ancestor's
method of transport.

The Blue Archduke always arrived, in Ulrich's imagination, in a flight of upturned cloak and hooves borne on an
upthrust of baroque horse-buttock. Of his own non-glorious
arrival (he assumed it would eventually be clinched as an arrival) Ulrich's imagination could make nothing. He was merely
enduring it.

His mount, a black mare dappled white, was no more than
serviceable. But then Ulrich was a no more than serviceable
rider. 'He remains', Ulrich had heard his father pronounce,
after he had at length worked the eleven-year-old Ulrich to the
point of putting his pony at a miniature fence, 'the most ped-
estrian equestrian I've ever seen.'

Luckily the mare was, except about making haste, obliging.
Ulrich had met horses who, as soon as they were deprived of
company, began inventing fantasies and taking fright at
them. This one made no fuss about the lonely and (to them
both) unfamiliar journey Ulrich was taking her on. Though

3

she must have been aware of it, she didn't pick up by contagion Ulrich's own anxiety, which was sharpened by the loneliness of the route: with not a building in view, he could frame not a hope of telephoning to his brothers the message that he was, though at the pace set by the mare, returning.

The broad, flat path they took, along which Ulrich could read for miles ahead the information that he was not yet within sight of town, was known as 'the Roman Wall'. It was raised barely a hand's span above the empty land it crossed. Seeing it now for the first time (photographs apart), Ulrich could believe it the site of a wall, but he could not construe it as the material remains of one—unless it was hordes of barbarian dwarfs that the Romans had been walling out from that part of Dacia or Thracia or whichever Latin term it was that had included what were now the eastern provinces of Evarchia. And were that so, Ulrich's thoughts added, some indigenous extra-mural strain must have mixed with the blood royal and thus accounted for his own stature, which only just rose to meet the requirements of 'average adult male' and did not meet his, Ulrich's, requirements at all.

From time to time the passage of Ulrich and the mare put up surprisingly large and loud-flapping birds from the naked hedge that bordered some stretches of the path. The mare continued unstartled. Her craftsmanlike paces did not falter even when she took one of them onto a just gelid puddle and its surface snapped and gave beneath her.

Since she required very few physical actions from him, Ulrich was a passive victim to the cold. It attacked, in particular, his knees, which he felt become haggard beneath his jeans. No more could he dodge or combat anxiety. Riding the mare demanded nothing of his concentration beyond that he remember to keep hold of the reins.

He had already noticed a constitutional change in his consciousness. The telegram from his brothers had ended an obsession which his consciousness had grown used to carrying and even content to carry. It put a sudden, simple STOP, like

4

its own international, spelt-out punctuation, to the play of voluptuous and affectionate thoughts with which, for weeks past, Ulrich's mind had been caressing the idea of Clara.

Squeezing the mare's sides with his thighs, he tried to start up the thoughts again, particularly the voluptuous ones, to serve him as a talisman against misery and the cold. Obediently, the images rehearsed. But the true and quite unwilled trend of Ulrich's fantasy went speeding out in advance along the road, there to pull up short, balking, as the child Ulrich (not his pony) had balked, at the unencompassable.

'No child of mine shall be afraid.' His father had distinguished each word in oral italics and, prodigal of his royal time and concentration, had set Ulrich to yet another circuit of the Royal Riding School.

'I can't, I *can't*', Ulrich had said, hiccoughing with sobs. Then, making his first attempt to argue with his father, he for the first time disclosed a corner of the content of his fear. 'How can I tell if the pony wants to?'

'*He* wants to', the king said dismissively, shutting down the opportunity. 'It's you who prevent him. All he wants is to do what you want. You must make your wishes known to him.'

The telegram seemed also to have stopped the play (or the work) of Ulrich's digestion. His breakfast, taken, admittedly, late that morning, seemed still to be lying between the base of his throat and the top of his breastbone. He could almost distinguish (which was nonsense, since he hadn't swallowed them whole) the palpable and discrete shapes of two brioches.

He acknowledged the brioches as a symptom of fear. Interdicted by his parentage from being afraid, Ulrich in fact and consciously was afraid, though no longer of horses. He considered it an irony that he should be making this journey home, of all journeys home, on horseback.

Yet through his fear, and through the disorientation his consciousness experienced on finding its centre shifted and its slow-grown obsession vanished, Ulrich was uninterrupted in his conviction that he had been right to go. Or at the least, he scrupulously amended his thoughts, he had had a right to go.

'You must do as you think right.' The worst, therefore, that Ulrich had done was take the king at his word. And had not the king brought up all his children on the maxim 'A prince's word is his bond'?

The grounds—or at least the stated grounds—of the king's objection changed too quickly and often for Ulrich to chronicle, let alone to counter. There was a point when it seemed implied that the obstacle was Advent. Ulrich conceived the reply that, as an unbeliever, he could not in conscience be bound to the revolutions of the liturgical year, a metaphor through which he perhaps figured himself as a martyr on the wheel. He inhibited that reply. Instead, more cleverly, he thought, he asked what article of state, church or concordat between them required the heir to the throne to reside at the Winter Palace throughout Advent. Advent vanished. No allusion in any discussion thereafter so much as hinted it had once been an object of consideration. Ulrich's immediate enquiry was replied to ('None, that I know of') as an irrelevance introduced by Ulrich ('Do *you* know of one, then?').

At the midnight before Ulrich's departure, the king appeared reconciled. Ulrich was summoned (in the king's language, asked, if he was not busy or asleep, if he would spare a moment for a word). His parents were in the Private Drawing Room. His mother was standing, looking, most of the time, into a tapestry forest more blue than green and populated by unclassifiable birds. His father sat: in a wing chair, a domesticated throne. He was wearing the scratchy-haired dressing gown Ulrich hated, and on his lap, beneath a tartan blanket, he cuddled a hot water bottle. 'Nothing. A very slight chill. It will be gone tomorrow—as will you, Ulrich. I felt I couldn't bear you to go with unkind thoughts between us.'

Ulrich had kissed his father's cheek and been surprised, not for the first time, that his father's beard, which looked so much more, was in fact so much less scratchy than the

6

dressing gown. And in token of his blessing his father had flourished a touch of that cold flirtatiousness which persuaded Ulrich that his father was (except, Ulrich had to presume, in relation to his mother) numb to sexuality. 'Make', he said in English, which he regularly claimed to be the language of gallantry (with the implications, both of which Ulrich suspected of being false, that he applauded gallantry and was himself expert in it), 'my regards to the fair Countess Clara.'

Though she uttered nothing, Ulrich's thoughts heard the queen's thoughts correct the 'make' to 'give'.

His father's hot water bottle, in its secret place, gurgled.

Ulrich was therefore bearing home to the Palace a sense of justification. He held it bold and upright in his consciousness as though he was carrying a banner as he rode. What sustained him was perhaps a proper pride, in which case the ironical likelihood was that it had been begotten (or, more probably, in-drilled in the Royal Riding School) by his father. Or perhaps it was the self-flattering obstinacy of a person without self-respect. Ulrich never knew whether the royal riding schooling of his childhood had made him or broken his spirit.

He did know that, even if he was truly (as well as believing himself to be) right, it was he who had put himself in danger of appearing truculent. Perhaps it was disingenuous of him to fight on the stated grounds, rather than force the true ones to appear. Yet it was his father who chose to do the stating. Why did the reproach of disingenuousness not fall on him?

The winter luminosity withdrew from the afternoon. The sky, of which a great deal was to be seen from the Roman Wall, became packed with a pale, thick yellow, a faint shade of the clayey colour of the puddles beneath their ice.

Ulrich decided the mare would surely not get him home before the early dark came down.

He hoped his siblings were not interpreting the absence of a message from him as the message that Ulrich was standing truculently on his rights and would not return.

How patiently, he reflected, people in history, up to the time of technology, must have waited for outcomes. The parents and lovers of all the soldiers must have trained themselves to work and dance on meanwhile, as though nothing were in suspense, as though the battle *had* no real outcome until an archduke galloped into town.

Ulrich felt ignorant of death. He could scarcely wonder, as his impulse suggested, what a dying person was supposed to *do*, since people died, he assumed, for the most part, involuntarily. But how could Ulrich's imagination pursue his father's imagination over the rim of its own extinction?

'You must commit yourself, let go, go with it, make up your mind to having passed the point where it was possible to change your mind.' Thus his father in the Royal Riding School; fatigued, impatient, shivering but perseverant. '*You* must do it, Ulrich. I can't do it for you.'

And I can't die for you, Ulrich's thoughts answered back a decade and a half later. It seemed that his pleasurable obsession with Clara had merely been chased out by this displeasurable one and that he must now, if he was not to go wastefully mad, break the adhesion of his consciousness to his father's, since his father's was about to vanish.

He was ignorant, equally, of what might be expected of *him*. People died, in history, in other people's arms: was that one of the duties of the eldest son? (But Ulrich had always been an egalitarian among siblings, insisting not at all on the privileges of the first born.) Or would his mother expect the arms to be hers? Or would she, even from the king's deathbed, have absented her mind?

In a cautious glide that could, at any moment of need, turn into a grip, Ulrich slid his right hand over the mare's shoulder. He was wearing string gloves which, like the mare herself, he had borrowed from the Countess Clara. They were too small for him, though only just too small, and there was a brief raw gap at his wrist.

Whether to thank, comfort or encourage her, he massaged

8

the trim, square top of the mare's chest, as though it were she who was carrying there the indigestible burden of two fantasy brioches.

The brioches signified, he supposed, in addition of course to Clara's breasts (an observation his thoughts threw in in a scholastic tone, without corroboration from his nerves), the two outcomes, the only two possible outcomes, of his ride, both to be dreaded alike: that he would arrive too late, and that he would arrive in time.

*   *   *

In his office in the Winter Palace the High Chamberlain said very loudly:

'The Roman Wall? Alone?'

He had raised his voice from the moment that he understood his interlocutor to be telephoning from Ketsch.

Not that the High Chamberlain entertained the pre-technological fallacy that, if you were speaking over a long distance, you had to shout into the machine. And in fact Ketsch was not a very long distance from Asty. He had unconsciously invented a technological fallacy of his own, according to which electrical impulses were conducted via density of human population. He shouted because he knew Ketsch to be a very small village surrounded by virtually unpopulated country, the sort of place where you would expect communications to be poor.

'The resources of the Countess's stables are limited to one horse', the detective replied.

'What?' the High Chamberlain said, temporarily deafened by the loudness of his own voice.

'I was not in a position to accompany his Highness in the course of his journey in view of the fact that the Countess is in possession of only one horse and it is not of sufficient size to accommodate two riders.'

'O. No. I suppose it wouldn't be. Well, where is he now? The

9

Prince, I mean.'

'Has he not yet arrived at his destination?'

'No, he hasn't. Why is all this taking so long?'

'The Castle is somewhat remote. An additional factor is that the Countess has not yet been successful in her application for the installation of a telephone. Due to this, the boy responsible for the delivery of telegrams found himself under the necessity of conveying the telegram to the Castle by bicycle. A further additional factor is that, on the arrival of the telegram, the Castle was unoccupied.'

'The clerk assured me it would be delivered first thing in the morning.'

'That expectation was fulfilled. However, prior to breakfast this morning, all the occupants of the Castle, including myself and the housekeeper, took part in an expedition to collect edible fungi. There was in consequence some time-lag before his Highness had sight of the telegram. I was not in a position to acknowledge receipt of the telegram, owing to the non-connexion of the Castle to the telephonic system. After his Highness commenced his journey on horseback, I effected repairs to the cars and then, by means of his Highness's car, made my way to Ketsch, the nearest point connected to the telephonic system, from which I am now reporting.'

'Cars?' the High Chamberlain queried. 'Did you say you mended cars? "Cars" in the plural?'

'I refer to his Highness's car and to the Countess's car.'

'They *both* broke down?'

'His Highness's car proved not to be in a viable condition. Prior to borrowing the Countess's horse, his Highness attempted to borrow the Countess's car, but the starter mechanism failed to operate.'

'Good God', the High Chamberlain said. 'Do you suppose it's sabotage?'

'No.'

'Why not?'

'It never crossed my mind.'

10

'Well it should have done. The remarkable coincidence of *two* cars breaking down—'

'With respect', said the detective.

'What?'

'According to information given me by the Countess, her car fails to start relatively frequently. Having carried out an inspection of the car in question, whilst effecting temporary repairs, I can confirm that that would indeed seem to be the probable situation. In the course of an oral account which the Countess gave me of her car, she alluded to it as a clapped-out old banger. She made use of the English words.'

'But there's also the Prince's car', the High Chamberlain objected, 'which is not a clapped-out old banger. I get regular servicing reports from the Royal Garages.' With his free hand the High Chamberlain reached, not with intent but as a gesture for himself, towards a pile of blue cardboard folders.

'With respect', the detective's voice said again. 'In recent weeks, in the course of a number of private and unofficial meetings with the Countess, his Highness has adopted the habit of driving his car himself. I formed the opinion that it was only a question of time before some mechanical defect made itself apparent.'

'I don't follow your line of reasoning.'

'Not to put too fine a point on it, and speaking entirely personally and off the record, his Highness is somewhat over-impulsive on the clutch.'

'O well then. If he brought it on himself I suppose it's all right', the High Chamberlain said. 'When do you suppose he'll get here?'

'I should estimate relatively soon. As I observed previously, I would have anticipated that he would have already arrived. However, I formed the impression that it was not a very fast horse.'

'Well, you'd better get back yourself. When you do, take his car to the Royal Garages and tell them I want it thoroughly overhauled. He won't be needing it for the next few days.'

11

As he put down the receiver the High Chamberlain rose, with the intention of going to report to the Family. After a moment he sat down again at his desk. He had already found it hard and embarrassing to get in touch with the Family while they were all clustered in the sickroom. There was no proper channel of communication. If the matter was prolonged, the High Chamberlain would create one. In the meantime he had to lurk outside, mistakable for an eavesdropper, and try to make a messenger of the first, and always hurried, medical attendant who came or went.

He decided that, although it might calm some Family anxiety to know that Ulrich was on his way, it would introduce a new and worse anxiety for them to know that his way was along the Roman Wall without the company of his detective.

Beyond that, the High Chamberlain perceived a yet graver anxiety impend. In principle, he was always happy to submit any of the staff appointments he had made to scrutiny. Yet he would deprecate an enquiry into the detective's competence at this particular time: the enquiry could almost certainly not be kept wholly private, and the particular time had, inevitably, a high potential for political instability.

The High Chamberlain's duties included being non-political. Indeed, he found it the easiest of all his duties to discharge, since he never understood what people found in politics to interest them. However, his tactical non-partisanship did not absolve him of the responsibility of making a grand strategic appreciation.

Briefly the High Chamberlain wondered whether his reticence was doomed: by Ulrich. If the facts were bound to come out anyway, then it would be better for the High Chamberlain to disclose them at once. However, when he tried to predict Ulrich's behaviour on reaching home (provided that he did reach home), the High Chamberlain concluded that Ulrich would, in the circumstances, have small social opportunity to chat to his Family about his adventures and that, in any case, it would be in Ulrich's own interest to minimise

12

their adventurousness.

Confidently resting the success of his policy on Ulrich's calculation of where his interest lay, the High Chamberlain swivelled his chair to the left and switched on his radio. He was in good time for the four-thirty bulletin on the king's health. He had written it himself. He liked hearing his sentences read aloud.

*   *   *

Ulrich rode into Asty through the eastern outskirts, a district he knew only sketchily and could now see only sketchily, because it was already dark and the globular street lamps, though alight, were sparse.

His dread of arriving retreated for a minute while his thoughts justifiably concentrated on working out that the road he was riding along must be the unfamiliar extremity of the Grand Boulevard, which virtually bisected the city, and that if he continued along it he must surely come to its junction with the Ring Boulevard.

For the moment the Grand Boulevard was unexpectedly taking him between rows of warehouses or small factories. The roadway stretched, flat, right up to their façades, presumably giving easy access to lorries. But no lorries were using it, and the buildings looked shut up if not positively closed down.

All Ulrich encountered was a scattering of peasants who, obeying the timetable of natural light even in their urban business, were walking or, more often cycling, out of the city.

Many had hung bunches of coloured ribbons from their handle-bars. But for themselves they wore caricatures (old-fashioned, double-breasted, unpressed) of the sombre suits of clerks. They rode, physically fatigued, in a slow wobble and their knees stuck out because they put their heels, not the ball of the foot, on the pedals.

The lamps became more frequent, confirming Ulrich's estimate of where he was. As the mare passed beneath each of them, the dappled contrast of her colouring was thrown into

13

vividness. She was a version in negative of the rocking horse that had stood or, strictly, had balanced (on two wooden half moons, like the Madonna in an Immaculate Conception) in the Royal Day Nursery—that, indeed, still balanced there, in the embrasure of a window, but minus, now, several of its dapples, which had been spurred off its flanks by the later born children. The window looked down on the courtyard of the Royal Riding School. Ulrich had often, rocking gently in side-saddle position on the rocking horse, watched his later born siblings overtake him in prowess with real horses as effortlessly as even the latest born began to overtake him in height.

In compensation, Ulrich became a virtuoso of the rocking horse. Not side-saddle now but hunched with the urgency of a jockey, he would work the horse into a frenzy of rocking, like an aeroplane revving up; then, without taking his feet from the stirrups, he would, by a technique of his own discovering which none of the other children ever mastered, cause the rocking horse to move, to make ground, consistently and quite swiftly, across the floor.

It was with the surprising tactfulness of children that the others invited the king to visit the nursery to witness Ulrich's feat. The king, too, no doubt meant to exercise tact—and also psychological acumen. He arrived visibly resolved to applaud. Ulrich was in fact only working through the preliminaries, and the rocking horse, though tilting violently, had not yet moved from the spot, when the king's hands burst into loud, agitated clapping and he cried noisily through his beard: 'Bravo, bravo! Well done, little Ulrich!'

That he eventually stopped being 'little Ulrich' in his father's vocabulary Ulrich believed he owed to some private and, probably, almost wordless intervention by the queen. But the epithet was not banished until Ulrich was eleven or twelve, by which time he looked, when the royal children assembled together, like a crocus among tulips.

The Grand Boulevard acquired pavements and, presently,

14

people on them.

Now his return was feasible, Ulrich felt less sure of his right to have absented himself. Or, rather, though he still felt justified, he saw, now that the circumstances of his return could be realistically conceived, that they would very likely never include an opportunity for him to justify himself.

Sedately the mare paced the gutter. She was perturbed neither by the cars that swished and sometimes hooted at her left nor by the pedestrians who, brisk in the cold, shouldered past her right shoulder.

It was Ulrich who felt confused in the sudden press of town—and who must look, he thought, like the centre of an episode, perhaps a desperate one, in a battle painting. There streamed past his waist svelte winter coats, buttoned militaristically to the neck and beyond, raincoats fashionably spun from by-products of petrol, whose light colours indeed gleamed, in the lamp light, like petrol on water, briefcases hugged beneath armpits as though they contained urgent dispatches. Furled umbrellas, held low in the same hands as handbags, pushed past his thighs like lances. Trimly boxed, then prettily papered and at last glitteringly but efficiently strung, a purchase from a confectioner's shop dangled for an instant alongside his instep, a ceremonial spur.

Ulrich now more or less recognised the neighbourhood, where he had once placed a wreath on a civic monument. He rode past a café, shuttered but with light leaking, from which he could probably have telephoned. He decided not to waste time on a message now that he was so nearly home himself. Almost instantly his orientation was confirmed. He saw ahead, swooping from the right towards the road he was on, a great curve of bare chestnut trees in shadowy silhouette, which must denote the Ring Boulevard; and indeed, as the road widened, in front of the mare's advance, into a multiple junction, he saw the curve repeated on the ground by tram lines.

As Ulrich approached, so, from the right, did a tram: two

15

canary-yellow, single-storey cars hitched together. The warm light inside illuminated the comfortable press of passengers, some of whom were reading the evening newspapers that were proffered on hinged racks (the headlines reporting, no doubt, on the king's illness); spilt from the windows it lit up the planks slotted into the tram's outer sides (they carried, in chocolate-coloured letters, advertisements for brands of chocolate now obsolete) and trickled down onto the road to glitter in the forming frost.

Ulrich was aware of a faint, momentary recession in the noisiness of the street, as though all the sources of noise had moved a yard further off. Snow began to drop.

Inflexible, the front of the leading tramcar bore down in a straight line towards the pavement. Ulrich watched, recovering a childhood delight in the inevitable avoidance of seemingly inevitable disaster, as the wheels at last found the point where the rails went into the sharpness of the curve. High above, the soft sucker that attached the cable to the overhead wire loosed a spark into the night. The tramcar tilted and then rattled and lurched as it obeyed its route, meanwhile sounding its bell against a cyclist grooved in the rail ahead of it.

The mare flattened her ears and kicked out with her hind feet, and for the first time Ulrich heard her voice.

For several seconds he was in danger of falling off. For a longer space, during the execution of sideways prances more elaborate than any of the steps rehearsed at the Royal Riding School, he was out of control of the animal.

Passers-by watched but continued passing by, their illuminated faces unalarmed. None moved to reach a hand up to the bridle. No doubt they were unfamiliar with horses and felt a perfect confidence that nobody would be abroad on one unless he was competent to control it.

When he did re-establish control of a sort, Ulrich used it to turn the mare down the nearest road on the right. It proved ill-lit and unfrequented and seemed to head obliquely away from the Ring Boulevard.

As soon as he dared lift a hand from the reins he soothed the mare, marvelling that she could plod unafraid through the eeriness of the Roman Wall and yet be fantasist enough to take fright at a tramcar.

With only the most general sense of his whereabouts, he tried to calculate a route that would bring him to the Palace by way entirely of back streets, without risk of trams. He realised he was going to arrive even later than he need have done and that the blame lay ironically with his incompetence as a horseman.

A snowflake landed on the mare's head and for a second, before it melted into her steaming body's heat, lent her an extra dapple.

*   *   *

In the Ministerium (which was in the Ring Boulevard, several doors along from its junction with the Grand Boulevard) for Parks, Ponds, Public Monuments and Culture, the Permanent Personal Private Assistant to the Minister finished with the eighth of the points he had jotted down to mention to the Minister and, having got permission to have the central heating in the Ministerium turned up, went on to the ninth.

'One doesn't want to be gloomy, but I gather from the radio bulletins that things are pretty serious. We must be realistic, Minister.'

The Minister thought he heard in the words and, still more, in the tone of his PPPA a conventional note of the funereal. The PPPA couldn't possibly feel grieved, so the Minister assumed the note was addressed to him and indicated that his PPPA took him for a sentimentalist, a royalist and a fool.

With deliberate roughness, therefore, the Minister said:

'Have we got anything on the new chap? The next one in line, I mean. What's his name? You know the one I mean, the dapper little man.'

Fairly certain that the Minister could in fact perfectly

remember the Crown Prince's name, the PPPA replied:

'I don't know. I'll find out.'

He pushed down the key on the buzz-box on the Minister's desk and said into the grille:

'Have we a file on Crown Prince Ulrich, please?'

As he pronounced the name, his gaze fixed on the Minister. The Minister turned his back.

To it, the PPPA said:

'There is one. They'll bring it.' In fact, the buzz-box's answer had been audible throughout the room.

Still facing the wall, the Minister asked abruptly:

'Who does state funerals?'

'The Interior, I think', the PPPA replied. 'Probably in liaison with the High Chamberlain. O, and, I suppose, with the church.'

'Huh', the Minister said enigmatically. 'Anyway, not us.'

Consenting to shew his face again, the Minister turned round and arranged himself in a waiting position, half sitting and half leaning on the side of his desk.

'If', the PPPA said thoughtfully, 'a memorial was erected, in a public place, the upkeep would eventually come to us—under Monuments.'

There was a knock. A voice and a hand but scarcely a presence briefly entered the room. 'The file for the Minister.'

The PPPA accepted the folder and proffered it to the Minister.

The Minister rather crossly nodded it back. 'Give me the gist of it.'

The PPPA opened the folder and thoroughly read the single sheet of paper it contained.

'Well?'

'It's curious', the PPPA said. He read aloud. 'Likes: coffee cake, fireworks even if noisy, music, jewellery, dogs, cats, asparagus. Dislikes: jelly, marshmallow, balloons (in case they burst), horses.'

'What do you make of that?' the Minister asked, giving a

challenging grin.

'I think it must be rather out-of-date. I seem to remember hearing we once had him to a children's party in one of our Parks.'

'Before my time', the Minister said quickly, dismissing the subject as though time before his ministry were pre-history.

'Before mine too,' the PPPA said, hoping to point the moral that, if the underling could, the Minister certainly should interest himself in the lore of the Ministerium.

'Well, one thing is clear, at least', the Minister said briskly, with a touch of a triumphant smile. 'Our file needs up-dating.'

'I can but agree with you, Minister.'

'Ask around a bit. Find out what the word is on the young man. Let me have a report.'

'Yes, Minister.'

'While you're about it, you'd better give some thought to getting *all* our files up-dated.'

'Yes, Minister', the PPPA said again. 'That, of course, will be a long-term project.'

'Even a long-term project has to begin in the short term', the Minister said, 'or one could put it off for ever.'

'Quite so,' said the PPPA.

He looked a question at the Minister, who looked back with a blankness that indicated he had no more business in mind to transact.

The PPPA left the room vindictively.

The Minister shifted himself more comfortably onto the top of his desk and went into a fantasy. The new king, an engaging young man, not in the least conceited, recognised his need of guidance. Childhood experience being so influential on later life, he applied, naturally, to the Ministerium that had so royally entertained him when he was (the Minister had to leave a blank for how old the Prince had been at the time). In the present Minister, the new monarch found exactly the mentor he sought, the one man, in a host of flatterers and intriguers, who would give him counsel both honourable and shrewd. It became known—The Minister cancelled that item and substituted: Though not publicly known, it was an open secret in circles political and social that Minister and young monarch entertained towards one another a comradely affection like that of ideal father and ideal son. One spring day, as they walked together in one of the Parks for which the Minister was responsible and Asty was famous, the youthful king diffidently invited the Minister to drop the formalities and address him as 'Ulrich' . . .

*   *   *

'Open up for me, please.'

Ulrich and the mare, both now physically tired, had arrived at the North-East gate.

It was not the gate Ulrich had been aiming for. It was the least used and least convenient of the ways in to the Palace precinct.

The soldier Ulrich spoke to was not the one who responded. Another soldier, who had been standing further off, next to a wooden hut where light glowed and a radio murmured, walked across and stood by the side of Ulrich's saddle.

His head scarcely reached to its level. He was a small man, of Ulrich's own size, but scraggy and untidy and rather older than you would expect of a soldier who had not advanced at all in rank. Between his pulled down hat and his upturned collar Ulrich could make out a pair of thick lips that were at variance with the stringy face and probably denoted something of the Islander in his blood.

'Cold night,' he said. 'See your pass, please?'

'I haven't one.'

'Then we can't let you in.'

All soldiers now wore khaki but Ulrich recognised the little diamond of bright blue cotton, stitched to the upper sleeve of the khaki greatcoat, that was all that was left to the Grenadiers of the blue uniform with silver facings reputedly designed for them by their first patron, the Blue Archduke.

'I think you can, Grenadier. I live here. My name is—' but Ulrich felt reluctant to pronounce his own name aloud. Instead, he said: 'I'm the Crown Prince.'

After a moment the Grenadier asked:

'Have you any means of identification on you?' He shone his sceptical gaze upwards as though it were a torch beam and ran it over Ulrich's jumper and jeans, as if to imply there was nowhere where Ulrich could have stowed a document of identification.

'For the sake of Christ, Saint Barnabas and all the infant angels', Ulrich said. 'I have come home unexpectedly, because my father is badly ill. I've been riding all day. I'm tired, the horse is tired, we're both cold and no one knows that I have at last managed to get here. Will you please go into your hut and telephone the Duty Officer and ask him to come down to the gate at once.'

The Grenadier considered.

'I'll see what I can do', he said, and he walked into the hut.

The second Grenadier stood silent and, apparently, unnoticing.

The mare shifted her feet, grinding the gravel with a noise like the attack of a spoon on coffee sugar. Perhaps she was responding to the impatience in Ulrich's voice.

Ulrich sat there on her back in the snow, feeling nothing, except the cold, thinking of nothing, not even his father

In the space between Ulrich and the light in the hut there was a swirl of snowflakes, making the currents of the wind for a moment visible.

Presently the Grenadier emerged from the hut.

'Is he coming?' Ulrich asked.

'I've done what I can.' The Grenadier strolled towards Ulrich and took up a casual, conversational stance, saddle-high, beside him. 'You could easily be a subversive.'

'I think you have an alarmist imagination', Ulrich said mildly.

21

'No', the Grenadier replied equally mildly, 'but I'm not politically naif, either. You have only to consider the geographical situation of Evarchia to see that we're at constant risk of subversion, from both sides—or, to put it less naively, from all sides. Well, whichever side you come from, tonight would be just the night for you, wouldn't it? I mean, with the old king dying (saving your natural feelings, if they *are* natural, if he *is* your father, that is), and with him being not so very old, either, so that it takes everyone by surprise—well, there's bound to be confusion and dislocation. And that's the very essence of a revolutionary situation—or a counter-revolutionary situation. If *I* were planning a coup, I'd think myself pretty clever to pick tonight, and to pick this particular gate, and have a man on a horse just appear out of the dark and say "Open up, Grenadier, for the Crown Prince"; and your naif Grenadier, who can't see very clearly anyway because of the snow and who doesn't want to be bothered because he's cold, just opens up; and all the time the real Crown Prince is sitting there inside the Palace unknowing.'

'You could', Ulrich suggested, 'telephone through to the High Chamberlain's Office and ask if the Crown Prince is in the Palace.'

The Grenadier thought and then shook his head. 'It wouldn't help. At least, it wouldn't *necessarily* help. All right, if the High Chamberlain says "Yes, the Crown Prince is here beside me eating his supper", then I know you're an impostor. But if he says "No, he's out on his wanderings", then I'm no better off. You could still be an impostor or you could be the wanderer returned. And the same is true of all the evidence. It all reads both ways. You tell me the king, your father, is ill. Well, you could know that from the radio. That's how you'd know tonight is the night to chance your arm. As a matter of fact, the way *I* know the king is ill is from the radio. And that's what makes it so hard for me to check anything. Suppose I say to you "Right, give me a piece of intimate information that only the Crown Prince could have" and you say "Right, the king is always addressed, in private, by his Family, as Bubbles"? Well, I'm still at sea. *I* don't know what the Royal Family call the king. It might be Bubbles. Or it might not.'

'Did you,' Ulrich asked, 'get through to the Duty Officer?'

'Ordinary soldiers don't just go telephoning duty officers unsolicited', the Grenadier said. 'I got through to my sergeant. I told him there was one point in your favour, and that is that you do, facially, resemble the Crown Prince—so far as I've seen the Crown Prince, which is only in the newspapers and on television. But even that's ambiguous, of course. I mean, naturally they'd choose someone with a resemblance to him. All the same, I'm not convinced the resemblance goes far enough. I know it's hard to tell, when a person's on horseback (and as a matter of fact that's probably the very reason why they *sent* you on horseback), but I've been looking at you carefully and my impression is that, when you're standing on the ground, you're quite a short man, like myself, whereas my impression of the Crown Prince, though, as I say, I've not seen him in the flesh, is that he's quite tall.'

'For reasons of vanity', Ulrich said, 'I always select for publication photographs that don't include anything that could provide a scale of comparison.'

'Well, that's only human', the Grenadier said, 'if you're sensitive on the subject, which I'm not, myself. I don't imagine you ever thought it would lead to problems of identification?'

'No', Ulrich said. He couldn't think of any further reply

The talkative Grenadier, however, began to talk again, but he was interrupted by two arrivals. The sergeant must have telephoned the Duty Officer before setting off himself.

The sergeant came forward from somewhere in the region of the hut. Ulrich could not make out the plan of the place in the dark. Simultaneously, the small wicket gate inset in one of the main gates was opened from the inside. The Duty Officer stepped over the four inches of wood, bound with a steel rim, that remained at the bottom and made the threshold look like a threshold in a ship, and hurried towards Ulrich.

23

'I must apologise, your Highness. I can only say we were not alerted to expect your arrival. Though we ought to have worked out for ourselves that you would be likely to come.'

He was young, with an elegant, egg-shaped face newly shaven for the evening. Still blushing under the sting of his after-shave lotion, it was now blushing further with embarrassment. 'Sergeant. Get the gates unbolted and opened.'

'Yes sir. Grenadier.'

The sergeant and the talkative Grenadier hurried into the darkness beyond the wicket gate. The silent Grenadier remained silent and remained where he was.

'I'm sure your Highness won't remember', the young officer said, 'but we have, actually, met.'

Ulrich performed a tired version of the gesture he had evolved to acknowledge such references without explicitly lying.

'It was at the regimental dinner last year.'

'Then you', Ulrich said, 'will have no difficulty in identifying me.'

'Indeed not', the officer replied, enthusiastic with nervousness. Only secondarily did it occur to him to read a significance in what Ulrich had said. 'I do hope the Grenadier didn't . . .?'

'The Grenadier did nothing but his duty. He did it admirably. I'd be grateful if you'd make a point of seeing that no blame attaches to him.'

'Yes, certainly. Yes, of course', the young officer muttered, his mind plainly already on what he had resolved to say next and say before the opening gates could cut him short. 'Your Highness. I hope you won't think me impertinent. I'd like you to know how much I—we all—sympathise with what you must be going through. We all feel—upset. Some of us thought we ought to cancel the dance tonight. But we decided that would be—'

While he hesitated over it, Ulrich conjectured with what idea the young officer could possibly plan to complete his

24

sentence: extravagant? unduly pessimistic?

But the young officer at last brought out: 'not at all what *he'd* want. He's always so concerned for people. He enters into everything about them, wants the best for them: a wonderful *man*, as well as a wonderful king. And if *we* feel that, one can well imagine what *you* . . .'

The great gates made a noise of yawning.

Ulrich hoped (he felt too weary to judge) his farewells were appropriate. As he urged the mare forward into the dark palatial precinct and heard the gates closed and bolted behind him, he considered that the most surreal part of the whole surreal episode was the presence throughout it, non-participant, unresponding, of the *other* Grenadier.

*　　　*　　　*

When he arrived to keep the appointment he had just made by telephone with the Cultural Attaché at the Bulgarian Embassy, the Chairman of the Communist Party of Evarchia gave some perturbation to the security staff (two men in square grey jackets who stood without apparent occupation in the marble and statued vestibule, where they looked like attendants in a museum) by refusing to divest himself of his top coat.

'I tell you, I shall be going out again almost immediately.'

One of the grey men had already taken a wire coat hanger from the rack against the wall. Now he waved it as he walked towards the Chairman: perhaps in threat but more probably in dumbshow and on the supposition that the reason the Chairman had not complied was that he hadn't understood what was required.

The other moved up behind the Chairman and, in a gesture half valet and half wrestler, slipped his arms over the Chairman's shoulders and tried to remove the coat.

He was foiled because the coat was still buttoned up.

Taking advantage of the setback to the grey men, the

25

Chairman broke free and all but ran up the stately, shallow-stepping staircase.

The grey men followed, and the three in succession burst into the Cultural Attaché's room where the man with the hanger made gestures with it towards the Chairman by way of explaining to the Attaché.

The Attaché said something in Bulgarian to the grey men which calmed and dismissed them and then continued, in Evarchian:

'All the same, Comrade, you will be too hot in here with your coat on. That sort of thing can give one a cold.'

'Come for a stroll in the Park', the Chairman said.

'Comrade, it is dark and, I believe, snowing. It's nearly time for the Embassy to close and for me to take my dinner.'

The Chairman simply stood in front of the desk. He seemed without animation—indeed, deeply tired. Perhaps it was his very lack of animation that implied he couldn't conceive of the possibility that the other will might prevail over his.

The Attaché sighed, stood up and shrugged. 'Very well. But now you must wait while I go and put my coat on. Please sit down while I do so.'

The Chairman waited, however, on his feet. He felt too tired to sit down and then have to get up again, just as he had felt too tired to take his coat off only to put it on again a minute later. Yet that attempt to hoard what energy he had left had betrayed him into his wasteful dash up the staircase.

When the Cultural Attaché was ready, they left the Embassy together, crossed the traffic and, side by side but unspeaking, walked up the mosaic path that marked the middle of the Metropolitan Park.

The snowflakes themselves made an opened-out mosaic, the Cultural Attaché considered, a mosaic in the act of disintegration, when they drifted from the unimaginable blackness above into the gentle, diffused sphere of influence of the lamps in the trees.

Except to pick out its blades more individually and in a

26

bleached shade of green (unless the light was bleaching it in any case), the snow had made no impression yet on what could be seen of the grass at the sides of the path. But at the edges of the path itself it was already compiling tippets.

Sometimes a light shone full on the dark, glossy leaf of a tropical plant bending under a paradoxical load of snow.

The Cultural Attaché wondered whether, somewhere in the unimaginable dark beyond the path, in a snowy-grassy depression or perhaps in an aromatic lair under the protection of exotic shrubs, the white peacocks were roosting.

The Chairman trudged, his legs resenting the slight upward slope of the path. He had chaired three meetings that day. His thoughts comported themselves with the rigidity of a drunk trying not to look drunk.

At the biggest meeting, he had ruled an opponent out of order under Clause 13 of the Party constitution. The opponent demanded to be heard not in terms of dry legalism but in the spirit of the Communist Manifesto. The Chairman could remember only the historical fact, like the date but not the outcome of a battle, of his own conversion by reading the Communist Manifesto in conjunction with Lenin's pamphlet on Marx. The argument convinced him that what it claimed as inevitable was inevitable, and he had resolved that Evarchia should be on the side of inevitability. Now he couldn't remember at all what the argument was—and only just what it was that it claimed as inevitable.

'Do they leave the white peacocks out in the winter', the Cultural Attaché asked, 'or take them into houses?'

'No idea', the Chairman replied.

He had declared that, as a matter of fact, the opponent was out of order also under Clause 30, and he had added that anyone who lacked the discipline to work through effective structures and by means of accepted procedures would do better to put his revolutionary fervour at the service of the Liberal-Democrat Party or indeed the Catholic and Pre-Canonical Parishioners' Guild for Boys.

27

Some people had giggled. The Chairman's opponent walked out of the meeting, leaving his supporters without advice about whether to follow him or stay so that they could tell him afterwards what took place. Some did the one thing and others the other, both uneasily. So the Chairman won. But he considered now that his opponent might have won, had he taken more thought.

At the top of the incline, the Chairman and the Cultural Attaché halted.

They stood at the stone rim of a basin which, large and circular, constituted the central rond-point of the Metropolitan Park.

The water inside reached nearly to the brim. It was lit by lamps beneath the surface, one of which focussed upwards on the naked nymph in the middle.

She was leaden, and nineteenth-century baroque.

In a gesture the Cultural Attaché would have judged lewd had it not been so matter of fact as to be funny, she was proffering her breasts on the palms of her hands. Through each of her nipples a thin lash of water arched into the air and then drooped, in individually audible droplets, into the pool. About half of each spout failed to become airborne. It trickled down the nether side of the breast, where it had long left brown deposits marking its route.

The upper sides of the nymph's breasts, which her gesture squared into positive platforms, had collected some snow. In the mild lighting, it was scarcely to be distinguished from the bird droppings that were always there.

'Well? What makes you think my Embassy is bugged?' the Cultural Attaché asked.

'I don't think it *is*, Comrade, I think it might be, and better safe than sorry', the Chairman replied wearily.

'It was mineswept quite recently—and found clean. This is, after all, Evarchia.'

'That scarcely guarantees you against electronic surveillance.' A distant creak of indignation began to sound through

28

the Chairman's fatigue. 'Both our universities turn out graduates fully conversant with the latest technical developments. You shouldn't rely, Comrade, on the myth of Evarchian incompetence.' He pronounced it 'Efarchian', using the soft *v* of the Islanders and some of the peasants. 'That is merely an offshoot of the myth of Evarchian insouciance and devil-may-care-ness, which is itself a deliberate propaganda exercise, carefully fostered for purposes of the tourist trade.'

'Really, Comrade', the Attaché said in surprise, 'there is no need for this nationalistic self-defence. You make me feel I ought to remind you that socialism is an international movement.'

'In which case I should remind you that it is agreed that a socialist state is fully entitled to preserve and develop its own cultural autonomy and individuality.'

'I scarcely need reminding', the Attaché said. 'I'm Bulgarian. However—'

The Chairman tried to interpose something but the Attaché began to feel an obligation to override him.

'*However*', the Attaché insisted, 'bugging, which is the subject under discussion, if you remember, is not part of the individual culture of Evarchia. The technique and practice are both, as I understand it, international. Perhaps I may now explain that, when I reminded you that we are, after all, in Evarchia, I did not mean to imply that Evarchian electronics engineers were not fully competent to bug the Bulgarian Embassy should they want to, but simply that I have the impression that the Evarchian government would very much prefer *not* to know what is discussed in the Bulgarian Embassy or, indeed, any other. The Evarchian government has won my and everyone else's admiration by keeping the most precariously placed national state in Europe in existence, and indeed in a condition of political stability, for very much longer than any political section in any policy-forming body in the world can have predicted. It has done it almost entirely through a rigorous technique of not knowing what other people predict about it. This quite brilliantly prevents the Evarchian government from falling into the error of over-reacting or of attempting pre-emptive strikes. You can't pre-empt what you have no reason to suspect is contemplated.'

The Chairman was silent for a moment, wishing he had not been too tired to understand the tone, as distinct from the meaning, of the Attaché's words. He could tell from the excitement in the voice that the Attaché had been enjoying himself in the construction of something like an intellectual fantasy. Its ingredients were evidently extravagant, if not positively paradoxical. In manner it was satiric. What the Chairman couldn't divine was the strategic plan it was meant to serve.

The Attaché, while he waited for the Chairman to answer, was visited by the thought that, seen from the back, the two of them might look, as they stood at the rim, as though they were standing side by side at a urinal.

The image displeased him. He turned sideways-on to the fountain and faced the Chairman's profile.

The Chairman went on gazing into the water in the basin as though its depths fascinated him. The Attaché was sure they didn't.

'As you say, Comrade', the Chairman eventually replied, his gaze unshifted from the water, 'bugging is international. That makes it all the odder that you seem to assume that the Evarchian government is the only organisation in Evarchia that might want to bug your Embassy.'

'No doubt you're right', the Attaché said concedingly, 'to be multilaterally cautious. In any case, here we are, safely beyond the reach of bugs, so no harm's done.'

'That is the point I was making in the first place.'

'Then consider it carried, Comrade.'

The Chairman said nothing.

The Attaché felt at a disadvantage applying to the Chairman's profile for a response that was not given. So he put away the displeasing image and faced the fountain again. Seen from the back they probably looked, after all, only like

30

two political agents in secret conversation.

The snowflakes made slight dimples when they touched the surface of the water.

'After all, I might have asked *you*', the Chairman suddenly said, 'what makes your security staff think I'm carrying a weapon in my coat pocket. I *don't* ask: I accept the principle of better safe than sorry.'

'They don't, actually', the Attaché said.

'Don't what? Who don't what?'

'The security staff don't think you're carrying a weapon. They just think that only peasants wear their top coats indoors.'

'What's wrong with being a peasant, Comrade?' the Chairman asked.

'Nothing, Comrade', the Attaché replied. He had begun life as a peasant. 'But peasants aren't renowned for their polished manners, whereas Asteans are, along with their insouciance and devil-may-care-ness. However, this is a sterile dispute. Tell me what you wanted to see me about.'

'The king is dying.'

'How do you know?' the Attaché asked swiftly.

'From the radio.'

The Attaché turned up his coat collar, felt, on the back of his neck, that it was already wet from the snow, and turned it down again. 'I never listen', he said, 'except when they're doing an opera.'

'Surely you have it monitored?' the Chairman insisted. 'I haven't had the time to sit listening personally, either, but I've taken care to be kept informed. I sometimes wonder, Comrade, if you don't plunge a little deeper than you need into your cultural cover. You don't think you're in danger of being seduced by the polished manners of Asty, do you? You're not succumbing to bourgeois elitism?'

The Attaché surmised that the Chairman meant to leave his retreat open by speaking as though he might be merely teasing, but it was difficult for him to get into his flat, fatigued

31

voice the bounces of tone that should indicate teasing.

'No', the Attaché answered blockingly. He had suspected for some time that the Chairman was himself bourgeois by birth and that the soft *v* in his speech was an affectation. But in a foreign language and a foreign society the Attaché was not versed enough in the indicators to be certain.

Ignoring the block, the Chairman said:

'Opera is scarcely an art of the people.'

'Ought one to be so condescending, Comrade, about the capacities of the people?'

'Studying operas is scarcely the most immediate way of advancing the cause of the people.'

'All struggles have both immediate and distant objectives, Comrade. Should we be correct if we lost sight of what we are building socialism *for*?'

'But *are* we building it, Comrade?' the Chairman asked. 'Here in Evarchia? Are we? I tell you: the king is dying.'

'May be dying', the Attaché corrected. 'And if he were to die?'

'Naturally', the Chairman said, 'I long ago formed plans to take immediate advantage of such a situation. Naturally, I've now brought them up to date, without, of course, informing more than a very few people. But of course I can't act—or can't effectively act—unilaterally. Some co-ordination of planning is now an urgent necessity. This is not the first time I've recommended such a course. But now I must recommend it with urgency, if the opportunity is not to be lost.'

'What difference', the Attaché asked, 'do you think the king's death would make—given that he's only a constitutional monarch?'

'Constitutional!' the Chairman replied, his voice flat even in exclaiming. 'The constitution is a superstructure, a mere front for capitalism.'

'Quite so. And as such unlikely, I should suppose, to affect the situation radically. However, I'll pass on what you say.'

'I must impress on you the urgency and the importance of

32

it, Comrade. A move at the right time on the other side of the borders, even if it were a move confined to diplomatic terms, could very strongly reinforce any move made here in Evarchia.'

'I'll pass on your views.'

'But there must be co-ordination', the Chairman urged in his unurgent tone. 'And it must be rapid.'

The Attaché looked upwards, at the water spouting and trickling.

'The king may die at any instant.'

As the Attaché watched, the spout from the leaden nymph's left nipple ceased.

The Attaché realised he had chanced to be watching at the exact, perceptible instant when the spout froze.

He drew a quick, strong breath and seemed to inhale ecstasy into his body, as though he had been a religionist who had witnessed a miracle.

He felt simultaneously satisfied and full of future purpose, a sensation on whose borders he recognised an impatience with the company he was in.

'To work, then, Comrade', he said euphorically. 'The cause of the people of Evarchia can't afford to have you catching cold in the snow.'

Ignoring or not recognising the facetiousness, the Chairman replied:

'I shall go back the other way, just in case we've been watched, though I'm confident we haven't.'

'Better safe than sorry', the Attaché said, nodding farewell.

'I'm glad you take the point. Goodnight, Comrade. I've given you the information. It's your responsibility now.'

Quick-marching in his euphoria, the Cultural Attaché set off down the mosaic slope, back to the Bulgarian Embassy where the statues wore marble frocks.

Che gelida manina, his thoughts sang, while his own hands snuggled inside his coat pockets.

As the vocal line in his thoughts rose, his chest swelled

against the constraint of his coat. Although his own bodily singing voice was a deep bass that could scarcely utter a note in the tenor register without strain, he could feel the high tenor notes of his mental aria buzz in the constricted bridge of his nose.

Perhaps those nasal notes, together with the gulp that projected them over the peaks of the tune, like a car taking a hump-backed bridge at speed, were what his singing teacher had meant by 'bad style', a phrase the teacher had shaken off the end of his forefinger not only at students but at record players while they uttered the voices of world-famous performers whose fame he judged unearned.

The Attaché formed, with triumph, the thought that, were *he* a tenor, he would be the most vulgar tenor on earth (thus making opera, his thoughts went on to enquire, an art of the people?).

In fantasy, he persuaded the Royal Astean Opera, several of whose directors he in real life knew by virtue of his cultural cover, to mount an open-air performance of *La Bohème* in the Metropolitan Park; the snow falling on the scene at the barrier would be real snow.

But he supposed that charcoal braziers, though pretty and though pleasantly confusing the stage scenery with the auditorium, would not keep the audience warm enough to keep them quiet. And the singers would complain of the fumes. Instead, his fantasy persuaded the directors to put on, in the opera house, a surrealist *Turandot* in which the role of the Princess should seem to be taken by a white peacock.

Returned to the Embassy, he warned the cook he might be late for dinner, hurried upstairs and locked himself in his office. Before he took off his top coat he withdrew from its breast pocket the micro-recorder on which he had recorded his talk with the Chairman of the Communist Party of Evarchia. He was surprised the Chairman had still not learnt, from one of the electronics graduates of Evarchian universities, that the gentle splashes from the nymph's breasts were not, even when

34

one of them wasn't frozen, loud enough to baffle acoustic apparatus of an advanced kind.

He now said, into the machine:

'Additional Notes. One. I imagine that the only organisation in Evarchia that is likely to try to bug our Embassy—it would probably not succeed—is the Communist Party of Evarchia. I think therefore that the Chairman's reason for always insisting that I talk to him out of doors, usually beside a fountain, is that he cannot be sure whether or not his own Party has yet succeeded in bugging our Embassy and whether or not someone from his Party regularly follows him and monitors his conversations. It is from some of his colleagues in his own Party that he is anxious to conceal his conversations with me. Two. My immediate thought was that there was only one way the Chairman could know for sure that the king is dying, namely that the Chairman himself has poisoned him. However, I do not think he would take such action unless he had received very firm instructions. If, therefore, no such instructions have been given, it can be assumed that the Chairman was merely trying to increase the apparent urgency of the situation. Three. The Chairman's implied threats to me are merely an additional pressure towards making me behave as though the situation were urgent. Four. There is, of course, no urgency in the political situation in Evarchia, which remains, and will remain for the foreseeable future, unchanged. The urgency in the Chairman's mind consists entirely in his own situation, which he has probably appreciated correctly, vis-à-vis his own Party. Five. Since you say your set is good at long range, you might like to know that, two days before Christmas, Radio Asty will be broadcasting the first night of the new *Norma* from the Royal Opera. I have heard a preliminary rehearsal and the production promises to be good. If the king dies, I suppose the first night may be cancelled. If so, that is likely to be the only major repercussion of his death.'

He extracted the cassette, noted on its label where, when and between whom the conversation it recorded had taken place, added the superscription 'For Evaluation—Not Urgent' and put the cassette in the safe.

He descended the handsome shallow stairs to dinner, humming aloud the music by which Siegfried journeys to the Rhine.

*   *   *

It seemed to the Crown Prince, as he forced himself to hasten through its corridors, that the Winter Palace lay under a silent impatience.

The corridors were empty, the doors shut. Yet he was aware of awareness throughout the Palace and of a sort of excitement, in which there was a tinct of pleasure.

He recognised it and felt revulsion. It was the excitement that had spellbound the Palace on the Christmas Eves of his childhood.

Up here on the fourth floor of the west wing the corridor was narrow, poorly lit and ill carpeted. The floor level sagged and recovered capriciously. Ulrich navigated by knowledge and a prickling in the fronts of his toes where they constantly expected to stub themselves against some obstacle.

It was thanks to knowledge alone that he did not stub his toes on the clumsy bump that marked his passage from the seventeenth-century wing into the thick block that had been cobbled onto it in 1869 in imitation, presumably, of a castle keep.

He wondered whether his father had chosen this least lovely quarter of the Palace to die in or whether it merely chanced to be the part he was in when he was taken ill or whether it in some way served the convenience of the doctors. Its lofty gothic emptiness might well remind them of a hospital.

As he approached the sickroom the silence deepened. Ulrich imagined a magical disaster in which the snowflakes from outside passed through roof and rafters and began falling silently within the Palace.

36

He tried to open the door quietly. But its designer had fitted it out, like a warhorse in armour, with heavy metal hinges and studs and a great latch that had to be raised by the turning of a huge metal ring, on which it was hard for a hand to get a purchase and which seemed itself to exercise little purchase on the latch. When he closed the door behind him the latch fell home under its own weight with a clang.

His father lay in a huge, brass-headed bed, propped on what seemed to Ulrich an uncomfortable mass of pillows, his eyes shut.

The room was almost without decoration, unless there was meant to be a decorative quality in the meanly pointing gothic windows, set in stone embrasures inches deep and intended, presumably, to defend the Palace against some fantasy long-bowmen of 1869, or in the gaping fireplace whose arch had been squashed until it followed the outline of a longbow lying face down. One picture hung on the wall, a triptych with religious subject matter by a painter influenced by the Pre-Raphaelites. It was difficult with the eyes of posterity to see how the painter had ever believed it to resemble quattrocento work.

The queen looked up when Ulrich came in and gave him her loving, abstracted, tragic smile. She was sitting on some sort of high stool beside the top of the bed. At the other side, like the other one of two angels flanking an altarpiece, and also on a stool, was a stranger whom Ulrich quickly surmised from her clothes to be nurse, nun or both.

For the others, Ulrich's siblings, no provision had been made. They squatted, were propped against the sides of the bed or lounged over the plain at the bottom of it out of danger to the royal patient's feet. A thin rug covered part of the floor. Two bars of heated coil were almost swallowed up in the fireplace. His father might, Ulrich reflected, have been dying in an upper room in a seedy hotel.

The orange quilt, scarcely thicker than the rug on the floor, was old, patched and faded. Ulrich knew it well. It had been made for and presented to the king on his marriage by the women of the southern provinces. Disposed round it were (in order of birth, not disposition, which was haphazard) their Devout and Imperial Highnesses the Archdukes Balthazar, Sempronius and Urban and the Archduchess Heather. Under it (for the most part), arms tucked down in evident obedience to the nurse, beard as if lately combed by the nurse over the top edge, lay his Most Catholic and Pre-Canonical Majesty King Cosmo III.

'My dearest', the queen said gently to the profile she was sitting beside, 'Ulrich is here.'

The longdrawn hollow face, face of an El Greco nobleman or saint, gave no sign of consciousness.

Balthazar and Urban made space between them for Ulrich to approach the bed.

Sempronius said:

'Papa. Ulrich has come.'

Several minutes later, without opening his eyes the king said, in a failing voice audibly hard driven to muster breath:

'Is that—little Ulrich?'

Ulrich flung his knees to the floor and his face into the orange quilt and sobbed.

Chapter Two

'Baa, baa,
Back Teeth,
Have you—'

'No, dearie', said Missy Five. 'I've told you ever so many times. That's wrong.'

'*Is* it?' the Archduchess Heather asked sceptically. She looked down at her fingers, bulky as Knackwürste, on the keys.

Though it was the English words she was trying to sing, it was with Mozart's version of the French version that she was trying, by ear, to accompany herself.

Her ear, like her small soprano voice, was true. Her fingers, despite their weight and lack of education, were musical.

'Not the music, dearie. You know I know nothing about music. The words.'

'O yes, I remember now. It isn't "Back Teeth", is it?' Heather pushed back the piano stool and splayed her long, weighty thighs, which were wearing corduroy trousers of sapphire blue. 'Well, as I told you last time, that was Missy Three's fault. It was her favourite expression. "I'm fed up to the back teeth with this." "I'm fed up to the back teeth with that." Naturally, when she began, at Mama's insistence, to teach me the nursery rhyme, I misheard it. Mishearings at an

39

impressionable age are virtually ineradicable. People mispronounce certain words all their lives, through having heard them wrongly in childhood. When Missy Three got cross with us during lessons she used to say "I'm fed up to the back teeth with the pack of you." '

'A very vulgar expression', murmured Missy Five.

'Is it? I wish I knew more vulgar expressions in English. Do you think Missy Three *was* vulgar, then—inherently vulgar, I mean? I know you never met her, but judging from the traces she's left in our English vocabularies?'

'It's not for me to criticise, dear. I think you should sing it again now, getting the words right this time.'

'Very well. What *are* the right words? Though it seems bizarre, somehow, to be singing English nursery rhymes on the day one's father is probably going to die.'

'Her Majesty said she wanted you to continue with your education, exactly as normal.'

'I know. Dear Mama. As if I were a child. It's "Black Sheep", isn't it?'

' "Black Sheep", dear, yes. That's right.'

'English nursery rhymes seem obsessed with sheep.'

'Do they?'

'Well. "Mary had a little lamb." '

'I expect it's because we were once such a great wool-trading people, dear.'

'Were you? Fascinating', Heather said. 'Still, you know, all this is going to stop on Christmas Day, when I become sixteen. My formal education, I mean. From then on it will be just a matter of idiomatic conversation in English, plus a certain informed cultural background.'

'Yes, dear, I *do* know.'

'Well, you've got a splendid job to go to. I'm sure the De Rigueurs will make you feel at home. The Count is said to know England very well, and the girl's awfully pretty. And anyway you're staying on for a bit, aren't you, to help Missy Six get used to our ways?'

40

'Only for a very little bit, dearie. I shall be off almost immediately after Christmas.'

'I expect Papa will have died by then. Do you ever feel there's something monstrous about me, as a result of my being born on Christmas Day? As though I'd been specially selected by Fate? Do you think, if I'd been a boy, my parents would have called me Noel?'

'I shouldn't expect so, dearie. After all, if they'd really wanted to, they could have done anyway. Noel's a girl's name too.'

'Is it? Anyway, I don't believe it would have made the smallest difference to me.'

'If you'd been called Noel?'

'If I'd been a boy.'

*   *   *

Snowflakes fell through the irregular segment of morning air which, unexpectedly bright and transparent, was enclosed by four disparate façades.

One was the severe, lofty brow of the domed Riding School itself. The left end of its roof rose, squared itself off and became a clock tower. The cube of brick below supported white weatherboarding suggestive of dovecotes or a rustic bridal crown, and almost, now, confusable with the snow.

At the right the full stretch of the Riding School was partly cut off from view, intercepted at a right angle by the Old Cloister (which was, on its outer side, closed).

The stone details were softened now into shapes rather than representations, the bays were lapsing out of true, but the vaulted ceiling still intersected and replicated according to the mathematics of wizardry if not positively of heavenly bodies.

The façade on the left was the handsomely invented flank of the Banqueting Hall, pilastered, corniced, cartouched.

Banqueting Hall and Cloister were linked by a block of the Palace proper, from one of whose windows, in the second

41

storey, the princes of the blood were accustomed, from as far back as their memories encompassed, to watch the first snow descend through the trapped portion of out-of-doors onto the courtyard floor.

To the two who stood there now it seemed that the unexpected lightness of the morning reflected the unexpected fact inside the Palace that the king was still alive.

Ulrich had kept waking up during the night. Each time, after his moment's pause in limbo, his first memory had been of his father's mortal illness. Each time he realised, much later, that his first thought had not been of Clara.

He was pausing in a limbo again now, mesmerising himself on the snowflakes, waiting for his consciousness to shew itself willing to set about a day of tasks—which must begin, of course, with a visit to the distant keep to see his father.

Beside him, between the window and the rocking horse, stood his immediately younger and very much taller brother Balthasar, the tallest, indeed, of the royal siblings—as yet; no one could be sure that Heather, who came next in height after Balthasar and only a couple of centimetres after at that, had stopped growing.

He was curly-haired; his long body and limbs, unlike Heather's, were bony; and so was his long face, which was to many people's taste good-looking.

By his parents' intention, which he endorsed, he was called BalTHASar. The royal parents were, however, almost the only parents in Evarchia with the forethought and the means to introduce their children to the English *th* (or, as the queen softly urged, the ancient Greek theta) at the early age when it had to be mastered if it ever was to be. Beyond his Family, Balthasar was almost universally pronounced BALtasar, and when he was reported in print he was usually spelt to match.

Perhaps because the sheer buildings about it made its area look, from above, smaller than it was, the courtyard of the Royal Riding School always reminded Balthasar of a tennis court. Thanks to the cognateness of *royal* and *real*, it was real

42

tennis that he had intellectually in mind, but what his imagination visualised was lawn tennis.

Now, as the snow compiled in the courtyard, especially in the corners, he saw it in terms of an extravagant—indeed, an impractical, a tripping-up—supply of unused white lawn tennis balls, amassed, especially in the corners, beyond the possible wants of any conceivable server.

He would have liked to gesture to his small, predominantly brown, rather Napoleonic-looking elder brother. What stopped him was the fact that they were standing. Any gesture must drop conspicuously from Balthasar's height to Ulrich's smallness and thereby undo the result Balthasar designed it to create.

He wished, as he often had before, that the Royal Day Nursery provided somewhere to sit—apart, that was, from the rocking horse and from the little painted chairs for infants that had now been pushed aside in a corner. Most of the little chairs were broken anyway, no doubt because attempts to sit in them had once been made by royal infants grown into royal adolescents.

'Whenever I see snow falling', Balthasar said, 'I think of that lump of snowflake obsidian you used to have. It always seemed a miracle that nature or chance or whatever one likes to call it had actually created a black rock with white spots on it, as though it had actually intended to design a snowfall in permanent form. Have you still got it? Have you still got your Collection?'

'Somewhere', Ulrich replied; and he smiled, to acknowledge that his brother's enquiry was the equivalent of a gesture of affection.

'You ought to get it out', Balthasar said, insistent that his interest went beyond gesture. 'The lump of snowflake obsidian, I mean.'

Ulrich had in fact collected and polished several pieces of snowflake obsidian, in sizes from lumps to chips, and had set some of them. Implying, however, for friendliness's sake, that his own memory was no more accurate than Balthasar's, he shrugged and said:

'It's years since I've had time to think about stones. Nature or chance or whatever you like to call it has picked on me for a different job at Court from the one that would really have suited me. I'd have been very happy as Court Jeweller.'

Balthasar gave him a grin of melancholic acknowledgment, and Sempronius entered the Royal Day Nursery.

Without turning to see it, his brothers were aware of the arrival of that blond nimbus that seemed thrown off round Sempronius less by his blond hair and flowers-painted-on-porcelain complexion than by his constant agree-ableness.

He stood at the far side from his brothers of the rocking horse and, dispensing as he always did with greetings, as though they were social cosmetics he did not need, said:

'I'm told Papa had a reasonable night. Better, anyhow, than the doctors expected.' He paused over what the doctors had expected and warned of, and then added: 'Mama sat up with him for most of it.'

'I must go to him', Ulrich said, as if reminded. But he went on looking out at the snow, his stance at the window frame miming that he was there only for one last moment more.

'By the way, isn't it absurd', Sempronius said, running his fingers through what was left of the rocking horse's nylon tail, 'that we have no chairs in here?'

'Quite absurd', Ulrich confirmed, leaving the window at last. 'We should take some from another room. Next door, per-haps.'

'There aren't any next door', Sempronius countered.

Without turning from the window Balthasar said:

'I'm going to speak to the High Chamberlain. Is that all right, Ulrich? Can you see any reason why I shouldn't?'

'None', Ulrich said from the Day Nursery door, which he was opening. 'It seems the only way.'

When Ulrich had gone, Sempronius moved forward into his

44

place.

He glanced into the courtyard. Between the angles of the buildings the snow was piled in the shape of (so far, low) triangular corner cupboards. Alternatively, Sempronius could almost imagine that a hampered or incapacitated person was squatting there and, using the walls as props, slowly wriggling himself upright.

'I've had a message from Mama', he told Balthasar. 'When she has caught up on a little sleep, she would like to see me and has a favour to ask.'

'I can guess what it is. The new English Miss is arriving today.'

'So she is. Papa's illness had driven it out of my mind. What a day to arrive. The girl from Girton. Or the new girl from Newnham.'

'Anyway, the classics graduate', Balthasar said. 'Having arranged it all on paper, Mama will have been taken by shyness. She will be feeling that'—he imitated the queen, and Sempronius grinned—'her own Greek is so dilapidated. And therefore she plans, my dear Sempronius, to hide behind your charm.'

'My charm', Sempronius said, spreading his hands in charming self-deprecation. 'Don't make light of it, in case it blows away. You know I have nothing else.'

Balthasar noticed that there seemed, in fact, to be no wind. The discs of snow fell straight, like carefully released coins. 'You wouldn't care to charm chairs from the High Chamberlain?'

'I'm already spoken for. Besides, it would come better from you. And be more likely to get us some chairs.'

They left the Royal Day Nursery and walked along the first corridor together.

'What', Sempronius asked as they went, 'shall you *say*?'

'O, that, though the popular imagination chooses to picture us as ethereal beings, we in fact have bottoms and should welcome somewhere to put them.'

45

For a time the snow fell without royal witness. It reinforced the outlines of the royal arms on the Banqueting Hall as though heightening them with white paint in a drawing on grey paper. By the time that the youngest of the archdukes, Urban, approached the window of the Royal Day Nursery, snow was standing solidly distributed over the whole courtyard pavement and was reflecting back the brightness above, making the courtyard look unnaturally illuminated, as though by underwater light.

The thought visited Urban that, were a miraculous thaw to melt the snow so suddenly and swiftly as to overwhelm the old (and, to judge from the bits that were visible, handsome) leaden drainage system, the courtyard would stand deep under water and look even more than usual like an indoor swimming pool.

He scarcely noticed that the dumbshow with which his imagination accompanied his thought consisted of his breaking violently through the Royal Day Nursery window, stepping up onto the snowy sill and diving into the pool-courtyard.

★   ★   ★

'This is—my boy Ulrich—my eldest boy. Ulrich, this is—Sister. Sister has been so good to me. You wouldn't believe what a—kind person she is.'

Ulrich smiled to the nurse.

She slid down from the high stool she was sitting on and bobbed him an inch of curtsey.

'And aren't you', she said in an Islander accent to the king, 'the lovely person to be nursing? Not the least little bit of trouble you are. Good as gold, you are, all the way through.'

Ulrich noticed that the second high stool, which had been in the room the previous night, had vanished. 'Do sit down again', he said awkwardly to the nurse.

'No, now that you've come, I'll take my chance to slip out and see to the flowers.'

When she had gone, Ulrich hoisted himself onto the high stool, which was almost too high for him to get there with ease.

'Ulrich?' the king asked feebly.

'Yes, Papa, I'm here. Don't bother to talk if it tires you. Unless you want to, of course.'

'I had—a dreadful night, Ulrich. Dreadful.'

'Papa.'

For a while the king lay still and silent against the massed pillows.

Suddenly he made a convulsive but weak attempt to sit up from them, twist round and reach his hand beneath them.

'Papa', Ulrich cried, cascading from his stool. 'What is it you want? Tell me. Let me find it.'

'Would you?' The king lay back again, panting. 'I feel— silly, being so—weak. That would be immensely—kind of you.'

'No, no, Papa. But tell me what I'm to look for.'

'The—list.'

'The list? A piece of paper?'

The king nodded, moving scarcely more than his eyelids.

Ulrich tunnelled between pillows behind his father's back, his hand constrained by his father's weight. He tried to keep his knuckles from impinging on the flesh, and he wondered whether the flesh would soon be insensate. He found a cotton handkerchief and two paper ones, the king's copy of the New Testament in Evarchian, containing the non-canonical as well as the canonical books, and eventually a sheet of pale blue letter paper.

'Is this it, Papa?'

The king made no move.

'Papa?'

'Sorry. Tired. Yes. I got Sister to—write it down. It may— not be clear. She's rather—stupid. Read me the—points, and I'll—explain.'

It was in fact very—quite roundedly—clear.

47

'Flowers', Ulrich read aloud.

'Yes. They're all—sending them. The ones from—Family—must be personally—acknowledged. Could—you, Ulrich? The secretaries may not—know who *is*—Family.'

'Shall *I*?' Ulrich asked, remembering how often he had stopped listening when his father had expounded their kin.

'Of course you will', the king said. 'You were—brought up to it. What comes—next?'

'The Cardinal-Patriarch and Father Felix', Ulrich read.

'O—yes. They keep—trying—to come and—see me. Keep them—away, Ulrich. I don't—want—to see them now.'

'I'll do my best.'

'Next?'

'Royal Blind', Ulrich read.

'Telephone them, Ulrich. Explain I can't—come to—their Christmas party. The secretaries—said they would—write, but the—blind can't read—letters. They'd be so—delighted to talk to—*you*. It's the—Royal Blind—Institution of—Asty or it may be the—Royal Astean—Blind Institution.'

'I'll find it, Papa.'

'I'm sure you—will. It will—be easy enough. Is that—all?'

'There's one more item. It just says "R.B.'s".'

The king closed his eyes.

'Are you too tired to go on, Papa?'

'No. R.B.s.' The king opened his eyes again. 'I told the girl to put that because—I didn't want her to—understand. It stands for "Royal Bibles". There's a stock. The—High Chamberlain will—shew you. Already—signed by me and with—the royal arms—at the front. I want one for—each of the—nurses.'

'Yes. How many nurses are there?'

The king was silent for a moment. 'Four, I think. Or—perhaps five.'

'It doesn't matter. I'll ask the doctors.'

'Yes. The plain—clothbound Royal Bibles, Ulrich, not—the ones with goldleaf on—the cover.'

48

'Yes.'

'Ulrich? Sit down for—a moment.'

Ulrich heaved himself back onto the high stool.

'Don't let—Heather—see me when—I'm dead.'

'No. All right, Papa.'

'Indeed, if you—can, try to avoid all that—morbid business, lying—in state and so forth, that seems to—go with our—profession.'

'All right. Yes, Papa.'

'Ulrich?'

'Papa?'

'Some of these—girls are very—stupid and—unimaginative. To move the—bowels, one needs a little—time, to—concentrate. They're so—impatient.'

'Would it', Ulrich asked, 'be less embarrassing if one of your nurses was a man? I could speak to the doctors.'

'No. That would look as if we—didn't think they were—doing their best. Ulrich?'

'Yes?'

'You must have lots—of affairs of your own that you want—to be busy about. Don't—waste any more of your—time on me.'

'I'll do the things on this list, Papa. I'll look in again later. The others will be coming, too, and, no doubt, Mama.'

'One thing—Ulrich, just before you—hurry away.'

'Yes, Papa?'

'Could you, very—kindly, put my—New Testament where I can easily—reach it?'

Ulrich negotiated it out from behind the pillows and put it at the king's hand, on the folded-down sheet.

He opened the heavy, studded door and found the nurse at the threshold.

She giggled over the accident of his opening the door so conveniently for her. Each of her arms was embracing a huge vase full of out-of-season flowers.

She carried them past Ulrich, leaving him a waft of their

49

sweetness, paused by the bed for the king to admire them, and then set them down in the gothic fireplace, which swallowed them as easily as it had already swallowed the electric fire.

'Glorious. Glorious', the king said. Ulrich noticed that his eyes were shut again.

*   *   *

'I realise', Balthasar said, trying to introduce paragraphing into a discussion that had been going on for fifteen minutes without, that he could discern, form or direction, 'we are the most down-at-heel, not to say pauperised, royal house in Europe. All the same. Nowadays every suburban clerk can afford seating for his family. And quite right too. Every peasant cottage contains some chairs. I'm told that even the Islanders, at least in the new generation, are giving up their traditional preference for squatting on their hunkers. So it really doesn't seem—'

'I have always maintained', the High Chamberlain interrupted, 'that the privileges of high position are accompanied by duties.'

Balthasar was halted by the irrelevance of the remark. Then he realised that the High Chamberlain had been reproving Balthasar's 'And quite right too'. He cursed himself for want of diplomacy; egalitarianism was unlikely to be the way to woo the High Chamberlain. He remembered and endorsed a dictum of his youngest brother, Urban, that people who said they were non-political always meant that their politics were of the Right. 'Politics itself', Urban had added, 'as a subject, is of the Left.'

'Well, in this case', Balthasar said, smiling, 'it's hard to see the privileges, and I really can't believe we have a duty to stand up all day. Must I really come into your office and take up your time with some such discussion as this whenever I feel like a sit-down?'

Refusing to acknowledge Balthasar's attempted joke, the

50

High Chamberlain replied:

'As I've already said, your case seems to me, personally, entirely reasonable. If it were up to me, you should have your chairs tomorrow. However, it isn't up to me—which is why I've asked the Comptroller to come and join our discussion. Jurisdiction over Mobile Household Effects, a category which I presume includes chairs, is shared between him and me. Luckily, our relationship is very good. We don't go in for demarcation disputes.'

For purposes of diplomacy, Balthasar didn't retaliate but smiled at the High Chamberlain's joke, which was directed against the Evarchian trade unions. When he had honoured the joke long enough, Balthasar said:

'If it really involves such a brouhaha, perhaps we'd better make our own arrangements privately. I daresay if my brothers and I and our sister were to club together, we could buy a few chairs out of our private allowances.'

'You might be surprised', the High Chamberlain said, 'when you see what chairs cost these days. I could arrange to have you sent some catalogues, if you'd like?' Without waiting for Balthasar's answer, the High Chamberlain made a note on a pad on his desk, meanwhile continuing: 'However, all that is quite beside the point. If you did buy some chairs, which of course you are entirely free to do, as soon as they were delivered they would have to go into the Royal Household Effects Depot and wait there until they had been entered in the Royal Household Inventory and assigned to one or other sphere of jurisdiction.'

'How long would that take?'

'Hard to tell. Jurisdiction is not a simple problem, as the precedents would have to be explored. And the Inventory is, I believe, considerably in arrears as it is. New entries would have to take their turn after it had been brought up to date.'

'It sounds as if it might take months', Balthasar exclaimed.

'It would certainly be wise to think in terms of months rather than, say, weeks.'

51

'And do you mean that all that time, however long it was, we wouldn't be able to use our chairs? Even though they would be our chairs and we would have paid for them?'

'Chairs', the High Chamberlain said, pushing his own back from his desk and tilting the seat slightly against its swivelling axis, 'are rather different in concept from the things you normally buy with your personal allowances, such things as, for example, your clothes or, to cite a very pertinent instance, the geological specimens your elder brother used to collect when he was a boy. All those can be called Personal Effects: they are for personal use or perhaps for giving away as personal gifts. A chair, however, is of its nature a Household Effect. It would be, though not impossible, unusual to give a chair as a personal gift. If you were to buy some chairs, it might be argued that they constituted Personal Effects were you to arrange to take them with you or have them put in storage whenever you left the Palace. I don't mean merely when you left for an overnight stay but whenever you left the premises at all. If, however, the chairs were to remain in the Palace on a more or less permanent basis, then plainly they would become part of the Household establishment. They would not and could not remain personal to their owners. One may have what is called one's personal chair, sanctified by usage and the courtesy of others when the so-called personal owner is present. The very fact that a chair stands—is placed—in a given room argues that it may, at some time, be used by whoever happens to be in that room.'

The High Chamberlain was interrupted by a knock.

The Comptroller came in. Balthasar received his salutations and his commiseration about the king's illness. He was settled into an armchair beside the one Balthasar occupied, and Balthasar was invited to put his case again.

When he finished, the Comptroller smiled with the corners of his small square grey moustache and wrinkled the lines at the outer edges of his eyes in a message of good will towards Balthasar.

52

'I should like first', the Comptroller said, 'to say how much I welcome this Royal initiative. And I think we should make it the opportunity for instituting a very much more radical enquiry. I apologise for using a word that I know inflicts pain on my colleague the High Chamberlain, but it does seem to me that nothing less than radical steps can meet the case. His Highness has, perhaps without quite realising it, put his finger on a field that opens up a great many other fields of enquiry. And I should like to say how grateful I am to him for doing so. There is for example the whole question of the Royal Household Inventory, now so deplorably in arrears. Then the question of jurisdiction, where the precedents have never been properly established. I think we should aim to get them established, and then consider whether the results seem to call for any reorganisation of responsibilities.'

'I must say', the High Chamberlain said, 'that I thoroughly agree. And I should also like to second, as it were, my colleague's informal vote of thanks to his Highness for raising these very important matters. It seems to me that we should regard our function as, in the general sense, advisory and, in the immediate sense, fact-finding.'

'Hear hear', the Comptroller said.

Balthasar, a little sunken in his armchair, realised that both men were looking, with meaning, at him. 'What facts are there to find?' he asked. 'They seem to me found. The facts are that we're short of chairs and would like some.'

'Facts are often more elusive than they appear', the Comptroller replied, amicably wrinkling the whole of his face at Balthasar. 'For instance: is the shortage endemic or epidemic—or sporadic? Was there once an adequate supply of chairs and have they now, to use a military expression, gone missing? Or was the Palace originally furnished with a certain sparseness of chairs, being intended no doubt for occupation by a generation made of sterner stuff than our own?' The Comptroller raised his hand from the arm of his armchair in order to forestall any reply from Balthasar. 'His Highness

53

doesn't know the answer to these questions. I don't know the answer. My colleague doesn't know the answer. You see how we are proceeding in a factual vacuum. We must have the facts before we can formulate conclusions. Would you not agree, High Chamberlain?'

'Absolutely', the High Chamberlain agreed. 'And while you were speaking I had a thought which I think may prove valuable. It occurs to me that the person we really ought to ask to sit in on our deliberations is the Royal Archivist. He wears two hats and can no doubt advise us under both of them—that is, both on the Inventory and on the precedents.'

'Excellent idea', the Comptroller cried, raising his hand again but with the purpose, this time, of thumping it down on the arm of his chair. 'Wouldn't his Highness agree that the advice of the Royal Archivist might be just the thing we need?'

'I don't see how I can judge', Balthasar said. 'I don't feel in need of advice. I feel in need of chairs.'

'Well said, well said', the Comptroller roared, thrusting his head into the back of his armchair as an indication of his applause. 'And now I'll tell you a thought that's just come to *me*, at the risk of my colleague's considering it a little too democratic. I think we should involve the Head Carpenter.'

'No, I'll endorse that, I'll endorse that', the High Chamberlain said, moving some pens on the top of his desk. 'I'm not the stick-in-the-mud you take me for.'

'Well, I won't endorse it', Balthasar said. He looked directly at the High Chamberlain. 'I believe I am probably the most democratic person present. But since I am not proposing to make chairs, but only to acquire some ready-made, I don't see the relevance of the Head Carpenter—or of anyone else you may try to drag in. Quite frankly, I think you are trying to obfuscate the issue.'

'I am quite sure', the Comptroller said in a peace-making tone, 'that that is a charge his Highness will want to withdraw as soon as he understands what prompted me to propose the involvement of the Head Carpenter. What I had in mind was that he would be the very person to help us arrive—and arrive *quickly*, which I'm sure is dear to his Highness's heart—at a definition of a chair.'

'A definition of a *chair*?' Balthasar repeated, half rising from the one he was sitting in.

'I think', the High Chamberlain said slowly, indicating that his words were considered, 'that our definitions ought to be on the generous side—that is, on the inclusive rather than the exclusive side. But naturally we must have exactitude in defining our liberality, or our endeavours wouldn't add up to anything.'

'Indeed, we can't work in the absence of exact concepts, any more than in the absence of facts', the Comptroller said. 'I'm sure his Highness wouldn't want to endorse sloppy thinking.'

'The definition of a chair', the High Chamberlain said, 'may appear to be a matter of commonsense. But the moment you begin to think about it, commonsense lets you down. For instance, not everything that people sit on is a chair. One can, for example, sit on a wall. Yet a wall is not a chair.' He leaned across his desk and directed himself at Balthasar. 'Is it?'

Balthasar looked deliberately over the arm of his chair at the floor.

'I suppose', the Comptroller said, indicating that he was weaving a very thin speculation for no purpose except to cover the rudeness of Balthasar's non-reply, 'it might be argued that a wall *is* a chair when someone is sitting on it. It becomes, so to speak, an *acting* chair . . .'

'Well', the High Chamberlain said, moving his pens again. 'Well. We seem agreed, more or less, on the Royal Archivist and the Head Carpenter. Is there anyone his Highness can think of who ought to be on the committee?'

'*What* committee?' Balthasar asked, and this time he wholly rose to his feet.

'The committee', the High Chamberlain replied in a tone that indicated Balthasar had injured him by refusing to understand something self-explanatory, 'to look into the problems you've raised.'

'And when is this committee to take place?' Balthasar asked.

The men he spoke to noticed that they were sitting while a royal archduke stood. The High Chamberlain leaned his knuckles on his desk and pushed himself up quickly but the Comptroller spent some minutes pulling on the arms of his armchair before he was fully on his feet. Meanwhile, the High Chamberlain had drawn his desk diary towards him and, while he turned over pages without looking at them, was replying:

'Well, for its first meeting, I would suggest—I'm merely thinking out loud, now—Well, we are, of course, in the period of run-up to Christmas, when it's always so hard to get anything achieved and to find a date that everyone can agree on—And of course at present there are certain personal considerations that will naturally take priority in his Highness's thinking—So . . .' He drew a second desk diary to him.

'I think the committee should take place tomorrow', Balthasar said.

'Not possible', said the Comptroller, a little breathless from pulling himself up. 'We haven't even got acceptances yet from those who are to serve. And we'll have to get out an agenda. And my colleague will want to appoint a representative from his department and I from mine—'

'Then next week.'

'Your Highness, too, will want to appoint a representative.'

'I shall represent myself.'

There was a pause.

'When', the High Chamberlain said delicately, 'a royal prince sits on a committee, he automatically takes the chair.'

'Or at least', the Comptroller said, 'he automatically has the *right* to take the chair.'

'I see', Balthasar said. 'Well, I waive my right to the chair on condition the meeting takes place next week.'

After a moment the others agreed to the bargain.

When Balthasar had left the office, the Comptroller sat down again, this time on the arm of his armchair.

The High Chamberlain sat in his swivel chair and swivelled it, creakingly, for a while, from left to right. Then he put his fingers on the edge of his desk and braked the chair the next time it reached the central position. He took a paperback off his desk and held it up to shew the Comptroller the cover. 'Read that?'

'No. Is it good?'

'Haven't begun it yet.'

'Spy story?'

'Mm. They seem to be all you can get nowadays.'

'I prefer thrillers', the Comptroller said.

'So do I. At least, what I really prefer, or used to prefer, is the old-fashioned *roman policier*. But they all vanished. Suddenly, all you could get was thrillers. I didn't take to them at first, but now I must confess I'm quite addicted to thrillers.'

'Violent', the Comptroller said, 'often very violent. But exciting. And, I must agree, the excitement can be addictive.'

'Well, now you can't get thrillers', the High Chamberlain said. 'The only ones you can get are the old ones, which I've read. It's all spy stories now.' He began to swivel again. 'Well, I shall see how I take to those.'

He swivelled in silence, apart from the creaks, until the Comptroller rose to leave.

'You *would* think', the Comptroller said, 'that he'd have other matters on his mind at the moment. Indeed, you might say this is a moment in his life when you'd expect him not to have any time at all for a subject like chairs.'

'Yes, I must admit', the High Chamberlain said, rising and accompanying the Comptroller to the door, 'I found him a little heartless, a little heartless.'

*　　　*　　　*

'How is he?'

'My father?'

'Who else?'

'Very ill.'

Ulrich stood in the straw, suffering the silence and enjoying the smell of horses that always lay between himself and Tom.

Tom was, in a precise and technical sense, the love of Ulrich's life.

It was in the smell of Tom's occupation and Tom's physical being that Ulrich had lost his dread of horses. Tom had taken him into shelter from his father's schooling.

The love Ulrich bestowed on Tom, who must have been then, though Ulrich didn't notice it at the time, a fairly young man, was complete and, Ulrich intended, irrevocable. Sexless in act, it was thoroughly sexual—indeed, specifically homo-sexual—in content.

Nowadays it lay between them in the form of an embar-rassment that accused Ulrich of being unfaithful. He had to accept that he had been unfaithful to Tom because he could not be unfaithful to the quality of his love. He found it im-possible to belittle his love by describing it in his own mind as calf-love or hero-worship. He had known as a child, and as an adult he merely knew even better, that it was indeed love.

'He's a fine man, Ulrich.'

Ulrich prised up a straw, balanced it across his toe-cap and bounced it away. He was aware as he did it that he wasn't really interested in doing it.

'And a fine horseman', Tom added.

Only since he had grown up and grown awkward with Tom had Ulrich wondered if Tom held him to blame for inveigling Tom into disloyal thoughts critical of the king's be-haviour to his child.

Even at the time, Ulrich had been surprised that the king, instead of frowning on, fostered the devotion. He had speci-ally told Tom to call the young prince 'Ulrich'. Tom still obeyed, since the royal command had never been revoked, though Ulrich could tell that Tom would have preferred,

58

nowadays, to highness him. Tom liked obeying princes and being obeyed by horses. He had failed to teach Ulrich to enjoy exerting command over beasts or men. Perhaps there, too, he accused Ulrich of inveigling him into disloyalty: he must have longed to issue to his royal pupil the insubordinate command 'Command!'

'About sending the mare home', Ulrich said, knowing he was approaching the very grounds of the mental divorce between himself and Tom.

His love for the mare's owner, he reflected, even at its most obsessive, had kept its distance—a distance in which he appreciated Clara and passed favourable judgment on the scents of her body and her parfumeur. In loving Tom, he had passed no judgment, even favourable. He had simply made over the whole world, so far as he was concerned, to be steeped in the smell of horses.

Perhaps in giving his love to Tom he had been faithless to some previous owner of it. He could not remember what he had felt towards his father before the schooling with the pony began or the first of his brothers was born.

As Ulrich had expected, Tom eventually replied:

'The lad can ride her home.'

'No', Ulrich said. 'I want her to travel in the horse box.'

Although Ulrich was bound to win, they wrangled a little further, like a divorcing couple indeed, Ulrich sardonically thought, in terms that masked whatever the true dispute between them might be and yet were dictated by it.

Ulrich insisted the mare had had a hard ride and a bad fright the day before. Tom's reply was a complaint that economies enforced by the High Chamberlain had reduced the Royal Stables to the possession of only one horse box. Ulrich pointed out that, in the present circumstances and the present weather, one could not be needed for any other purpose, Tom that the immediately future weather might make the roads impassable to a horse box, Ulrich that that was an argument for the horse box to set off without delay while the roads were still clear.

Ulrich broke off the wrangle by telling Tom that he wanted a packet delivered to the mare's owner along with the mare. 'I'll get it ready at once, while you get the horse box ready.'

Although Ulrich had won, he counted Tom the victor. Tom had ceded not in concern for the mare but to the fact that Ulrich was Crown Prince—the fact which Tom always wanted Ulrich to exert.

Moreover, Ulrich realised as he walked back to the Palace proper, he could not even be sure that his concern for the mare had served her wishes or interest. He might merely have robbed her of a day's exercise she would have liked.

*   *   *

As they usually did when she asked for an improvised meal, they had forgotten, in the Royal Kitchens, that the queen was a vegetarian.

She looked at the stewed wing the Kitchens had sent, felt sick with pity, reburied the dead flesh under the tin tumulus meant to keep it warm, ate the roll from beside the plate, drank the glass of the red wine grown in the western provinces and then put the tray outside her study door.

When she came back, she put on her winter coat and approached her study window.

From the coping that bordered the enlarged window ledge she was watched by three pigeons, six orange narcissus eyes.

She raised the window.

Though they had all known what she was going to do, only one pigeon had the self-control to sit it out. The others rose into the air and circled, their wings making mewings that might have been mistaken for cries.

They were joined by a great tumble of pigeons from the out-of-sight ledges on the façade behind the queen. Rowing wings squeaked. There were noiseless collisions with snowflakes, sharper ones, and flapping, between pigeon bodies.

60

Having precipitated themselves from the façade as if from a sling, they slewed in mid-air and approached the ledge, leaning backwards, feet extended forwards, for a landing. At the last moment they broke off (usually downwards, sometimes nearly catching the underneath of their chins on the coping) because the queen was trowelling aside the accumulated snow on the ledge, breaking up the solid ice in their bath (which was, ironically, she thought in the memory of her meal, a huge tin roasting dish) and refilling it with water from a ewer.

At sight of the ewer, which the queen had to heave up onto the bottom of the window frame, even the self-controlled pigeon took to the air. She (putatively she) was a sleek, plump bird with a smooth speckled head like an egg. Six months before, she had arrived limping. The queen had taken pains to feed her individually until the leg mended, and the pigeon had gone on expecting individual care ever since.

The queen ascribed femaleness to her only tentatively. Pigeons were admirably, she considered, sex-egalitarian, in that no bodily sign distinguished the genders to the human eye; she was not sure whether any did to the pigeon eye. She had never seen the speckle-headed pigeon woo anyone, but she had seen her much wooed by others. On the whole, the queen thought, only the males puffed out their necks, fanned their tails downwards, like mud flaps over rear wheels, and, cooing, walked in swift, strutting circles after those they wooed; but as she suspected they were liable to woo female and male indiscriminately, she was cautious about taking the fact of being wooed as a guide to sex.

She put her hand, palm full of nuts, onto the ledge.

Two pigeons landed just beyond reach and edged away from her hand for a few sideways steps and then back towards it.

She remained immobile.

The ledge was large enough to indulge their shyness. It was, though you could not see so without leaning dangerously out of the window, a platform between two capitals borne up by

61

giant and, the queen believed, hideous caryatids in the form of Red Indians that had been stuck on, during the nineteenth century, to the outside of the eighteenth-century block of the Palace, perhaps because it had seemed, to the prevailing taste, too plain.

One pigeon craned his neck sideways, snatched at a nut, missed, and returned to snatch again. The queen watched the yellow and red flash of the inside of his beak as he swallowed; and suddenly her hand was surrounded by pigeons and pigeons filled the ledge.

They pressed their warm breasts, damp from the snow, into the edges of her hand while their necks swerved down to her palm. On the flattened backs other pigeons landed, so that pigeons stood two layers deep, upper layer almost up-ended in its anxiety to reach down, lower layer, though squashed, scrabbling on the ledge, between one another's feet, for nuts spilled and rolled. One hooked his beak round the queen's wedding ring and tugged.

'My children, my children', the queen murmured, almost as if she were cooing in among them.

Two handsome light grey birds with black barred wings, whom the queen took to be father and son, the elder distinguished by deeper and more gnarled white encrustations on his beak, stood upright at one side of the ledge, waiting with confidence in the queen's impartiality. She picked out a handful of small peanuts to offer them. The light grey birds were unable to swallow large nuts. If she offered them, they kept trying and kept having to spit them out—or, more exactly, to roll them from their beaks onto the ledge.

At the other side, the speckle-headed pigeon waited for the queen's individual care. She was standing up, alone, on the window frame, her head tilted as she peered into the interior, which must look dark to her, of the queen's study, which always provoked her curiosity.

Knowing the birds liked her to speak while she fed them, the queen, who sometimes said poetry among them and sometimes the opening two paragraphs, which she knew by heart, of what she believed to be the only great novel written in Evarchian, chose today to rehearse, murmurously, what she could remember of the paradigm of the Greek verbs.

'Lelumai, lelusai, lelutai', she recited softly, holding her palm in a group of gleaming dark birds, the colours of slate roofs wet with rain, who were the most aggressive with other pigeons and the most shy with the queen and whom she found the hardest to recognise as individuals. Her memory stumbled, as it usually did, at the dual. 'Lelusthon, lelusthon?' she pronounced uncertainly. She held out another palm-ful to be shared by, as well as any edgers-up who could force a way in, two birds who had not yet had their due. One was a still ragged baby; the skin at the top of his (or her) beak was still pinkish and the beak itself still long and naked, for thrusting into his parents' beaks, and when he took the nuts he still made tremors with his wings and squeaked a little, as if it were his parents he was demanding the food from. The other was a black-eyed bird the queen had loved particularly in his babyhood, for his lack of instinctual fear of her and a sort of clever idiocy in his behaviour. He had grown big and well able to protect himself if not positively aggressive, but he was still eccentric, as if absent-minded, and his eyes were still black. 'Lelumetha', the queen said as he gobbled, and then, suddenly confident of, at least, the ending of the Perfect Middle tense, she hastened home: 'lelusthe, leluntai'.

Just as she knew that, if she didn't manage to get food to a pigeon who was maimed, it would almost certainly die, she felt today as if (but she hoped it was not true) the survival in living consciousness of the whole painstakingly recovered language and literature of the ancient Greeks depended on her limping memory of its forms.

The black-eyed bird's crop swelled as she watched. After a moment he stopped eating and, as the queen had expected, began to hiccough. With each spasm of his chest, he gave out a little contralto hoot with a timbre like that of a french horn.

Besieged by birds, her hands hurried to renew provisions. Above them, her recitation moved on to the Future Perfect Middle, which was easier. She reached specially—and slowly, unstartlingly—out to coax a shy bird coloured (the only one of her flock who was) like a sepia photograph.

At last she saw (with the satisfaction, she self-satirically thought, of a hostess at a dinner party) that all their crops were bulging. She scattered the ledge with corn and a few secret heaps of nuts which she hoped would remain hidden and therefore to be eaten later, closed the window and watched through the glass, meanwhile rubbing her hands back to warmth.

The birds pecked at the corn. It took them thirty seconds to find the hidden nuts. Given the shortness of the winter day, the queen was not sorry; within an hour or two, at some advance sign, detectable by them though not by a human, that the light was about to begin to fail, they would turn lethargic and lose their appetite.

The black-eyed bird pecked once, sharply, sideways, at the cheek of the baby.

A mottled grey and black bird expanded his neck feathers, thereby losing to sight their variably coloured sheen, and marched to and fro on the ledge in straight lines, uttering the territorial coo which the queen was fairly sure was used, unlike the mating coo, by both sexes. He marked out the area of grains he was claiming as his, though with his neck expanded he could not eat them. A dark bird infringed his rights. The owner slapped him, fiercely and swiftly, with his wing. It made the sound of a fan being shot open and reminded the queen of arch productions of eighteenth-century operas. Having delivered the slap, the mottled bird stood with his wing slightly raised at the shoulder, threatening the intruder with a further slap or a shoulder charge. Meanwhile other birds were eating his store of grains behind his back.

The queen could never explain to herself in terms that

64

satisfied her reason why she considered the birds' egoisms and aggressions more innocent than human ones.

Two birds jumped down from the rim into the bath, where they met chest to chest and neither yielded. They stood for a moment upright and then, in unison, lowered their bodies into the water. A third pigeon waited on the rim for his turn.

The speckle-headed bird flew away. She was usually unwilling to mix with the other birds, though once, when she was being followed by a cooing wooer, the queen had seen her stop, turn and swiftly kiss her pursuer before walking on.

The others, for the most part, marched or fluttered about the ledge. The falling snow exhilarated them. The two in the bath gave no sign discernible to the queen (who herself was only now feeling warm enough to take off her coat) of noticing the cold.

The pigeon on the rim stuck his beak into the water, between the side of the bath and the side of one of the bathers, and took a long drink, sucking up the liquid and not needing, as birds of other types did, to tilt his head back in order to swallow.

A pigeon settled on the coping stone, sank his chin into his fluffed-out, crop-full neck and raised one foot (for warmth or to rest it?, the queen wondered) against the underside of his body.

First one of the bathers and then the other extended his wings, tipped, with a comic solemnity, forward, almost onto his forehead, and then whirled his wings to splash the water all over his body.

They clambered out, leaving a white scum on the surface of the water from the grease of their feathers. The pigeon who had been waiting jumped in.

Beside the bath, the two who had already bathed shook themselves. Then they made each feather stand out individually, reminding the queen of the feathers in angels' wings in paintings, rippling and shaking each area of plumage in turn like a bodybuilder displaying the repertory of his

65

muscles. The size of the birds was magnified; the pattern of their markings was no longer coherent; the queen could no longer recognise which, of the birds she knew, they were.

One of them lay down. He lay tilted to one side, leaning on the wing he had bunched against the floor of the ledge. The other wing he stretched full out, resting only its tip on the floor.

Hoping the tray had been removed from outside her study, the queen prepared to go and visit the king. Just before she left, she saw the pigeon who was lying down tilt yet further onto his side and raise his extended wing almost to the vertical, so as to allow the snowflakes to drift down into his armpit.

*   *   *

'Of Kings' Treasuries', Ulrich thought, quoting John Ruskin.

He squatted in front of the triangular cupboard in the corner of his dressing room.

On the next to bottom shelf he found his soldering instruments and the barrel-shaped tumbling machine, not unlike a small-scale locomotive, which had shaken his stones for days against grains of coarse sand until they were polished. On the bottom shelf, bulged into cardboard boxes whose walls had now split, wrapped in old, odd pages of *The Times of Asty* and (the paper in this case shiny and hard to screw up) *Evarchian Gem Collector Monthly*, 'the paper for the enthusiast of small means', he found the stones themselves, a few of them semi-precious but most just pebbles or lumps he had picked up, cut and polished for the sake of their patterned veining.

He found what he was after: a smallish flake (or largeish chip) of black obsidian whose polished side was irregularly dotted with small white spots, their edges sputtered as though they truly were snowflakes just landed. It had been too roughly shaped to set; Ulrich had simply mounted it naked on a steel ring. The ring was open and therefore adjustable, which suited Ulrich's present turn because, though he knew

66

them well, he could not have gauged, in her absence, the size of Clara's fingers.

At the desk in his bedroom he wrote briefly of his hope that Clara would sometimes wear the ring when she rode the mare, whose colouring and pattern it matched in miniature.

From his desk drawer he took the string gloves Clara had lent him, hesitated about which finger to choose, decided on the little finger of the right-hand glove, and drew the ring over it.

He made the assembly, together with his note, into a package, which he waxed and sealed and then addressed to the Countess Clara Claribond.

He could tell he was no longer in love because of the elegance and economy he had managed to impart to his gesture. The very handwriting was the neatest he had ever addressed to Clara.

As he walked the corridors looking for a footman to take the package out to Tom (it would have cost him hours had he rung and waited for someone to answer), he wondered if all the love he was capable of giving was devalued, reduced to the semi-precious, by some liability in it to stop. He wouldn't have censured other people for faithlessness in love, since he recognised that love was not within the power of the will, but in his own case it was as if he knew, even if he could not quite remember, some secret and remote past history that made the behaviour of his emotions discreditable.

*   *   *

The writer of the only great novel in Evarchian (in the judgment not only of the queen of Evarchia but also of several professional critics) opened the door of the pretty little terrace house he occupied within the precinct of the Winter Palace and found on his doorstep, overtopping him (even though the doorstep was on a lower level than the hall of his house), the Archduke Sempronius, the Archduchess Heather and, behind

67

them and happily, he thought, a little shorter, an unknown young female.

'You have such lovely snug armchairs, cher maître', Sempronius began straight away, snowflakes standing in his blond hair as though he had arrived through a storm of sequins, 'whereas we appear to have virtually no chairs at all and nowhere, in consequence, for the new English Miss to sit down for an hour while she recovers from her journey. So we ask your mercy. Besides, you speak such excellent English and'— Sempronius began to speak in English himself—'your Mrs knows how to make tea.'

It took a little time to get them ushered, in single file, through the narrow doorway, to get their wet coats (and the English girl's wet headscarf) off and hung in the narrow hall and, after he had made a whispered enquiry of Sempronius, in their native language, about the king's health (the answer was not hopeful), to get the writer's English flowing again. It was like, he thought, a fountain pen that did contain ink but which one had not used for some weeks.

They were all, in the end, thoroughly ushered and seated, and without too much violation of precedence. Gratified that he and his wife made an afternoon habit of dressing neatly even when they expected to be on their own (he was in his carefully tended velvet suit, she in her soft, pleated dress of dove grey which indeed made her bosom look plump and yielding like a pigeon's breast), the writer, as his anxieties retreated and his English idioms advanced, began to feel not unpleased by the royal visitation. There was nothing he imperatively had to do that afternoon; and he was always happy to have his drawing room, which was neat at all times of day, seen by others.

Sempronius sat in one of the rose-strewn armchairs he considered snug, Heather and Missy Six (as the writer calculated this new one must be) side by side, but well distanced, on the sofa, whose tall, rigid drop-ends were bound up by tasselled shoulder knots like those on the dress uniforms of Evarchian

68

officers.

Heather's hair, the writer noticed, looked merely dank from the snow, whereas her brother's, as the sequins dried, fell into finespun rococo ringlets.

The host himself sat on a pouffe: not for want of choice (his drawing room was, if anything, slightly over-furnished) but because it seemed aptly lowly and allowed him to be easily mobile.

His crouched position was perhaps a reminder to himself that, should the opportunity flower from the unforeseen visitation, a single question to Sempronius might settle the serious anxiety that had been besetting him for forty-eight hours.

The front plane of his mind, however, was still bustling with small, immediate and social anxieties, and his upward gaze was directed less often at Sempronius than at the two girls, who took a sort of social priority in his concern through being female. Behind or between them the writer glimpsed from time to time an undulation, as if of an overtowering monster, of his black but half siamese cat as she stalked hazardously to and fro along the thin, braided top of the back of the sofa.

The writer's wife sat up, on a hard chair, to the tea table. Because the conversation was predestined to be in English, her part in it was limited in advance to pouring tea from the energetically worked teapot of English Victorian silver into the floral and also English china cups and miming to each guest the question whether she should add milk or one of the slices of lemon that were aromatising the room.

After each answer was given, the writer sprang up from his pouffe, steered the cup and saucer to its destination and followed it with a delivery of the sugar basin and tongs.

'Your Mrs does indeed', Sempronius said after his first sip, acting out his appreciation socially, 'know how to make tea. Do you not think so, Missy Six?'

'Excellent', Missy Six confirmed, accepting the cue, after a

69

moment's difficulty, under her new name. It was almost her first coherent utterance in Evarchia.

'My wife will be so pleased', the writer replied, and he spoke to her in Evarchian.

The hostess blushed plumply to her royal guests, smiled with particular kindness to Missy Six, who, she realized, was bewildered, no doubt because part of her consciousness was still following the rails of her long journey, and spoke in Evarchian to her husband.

'She says it is because she obeys the English method, whereas in Evarchia most people use tea bags.'

'You see', Sempronius said with a shrug to Missy Six. 'We are an under-developed people.'

Missy Six considered remarking that tea bags had now invaded England itself but she feared that the intended self-depreciation might be construed otherwise. So she merely smiled at Sempronius and took a demonstrative gulp from her teacup.

'I ought to be explaining to you', Sempronius said. 'I hope we are not all too disconcerting for you at first. Well.' He looked about for somewhere to transfer his now emptied cup to from the arm of his chair. His host sprang up and mimed the offer of more, which was in mime refused. 'As you know, the chief job is to read Greek with Mama.' Silently the writer transferred Sempronius's cup back to the tea table. 'Mama is very worried that her Greek will fall far below your standards. She has asked us to warn you that she has forgotten a lot, that you will be dealing almost with a beginner again.'

'I'm sure', Missy Six said, 'that—', and she purposely mumbled the end of her sentence.

'Perhaps she is being modest. She is a very modest woman, especially for a queen', Sempronius said. 'I can't judge. Although we all learned a little Greek from Mama when we were young, we have all forgotten it all. Except perhaps my brother Urban. He may well remember. Anyway—'

'Ow-ah', the black cat said.

70

The writer's wife spoke in Evarchian.

'My wife says she hopes you do not have an objection to cats?'

'No, I love them, thank you', Missy Six replied, trying at once to be polite to her host and to indicate to Sempronius that her attention was still his.

'You will discover', Sempronius pursued, 'that Mama has two intellectual passions. One is ancient Greek literature. The other is modern English life. She has never been in England. We have none of us ever been in England.'

The black cat leapt from the back of the sofa to the window ledge, where she landed noisily and began to walk to and fro, flowing round, almost rubbing her flanks against, threatening, but not quite dislodging a Worcester jug that stood at the exact centre of the ledge, bulging yet upright and svelte, and undamaged apart from a mended lip.

'Mama says that actually to go there now, to see England in reality, would break her heart or at least her imagination. Suppose, she says, it proved to be not as she imagines it? However, nothing can sate her appetite for information about it. When you meet Missy Five, as you will do this evening, when she will have returned from the cinema, she will no doubt tell you how Mama has wearied her with demanding to hear about a typical day in London, how I go for a walk along Bond Street, how I go into a pub for some beer, and so on and so forth. And then, besides Mama, who, despite the demanding nature of her intellectual passions, is very gentle and easy to deal with, you will have to deal with all of us.'

Turning to face the nearer corner of the sofa and thereby virtually turning her back on her companion on it, the Archduchess Heather heaved her huge legs into a triangular shape on the sofa seat behind her.

From his crouched perch the writer watched minutely and in horror. Her boots, still damp and stained from the snow, approached the clear yellow silky covering of his sofa.

Heather had allowed her imagination to extrapolate from

71

the fact that the new girl had read classics at Cambridge to the expectation that she would be a classical beauty. Imagination had been belied at the first, through-a-window glance, as the chauffeur handed the girl out from the car that had met her at the Eastern Station. The girl wore her hair long and loose in a manner Heather found unattractive. (It was the way she wore her own.) Heather took no further interest, addressed to the new arrival not a sentence more than politeness obliged and was content now that Sempronius's charm should rise on the girl like an early summer sun.

'. . . our several passions', Sempronius was saying, 'in English literature.'

For her part, Heather turned yet further away—in order to look, over the back of the sofa, at the cat on the window ledge.

As she turned, she put one of her big pink hands over her trousered kneecap and pulled it towards her.

Her boots continued to stick out beyond the edge, a millimetre short, the writer observed, of the yellow upholstery—not, he felt sure, through scruple but merely because her thick legs would not fold into the space available to them.

Heather's gaze met the wide, luminous stare of the cat. The cat sat down on the ledge but without breaking her stare.

'Ulrich prefers Milton', Sempronius said in answer to the question he had at last coaxed from the English girl. 'Balthasar's favourite is Crashaw. My sister likes Marvell.' Heather turned her head briefly towards the middle of the room and nodded, acknowledging Marvell rather than the living company. 'Urban is most fond of Dryden.'

'What sophisticated tastes', the English girl said.

'I suppose so. But I don't think that is wrong. Do you?'

'No.'

'And in any case', Sempronius said, 'the simplicity of my own taste compensates for it.'

'I was just going to ask you about your taste.'

'Can you guess? Can you guess what I consider the most beautiful of the many beautiful poems in English? The most,

72

in a way, surreal, the most'——Sempronius strained, almost visibly, his command of English—'merely *there*, take-me-or-leave-me?'

'Something', she hazarded, 'by William Blake?'

He shook his head. 'It is also, this poem, I ought to say, very neglected, very unappreciated.'

'Perhaps it's a poem I don't know. You have probably read far more English poetry than I have.' She made a little, uneasy stir of skirt.

'You know it. I guarantee you know it. I will say it for you. It is very short: and perfect.' Sitting very upright, still and beautiful against the bowery back of his armchair, Sempronius recited:

> 'Little boy blue
> Come blow up your horn.
> The sheep's in the meadow,
> The cow's in the corn.
> Where is the boy
> Should look after the sheep?
> Under a haycock
> Fast asleep.'

A little silence came down on the end of the poem.

To her astonishment the English girl felt a start of tears behind her eyes.

'It *is* beautiful?' Sempronius asked quietly, a touch anxiously.

'Yes', she replied in a serious tone, though she was mentally trying at the same time to set her emotion down to fatigue and disorientation. 'You were right.'

Moving suddenly in his chair, demonstrating perhaps that he could break, even if he had not quite been in control of, the spell he had cast, Sempronius alluded with his head to their host while he said to the English girl:

'Speaking of literature, perhaps you do not know, Miss,

73

that we are the guests of the finest writer in Evarchia?'

'Really? No, I'm afraid I didn't know. Please tell me what—tell me about it.' Her voice had taken on again a tone of politeness and bewilderment, as though she had shifted vocally forward onto the edge of the sofa.

'A novel', Sempronius replied. 'It has been translated into English. You still have'—he fired a look down at the pouffe—'the English edition?'

Bodily signalling reluctance yet obligingness, the writer slipped through the pretty thicket of his furniture, stroking his cat as he passed, to a glass-fronted china cabinet that held not china but books.

Everyone seemed socially overweighted with expectancy—except the writer's wife, who sat plump and pleased, having followed in arrears the drift of the conversation from the direction of her husband's search along the shelf.

At last he returned with the book, which he slid, open at the title page, onto the English girl's lap.

Neither title nor author's name was known to her.

'How interesting', she said, turning the book meaninglessly about, glancing at the front of the matt, pastel-coloured jacket, which had a layer of dust impressed into its texture like face powder into skin.

It was quite a thick volume, published by the Grey Walls Press in 1954.

'You have not read it?' Sempronius asked.

'No. That is, not yet. Perhaps, after I've properly settled in, I might borrow it?'

'I should be honoured', the writer said, giving a telescoped bow from his pouffe.

'And yet', Sempronius said, 'it was reviewed in an English journal, was it not?'

'In two', the writer said, gazing between his knees at the rim of his pouffe and, beyond that, at his Persian carpet.

The English girl slid her palms beneath the halves of the still open book and made as if to return it to its author. But he was still looking at the floor. Instead, therefore, she proffered it sideways, towards the Archduchess, almost as if she were proposing to transfer a sleeping cat or baby.

'I've seen it', Heather said.

Alerted, the writer sprang up and took the book away.

'And then', Sempronius resumed, 'there is the job of our English conversation, Miss. You must please give your solemn promise that you will correct each of us whenever you hear us say anything wrong.'

'Really?' she asked.

'Why? Are there so many errors that you feel you will be always correcting?'

'No, no. Your English is marvellous. I only wish I spoke any foreign language as well. All I meant was that it would surely be annoying for you, inhibiting . . .'

'It is the only way to improve us. Is there, perhaps, one thing that you have already noticed that I always do wrong?'

'How shrewd of you', she said, surrendering. 'Or how transparent of me. Yes. In England, one doesn't use the word "Miss" quite as you've been using it. It isn't the equivalent of "Mademoiselle"—for which we, very awkwardly, *have* no equivalent.'

'In*deed*?' Sempronius asked. 'You are serious?'

'Missy Three', Heather pronounced, suddenly attentive to the conversation. 'That's where we got it. Missy Five always *says* she must have been vulgar.'

Sempronius enquired:

'Is that correct? "Miss" in the sense of "Mademoiselle" is vulgar?'

'Technically, I suppose, yes', Missy Six said, and she sighed.

'You sigh?'

'I don't know what I think about this problem myself. You see, I tell you that in England we don't use "Miss" in the sense of "Mademoiselle", but in fact we do. About eighty per cent of us do. How can I tell you that what they do isn't the English language? English is their language as much as mine. After all, they have no other.'

'Unless what they speak *is* another?' Sempronius suggested.

'Quite so', Missy Six replied. 'Is it a wrong version or is it merely an alternative? And in this particular case one can't even say they have corrupted or replaced the received form. In modern English there *is* no received form for it, but there is a need for one, as French, German and Italian all testify by having one. This is a case where received English offers not a ruling but a vacuum. And the problem is just as difficult when it comes to grammar and syntax. Half the population says "you was"—in place', Missy Six thought it as well to explain, 'of "you were". And as a matter of fact "you was" has been acceptable, even among educated people, for many more centuries than it's been unacceptable. When I was up at Cambridge—it may all have changed by now—there was a great fashion for permissiveness in language. It was always being said that the language is whatever people actually say, that the so-called rules in English were merely imposed by grammarians, who with no good reason tried to make English conform to Latin . . .'

'And what do *you* say?' Sempronius asked.

'I find it hard', Missy Six said, her face wrinkling with worry, 'to be as permissive about language as about life. I find it hard to believe that Latin is necessarily a bad model. . . . But then I am a latinist . . .'

The writer had gone back to looking at the carpet. The problem being discussed interested him. What was a language, a dialect, a patois, an error? At what point in evolution did a deviation separate itself from the stock and become an independent species? In his own novel he had introduced certain Islander expressions and forms of words not merely into dialogue spoken by Islander characters but into his own narrative, vouched for by himself as writer. It was the first time that had been done (except by illiterate accident) in written Evarchian. He reminded himself to look again, after the royal

76

departure, at the English translation of his book to see into what sort of English the translator had transposed his Islander words. Yet he did not raise his head to join in or even to follow closely the conversation between Sempronius and Missy Six. He was aware Sempronius would soon rise to conduct his party away, and he was preoccupied with whether he would or wouldn't manage first to ask Sempronius the question.

'But I suppose in practice, for the purposes of my job here', Missy Six said, 'it's simple enough. I imagine what you would want to learn from me is the received usage?'

'No', Heather said loudly. 'I'd much rather learn the vulgar usage.'

'I think', Sempronius said, 'we would at least wish to learn which is which.'

'True', Heather allowed. 'I shouldn't get much pleasure from speaking vulgarly if I didn't know I was doing it.'

'Yet you must not, please', Sempronius said to Missy Six, 'make deductions from the office to the person. As a matter of fact, although we are, insofar as our office is concerned, non-political, we are all, insofar as we are persons, democrats and socialists—and, indeed, republicans.'

'And also militant atheists', Heather said. She accepted a tiny signal from Sempronius to rise, an example that was at once copied by everyone in the room.

'Except Papa', Sempronius added. 'Papa is a Christian. In fact, he is a Catholic and Pre-Canonical Christian. Politically, he is probably a Christian Democrat and a Christian Social-ist—which means, as you will realise, something very different from being a democrat and a socialist or even from being a Social-Democrat. Whether Papa is also a Christian Repub-lican, and quite what such a thing would be, I don't know.'

'I don't know what it would be, either', Heather said. 'In fact, it probably has no meaning. But I think Papa *is* one.' She turned to Missy Six. 'When we were very young indeed—well, I suppose Sempronius wasn't, but I was practically a baby still and Urban wasn't much more—Urban—that is, the youngest of my brothers—came to the conclusion that he could recognise no sovereign authority except the will of the people. He went to Papa and declared his conclusion. "Yes, my darling", Papa said, "I completely agree with you." Urban was just opening his mouth to argue or, probably, to ask how Papa reconciled such a view with continuing to sit on a throne, when Papa added: "Unfortunately, the will of the people is that I should be their sovereign." '

Laughing politely, murmuring that he would fetch the coats, the writer, followed by his smiling wife, manoeuvred behind the standing people and between his chairs and made for the hall.

'And what', Missy Six asked Sempronius while they waited, 'of the queen?'

'She is', he said consideringly, 'a woman very sensitive to other people's rights and very anxious not to use emotional power to influence their views. That is probably why she says so little. And because she says so little her own political opinions remain a matter of conjecture.'

'I conjecture she's a communist', Heather said. She turned abruptly aside and began to stroke the cat.

'That would not greatly surprise me', Sempronius agreed. 'Her views on religion go equally unexpressed, but perhaps one can deduce them from what she says about the New Testament.'

'Which is?' Missy Six asked.

'That it is written in deplorably bad Greek.'

'My wife asks me to say', the writer said from behind Missy Six as he helped her into her coat, 'that we are very sorry that neither of our two daughters was here. They would have liked so much to meet another young lady from England. They are not here because one of them is at each of our Evarchian universities. The elder is teaching chemistry and the younger is studying mathematics.'

'I hope I shall have the opportunity later on', Missy Six said

78

and, having reminded herself, she added: 'And also the oppor-tunity to read your book.'

After the guests had left, the writer and his wife carried the tea cups, one by one, into the kitchen and washed them up, also one by one.

The question the writer had wanted to ask was whether the queen's patronage, thanks to which he occupied his house in the Palace precinct and received, as an unofficial prose lau-reate, a small stipend, was personal to her or whether her power of patronage would cease when her husband died. He had not asked the question because, although Sempronius had placed himself under an obligation to the writer, it was part of Sempronius's charm to make favours taken seem gifts given.

When the tea cups had been stowed, the writer filled a small plastic watering can and returned to his drawing room.

He began to water the trailing indoor plants whose pots stood inside a large porcelain bowl and some of whose tendrils trailed through the gaps in the bowl's basketwork edge.

The black cat sat alongside. At first she simply watched acutely. Then she curved one of her black paws into a hook and played at catching the jets of water.

Since his novel, the writer had written only a few short sto-ries, not enough to collect into a volume, and, at roughly the rate of one a year, some essays and papers for critical journals, which no publisher wanted to collect into a volume. Nowadays he exercised his taste—and came thereby to know what his taste was—chiefly by choosing between other people's crea-tions, preferring one book to another when they were sent him for review, deciding to spend his very small amount of spend-ing money on this piece of china while leaving that in the shop, rather than by imagining scenes and personages of his own invention and choosing between those.

He admitted he was, about his not very distinguished pieces of china and furniture, a little old-maidish, and that he was exploring his own taste more at second-hand, less creatively, than he need.

79

He knew that many people in Evarchia ascribed his retreat from creativeness to the fact that the queen had made him financially secure. From his history they argued to a general rule that creative artists could be kept creative only by being kept on the tenterhooks of poverty.

He considered the argument invalid without being able in his own mind (the charge was never put to him explicitly in conversation) to combat it.

He knew that, although he had been congratulated on vividly conveying, in his novel, many different types of experience, he would never convey to anyone his own experience of writing it. He could only allude to it, in his memory, in a quick deep slash of horror. He had been, the whole time, so preoccupied.

One of his daughters had been learning to walk. The other was swelling out his wife's belly. He had been unable to give more than mechanical heed to any of them, his wife included. While he kissed her he invented or re-cast passages of narrative; it was to the rhythm of passages of dialogue, senselessly repeated by his thoughts, that he made love to her. And then he lay half-awake all the rest of the night, shaping his invented world in advance of the point he had reached in the writing, often in a near-paralysis of dread lest he forget an important invented fact before he reached the moment of writing it down.

His concentration frightened him, threatened him, he thought, with lunacy, because it was compulsive: not merely unwilled but defiant of his will. When his wife recounted something or consulted him about something, when the toddling or, more often, stumbling child solicited his attention, he resolved to attend—and then was pulled away backwards, by a force he could not see, into his other world, from which he did not hear what the real world addressed to him.

He did not know whether his wife had resented—or even whether she had noticed—his mental removal from her. Perhaps she would gladly undergo such another absence for the sake of another novel. She was very proud of the first.

It was not, however, for her sake but for his own that he abstained, developing a technique for dealing with his imagination when it, uninvited, proffered nuclei of fictions: a few he compressed into short stories, which took only a day or two to imagine and write down, but most, even more cleverly, he distorted into sometimes rather brilliant critical perceptions about other writers' work. 'All critical insight', he began one of his critical essays, 'is autobiography by the critic.'

He thought his refusal to write again quite a reasonable and pardonable decision by a man who loved his wife, his daughters, his cat, his home and his own intense consciousness of them all. No one could blame such a man for refusing to take a job in a distant country from which no postal, telephone or return-train service existed.

The cat butted her face into the rose on the watering can, which had run dry.

He put it down and stroked the cat where she idiosyncratically enjoyed being stroked, on the bridge of her nose.

He knew by imagination exactly what it was like to be a cat. The intensity of his knowledge sometimes tempted him to fiction. He refused, of course. To invent a cat would be to absent himself from, to be faithless to, *this* cat, who was the cat he loved.

*   *   *

The Permanent Personal Private Assistant from the Ministerium of Parks and other things said:

'That one.'

He pointed down through the glass at a frail boat that was navigating a gaudy (or perhaps a risorgimentesque) cargo of cherries and angelica through the channel between two coffee confections shaped like the velvet caps inside royal crowns.

The woman behind the counter handed him a sepia ticket with a number stamped on it.

He set off for the inner room and then, changing his mind, returned to the counter—where another customer, a thin man with greyish hair, was by now pointing to a green object that mimicked the spiked case of a horse chestnut split just enough to reveal a glossy brown roundness within.

'I'll have one of those too', the PPPA said when it was his turn again, and he received another sepia ticket.

In the inner room he saw that the grey haired customer had just taken the last wholly vacant table. The PPPA felt resentment. Yet the grey haired customer hadn't bothered to remove his coat: perhaps he meant to be quick and his table would soon be heritable.

However, beyond that customer, a cane was hoisted into the air and waved like the last hope of a marooned sailor. It meant that Karyl Frumgeour was, as the PPPA had hoped, present. It also meant, the PPPA reflected while he crossed the bare floor boards, peril to the close packed customers round about, including an immediately neighbouring pair of middle-aged women who, in their thick tweed suits and deep, marzipan-textured, quasi-tyrolean hats, looked like part of the tenor section of the chorus in *Der Freischütz*. He supposed that the self-assurance (a polite name, he considered, for selfishness) of Frumgeour's manners was licensed by Frumgeour's inherited income and he surmised that, if Frumgeour's carelessness did one day let that emblematic cane of his come into contact with a fellow-customer, it would somehow fall out that the victim of the accident was a woman.

The PPPA hung his coat on an overloaded stand whose wooden branches, several of them snapped short, imitated antlers and edged his way, between marble topped tables with swollen wrought-iron bases, back to Frumgeour's—which, he now saw, already had three people sitting at it.

With difficulty, because of its wrought-iron weight, he pulled up a fourth chair.

'Greetings, dear boy', Frumgeour said, half-hoisting his cane again. 'You know Skimplepex.'

82

'Of course', the PPPA replied, nodding to the author—or, at least, the editor—of a daily column in *The Times of Asty* or *The Astean Times* (one of the PPPA's duties was to read both each morning noting passages his Minister ought to see, and he could never distinguish between them by either literary or visual style) and whose personal name (if, the PPPA thought, he had ever possessed one) had long been swallowed up by the sobriquet that appeared, in printer's cursive, beneath his work.

'Haven't seen you for a long time', Skimplepex said. 'Your lot haven't given any good press conferences lately, I suppose.'

The Skimplepex column was said to keep up the pre-war Astean tradition of bitingly satirical journalism combined with inside political information. The PPPA had once, on his Minister's instructions, tried to leak a story to Skimplepex. The facts had come out wrong and the slant unjustifiably anti-Ministerial.

'But I don't think you know my young friend', Frumgeour added.

'Coffee?' the waitress said from behind the PPPA. 'Or chocolate?'

'Coffee', the PPPA replied, and noticed that everyone else at the table was drinking chocolate. Then, wondering whether it was in contempt, secrecy or possessiveness that Frumgeour had neglected to allow him a name, he greeted the young friend, whom he found a diffident, mildly pretty youth dressed in pretty but retiring clothes of pearly colours that made him look as though he had been deposited, not very conspicuously, by the passage of a snail.

'Well?' Skimplepex demanded of the PPPA. 'Are you here to seek information or impart it?'

'Primarily', the PPPA said fendingly, 'I'm here for coffee.'

'Are both these for the same person?' the waitress asked. She was holding two plates above the customers' heads. Each contained one of the confections the PPPA had ordered, with its own mermaid-tailed fork alongside.

'They're both mine', the PPPA said crossly, pushing the other people's chocolate mugs away in order to make room on the marble table for his two plates. The waitress tucked the counterfoils from his two sepia tickets under a rim.

'And not only coffee', Frumgeour said. 'I suppose you have no need to resist temptation. But that's not true of us all. *Is* it?' On his '*Is* it?', he half-hoisted his cane again, avoiding by merest chance a collision of its handle or his elbow with the waitress, and bored its end towards the large pearly button that secured the top, above the fly, of his young friend's trousers. The youth winced away as if from—or perhaps indeed from—an assault on his sexual integrity.

The PPPA began to eat his cherry boat. 'I wondered', he said to Frumgeour, 'if you had any particular impression of what Crown Prince Ulrich is like.'

'Is the king dead, then?' Skimplepex interrupted.

'Not that I know of.' The PPPA was annoyed that Skimplepex was present, because any information Frumgeour had would go also to Skimplepex. On the other hand, Skimplepex himself might have information to give. It would probably have been already published, but since the Minister, unlike espionage systems and the press, had no funds for buying information, he could not expect to fill his files with exclusive knowledge. As a gesture, almost, of disgruntlement with his Minister, the PPPA filled, instead, his own mouth with the last third of his cherry boat and looked a renewed enquiry at Frumgeour.

He's heterosexual, I believe', Frumgeour said disparagingly.

'It's not a disease', the PPPA said, and a few crumbs and drops of spittle shot from his mouth. So far as he knew, the PPPA was heterosexual himself. He considered it part of Frumgeour's bad manners that he never made allowance for the fact that people he talked to might be. All the same, the PPPA was disconcerted that the crumbs continued to lie noticeably on the marble in front of him, with a couple of small but glinting blobs of liquid between them. He couldn't quite bring himself to accord them an explicit enough acknowledgment to brush them away.

He swopped plates and began very cautiously, with his second fork, to pierce the horse chestnut. Looking at what he was doing rather than at Frumgeour, he said:

'If you think that, you must know of women in the case.'

'*A* woman', Frumgeour said.

'The Countess Clara Claribond', Skimplepex said in a tone he made sound bored. 'Lives in a large tumbledown castle and has no money. It was all in my column months ago. If your Ministerium took the trouble to read me, it wouldn't have to send you on these scavenging expeditions.'

'We do', the PPPA said, taking a small fragment of the chestnut, 'read you. It just didn't arise till now.'

'As a matter of fact', Frumgeour said, 'the person who can brief you is my young friend. He works at the Winter Palace. In the High Chamberlain's department.'

'Only in a very lowly capacity', the youth said. 'I'm afraid I've never even met the Crown Prince. The only one I've had any dealings with so far, and that very remotely, is the Archduke Balthasar.' He pronounced it BALtasar. 'It seems he doesn't think there are enough chairs in the Palace, and there's to be a committee, which I'm to service.'

'Mm', said the PPPA, daring to take a larger piece of the chestnut and deciding that his Minister could scarcely require him to open a file on each of the innumerable royal siblings. He turned back to Skimplepex. 'Claribond, you said?'

'Claribond.'

'I remember your article now. It was just the name I couldn't remember.'

Two tables away, the grey haired customer looked at his wrist and drew the open halves of his coat together over his chest. He had five minutes in which to return to the clinic for his appointment with Petrus Squinch. He had noticed that it was only before his appointments with that most worrying and most pitiable of his patients that he experienced a longing for rich cakes and a dilatoriness about eating them. On one such occasion he had produced an actual parapraxis, by forgetting to wind his watch that morning and sitting on in the café, confident that he still had time to toy with like a cake, while in fact his patient waited at the clinic.

The PPPA watched him surrender his ticket and counterfoil, pay the waitress and leave, again drawing the two halves of his coat together over his body, evidently postponing the buttoning up until he reached the cold outside. The gesture reminded the PPPA of the split case of the mimic chestnut which he had gone back to order almost, he almost persuaded himself, on the advice of the grey haired customer. Had he been content, he accusingly remembered, with the boat, he could have had a table to himself. Though the confections were light, the best in Asty or indeed, some people claimed, in Europe (no one claimed, however, to know whether it was through traditionalism or insolence that so famous and prosperous a place had never changed its décor—or even given a new coat of paint to what it had), the PPPA felt slightly overfed. The constrictions of four at a table made his feeling worse; and he, unlike the unknown customer, could not just abruptly get up and go. He had learnt only a name that he might eventually have remembered for himself or, at worst, have looked up in the back numbers of Skimplepex's paper; and in return both Skimplepex and Frumgeour must now think they stood in credit with him for favours to be drawn later.

*   *   *

Without design or even complete awareness on their part, the order in which the royal siblings visited the king was the order of their birth.

To Urban, therefore, youngest of the sons and next-to-youngest of the children, fell the penultimate slot: at a time when it was dark outside but, since it was early winter dark, not yet night; before dinner for the healthy members of the Family but after it for the royal patient—so far, that was, as he could be brought to eat at all.

Urban understood the tears his eldest brother had shed the night before. But for himself he sat at the bedside clenched round a conscious determination not to be so deeply invaded by pity.

Without knowing whether the thought softened or sharpened pity, he considered that it was because his father had already lived so long and so forcefully that death was able to ambush him now, unfairly, at his weakest.

No nurses were present but Urban could hear distant movements, scrapings away, perhaps, of food the king had repulsed.

The king lay silent, seeming more wan and fatigued than ever—than possible.

The stony air of the fake gothic bedchamber was unwarmed by the fire, unenlivened by the flowers or the weak painting. To Urban it seemed already the air of the tomb. It didn't stink. It had, unnaturally, no smell.

'I was', the king eventually said, 'reading. But it—was too heavy to—hold.'

Urban picked up the New Testament from the bed.

'I know you aren't—religious, Urban—none of my children is—but, in the circumstances, would you . . .'

'Read to you, Papa?' Urban's brothers had forewarned him of the likelihood. 'Yes. Where were you?'

'The—gospel according to—Saint Thomas. Chapter Four.'

One of the earliest in the Missy sequence had asked her infant charges how the Family could call itself Catholic and yet not acknowledge the authority of the Pope. Not knowing the answer himself, Urban had relayed the question. The king had replied, sorrowfulness brimming over his beard: 'I am afraid the Pope is a very bad Catholic.'

87

It was only in arrears, when he attained puberty and the elements of worldly perspective, that Urban found the answer funny.

'You don't—mind that it's one of the—non-canonical—gospels?'

'They're all the same to me, Papa.'

As he opened the book, Urban was submerged by an involuntary, very strong but quite imprecise reconstitution of the mental mood of his early childhood. He knew his way round the contents of the book. And yet, now he was put to the test, it turned out he didn't *exactly* know. What he was really recollecting so strongly was the fact that he had once known. And when, half stumblingly, he came upon the required place, his memory found it could not quite anticipate the events of the story he was to read aloud but told him only that he had once known it almost word for word, in the indeed rather wordy Evarchian translation, and that it had regularly provoked in him some secret, teasing excitement.

He began his reading. A great rain fell on Nazareth. Jesus, who was five at the time, collected the surplus water into a large pool. The pool was muddy. By a miracle Jesus made it clear.

However, it was with mud from the pool (which the miracle had, presumably, precipitated rather than abolished) that the little boy then fashioned twelve clay sparrows.

This handwork he carried out on the Sabbath, and his adoptive father, Joseph, therefore reproved him for Sabbath-breaking. But the miracle-working child waved his hands (Urban remembered, as he read, his mother's comment that it was the one intelligent act recorded of him, as well as the most charming) and exculpated himself by removing the evidence: he transformed his mud sparrows into real ones, who flew away twittering his praises.

Then a Pharisee arrived and set about emptying the pool Jesus had made. Jesus struck him dead.

At the end of the chapter, Urban stopped reading.

88

'I suppose', the king said in a voice sad as well as enfeebled, 'that seems a—very difficult—passage to you.'

'Not more than any other.' Urban turned the end of his sentence down in pitch, hoping to turn away the challenge to wrestle with a dying man.

'Yet who', the king pursued as though Urban's answer had never been given, 'are we humans—to say that we—will accept some passages—of the scriptures but—reject others merely—because we—find them hard or—disagreeable?'

Urban made a mm sound in acknowledgment but he thought it strange of his father to press the argument on him when his father had begun by conceding that Urban wasn't religious.

'What is—called the canon of the—scriptures is in fact a—selection from—the scriptures. The—selection was made by—human choice, indeed by—arbitrary choice. It represents—merely the—consensus of personal taste—over a number of years—in the Roman—Catholic Church.'

'Yes, Papa. But I'm not a Roman Catholic, you know.'

'And the Protestants, Urban! Many—of them take—the scriptures as—a literal guide to life. They forget—that they allow themselves to—consult only—part of the guide and that—the selection was, in—the main, made—on an authority they do not—recognise, that—of the Roman Catholic Church.'

'Yes, I'm not a Protestant, either, Papa.'

'No—doubt they had—pious motives. They—did not want to put Christians in the position of judging Jesus. But—they took it on—themselves to withhold—some of the word—of God. Perhaps such—passages are—intended to—try our faith. If—you withhold the trial—from the—people, you—may be—withholding—salvation.'

Urban found he could make no further reply. The king's inability—or refusal—to conceive that Urban did not believe any part of the scriptures seemed to have wound itself round and round him until he was swaddled immobile.

89

At the thought that this non-exchange might be his last conversation with his father, a disagreeable sense of comedy swelled up against Urban's swaddling bands and he remembered how, as a small child tickled by Balthasar, a larger child, he had lain heaving, immobilised in the bondage of unwilled laughter, beyond self-protection or even protest.

'Urban?' demanded the urgent, invalid's voice.

'Yes, Papa?' Urban responded with a promptitude that might have been gulping down a giggle.

'In case we—are tempted to judge, we—should remember—that we humans—do not know what—that Pharisee—was spared—by being—at that moment struck—dead.'

Urban nodded, and the quaking of his emotions stopped. He recovered the more serene excitement the story had prompted in him as a child.

He realised that his father was probably thinking that what the Pharisee had been spared was a slow dying, but even that thought presented itself with only a gentle melancholy.

'I suppose these—scriptural reflexions bore—you and you want to—be off to your—dinner. But I—cannot conceal my—true personality—from my—children, even though—all my children conceal—theirs from—me.'

Urban felt that the secrecy his father reproved him for was gathered round some concealed, sly method whereby he could, if he needed, escape reproof, the constrictions of cross purposes and even the trapped, still air of the gothic chamber. It was as though he held concealed an ultimate, cheating trick, a miracle-working hand that needed only to be waved to get him out of trouble.

*   *   *

Petrus Squinch was already at the clinic when the grey haired doctor returned from the café.

For the first time the patient was accompanied by his

90

mother. Her taut, wasted little body was standing in an attitude of protection beside the tall, thin, worried and stooped young man she had given birth to.

It was the mother, whom he had long wanted to meet, that the doctor invited into his consulting room.

'No, no, I *only* came to explain, *very* briefly, just to let you *know*, doctor, that I'm taking Petrus away, *just* to the country, *just* for Christmas.'

Looking down on the top of her head, where the hair, dyed orange, was coarse and the scalp, at the many places where it shewed through, was tinted a light scarlet, the doctor wondered if her bizarrerie were mother to Petrus's delusions.

He sighed for the responsibility that had fallen to her, which he did not think she could carry or he could alleviate.

'Just for a brief chat', he said. 'Petrus won't mind waiting for a minute or two.'

'It would be *too* naughty of me. To cut into your time with Petrus, which does him *so* much good.'

In the end she agreed, because Petrus said:

'Go, Ma. You explain to him. I can't. How they burgle my brain.'

'*Just*', she repeated as she sat down, 'to the country. *Just*'— she leaned forward and almost whispered across the doctor's desk—'during the Christmas holiday.'

'I think it would be wiser to stay in town.'

'But you won't be seeing Petrus over the holiday.'

'Yet you could always get in touch with me. If you telephone here, the clinic can always contact me.'

'But the *country*, doctor. It's *so* healthy.'

'Let's discuss it in a moment', he said. 'I wanted to ask whether you could give me some idea, just a general impression—or perhaps some incident that stands out in your memory—of what Petrus was like as a child.'

'*Terribly* good', she replied quickly. '*Never* naughty. Not the least bit of trouble at all.'

'He isn't, you know, being naughty now. He's not bad, you

91

realise? Just ill.'

'You see, doctor, I feel the country will make him well.'

'His is not a physical illness.'

'But the *peace*, doctor, the peace of the country.'

'To revert to his childhood. Did he have friends among other children? Was there any one particular friend? What were his interests?'

'When Petrus was a child, doctor——. That was when we were living in Vienna.'

'Yes?'

'O yes. Although I am Evarchian, I am *also* Viennese—by adoption. I didn't bring Petrus back to Asty until—O, I can't remember. He was quite a big boy by then, I think. But still *good*. That was when his father left us.'

'Would you tell me about his father?'

'His *adoptive* father. Well, he was also his real father, but he had to adopt him later. I always told Petrus to call him "Father", even before he adopted him, but Petrus never would, and do you know, doctor, I think it was all for the best, after all, because when he left us Petrus never missed him.'

'How do you know?'

'He just went on playing. He was *so* good.'

'What did he go on playing *at*?'

'At? He played with his animals.'

'What sort of animals?'

'Just—animals, doctor.'

'Cats? Dogs? Mice? Guinea pigs?'

'O *no*.' She sounded repelled. Then she gave a loud giggle, which ended in a small shriek. 'Fancy you thinking that. No, no. Toys. Toy animals.'

'Of what kind were they?'

'Teddies, I think. Teddy bears.' She giggled again. 'I baked one once.'

'Baked?'

'After Petrus had had the measles. However, that was not a teddy. It was a'—she cast about—'duck.'

'The duck was his favourite? If it had been so much with him, during his illness, that it had to be baked, it must have been his favourite?'

'Really, doctor, I can't recall which was his favourite. He was silly about them all. But never naughty. Never *never* naughty. He had several. Three or four. Or five or six. He called them the Bear Family. Or the Duck Family. I simply *don't* recall.'

'Did they return with you from Vienna?'

'Who? No. Petrus's father had left us. Didn't I tell you? It was just Petrus and me, as it has been ever since.'

'I meant the animals.'

'I haven't, doctor, the very least idea. It is of absolutely *no* importance. And here's naughty, naughty me prattling to you about toy ducks when it's Petrus who needs your help. I'll just creep away now and send him in. And *do* tell him, doctor, that *you* want him to go to the country for Christmas. He sets *such* store by what *you* say, you know. And it *will* be *so* good for him. Tramping over the hills, walking in the winter woods, the cold clear clean air—he knows all the farmers round about, you know, doctor—they're all *ever* so kind to him—O, I'm sure he'll come home *quite* healthy.'

The doctor said nothing. He had no power to compel and not even any articulable reasons to put; only a pre-logical intuition.

'Did she explain?' Petrus asked when he came into the consulting room.

'Yes. But what I would like us to talk about this evening, Petrus, is the toy animals you had when you were a child.'

'I don't remember them.'

'You didn't have any live animals?'

'My mother thinks dogs and cats are dirty to have in the house. Am I going to the country?'

'Do you want to?'

'Yes, it will be very healthy for me. I shall tramp through the winter woods, in the cold, clean air.'

'Was it a family of bears or of ducks?'
'Ducks', Petrus said definitely.

*   *   *

'Yes, all right', Heather said. 'What are you reading?'
The beautiful, emaciated hand gestured faintly across the orange quilt towards the New Testament.
'Don't be silly. You've read it. You need a crime story or a spy story, something that will hold your attention.'
'I can't—concentrate. Will you—just talk to me, perhaps?'
'All right.' Heather sat grossly down on the side of the bed and the inert, invalid's body rolled into the hollow she had caused. 'Woops', she said. 'What do you want to talk about?'
'Is your eldest—brother very upset at being—snatched from the side—of his fair—Countess?'
'I haven't asked him. It's none of my business.'
'But—guess.'
'How can I? I've nothing to go on. Incidentally, it's none of your business either. He doesn't *seem* upset. You haven't asked about Missy Six, who arrived today.'
'What is—she like?'
'Nothing', Heather replied. 'This quilt is shabby. And a quite hideous colour. You need a new one.'
'It was made by—the women of the—eastern or perhaps it was the—southern—provinces.'
'But not recently. Sempronius's favourite poem in English is "Little Boy Blue".'
'Is it?'
'"Where is the boy Should look after the sheep?" All English nursery rhymes are about sheep.'
'Really?'
'*I* can't think of anything else to talk to you about. If you don't feel like reading, you ought to listen to the radio. Where is it?'
'There isn't—one, so—far as I know.'

94

'Nurse!' Heather shouted.

'Heather', the king whispered. 'You should—have gone to—fetch her. Princes—should never be—impolite—to inferiors.'

'She's not my inferior', Heather said.

'No, of course—not, really,—but in social terms . . .'

A girl came into the room, looking timid. 'Highness?'

'Is there a radio for the king?'

'No, Highness.'

'Can you get him one?'

'I don't know, Miss—Highness. There was a gentleman here this morning who said if we want any non-medical supplies we should indent for them, but I don't know how—'

'It would take an age, anyway', Heather said. 'All right.' She gave a nod to the nurse, who went away.

To the king Heather said:

'I'll get you one.'

'Heather, please—don't upset—I don't need—', the king protested, but she had already marched to the door.

The High Chamberlain was not in his office but his transistor was.

On a scratch pad she found on his desk, Heather wrote:

> Have taken your radio for
> the king.—Heather A.

She carried it back up the grand staircase and along the numerous corridors between the centre of the Palace and the keep.

'How unfair this royalty business is', she said to the king, who was lying with his eyes shut. 'I'm just reaching the age when, if I was anything else, I could refuse to disclose my first name and insist on being called Miss Whatever-my-surname-might-be, as a mark of respect to an adult. But being royal is like being a perpetual child.'

'The royal Family is everyone's—family', the king said.

95

'All our people feel—related to us.' He opened his eyes. 'Where—did you get—that?'

'The High Chamberlain. Incidentally, I forgot to tell you, Balthasar went to him earlier today, to try and get some more chairs for the Palace. But he didn't have my luck.'

'Chairs? For the—Palace? I've never noticed—any—shortage.'

'No, because if there *is* a chair you sit in it.' Heather switched on the radio and tactfully turned the dial from the station that carried news bulletins, including those on the king's health, to the one that broadcast only music.

Music came through.

'Beethoven', Heather pronounced. 'I'd hoped there'd be something good. They're broadcasting the new *Norma* some night soon.'

'Symphony number—seven', the king said. 'Gorgeous stuff.' He closed his eyes again. 'Gorgeous.'

'O well, if you like it. It's the eighth, actually. The minuet. I find him clumsy.' Clumsily, Heather put the radio down on the bed. It tilted into a valley of bedclothes and the music faltered. 'You need a bedside table for it. I'll tell the nurse tomorrow.'

'Are you leaving—me already?'

'You've got Beethoven.'

'Heather. If you won't—stay with me, will you—do something—for me?'

'What?'

'Comfort—Ulrich.'

'What for?' Heather asked unthinkingly and rhetorically before she slammed the door. The nurse in the next room heard her clearly, the king only faintly through the sound of the orchestra, as she sang down the corridor:

Baa, baa
Back Teeth . . .

96

Chapter Three

The Cardinal-Patriarch appointed the Feast of the Epiphany to be observed as a day of national thanksgiving for the king's recovery.

*　　　*　　　*

(In green ink on cream paper, deckle-edged; die-stamped at top left 'The Countess Clara Claribond' and at top centre 'CCC' surmounted by small emblematic coronet; spots, presumably of coffee, on paper, causing ink to run in places.)

Ulrich dear—I was so delighted when Martha told me the good news—She heard it on the radio—Even so, I held up this letter until I had heard it for myself, because you can't always be sure people have got it right when they tell you things they've heard   I was so glad for your sake—and of course for *his*, too   Although I don't know him at all well in the personal sense, I have always thought him a marvellous person—and so charming—

When you read that I 'held up' this letter you will probably think that I have indeed 'held it up' quite long enough anyway—

But you see, my dear, I didn't want to write anything to distress you while you were feeling worried and 'gloomy'—and I knew you would realise straight away, from the

97

packet (I mean, it being not just an envelope) that I was returning your ring—your very dear ring—

But you will see, Ulrich dear, that I must return it because it is a ring—I know it is not a precious one—though very precious to me—but even so, it is a ring—and if I wore it people might assume things—or even ask, and you know that discretion is not my strong point!

Ulrich, after you left the castle so suddenly and in such a state of worry—well, in fact, during all this worrying time—I have had time to think, and it brought it awfully near to me how close you were to becoming king—

Well, I know you will say that it has always been on the cards—and of course you are right—but in the normal course of events one tries not to think about eventualities—

And you see, Ulrich, what I thought was that I just could not bear to be queen—

All the cafuffle with your detective and the telegrams and so on—all of which would be so much worse if you were actually king—one would be so much less *free*—

Well, I know you will say why shouldn't we just go on as we are now—

But, Ulrich dear, it could never be the same—You and me having a love affair—and it has been a *love* affair, my dear, so far as I am concerned, please believe that—it is quite a different thing from me being the king's mistress—Do you understand? When you are king you won't be able to have a love affair, even, without it being in a way '*official*'—

I realise you will think I am being very unfair to you—penalising you for the accident of your birth or something—I can just hear you saying it—

And in many ways I feel I am a coward—

But I have to tell you the truth, Ulrich—I just cannot face it—

I am just not cut out to be a queen—or a king's mistress.

Goodness knows what I *am* cut out to be—But in some

way I have managed so far to be myself—and though I have tried to imagine it I cannot feel I would be free to be myself any more—

I realise I have explained very badly—but please try to understand—and to forgive—

your

C.

PS. Martha thinks I am cut out to be a mushroom grower! She is full of the idea we should grow them here in the old dungeon—Apparently, they grow well in basements and if the dungeon is not a basement I don't know what is! Certainly, *some* help with the finances is needed! Perhaps Martha is afraid I won't be able to go on paying her wages! But I don't know where we would sell them—It is no good having a stall by the side of the road out here, because there is hardly any traffic, as you know—and what there is is mainly lorries—What do you think of the idea??

PPS. Ulrich, please let me know that you have had this letter and that you *understand*, even though I've put it so badly—Please write *soon*—Don't keep me waiting as long as I kept you—I had to, because of not wanting to upset you more than you were already—

*   *   *

Daily, it seemed now, the decades-old Daimler, flying the discreet pennant of the patriarchate, drew up in Ceremony Square.

Father Felix descended first, from the seat next to the driver, and held open the rear door for the Cardinal-Patriarch's descent, in the course of which he would render the Cardinal-Patriarch little courtesies (a palm beneath an elbow or sometimes even a swift stoop to pavement level to uncurl the hem of the Cardinal-Patriarch's robe) that put old-fashioned passers-by in mind of the great days of grand arrivals, when, by lurking outside the Winter Palace of

99

an evening during the party season, you had been able to count on seeing grand-scale unshippings, by gentlemen in white gloves, of wives or (perhaps the closer analogy) mothers.

Of course Father Felix himself wore a long skirt, though as it was merely black and tolerably narrow in cut (without, anyway, the least suspicion of *train*) it seemed to need less continuous protection than the Cardinal-Patriarch's from the elements. The memory that the double descent from the Daimler provoked in the very oldest-fashioned of the passers-by was of the days of dutifulness, when dowagers had exacted escort to balls from their unmarried daughters or from half-paid lady companions.

Although the Palace gates would willingly have opened to their car, the two ecclesiastics always got out in the public square and, in a gesture generally interpreted by the watching Household staff as one of humility, tramped on foot across the snowy forecourt.

When fresh snow had fallen overnight, Father Felix would march ahead and the Cardinal-Patriarch would follow his tracks. (Eyeing them from a Palace window the Archduchess Heather noticed herself humming the Wenceslas carol, and giggled.) Invariably Father Felix paid the penalty of arriving with a damp hem. And his sacrifice did not always save the Cardinal-Patriarch from having to hitch up his vestments by taking a handful of them at the hip, causing the disclosure further down of disappointing grey trouser legs with turn-ups.

When, however, the snow was stablised, which it usually was these mid-winter mornings, the two would walk side by side, Father Felix turning his head to chatter to his patron. The only exception was when the Cardinal-Patriarch was carrying the sacrament to the royal convalescent. Then *he* would lead—and Father Felix would follow, eyes cast down and tongue stilled.

On these occasions the Cardinal-Patriarch would walk—or perhaps stalk—with a particular slow and rigid gait, as

100

though he did not want to jolt the sacred vessels, which, covered by a fringed cloth of violent colour, he carried, bracketed between an upper and a lower (much ringed) hand, just above that early-pregnancy paunch that paradoxically increased instead of spoiling both his vested dignity and the impression he made of being personally austere.

In whatever order they crossed the forecourt, the two always, before they reached the portico, formed themselves into a procession.

The Cardinal-Patriarch received the salute due, under the concordat, to his office and, once inside the Winter Palace, bored undeflectably through its corridors.

The colour combinations of his needleworked robes changed weekly. If one of the footmen who variously bowed and genuflected as he passed had been learned in liturgy but had lacked a calendar, the changes would have informed him how Advent was advancing.

The cloth that draped the sacred vessels changed from violent purple to violent turquoise, and its fringe ripened from silver to gold. The queen remembered the beaded squares that had hung over milk jugs before refrigerators were common in Evarchia. And Missy Six, turning a corridor corner unawares, was reminded by the solemn port of the vessels of how one carried a cup of coffee from a self-service counter, with its saucer balanced on top.

The procession made its way to the former sickroom, where the king now sat up, for increasing portions of the day, in the wing chair from the Private Drawing Room (agonisingly manoeuvred up a twisting stair by three footmen), wearing his bristly dressing gown (a hair shirt, Ulrich considered it, turned inside out, the penance being imposed on others) and eager, to the limits of his recuperating strength, to discuss with the Cardinal-Patriarch the details of the thanksgiving ceremonial.

It was by his dignity, his austerity and also the intensity of his visits that the Cardinal-Patriarch contrived, without ever putting the idea into words, to propel through the Palace the belief that the recovery for which thanks was to be given was miraculous.

*   *   *

The Archduke Balthasar drew, on his copy of the Agenda, a repeating pattern, one of whose motifs was phallic; a just recognisable Donald Duck; and a solid cube, its sides cross-hatched each to its own degree of shadow—an academic exercise of a kind which, as a matter of fact, had never been required of him during his schooling.

His long chest descended lower and lower over the table top. His by nature long-sighted vision became unable to focus on his drawings. He was attending acutely to the words uttered round the table and at the same time he was recognising, with astonishment, his own response to the experience.

The chairman (the Comptroller) having set the precedent, each speaker felt obliged to begin his first contribution to the meeting by felicitating Balthasar on his father's recovery. Balthasar was therefore alert for the cues at which he must sit momentarily up and grin, murmur or make an acknowledging movement of his hand on the table.

He was on the alert also for a cue that wasn't given. From the preliminary talk in the High Chamberlain's office Balthasar's memory had afterwards isolated three subjects (the Inventory, the precedents and the defining of a chair) about which, he considered, the obstructionism accumulated like silt round the stilts of a bridge. He believed he could shew all three theses to be nonsensical. On a square of jotting paper (now hidden beneath his Agenda) he had carefully written the headlines of his arguments against each. The words in which he planned to present his arguments he had rehearsed, compulsively and all but involuntarily, while he bathed and while he shaved. He arrived at the first committee meeting secretly effervescent with excitement and a sense of risk. He could not

102

quite trust his pencilled and abbreviated headlines to prompt him to the full fluency of his rehearsed speeches and he felt in danger of doing his case less than justice. He took his place (at the chairman's right hand, in tribute to his rank), read the Agenda that had been laid on the table in advance like the cover plate in a restaurant and found in it no subject-heading that had anything to do with the three subjects he had picked out.

The members of the committee arrived piecemeal, each making his separate obeisance to, and requiring his own acknowledgment from, royalty before he would sit down. The Head Carpenter, whose office had been so cardinally linked to the definition of a chair, did not arrive. His absence went unexplained.

Several presences were also, from Balthasar's point of view, unexplained and unnamed, including a youth in grey who sat at the far end of the table and wrote what Balthasar took to be the minutes of the meeting, doing it all with a gesture that could not have been easy to accomplish of distancing himself both from the committee and from his script.

And still, as the meeting went on and speech endorsed, politely differed from or shewed no traceable connexion with speech, none of the three subjects was mentioned. Utterances of gracious acknowledgment were several times required from Balthasar. But occasion never seemed to be given him to speak pertinently about the chairs.

Balthasar asked himself what his own sensations were and discovered that he was feeling, as he had never done in his life before, simultaneously fascinated and bored out of his wits.

The speeches fell from all directions on his lowered head. An ache began at the back of his neck and his limbs were stiff. And yet the thought of shifting his bodily position and, still more, his concentration was disagreeable to him and he was specifically conscious of not wanting the meeting to end yet.

He seemed to be pursuing and always on the verge of catching some thread of hidden logic in the discussion—which, if

103

he could only concentrate enough to trap it, would disclose to him a connexion between what was being said now and his own original perception that the Winter Palace was short of chairs.

He wondered if he was listening to the speeches in the same spirit as a flagellomaniac received the blows of the whip.

When the meeting did end, Balthasar discovered by consulting his watch that it had lasted over three hours. And nothing, to Balthasar's mind, had emerged except the date of the next meeting.

That he remembered agreeing to in a state almost of trance, with both his this year's and his next year's pocket diary open on his Agenda sheet in front of him. 'We mustn't', the Comptroller had said from the chair, 'inadvertently pick on Epiphany, a date that is reserved for a much more important occasion.' The committee had laughed, and its members felt obliged—or took the opportunity—to felicitate Balthasar all over again.

They slipped away piecemeal, some making Balthasar an embarrassed half-bow before leaving the room.

'Well', the Comptroller said. 'A useful meeting, I think.' He straightened a large clutch of papers by tapping their ends on the table-top, fitted them into a cardboard folder, and stood up. 'Yes, I think we progress, we progress.'

Balthasar wondered what papers the Comptroller could possess on the subject of the shortage of chairs, since the subject hadn't really been discussed.

He retrieved his own unused scrap of notes from underneath his Agenda and scrunched it secretly inside his coat pocket.

When he got back to the Family part of the Palace, he found that one of the private secretaries had left him a message propped on his dressing table.

It was written on the bottom, torn off with the help of a paperknife, of a sheet of foolscap and said:

104

Times of Asty rang about cttee about the chairs. Said I wd ring back and tell them when you can give them interview. Wd you let me know please?

It seemed to Balthasar ironic that, after three hours of committee, he had no news whatever to give.

He wrote on the bottom of the paper:

Please ring back and thank them for their interest but say that the chairs (or the lack of them) are a purely domestic problem.

BA.

Between the *t* and the second *a* in the secretary's version of his name he made a caret sign and inserted an *h*. Then he put the message on the silvergilt tray that stood on a table in the East Anteroom, where the whole Household's letters waited for the secretaries to sort them.

*   *   *

The Cardinal-Patriarch's return journeys, from the convalescent's room back to the portico (where his driver usually proved to have defied instructions, brought the Daimler into the forecourt and thus spared him a second tramp over the snow), were much more diffuse affairs than his arrivals.

No longer intent, no longer implying, in silence, a single-minded message, he moved without haste through the Palace, sprinkling through the corridors specific items of information as though they had been droplets of holy water. The king would, on the day, leave the Palace building at ten forty-five and the forecourt gates at ten forty-three, and, while the great bell rang out, would ride, on his white horse, across Ceremony Square to the steps of the Cathedral . . . No, that plan was, on the advice of his doctors, which was endorsed by his

105

security officer, cancelled. It was now into the Jewelled Coach that he would, at twenty to eleven, climb . . .

While his robes changed colour for liturgical reasons, the Cardinal-Patriarch's face, for no guessable reason unless it was the sheer excitement of having so much elaborate ceremonial in his charge, took on daily a more transparent, a more nudely babyish pink. At the same time it became plumper and softer, until it resembled the pink lumps in a box of turkish delight—down, indeed, to the dusting of white, for such bristles as survived even his close shaves were white in colour and the Cardinal-Patriarch was in the habit of smoothing them over, as though to paint them out, with well rubbed-in handfuls of talcum.

Accessible though he was, even genial, he couldn't of course stay for ever. All the designs and details arrived at in his consultations with the king had to be set moving towards execution beyond the Palace walls, and the Cardinal-Patriarch always had, in the end, to drag himself away in order to broadcast the latest decision through memoranda to the Cathedral staff, through pastoral letters to the provincial clergy, and even, as the time drew closer, to the public through press releases.

Often, however, he left behind him, within the Palace walls, Father Felix.

After the kingfisher passage of his vested superior, Father Felix, in his simple black (occasionally with white lace collar), looked like an underskirt. He might have been an unneeded petticoat which the Cardinal-Patriarch had simply stepped out of as he went and discarded in one of the Anterooms, where he could often be found draped, in the general absence of chairs, on the marble top of a console table.

He was young, and of a saintly thinness. Brown hair rose en brosse from his brow and descended en brosse from his cheeks. The lips sandwiched between were as soft, as startlingly pink, as palpably pored as raspberries.

His personality, too, made an impression of uncalloused

106

candour and naturalness.

'I think', the Archduke Sempronius whispered to Missy Six, 'he is a character trying to get into a Dostoevsky novel.'

It was Missy Five who drew the most comfort from Father Felix's gift of sympathy. His beautiful deep brown eyes often tottered on the edge of tears of fellow feeling. He was prepared not simply to listen to but to enter into emotional turmoils that other people (Heather perhaps) would have dismissed as cases of hysteria or self-indulgence.

More and more ('though of course it isn't', as she told Heather, '*my* religion'), Missy Five confided to Father Felix the anxieties of her departure or dismissal, and his soft-voiced sympathy lapped towards her over the marble top, in the susurrus of an unofficial, standing-up confessional.

Upstairs, a doctor said to the queen, diagonally across a wing and the back of the wing chair:

'I see no reason why the strength should not be almost fully recruited by the time Epiphany comes.'

(But then, so Ulrich construed his mother's unvoiced thoughts, the doctors had seen no reason for the illness in the first place—or for the recovery, either.)

'Always provided', the doctor pursued, 'that the appetite can be tempted a little.'

The queen therefore asked the Kitchens to send up one of the little *pots de chocolat* with which the king usually, by his own avowal in English, made a pig of himself.

But at the sight of the earthenware pot, with, just below the rim, its froth of solidified bubbles, some of which had burst and set into tiny, delicious craters, the king, though very politely, turned his head away.

At Sempronius's suggestion, the queen asked the chef the next day for profiteroles.

Again the king directed his gaze to the inside of the wing of his chair.

Ulrich, on-looking, spluttered a sudden recognition. 'Papa. You're not still trying to fast for Advent?'

107

The king's face took on a look abashed but not at all ashamed. Indeed, he stared more fixedly than ever at the wing, as though trying to control a smile.

It was Balthasar who, acting on his mother's thoughts, sped out of the room and down corridors and stairs, thrusting open doors until he arrived at the one that disclosed that Father Felix was indeed still in the Palace and snatchable away to the keep, there to pronounce an absolute, unconditional, in fact virtually mandatory dispensation.

Missy Five, to whom, as so often recently, he had been talking, let the Father be snatched from her without complaint. The questions he had been asking her had suddenly changed her vision of him. The compassion, the simplicity of heart, the unsnobbish willingness to linger in the Palace and discuss their personal concerns with people of high rank or low: in the new perspective, all seemed the traits of triviality. Missy Five had lost faith in Father Felix as a saint. She now saw him as a gossip.

Perhaps that, willingly on his part or, more probably, artlessly, was his usefulness to the Cardinal-Patriarch.

In his snug little office (which, as winter set hard, was much remarked to be the warmest and most comfortable room in the Palace), the High Chamberlain said:

'I still think Epiphany a poor choice, and I don't care who knows it. With all respect, you can't trust the church with ceremony. They're not professionals. They always have an ulterior motive—nothing sinister, of course, merely something spiritual, and quite right too by their lights. But the result is they don't give the ceremony priority. And so they botch it. What they've botched in this case is, of course, the timing—the psychological timing.'

'You mean in relation to Christmas?' the Comptroller asked.

'Precisely. In close relation, in close-after relation, to Christmas. The whole nation works itself up to Christmas. And then the Cardinal-Patriarch calls for a day of national

108

rejoicing twelve days *after* Christmas. It'll be a national anticlimax.'

'I must confess', the Comptroller agreed, 'it seems a little inept, a little inept.'

'Only the church', the High Chamberlain said, 'would choose, for a day of national jubilation, the day on which, by tradition, one takes the Christmas decorations *down*.'

A few days afterwards it happened that the Cardinal-Patriarch seemed to have more time than usual for lingering in the Palace, time enough to come upon, severally, many members of the Royal Household and even the Royal Family. Smiling more affably than ever, talcumed even more liberally than usual (to the point where an interlocutor could distinguish that the scent was of lilac), he mentioned conversationally that, by the tradition of the Catholic and Pre-Canonical Church of Evarchia, the major winter festival was Epiphany; under western and perhaps commercial influences, Christmas had now, of course, increased in popular importance; but among the peasants and Islanders, as well as in some provincial families of the nobility, the older custom still held sway, Christmas was a comparatively minor feast and it was at Epiphany (the English Twelfth Night) that families gathered to feast and parents gave presents to children.

'Do you think', the Archduchess Heather said, that afternoon, to Missy Five, 'Fate slipped up in having me born on Christmas Day? Oughtn't it to have been Epiphany?'

'Perhaps it ought, dearie.'

'And then I could have been called Viola, after *Twelfth Night*. Or Epifania, like the Millionairess.'

Missy Five understood neither allusion but she made no enquiry. She was preoccupied by lamenting that, whether through evasion or heartless forgetfulness, Heather should muse on thus without once acknowledging the fact that Epiphany was the date appointed for Missy Five's departure.

* * *

109

The Crown Prince's suite (in effect, his bedroom and dressing room, since his bathroom was shared with Balthasar) contained, apart from the bed, only one place to sit: a hard, upright wooden chair with a somehow 1919-ish look to it. Perhaps its severely elongated back was a belated tribute to the influence, received into Evarchia by way, no doubt, of Vienna, of Charles Rennie Mackintosh. When he sat there, the high back overtopped Ulrich's brief torso, yet the seat raised his knees too high for them to get comfortably under the in any case shallow kneehole of his little davenport-type desk.

As he sat on it trying to reply to the Countess Clara, the chair felt to him as hard and discomfiting as a stool of penitence—though his must have been an oblique penitence, since his legs had to be slewed sideways-on to the desk. What he began as a letter he was forced presently to think of as merely the draft of a letter. He was oppressed by Clara's post-postscript, which spurred him as a point of honour to write *something*, soon. Yet the more he hastened, the more, he realised, his exposition became repetitive, self-contradictory and full of inverted constructions he could see no way of wrenching to a syntactical conclusion. Eventually, there was no letter and not even a draft. They had disappeared into their own maze of arrows and loops signifying insertions and transpositions.

When the doctors declared his father's recovery Ulrich had expected to be repossessed by his infatuation. But though he listened minutely to his own sensations he could detect nothing of his former obsession creeping back into his thoughts. He did not even want with any urgency to see Clara again. His mental landscape, when he considered Clara, was like a naturalistic painting by an amateur: it depicted features recognisably but captured no illusion of light.

He re-read Clara's letter to him. He remembered that,

110

when he had been in love with her, her half-literate punctuation, which was common enough among the ill-educated daughters of the upper class, had provoked in him a particular affectionate response, as though mentally he had always read it with his head tilted to one side. But he could no longer remember quite what his response had been.

In the new coldness of his feelings he was aware that Clara's letter offered him honourable release. He had only to accept.

Yet his very coldness calculated, coldly, that that would be a waste. He had never taken all the pleasure he was capable of from Clara's body, because his pleasure had been liable to be overwhelmed by great springtimes of joy. He found himself plotting how much more efficient he could be, now there was no question of love, at lust.

His flesh rose to the thought.

Suddenly Ulrich was berating himself as dishonourable and craven, and his cold excitement had been replaced by cold nausea. All the loves to which he had been unfaithful accused him. He was tumbling down a rocky hill and at this point, at this love, which he had so nearly already slid past, he must be stern with himself and, even if it barked them, dig in his feet.

He could overcome Clara's objections by the simplest (so it seemed as his mind sketched it) of acts, the renunciation of his inheritance. And if he embraced his true love after his affection had in fact ceased, the abnegation of the rest of his life was no more than the perpetual martyrdom he owed to all the other true loves he had slid past among the stones.

His resolution was subverted by his recognising what a comfortable martyrdom his would be, given that his lust still lived and that he had always dreaded being king anyway.

He sank his head onto the uncomforting slope of his desk lid.

A nostalgia took him for his own feelings as they had been before his father's illness, when love, lust and honour had all (or so it seemed to him now) been plaited into a single silken bond.

111

He was afraid that any relation he might now pursue with Clara would be haunted by his regret for his previous, perfect love for her, like an unimportant country with a splendid history.

Longing, suddenly, for someone to recount his own history to, he passed his siblings in review.

The thought of Balthasar, he found, was almost wholly a conjuring of his bodily, bony, likeness. Ulrich had almost no concept of Balthasar's personality and couldn't therefore assess Balthasar as confidant.

Sempronius would give his charm generously. But it would be the same charm as always, undeviating, a panacea that could not adapt itself to a particular suffering or sufferer.

Urban—. Ulrich's thoughts halted. If he was ignorant of Balthasar, it was through a dereliction on Ulrich's part or perhaps just an unavoidable blurring of his vision as a result of their proximity in age. But Urban, whom Ulrich took to be certainly the cleverest of the brothers, was also the most furled. He wasn't silent or ungiving. But he answered questions economically, Yes or No, and the utterances he volunteered came pre-cast in elegant shapes, so that you remembered them as dicta and considered them for their content (hence, perhaps, the impression that Urban was the cleverest brother) and got from them no indications of the birthpangs of the personality that had brought them forth.

Ulrich had previously felt an affinity with his youngest brother because both their names began with U, as though their parents had decided to initiate and close the series of royal sons with that open-ended and enquiring vowel. The initial now seemed all that Ulrich could be certain of sharing with Urban. Enough the elder to do so without condescension, Ulrich had watched Urban becoming adult and had expected his personality to set firm and declare itself. Yet though it obviously was firm it declared itself only inwards. Urban seemed to find himself a sufficient spectacle or, alternatively, a sufficient audience.

112

Ulrich's thoughts moved to and, surprisingly, fixed on Heather: younger and yet, compared with the unopening bud that was Urban, overblown. All her secrets must be open secrets. Yet to his astonishment it was in Heather that Ulrich suddenly discerned a particular concentration of the life force and from her that he was suddenly convinced he could get, if he knew how to accept it, an *elisir d'amore*.

On a fresh sheet of paper he obliged himself to write, quickly and without second thoughts:

This is just to assure you I have your letter and the ring. I will write properly as soon as I can. For the moment I'm a bit lost beneath all that's going on here in preparation for Epiphany. A bientôt—U

He went to look for Heather, intending to ask her for an appointment for a private conversation.

*   *   *

The first night of the Royal Astean Opera's new production of *Norma* was indeed postponed: in deference not, however, to a royal death but to the militancy of Evarchian trade unions and the perfectionism of the designer. A dispute about whether the sickle with which Norma was to cut the mistletoe was a Schedule One property (which artistes might carry off-stage themselves) or a Schedule Two property (to be deposited on stage and removed later by stagehands) passed the point where anyone could back down unscathed at almost the same moment as the designer, seeing the Roman soldiers' costumes for the first time, condemned them to be torn apart at the seams and re-cut, on the grounds that he could not lend his name to the transformation of respectable tenors into gym-tunicked girls from an English school story by Angela Brazil.

The Bulgarian Cultural Attaché, though not surprised (it was a *mot* in Asty that the advance programme of the Royal

113

Opera was as likely to be fulfilled as the weather forecast), was disappointed.

On Christmas morning he walked across Ceremony Square staging the *Casta diva* scene in his mind.

Feet, wheels and shovels had removed the snow from the centre of the square, but round the edges, as well as in the forecourt, which bordered one side of the square, of the Winter Palace, it lay opaque and compacted.

The morning sun added a layer of luminous gold to its surface.

In the Cultural Attaché's mind, however, that was, by Bellini's and his own imagination's alchemy, transmuted to silver.

His mental voice growled the deepish, almost transvestite notes with which Norma first enunciated the melody.

'Casta diva, che inargenti queste sacre antiche piante . . .'

And suddenly he was *in* the ancient sacred grove which the chaste goddess of the moon ensilvered: he was forrested about by the tall, thin, strong, steel stanchions that were to support the temporary stands from which the crowds would watch the thanksgiving ceremonial.

He emerged into the clear and passed the Cathedral steps. Last-minute-comers were hurrying up them to one of the Christmas morning masses, chivvied by the swift, monotonous nagging of a lightweight, raucous bell. The Attaché's thoughts expunged them. Norma alone mounted the steps, approaching *her* altar, to the tones of *her* rite.

He passed a real, though also in a sense sacred, tree: the large Christmas tree that stood at the side of the Cathedral steps as the Cardinal-Patriarch's gift to the people of Asty.

It faced, across the square, another large Christmas tree, the one that stood outside the gates to the forecourt of the Winter Palace as a gift to the people of Asty from the king. (Would the gift, the Attaché wondered, have been made posthumously if the king had died?)

He approached the corner of the square and realised that

114

his rendezvous could not be literally kept. The fountain that was his destination had been covered by a tarpaulin, and a stand for the crowd was being built round and over it.

As the fountain had been turned off, and as the machine in his pocket would not have been baffled anyway, it made no difference whatever.

He got as close as he could and turned to survey the square.

He stamped softly in the snow, to signify the entry, in the progress of the music in his thoughts, of the chorus.

And then he at last loosed his mental voice into its soprano upper realm, as he floated Norma's high, shimmering vocal line above the dark, melted-together sounds of the chorus, and, in his mind as it listened to itself, the sequence of notes lay on the air like one of those ripples of moonlight-coloured paint that were sometimes imposed over the black lacquer ground of Chinese cabinets.

The Chairman of the Communist Party of Evarchia approached from the opposite direction.

He came not across the square but along its sides, weaving between stanchions and sometimes looking upwards into their heights, as though searching branches for birds.

He reached the Cultural Attaché, halted beside him and kicked at the base of the nearest stanchion, which gave a brief, steely ring.

'Happy Christmas, Comrade', the Cultural Attaché said. 'So the king didn't die.'

'No', the Chairman replied, apparently neither giving nor receiving any resonance of irony. 'He's going to make a public demonstration of his robust health. And proletarians have to build stands so that proletarians can get a good view of it.'

'If the first proletarians get the work finished in time', the Attaché said. 'But perhaps these affairs are better organised than the Opera.'

'I heard there was a strike there', the Chairman said.

'A go-slow. If they resolve the dispute, perhaps they'll have the new production ready by Epiphany.'

115

'No doubt', the Chairman said. 'No doubt the union will accept another bribe.'

'Does it accept bribes, Comrade?'

'All bourgeois unions accept bribes, Comrade. What do they fight for, except bigger bribes? More leisure . . . You'll notice work on these stands has stopped for Christmas—'

'Most people do stop work at Christmas, Comrade. Except you.'

'If the date doesn't suit you, you should have said so. Did you want to keep it free for going to mass? More leisure, higher wages: bribes. In return, they agree to forget they belong to the working class.'

'I don't follow your drift, Comrade', the Cultural Attaché said. 'Are you arguing that the working class should be forced to work over Christmas?'

'In bourgeois countries—', the Chairman began. He stopped and turned away. In fact he wished precisely that the workmen had been kept at work either by the press of poverty or, better still, by a feudal and personal caprice on the part of the king.

The Chairman himself was feeling, as he supposed the king to be, in robust health. He had suggested Christmas Day as the date of a meeting to several people. It was his private test of their objectivity. The Bulgarian Cultural Attaché was the only one he had been able to cajole into accepting. The others, even his colleagues in the Party, had rejected not only the day itself but the surrounding days on both sides, pleading the rush to buy consumer goods in time for the day or the need for the leisure to consume them after it.

As a result, the Chairman's engagement book did not shew a meeting during an entire fortnight and he had not felt so well-rested for a year.

Grudgingly, he said to the Cultural Attaché:

'The appreciation I gave you of the situation last time we met was correct according to the information available at the time.'

116

'Yes, of course, Comrade. No one thinks you ought to have been able to predict the king's recovery.'

'If it *was* a recovery', the Chairman said. 'If he was ever ill in the first place.'

'Have you reason to think he wasn't?'

'I can see what would be to their advantage. If, for instance, they knew that a move was in preparation on the other side of the border—'

From behind the two men a voice said:

'Merry Christmas.'

They turned.

Scarlet hung swaying between two stanchions. A young man dressed as Santa Claus had gripped a stanchion on each side of him and let his body lapse forward, so that his white-bearded young face, under its hood, intruded into the conversation.

'Bluntschli's Emporium is reopening its Christmas Fair after the holiday', Santa Claus said. 'It'll remain open till Epiphany. Bring the children.'

He moved off.

As he went, the Chairman commented:

'Suffer the little children to come unto consumer capitalism.'

'You should be pleased, Comrade, that some workers do work over Christmas. An actor, I expect, between jobs. Or maybe one of the chorus from the Opera.'

'Do you think he overheard what I was saying?'

'No.'

'How can you be so definite?'

'The hood', the Cultural Attaché said. 'The hood must muffle his hearing.'

He had no idea whether it really did.

The Chairman, however, nodded, satisfied, and resumed:

'I wish to urge, Comrade, that, given it would be the easiest thing in the world for them to do, and given that to do it would be to their advantage, we should not discount the possibility

117

that they invented the entire illness and recovery.'

'They?' the Attaché murmured. 'The Royal Family? But I don't quite see the advantage to them.'

'To engineer a resurgence of royalist feeling. Combined, perhaps, with a religious revival. People are saying it was a miracle, you know.' The Chairman gulped, as if swallowing back a little rush of vomit. He hated the superstitiousness of the working class, together with the profit shopkeepers made from it at this time of year.

'Indeed?' the Attaché said. 'I don't move in religious circles.'

'What easier', the Chairman pursued, 'in fact, what *cheaper* way could they find of countering any help they got wind of on the other side?'

Pretending to reach for his handkerchief, the Attaché switched off the recorder in his pocket. He prepared himself to tell the Chairman that he was pretty sure no help had ever been mustered on the other side of the frontier and that a coup in Evarchia could not be considered a simply desirable event, since it would alter the balance of power, shift the buffer zone forward, require a new strategy for and higher spending on defence, re-jig the budgetary compromise between weapons and industry . . .

But when he sought the Chairman's eyes, in order to command his attention, he decided they were the eyes of a man too old to take telling.

The Chairman was feeling, however, less old than he had done all year.

His rested mind was able to experience, instead of merely remembering the existence of, his emotions.

He stamped in the snow and drew a deep breath of frosty air, which scratched his lungs and awakened in his chest a pain that he interpreted both as his passionate, nostalgic love for the solidarity of the working class and as his indignation that the solidarity should be broken off—bought off— piecemeal.

118

His opinion was that Evarchian trade unionists translated their power into new pillars that merely performed the same unaltered structural functions in society, translated their high wages into full larders, title deeds and share certificates, and never noticed that they had thereby translated themselves into dwarf capitalists.

Certainly he wished for an oppression of the Evarchian working class bitter enough to make it notice that it was being cheated.

He was proud of the depth of his love, which enabled him to be ruthless.

The Attaché said:

'Your view will be noted, Comrade.'

'That's all I ever get from you, Comrade', the Chairman answered.

The Attaché began to counter, but the Chairman said, compassionately:

'I know it doesn't fall within your sphere of responsibility to commit yourself to more.'

He made an abrupt sketched salute and marched away between the stanchions.

The Attaché walked back across the square, debating the staging of the second act of *Norma* and wondering that Bellini could move him by dramatising an obdurate adhesion to an old religious superstition and to a nordic nationalism.

An Islander was squatting shabbily on the snow huddled at the Palace railings. As the Attaché came abreast of him, he sprang upright, held out his arm in the air and said:

'Season of goodwill, brother. Give us a kiss of brotherly love.'

The Attaché looked up and saw the man was holding over his head a few leaves and a couple of berries of mistletoe.

'Ah, Norma', the Attaché murmured as though recognising a discarded love now grown middle-aged, and he put forward his left cheek deliberately, though puritanically, to be kissed.

*   *   *

Inside the Palace, on Christmas afternoon, the Archduchess Heather gave notice that she had that day become adult. She had, she disclosed, told the chef in advance that this year she did not want a birthday cake with candles.

However, since it was Christmas, there were plenty of other rich cakes.

After tea, when the king had removed himself, and his favourite chair had been removed with him, from the Private Drawing Room back to the chamber in the keep, Ulrich waited for Heather in the Royal Day Nursery.

Twenty minutes after the time of their appointment he went to seek her.

He found her in a corridor beside a table where the servants had temporarily deposited, on their passage to the kitchens, the trays onto which they had cleared away tea.

Missy Five was standing beside Heather, talking intently. Heather was collecting crumbs from a plate that still bore three quarters of a cake intact and lowering them, clutched between the tips of straight fingers, into her mouth.

'You didn't keep our appointment', Ulrich said.

'Fuck', Heather replied in English. 'I forgot.' Ignoring the top layer, which was of icing, she dug her forefinger into the marzipan stratum of the cake and managed to form and get out a lump. 'Let's make it next week, Ulrich. I'll let you know which day later.'

Ulrich agreed, but he lingered a little, still hoping that Missy Five might take herself off so that he could have his private conversation with his sister immediately.

However, it was Ulrich who in the end took himself off.

After listening for the recession of his footsteps, Missy Five said:

'I wish you wouldn't use that word, dear.'

'Why?'

Missy Five turned away her head, hiding incipient tears of

120

hurt, convinced that Heather pretended not to understand many things she understood perfectly well.

*   *   *

The Archduke Urban, whose room did not contain even one chair, lay fully clothed on his back on his bed and from time to time, virtually without noticing he was doing so, nibbled at his favourite food: himself.

An after-Christmas lethargy, resembling the sound-padding girdle of the snow itself, held the Palace in a spell that seemed to exert its force particularly in the afternoons. Urban knew that the queen was working at her Greek with Missy Six and that, in some other part of the Palace, Heather would be listening indifferently to the whispered secrets of Missy Five. But the king had taken to a regular and quite official after-noon sleep while he collected his strength for Epiphany. The High Chamberlain and the Comptroller, though due to return in good time for Epiphany, were on leave. Not that Urban conceived the liveliness of the Palace to rest on them. Yet by mid-afternoon, when the brief winter sun was at its maxi-mum, Urban was aware of a general silence and a sense of there being nothing to do.

At the junction of his left nostril with his cheek there was a tiny, wintertime sore. Inserting the edge of a fingernail under the border of the scab at a point where it was beginning to rise, he managed without very strong pain to detach the scab almost whole. His front teeth received it from his fingernail. It was chewy and took a long, pleasurable time to soften for swallowing.

There was no more scab available. What was left of it was attached to quick flesh and would have hurt to take off.

Then Urban remembered there was a pimple on the crown of his head which, by regularly culling it, he had managed (though again without full awareness of doing so) to keep pro-ductive. With a little difficulty he located it beneath his hair,

121

decapitated it, lost the scab, which stuck on the middle of a strand of hair as he was removing it, recovered it, and ate it.

It was grittier in texture than the previous scab and gave a sharper though shorter pleasure to chew.

While he ate, he read the timetable for the Royal Household for Epiphany. He held it (it was on photocopying paper and smelt sour, faintly like a fruit caramel) close above his recumbent face. He was the only one of the siblings to be short sighted.

The engagement to get the siblings excused from the service of thanksgiving in the Cathedral had been fought by Ulrich, Balthasar and Sempronius, though in Sempronius's case 'fought' was perhaps too aggressive a verb: Urban's thoughts formulated in English that Sempronius was one of the few people who could be said to be winning without first having to be combative.

Urban himself had stood by, holding in his mind an argument prepared in advance which, like a reserve force of cavalry, he was ready to rush to wherever it might be needed. In the event, it wasn't needed and it was Heather, arriving late at the discussion, who carried the point. She simply told the Cardinal-Patriarch ('like', Sempronius said afterwards, 'a trade unionist declaring a strike') that she *wouldn't*.

The concessions the siblings yielded at the patching-up afterwards were merely that Ulrich, as Crown Prince, would appear at the gates of the Palace forecourt to welcome the king home from the Cathedral and that they would all share with the king, who would probably by then be fatigued, an appearance afterwards on the balcony that overlooked the forecourt and Ceremony Square.

There was not much, therefore, that Urban had to note as being to his personal address in the timetable, except that he obviously could not treat Epiphany as an ordinary day and must remember to put on a suit.

Though the king implied he was being bereft of the support of his children, Urban suspected he was not displeased not to

122

be sharing the public's attention with them.

Urban let the timetable descend onto his face.

He wasn't, however, tired and he kept his eyes open though they could see nothing.

On afternoons like this he often masturbated. Briefly he coveted that violent pleasure now. But almost before they had framed the wish his thoughts turned out to have moved sideways, towards some other wish, related but not definable, which frightened as well as tempted him.

He meditated for a moment on the magic power of sexual acts to change the texture of consciousness. The mind flowed, like velvet, so uniformly and urgently in one direction—and then, by an almost literal wave of a practised hand, its tendency was reversed. (About a year before, Heather had made Urban her confidant while she temporarily took an interest in drugs. He did nothing to dissuade her, did not join in, and said he did not believe any injection could produce such a startling change in consciousness as an ejaculation did. His thoughts now added that there must be only one greater and more magic change, the one procured by death.)

His mind felt teased, curled up at the edges, by whatever thought it was he had approached. He had a sense of danger so strong that he moved the timetable and looked at his hands and was surprised that he could not see them tremble.

For refuge he re-read the timetable.

To celebrate his father's recovery seemed to Urban insensitive, given that the supposedly miraculous recovery had not guaranteed its subject immortality for ever after. Was it matter for congratulation that the king, having gone so far into the abominable process of dying, had been snatched back—only to wait passive until he was forced to go through it again, the next time thoroughly?

The miracle of which the Cardinal-Patriarch had persuaded himself was, to Urban's mind, a cruelty; and the miraculously recovered or even miraculously resurrected figures who peopled the Cardinal-Patriarch's mythology were, Urban

123

considered, a legion of the half-hanged, the most ill-used of all victims, since they were destined to die twice.

There was, Urban thought, something craven, something which rendered life less valuable, in the passive obedience to the instinct to live with which people waited for that date they could not influence, the date of their natural death.

Only for his mother's sake could he rejoice in his father's recovery.

He got up and went to stare at the snow on the Palace roofs through the small, high-up window of his bedroom.

He disliked having promised to appear, at Epiphany, on the ceremonial balcony. He was liable to (he supposed) vertigo. On balconies he often had the illusion, which he could never believe at the time was an illusion, that the material he stood on was shifting and quaking before collapsing into the drop.

Comforting himself, he found, while he stood staring at the whiteness that was already touched with evening, another piece of himself to eat. Most of the little flanges of half-dead skin at the sides of his fingernails had been recently cropped. But on the ring finger of his left hand he found one that had been given time to renew itself. His front teeth seized it and incised, giving him sharp pain and a moment's mental ease.

*   *   *

'Of course, I've only met her a couple of times', Heather said consideringly. 'I thought she was sexy, but not, if you see what I mean, absolutely super.' Heather was standing, as she spoke, on one leg, leaving the other dangling, as she tried to get a side-saddle purchase for one of her huge buttocks on the saddle of the rocking horse. 'However, though I don't think you ought to do it for *her* sake, I like the idea of your renouncing your claim to the throne. Have you talked to Balthasar?'

Ulrich assured her he had mentioned none of his present concerns to anyone except herself, and he begged her to *keep* them to herself.

'Yes, of course I will', Heather said. She put too much weight on it and the rocking horse rocked. Her buttock slid off and its undisciplined flesh quivered under the shock. 'But you'll have to consult Balthasar. He's the one whose life will be ruined if you do it. Unless, that is, we *all* do it. Would that be rather magnificent? Suppose we all signed renunciations. Surely they'd have to pack the whole thing in and become a republic?'

Ulrich agreed that in practice, through purely psychological responses, such an unprecedented mass renunciation might well provoke a constitutional crisis, though technically the crown should simply pass to the collateral branch of the Family.

'Yes', Heather said, 'what Papa always calls "the other line", as though we were all tramcars. Still, when they saw how we felt about it, the other line might hesitate to take on the job.'

Working out his own thoughts, and referring back to Heather's view that it shouldn't be for Clara's sake that he did it, Ulrich said he couldn't in honour conceive of renouncing his inheritance and then *not* marrying Clara; it would be, he said, as dishonourable as letting a woman be cited in a divorce that freed one and then using the freedom for some purpose other than to marry her.

Heather would barely hear him out. Standing impatiently beside it, she gave a great nudge with her thigh to the rocking horse and set it tilting and creaking 'Ulrich, your concept of honour is *ludicrous*. I wouldn't be surprised if you got it from the divorce courts, it's so punitive. I expect you think it's only yourself you want to punish, but in fact you're passing it on. It's as if you were in a sulk because Papa got ill and gave you a fright that scared your love away, and now you're looking for someone you can kick in your turn . . . What good would it do Clara to marry you when you didn't even expect to be happy? Is it an act of honour to put her in the rôle of the person who makes you miserable?'

125

Ulrich acknowledged the truth in what Heather said but countered it by trying to explain his admittedly romantic belief that to pass from one seeming true love to another was to devalue them all, since it was to admit that one's love had been founded on illusion.

'Well, of course it is', Heather said. 'Illusion or ignorance. Why does it worry you? Nobody's more romantic than I am. I'm in love all the time—romantically in love—with someone. I've been through *thousands* of people. I don't feel *guilt* for it. After all, when you start to read a spy story, you don't know who anyone is or which of them is a double agent, so they're mysterious to you, and you feel intrigued and you read on to find out more about them . . . But when you've finished it, you know all about everybody, and the story goes dead on you, and you don't want to read it again . . . You want to read another one.'

Ulrich said he was perhaps afraid of just that: that when love ceased he was wishing the once loved person dead.

'But it doesn't rest with you to keep them alive', Heather expostulated. 'People will go on living, even if they're no longer loved by you.'

Ulrich admitted that she had perhaps picked on something arrogant in his attitude.

'Not so much arrogant as childish', she said. 'You seem to think you hold the gift of immortality and can bestow it on the person of your choice, as if you were one of the gods. But people will grow old and change and die, whether you continue to love them or not. Honestly, Ulrich, you're older than I am, and I would have expected you to have found this out long before I did. We're mortal. We're human. One of the dimensions we live in is time. *Tout passe, tout casse, tout lasse.*'

She looked straight (down) at Ulrich. Either the obstinate misery she met in his face or accumulating muscular fatigue or a culmination of annoyance at there being nowhere in the Royal Day Nursery where they could sit down to talk in a civilised way seemed to prompt her to an ultimate impatience. She

126

flung her leg over the rocking horse and her whole weight into its saddle, as though by picking up the reins she could gallop away from the unsatisfactory conversation.

One of the delicate dappled wooden forelegs made a splintering sound and the horse sagged forwards.

'See. *Tout casse*', Heather said. She giggled and dismounted clumsily.

Ulrich stared at the rocking horse's leg. One splintered section of the shaft was now overlapping the other, painfully suggestive of bone. He felt Heather had broken his childhood.

'And now there's absolutely *nowhere* to sit in here', Heather said.

★   ★   ★

On the morning of the day before Epiphany, the fourth item of the Skimplepex column in *The Times of Asty* read:

> Those of my readers who remain in touch with their childhood may recall a fairy-tale character named Prince Charming. Indeed, the more naif among them may have supposed (especially in view of all the niceness and cosiness that's been flying about, these last few weeks, over the royal recovery of health) that we here in Asty rejoiced in the national possession of a whole family, a positive nest, of Prince Charmings. And who wouldn't, you might wonder, be charming in the circumstances? Free from material care, free from the grind of earning a living, inhabiting one of the most splendid (and huge) architectural monuments in Europe . . . To many minds, the very idea of a Royal and Imperial Archduke will be equivalent to 'the man who has everything'.

> But everything, it appears, is not always enough. Word reaches me that the Archduke Baltasar (he's, for the benefit of those who can't keep up with the royal birthrate, the second of our Prince Charmings) is dissatisfied with the

127

royal environment. Not content with living at public expense in the lap of luxury, Archduke B. is trying, it seems, to get the whole interior of the Winter Palace made over into something more up-to-date and yet more luxurious. Unwilling to settle for a few modest mod. con.s, he's insisted on the appointment of an entire commission of enquiry (at what cost, one wonders, to the Privy—that is, ultimately, the public—purse?). Pushed into existence, the commission is now being pushed by the imperious Archduke to seek tenders for what one member of the commission calls 'a complete overhaul job, fitted carpet, air-conditioning, the lot' from firms not only inside Evarchia but abroad. The country's foreign exchange problems evidently don't weigh with the man who's always had everything. Prince Charming, did I hear you say? Or was it Prince Greedy?

*　　*　　*

On the night before Epiphany Missy Six peered towards the glass on her dressing table. She was trying to see, through the poor light that came from the old-fashioned table lamp, impeded by an old-fashioned shade, whether her hair, which she had washed a couple of hours earlier, was yet dry enough for her to go to bed without risk of its re-setting itself, overnight, awry and thus turning out fluffy on the day of the celebrations—which she would consider, though also considering herself absurd for doing so, an act of disloyalty to Sempronius.

She was possessed by an effervescent, lyrical and somehow forward-pressing excitement.

On the dressing table, bedraggled, lay the tokens she had had from Sempronius. They included: an Evarchian-English dictionary in a pocket edition (it placed a disproportionate and, to Missy Six, useless emphasis on the technical terms connected with sailing vessels); a pink paper fan (given away free to female customers at a restaurant where he had taken her

128

for supper); and a white feather which, in the course of shewing her the sights of Asty, he had picked up for her out of the
snow in the Metropolitan Park and which had presumably
been shed by a white peacock.

Next to them lay *The Times of Asty*, folded back to the
Skimplepex column as though to a crossword. When Missy
Six had, with Sempronius's help over the Evarchian, finished
reading it, she had felt in her eyes the unbearable tears of
injustice.

Now, a little belatedly, she tried to caution herself against a
precipitate espousal of the Family honour. No one had, yet,
invited her to feel ill-used on Balthasar's behalf.

She added a caution against the banality of taking a job as
(to all intents and purposes) a governess and immediately falling in love with the most handsome of the sons of the house.

She was quite aware that she might become a victim of the
disparity in fortune between herself and Sempronius—a disparity that consisted, of course, in her being averagely attractive and his being as instantly and conspicuously meet for
adoration in every eye that beheld him as an archangel.

Yet for all her deliberate prudence she was swirled forwards
by her excitement.

Moreover, she could detect in herself not a trace of envy of
Sempronius's social radiance and not a trace of distrust of
him. She was daily the more convinced that she had, whether
she wanted to or not, committed her heart to him—and that
there was not in fact the least reason in the world why she
should not want to.

Somebody knocked at her door.

Missy Six remembered (with shame at having forgotten)
that Missy Five had promised (as she had put it; the offer was
really an insistence) that she would come to make her final
private farewells.

Just before she opened her door Missy Six also remembered
(with a despond that again occasioned her shame) that Missy
Five was bound to be wearing her burgundy woollen dressing

129

gown that zipped all the way up from its ankle-length hem and had light blue facings on the collar.

Missy Six insisted on installing Missy Five in the sole chair, a politeness of which the truth was that she did not want to see Missy Five on her bed.

Missy Five declined her offer to try to find someone to convey an order to the Royal Kitchens for tea or cocoa. (Both Missys knew they had small chance of getting anything so late at night.) Missy Six felt relieved but also deprived of something to do and talk about in relation to her visitor.

She blamed herself for the fact that, though she knew how momentous Missy Five's departure was to Missy Five, she could not receive the farewell visit as anything but an interruption to the progress of her thoughts about Sempronius.

She marked her absurdity in supposing that her very thoughts about him should be held sacred against interruption, as though her relationship with him could progress in his absence, merely in terms of her image of him.

She forced herself to put to Missy Five an enquiry, to which she already knew the answer, about the time and mode of her departure the next day.

While Missy Five answered, Missy Six noticed that it was in fact one of the absurdities of the state of being in love that it always insisted on progressing. Her love for Sempronius collected not only material tokens but looks, disclosures, half-avowals—and not only collected but accumulated them. They were always adding up to something, just as the relationship, as if pressed for time, was always hastening to something. She knew, of course, that one of its destinations was bed. (Would it be *this* bed, from which she had averted Missy Five, or would Sempronius find them a place for making love outside the Palace precinct?) Yet even in bed, Missy Six was convinced, she and he would be hastening on, daring themselves further, as though the essence of love were in its progress and love could never spare time to enjoy its own state of being.

'There is just one thing, dear', Missy Five was saying, 'that

130

I ought to warn you about. At least, I think I ought. I know I'd have been very glad if one of the previous Missys had warned me. Heather—'

'I haven't really yet', Missy Six said, forcing herself to take part in the conversation though only, in effect, to cut it off, 'come to grips with Heather. Most of my dealings so far have been with the queen—who has, I must say, some very peculiar notions about life in England.' While she spoke, Missy Six's thoughts were deliberately saying 'Sempronius, Sempronius, Sempronius', as though he were a note or a number which she had to carry in her mind during this tedious bridge passage in time. And yet, she reflected, there was not the very smallest danger that she would forget him. 'She seems', she meanwhile continued with only half her attention on her words, 'to suppose that one makes a telephone call by hiring a *jeton*, that in a pub one sits down at a table and waits for the waiter to come, that one buys stamps for one's letters at a tobacconist's . . .'

She became aware that Missy Five was gazing directly up at her (Missy Six was raised because she was sitting on the side of her bed) and was, from the jaws of the armchair, gawping.

'*Doesn't* one?' Missy Five eventually whispered.

'No', Missy Six said, frowning as much, still, in an effort to marshal her own attention as in puzzlement.

Suddenly Missy Five was tilted forward from the armchair, was kneeling with one knee positively at Missy Six's feet, scrabbling at the skirt of Missy Six's nightdress and sobbing.

'Don't tell them, please don't tell them, I know you'll think I've cheated them, but I haven't, or only in a way, I *am* British, English is my native language, I've never spoken any other, it's true I've never been to England but I was born British, I can prove it, my passport is British, I'll shew it you, only I generally keep it hidden because of course it shews one's place of birth . . .'

Missy Six condemned herself because her feelings responded only to the grotesquerie before her, not to the compassion she knew she felt.

131

'*Please*, Missy Six, don't tell them, *don't* tell them.'

Missy Six controlled her wish to shake her nightdress free and to say that Missy Five's present behaviour was unBritish.

'Beirut', Missy Five enunciated through blubberings of eyes and nose. Missy Six reconstructed that it was the place of birth mentioned in the passport. 'And then we moved to Alexandria, I went to the English school . . .'

Missy Six obliged herself to put an arm about the heaving back and help Missy Five up and into the armchair again.

She fetched a handkerchief and the bottle of Scotch which she had bought duty-free on her journey from England and which was still almost untouched because she didn't really like it.

'You won't feel you must tell the De Rigueurs? Promise.'

'The De Rigueurs?'

'My new employers.' The phrase (or the concept) provoked a new eruption of tears.

'No', Missy Six promised above its noise, thinking that she was unlikely ever to meet the De Rigueurs and on the heads of the rich be their own extravagances and vanities like employing (supposedly) English girls.

'Heather says the Count knows England ever so well.'

'Then he'll want to talk about his own experiences, not bother with yours.' Or alternatively, Missy Six's thoughts added, the Count might be an impostor himself.

She managed in the end, using the protective arm again, half as propellant, to get a sufficiently dried-out Missy Five back down the corridor to her own room.

She found that, through it all, her thoughts had been holding the note faithfully: Sempronius, Sempronius, Sempronius.

*　　*　　*

'He must be tired—and cold', the queen said, as if apologetically.

She pushed open the glass doors (for which 'french windows' seemed too suburban a name) that separated the ceremonial balcony from the Throne Room, stepped diffidently out and placed her hand, in the gentlest of remonstrances, to the elbow of the king's *other* arm, the one that he wasn't using to wave to the crowd.

At her appearance and, still more, her gesture, the crowd made a huge murmur of inarticulate appreciation.

After a moment the king let himself be persuaded inside, leaning a little on her arm in his fatigue yet courteously gesturing her through the door first.

Some of the vigorous chill from outside came in at the door and ran round the grand emptiness of the Throne Room, but some of the splendid sunlight entered, too.

It was perfect weather for the celebration. (Had there been, when the Cardinal-Patriarch remarked on it, the tiniest of smug hints of an extra, a bonus miraculous answer to his prayers?)

The king stood, for a moment of deep fatigue, where a burst of sunlight coldly illuminated those slices of variously coloured marble whose pattern made the Throne Room floor at once chessboard, compass face and diagrammatic cross-section of a fruit. Seeming as though he could walk no further, he murmured into his beard:

'It's touching. Such affection.'

One of the doctors stepped forward and spoke to him and the queen.

'It seems dreadful to disappoint them', the king said. He raised his beard and wagged it in an unspecified direction that seemed to comprehend all his children. 'Perhaps? Would some of you . . .?'

Ulrich hung back. He had already been greeted by the crowd when he had welcomed the king home at the gates.

Sempronius gave Missy Six, who was standing next to him, a smile of temporary farewell that was equivalent to a kiss of the hand, and went onto the balcony.

Balthasar followed him, uncertain, however, of facing a crowd that might contain readers of Skimplepex.

But the crowd's reassurance echoed—at one remove, like the sound of the sea in a seashell—inside the Throne Room.

Missy Six waited, everything suspended for her while Sempronius was absent.

Missy Five circled the room, everything ending for her.

Skirting the columns and the busts, scouring the niches, she visited all the little clumps in which people, like flexible statues, stood—stood because, of course, there was nowhere to sit, unless you counted the two angular thrones which were obviously uncomfortable as well as forbidden.

She had already taken her private leave of the king (he gave her a Royal Bible—with gold leaf on the cover) and the queen (who had secretly given her a cheque, which Missy Five had in her handbag, along with her ticket) and the royal siblings. She was now descending the circles of the hierarchy, like the circles of hell.

Her goodbyes to the High Chamberlain were scarcely heeded. He was in a fuss because the timetable was lagging and because, once the king and Ulrich were safely back inside the Palace, the crowd had, as the gendarmerie had half expected them to do, scaled the railings of the forecourt and advanced towards the façade of the building itself, to be met half-way across the forecourt by a cordon of gendarmes and restrained there in an untidy splurge whose front border sagged in the middle.

'My dear High Chamberlain', the king said, as he suffered himself to be led, by the queen and the doctor, past, out of the chilly grandeur and into somewhere where he could sit down, 'you should count our blessings. Remember that in other countries when a crowd storms the winter palace it's with hostile intent.'

Missy Five encompassed another circle. She was down, now, to the High Chamberlain's entourage, to the very detectives.

Sempronius came in from the balcony and Balthasar followed him.

Sempronius's vision sought, first, Missy Six and then the rest of his siblings.

'Ulrich, your turn', he said. 'Heather. Urban.'

As if obeying the order of his nomination, Ulrich went first onto the balcony, then Heather ('I hate this sort of thing', she said to anyone in earshot, 'because I know I'm so bloody different from the ideal they cherish in their bloody fantasy lives'), and Urban last.

Missy Five knew the royal car would be waiting for her, though not at the ceremonial door, and she still had her coat to fetch from her room on the top storey.

After only a moment out there, Urban came in from the balcony.

'I'm sorry', he said to Sempronius, 'but could you take my place? It makes me feel ill.' His face was grey.

Sempronius gave Missy Six another of his flowering looks and went out again.

Ulrich was aware that the space between himself and Heather had been vacated by one brother and reoccupied by another.

Sunlight dazzled at him: from the marble of the balustrade and from little heaps of snow cradled between the balusters, which hadn't been swept when the floor of the balcony was cleared.

He looked down through the dazzle at the crowd. It touched his emotions by its numbers. It half-filled the forecourt and wholly filled Ceremony Square beyond, oozing out to occupy the irregular spaces at the corners. It filled, and was raised up on, the Cathedral steps; filled and was raised yet higher, like choirs of angels, by the viewing stands that flanked the steps; filled, indeed, everything in sight except the great dome itself of the Cathedral, which bulged directly towards Ulrich across the square, looking in the calm light less distant than it was, one side plunging down like a ski-slope

135

under its close cloak of snow and the other, which the sun-shine had temporarily bared, lacertine and twinkling with (where the gilt twinkles let you decipher the colour) turquoise tiles.

Ulrich wondered if a document composed, written out and signed by himself would suffice. It seemed simple and fool-proof enough just to renounce the throne for himself and his heirs, should he ever beget any, in perpetuity. But he won-dered if, to make it binding, he needed to have his signature witnessed, which would require explanations to the witnesses even if he didn't shew them the text; and he suspected that, if he didn't seek anyone's advice about the wording of the text, someone, probably the High Chamberlain, would find it easy to pretend to see some flaw in it.

In the square there was a report, followed by a prompt echo. It sounded like a grotesquely gigantic fart and was in fact, Ulrich for a moment assumed, the fart of an internal combust-ion engine.

Pigeons rose hastily and their wings creaked above the square.

But Sempronius fell down onto the floor of the balcony, shot dead through the heart.

Dead March

Chapter Four

The soldiers marched with the ceremonial step that imposed a drilled hesitation on them in mid-stride. The impeded action seemed (and had perhaps originally been designed) to betoken the unnatural cutting short of the natural forwards impetus of a life.

It would have been absurd and even perhaps, in military eyes, impertinent for the man in the civilian suit, who walked behind the leading detachment, to try to keep in step with the soldiers.

He adopted, therefore, his own rhythm, but that was necessarily irregular. Three of his paces took a very slightly briefer time to complete than one, plus hesitation, of theirs. Every now and then, therefore, he had to slow down or take shorter steps than usual in order to avoid running into the rear rank of the soldiers in front or being over-run by the detachment behind.

Against encroachment by his pursuers Ulrich was, however, always forewarned, since they consisted of the massed drums of the Blue Grenadiers.

Always a fraction of a second after his ear expected it, as though he was incapable of learning to allow for the protracted pace, the Grenadiers' every footfall was reinforced by a drumbeat; and with each empty, repeated non-note, peppered by the noise of the snares, Ulrich felt himself inescapably chased by the repetition of dread images in his mind.

Document 27, Group III.

Deposition (2).

I, Nathan Georg, independent farmer, make this deposition before the notary public in the sub-district of Ketsch in the Eastern Provinces. This is my second deposition. In it I shall try to answer the questions forwarded by the Office of the Examining Magistrate. I desire this deposition to be taken in conjunction with the one I made previously.

I did form the impression that Petrus Squinch was not in his right mind. You had only to look at him to know it. Everyone in the district knew it.

His mother did not say it in so many words. She called him 'ill'. But you could tell what that meant.

It was not irresponsible of me to lend him a firearm. The first time I let him shoot over my land I went with him and made sure he was a skilled shot.

We were after pigeon, duck, rabbits—whatever there was.

After the first time, I let him have the key or, to be precise, I shewed him the shelf where the key is always kept. It was not possible for me to be there myself all the time, as I had my farm to run. He was doing no harm and it is always useful on a farm to have someone keep down the vermin.

My motive was as above and, in addition, to do him a kindness. His mother said country life was good for his health.

Originally he was going to stay in the country just for Christmas, but when the celebration of the king's recovery was announced his mother decided to let him stay on till Epiphany. She herself went back to Asty after Christmas. She was going to come and collect Petrus, to take him home by train, on the day after Epiphany. She did not want him to be in Asty during the celebrations because the crowds would make him nervous.

He continued to shoot over my land after his mother had gone back to Asty.

He never borrowed anything heavier than a fowling piece before. (Marginal note: 'Before': sc. before Epiphany.)

On Epiphany I got up very early and drove, in the farm truck, to Ketsch, in order to attend the early mass in thanksgiving for the king's recovery.

How was I to know (crossed out and 'I had no means of knowing' substituted) that he would help himself to the larger rifle and hitch a ride to Asty.

I have firearms of several kinds. A farmer in a remote district has to be prepared for emergencies.

Note: It is from my own observation that I know that the rifle was missing when I got back from mass. I looked because I was thinking of spending the rest of the morning shooting. It is not from my own observation that I gained the impression that Petrus hitch-hiked to town. I heard it on the radio. But I do know that he never had any money on him, so that must be how he travelled.

*   *   *

'Comrade, there is one thing you *must* tell me, because I *must* know. Did you do it?'

The Bulgarian Cultural Attaché evidently shewed his astonishment in his face, because the Chairman of the Communist Party rushed on:

'O, not you personally and in the singular, Comrade, but— You know quite well whom I mean.'

'But why on earth', the Cultural Attaché asked, 'should you suppose they'd *want* to?'

'To induce a revolutionary situation', the Chairman replied as though the answer was obvious.

'Even supposing that was their objective', the Cultural

141

Attaché said, 'it doesn't seem an appropriate or efficient method.'

'Then you give me your assurance?'

'I'm not omniscient, Comrade. But so far as my knowledge extends, yes, I give you my assurance.'

'Thank you, Comrade. I had to know where I stood. I'll keep you informed.'

'What of?' the Cultural Attaché asked, catching him back by the sleeve.

'What do you mean?'

'What will you keep me informed of?'

Instead of answering, the Chairman narrowed his eyes as if taking a pride in his own shrewdness and asked:

'Who do *you* think did it, Comrade?'

'I've absolutely no knowledge of the affair, no evidence at all to go on. I suppose—I assume—it was this poor lunatic whom the police caught on the spot. *The Times of Asty* says he didn't even try to run away.'

'Do you believe what you read in the bourgeois press, Comrade? Do you believe the stories put out by the bourgeois police?'

The Cultural Attaché sighed. 'I imagine all newspapers and all police forces sometimes tell the truth. After all, it must often be easier than making something up. And occasionally, no doubt, it serves the purpose just as well.'

*   *   *

As soon as he realised Sempronius had fallen, Ulrich dropped to his knees beside him. Heather on the other side did the same—and was, indeed, half supporting his weight, which had lurched against her as he went down. Ulrich was aware of her sobbing and saying 'Fuck, fuck, fuck.'

Ulrich was then, as he thought at the time, attacked from inside the Palace, his ankles pulled from under him as he knelt.

142

It quickly turned out that his detective was bidding and in fact forcing him to keep his head down. But for a second or two Ulrich experienced an almost euphoric emotional release as he kicked out in the blind belief that he was injuring the enemies of his brother.

The feeling of release he never recaptured. Its vividness was cancelled by his discovery that it had been an illusion. It was the other events that forced themselves, again and again, through his mind, and however often he involuntarily re-lived them he could not turn those into illusions too.

The images were in his mind as he walked in front of the drums and as he kept vigil at the bier. (He noticed but did not seem to make any inward comment on the paradox that the king, who had wished away ceremonial from his own expected death, insisted on draping his son's obsequies in every last rite at his command.) At nights Ulrich was convinced that the reiterated images would prevent him from sleeping. Yet he did, in the end, sleep, noting with surprise, as he reached the last promontory of consciousness, that he was about to do so. And yet again, the next time he woke, which was not always in the morning, it was with an awareness that the memories had never wholly left him even in sleep.

He came to think that between sleep and waking the distinction was much less absolute than he had previously— perhaps childishly—assumed.

The last image, which always prompted the first to recur again, was always of the unaccustomed view he had had from floor level of the bottom of the balustrade. A drop of Sempronius's blood had splashed onto the snow between two balusters and, as it sank in, its colour became diluted.

*   *   *

Document 9, Group I.
Squinch, Petrus. Interrogation by Examining
Magistrate (verbatim), Session 3.

—Why did you take the gun into the square?

—Because I'd heard.

—What had you heard? Where did you hear it?

—On the radio.

—You'd heard on the radio that there were to be celebrations in the square?

—Yes. They must have heard, too, possibly by radio. It would be a secret radio. Things I always kept private they found out about and made public. They stole.

—Who are 'they'?

(No reply.)

—You say that 'they' stole. But you stole, too, didn't you? You stole the gun?

—O no. That was for shooting.

—For shooting? Shooting whom?

—Pigeons. Or ducks. They're dirty. It was very healthy for me to shoot them.

*　　　*　　　*

The pigeons outside her study window pressed their breasts, which felt frosty to the touch, against the queen's hands, taking warmth from her at the same time as food.

'My children', she said to them. 'O my children.'

*　　　*　　　*

Document 10, Group I.
Squinch, Petrus. Interrogation by Examining
Magistrate (verbatim), Session 4.

—You said, at our last session, that the gun was for shooting duck or pigeon.

—That's right.

—But it wasn't a duck or a pigeon you shot in Ceremony

144

Square, was it?

—O no. In Ceremony Square I shot the Crown Prince.

—Your answer has been noted and written down. However, I must now tell you that the man you shot was not the Crown Prince. It was his brother, the Archduke Sempronius, who was the third in age of the royal brothers.

—No. I shot the Crown Prince.

—What makes you think it was the Crown Prince you shot?

—He was the tallest of them. The tallest is the eldest. Anyone can work that out.

*   *   *

To all members of the committee of enquiry on the subject of chairs in the Winter Palace.

On account of the recent tragedy, the next meeting of the committee is cancelled. The committee is suspended until further notice.

Comptroller, Royal Household
(Chairman, Committee on Chairs)

*   *   *

'I turn now to the subject of Personal Security. For the purposes of our studies, this may be defined as the problem of ensuring the personal safety of such public personages as are likely to be the targets of assassination or kindred attempts.'

The visiting lecturer who gave the course on Security at the Evarchian Academy of Advanced Military Studies was popular with his students. The rather schoolroomy small desks in Seminar Room B were all occupied for his lecture.

He wore civilian clothes. Officially, he was seconded to the visiting lectureship from the police (the police proper, as distinct from the gendarmerie, whose responsibility stretched scarcely beyond traffic and crowd control together with the pettier strata of petty crime). It was rumoured, however, that originally he had been seconded to the police from the army.

The rumour might, on the other hand, have been based on nothing firmer than the type of civilian clothes he wore and the way he wore them. Whether by habit or by choice he had adopted both the cut and the bearing that were fashionable among officers for their off-duty hours.

Indeed, one of the reasons why he was popular with his students was that he strongly resembled his students—who were without exception men of thirty-five or older and, with one exception, officers of the rank of major or higher.

The exception sat at a desk that had been crammed into a window recess, where he was slightly separated from the others. He was or purported to be a private soldier, though he could and did present all the right passes and papers to get him admitted to the course.

Among his fellow students he was nicknamed (though not to his face, since the opportunity never arose) 'the silent Grenadier'. When directly questioned, he answered in the fewest words that would suffice; and none of the students had ever heard him initiate a conversation with anyone. He would not have been allowed, of course, into the officers' mess where the other students dined at night. But in the canteen where everyone, lecturers and students, helped themselves to luncheon he was as silent as if he had not been present there either. He was silent even during the break in the middle of the morning's lectures, when everyone queued (with considerable good-natured pushing) for the little spiced biscuits that were brought in on a tray and queued again for the use of the lavatory (though here the queue was less explicit, as if to admit to a bodily urgency of that kind were to display a lack of soldierly hardihood).

Because he never became entangled in conversation, none of his fellow students ever saw a chance to question the silent Grenadier about his status. To pounce on him without preliminaries would have been to address him as from officer to

146

man, and in the studentish, not rigorously disciplined atmo-
sphere of the Academy that would have seemed bad form.

'All attempts to ensure Personal Security', the lecturer said,
'are predicated upon the presumption of a degree of rationality in the intending assassin. This is a pivotal concept in
thinking about Security.

'We assume rationality in the would-be assassin in two
main departments.

'The first is his motivation. The long-term objectives of certain groups may appear to us irrational. That is a value judgment on our part.

'But if we postulate that, in trying to achieve those objectives, they will employ the weapon of assassination or kindred
weapons, then we postulate that, in choosing the target to
direct the weapon against, they will make a rational assessment.

'Their assessment will not necessarily be correct. We assume, however, that it will be rational, to the extent that the
groups will have asked themselves the rational question, "By
the elimination of which persons will our path to our objective
be made easier?"

'When, for example, a foreign head of state visits our
country, it is by projecting ourselves into the minds of various
groups and asking that question that we, the Security forces,
know which activists, from which groups, we should be wise to
place under temporary arrest until our distinguished guest has
gone home.

'The second area in which we have to postulate rationality
in the would-be infringer of Personal Security is in the plan he
makes for his own conduct after the commission of his deed.

'The assumption we make is that he is rational enough to
want to get away afterwards and escape the consequences to
himself.

'If the intended crime is a kidnapping or abduction, our assumption is invariably correct. It is not possible to conceive of
a successful kidnap without conceiving that the kidnapper

makes good his escape—*with* his victim.

'Assassination, however, is a different matter. All Security efforts against assassination pivot on the assumption that the assassin wants to be able, afterwards, to escape detection and capture.

'It is not, however, necessarily the case that he does so want. The assumption of that degree of rationality in him cannot be relied on.

'And I must say to you, gentlemen, that no Security system in the world can, except by pure, blind accident, protect anybody from the assassin who does not mind if he is caught.

'A very recent, very tragic example will occur to everyone.

'One does not want to anticipate the conclusion of judicial enquiries now in progress. But all the evidence suggests that there was not in this case sufficient rationality to prompt any attempt to avoid the consequences of being known to have committed the act.

'When I say "all the evidence", I am not talking loosely. I see no harm in disclosing that the police officer who made the arrest reported directly to me.'

(The second reason for the lecturer's popularity with his students was that he often saw no harm in disclosing to them items of information of this kind that were not generally available.)

'What apparently happened was that the people standing next to him in the crowd detained him. It was as easy as that. Although he was actually still holding the weapon, he made no attempt to use it to defend himself.

'So these citizens hung onto him and called the gendarmerie, who called the police.

'All this was of course already known to me by the time the funeral arrangements were made.

'I don't know if any of you saw the funeral and thought to yourselves it looked like bad Security? I mean: with the Crown Prince marching through the streets virtually on his own? Well, of course there were troops in front of him and behind,

148

but there was no one on each side. You might have thought he was positively inviting an enfilade. And then, between the next two blocs of troops, there was the rest of the younger generation of the Royals, looking like a marksman's dream. It must have seemed an awful risk after what had just happened.

'But then, you see, I knew that what had just happened was a one-off—the fluke, the irrational case you just can't guard against. And I knew that the man who did that was not in a position to make a second attempt.

'So the chances of its happening a second time were neither higher nor lower than the chances of its happening the first time. The chance is always there, and the odds are always exactly the same, and either you ignore it and risk it or you tell your potential target people that they're never to go out in public, never to go out of doors even, at all. And of course if you tried to tell them that they'd disregard you, quite rightly.

'Perhaps in one respect there was an enhanced risk. Some people think that the irrational cases can be set off by one another's example. I've heard it argued that you can have an epidemic of irrational cases, through the phenomenon of hysterical imitation.

'However, I've never heard the theory backed up by anything solid in the way of statistics.

'So I reckoned that the extra risk, if there was one, was pretty small and that it was outweighed by His Majesty's deep and very natural wish that every possible respect should be paid to his late son.

'And I should add that the Crown Prince himself had no qualms but was quite happy to go ahead.

'So we went ahead, and as you know it turned out all right. We took all the normal security precautions, of course, against attempts based on a degree of rationality.

'But the irrational, the man who doesn't try to avoid the penalties of his act, is the contingency which the science—or the art—of Security can do nothing about.'

There was a silence.

An arm rose.

The other students were astonished to recognise that it had risen from the desk in the window recess and was khaki-battledressed, with a blue flash.

The lecturer gave it the nod of a conductor signalling the entry of the woodwind in a passage of no great importance.

'Would the lecturer agree', the silent Grenadier asked, in a voice that, now it was extensively heard for the first time, turned out to be deep, quiet, clear and cultivated, 'that, if Security is not simply to resign from its responsibilities, the only effective action it could take, in the type of case in question, is to advise that the penalty should be increased to the point where even an irrational person *would* understand and dread it?'

The lecturer seemed as surprised by the question as the audience by the questioner.

'I suppose you *could* argue that, I suppose you *could*', he said, sounding flustered but in fact giving himself time to mount a counterattack. 'But, of course, whatever you threaten you've got to be prepared to carry out. Otherwise, someone will call your bluff, and you'll be exposed as defenceless.'

The silent Grenadier seemed to receive the answer as confirming, instead of countering, his own point—or at least some point of his own, not necessarily the one he had expressed.

He gave the lecturer a nod as curt as the one he had received, though technically it could have been interpreted as thanks for the answer.

He looked down at his desk top, apparently not at all disconcerted by having indefinably disconcerted everyone else in the room.

*   *   *

Extract from Document 103, Group V (Table to Establish

Timing of Principal Events and Movements).

12.52 Archduke Urban leaves balcony (time established by telerecording made for television news bulletin which includes view of clock on façade of Palace).
NOTE. Times given in this document have been adjusted to allow for the fact that the Palace clock was subsequently found to be 34 seconds slow.
12.53, 10″ Archduke Sempronius takes Archduke Urban's place on balcony.
12.54, 50″ Archduke Sempronius is shot.

★   ★   ★

The Royal Astean Opera announced last night the postponement of its new production. Cause of the postponement was said to be 'the national mourning for his Devout and Imperial Highness the late Archduke'. No new date could be given, a spokesman for the management said.

Despite the official reason, operatic circles in Asty were last night treating the postponement as a victory for the Chorus Section of the Singers Union, which last month organised a go-slow in protest against what they regard as the exorbitant fees commanded by opera conductors of international standing.

The new production was to have been *Norma*.

The Astean Times

Music lovers were doubtful yesterday whether the Royal Astean Opera's new production will now ever reach the stage. The opening night of Verdi's *I Normani*, sequel to *I Vespri Siciliani*, has now been postponed three times. It is believed that the Board of Management does not see eye-to-eye with the designer's wish to stage the opera, which is set in the medieval period, in modern dress.

The Times of Asty

151

*   *   *

Document 8, Group IV.
Evidence (continued) given before the Examining Magistrate by Dr Etzel Duschek, Therapist in Charge, Asty Clinic of Psycho-Therapy.

—Let me ask you this, doctor. Have you read the evidence of the lorry driver with whom Squinch got a lift to town?
—Yes.
—Then you will remember that Squinch was carrying what later proved to be the firearm, that it was wrapped up in brown paper, and that, when the lorry driver asked him what the object in his possession was, Squinch replied 'A fishing rod'? Now what I want to ask you, doctor, is whether you would agree that this shews that, in accomplishing his purpose, namely getting to Asty with a firearm, undetected, Squinch exercised a degree of forethought and, indeed, cunning.
—A degree, certainly.
—Would you care, doctor, to indicate *what* degree of cunning you would say was involved?
—I should like first to make it clear that Petrus believed he *had* to exercise cunning, because he thought that cunning—indeed, advanced technology—was being exercised on him.
—You are referring now to your belief that he thought images were being stolen out of his mind, by some process connected with radio waves, and were being 'projected', I believe you said, 'in terms of public life'?
—I am referring to his systematic delusions, yes.
—Very well, doctor. You will understand that it is one of my duties to make sure I have correctly translated what I may call your jargon into language comprehensible to an ordinary intelligent person. I take you to be saying that

Squinch intended to behave cunningly. Would you now answer my question by telling me what level of cunning you think he achieved.

—Only a very elementary level, the level you would expect from a pre-pubescent child. The emotions to which Petrus was responding belonged to his own childhood. In relation to these emotions, his intellectual processes were fixated at childhood level. I call them elementary because, for instance, when he was asked about the gun he said it was a fishing rod—a very simple disguise indeed, involving the substitution merely of one type of lethal weapon for another.

—If I understand you correctly, doctor, you are calling a fishing rod a lethal weapon. Can you explain in what sense, please? I have yet to hear of anyone being assassinated with a fishing rod.

—Fish are assassinated with a fishing rod. It is a weapon lethal to fish.

—I see, doctor. You were speaking from the fish's point of view. In this tribunal, however, we must confine ourselves to the human point of view. I shall therefore ask you whether you would agree that Squinch evidently knew that his purpose, in taking a firearm with him to Asty, was reprehensible, since he had the forethought to conceal it from sight by wrapping it in a brown paper parcel.

— I should be extremely interested to know whether, on what I might call his first return journey to Asty, the return journey he made, as a child, from Vienna, his collection of toy animals, which he called the Duck Family, was wrapped up in a brown paper parcel. Have you asked him that?

—My enquiries have been directed to more recent and more momentous events. I have already noted, from the evidence you gave earlier, that you are asking me to believe that Squinch, who, according to his own evidence,

153

thought that the Archduke was the Crown Prince, also and simultaneously thought him to be (a) a pigeon and (b) a toy duck.

—I am not asking you to believe anything. You asked me, as Petrus's therapist, to explain by what mental process Petrus could have arrived at the idea that he ought to kill the Archduke. My view is that he conceived the Royal Family to be a projection of the Duck Family, of which he had made a totem in his childhood, and that he acted on the hostile component in the ambivalent feelings he entertained towards the family of toys, towards his own family and, primarily, towards his adoptive father. Whether you accept my hypothesis is of no moment to me, though I am anxious that you should realise that it would be an injustice to take punitive action against my patient. Some preventative action, some detention, is of course inevitable, and I only wish it had been in my power to arrange for it *before* the Archduke was killed.

—We must all echo your wish, doctor. I see that, in your previous evidence, you stated that you would have been even more firmly opposed to Squinch's visiting the country had you known, and I am now quoting you verbatim, that 'his mother's conception of country life consisted of dealing out death to birds'. Today you have given us an example of your remarkable propensity for seeing the world from a fish's point of view. Would you tell us therefore whether your earlier statement was made in the interests of a potential human victim or in the interests of birds?

—Both.

—We have all heard, doctor, of cases where the idea of a patient's illness has in fact been put into his head by his psychiatrist. Would you consider the possibility that the confusion between animals and humans which you ascribe to Squinch was, so to speak, caught by him from some similar attitude in yourself?

—As a post-Darwinian scientist, I regard humans as a

species of animals. You will perhaps allow me to add that I am not a psychiatrist.

—How would you describe yourself, then? Simply as a post-Darwinian scientist?

—I must take the risk of annoying you again by using jargon. Technically, I am a psychoanalytically-orientated psycho-therapist.

—That is highly illuminating. Let us return, however, to our subject of prime interest, namely Squinch. Would you say that Squinch's confusion of men with animals was the result of Squinch's being a post-Darwinian scientist?

—Mentally, Petrus is a *pre*-Darwinian scientist. He lives in the world of magic-making, though he naturally gives his fantasies a rationalising colour—his talk of radio waves, for instance—that is borrowed from the age of science.

—And his belief, as you hold it to be, that a man can be a bird: is that a scientific belief?

—It is a very common pre-scientific belief. Anthropology throws up numerous instances of tribes who hold their ruler to be both a human king and the tribal totem animal. You will recall that the ancient Egyptians depicted gods with human bodies but with heads of animals of other species. Illuminated manuscripts, produced, during the eleventh and twelfth centuries, in Evarchian monasteries, include scenes painted by men who apparently found no difficulty in conceiving that the Holy Ghost was, at one and the same time, a third of a god, an invisible spirit and a dove.

—I must regret, doctor, that this judicial enquiry cannot make time for your instructive reflexions on anthropology and art history.

—May I make one more point?

—Briefly.

—I should like to make it for the sake of intellectual completeness or, if you like, for the sake of my own reputation. You were implying, I think, that what I claimed as a scientific point of view in myself I described in Petrus as a

155

delusion. I think you were trying to shew me up in a contradiction. What I want to say is that the images in which a human is mixed with an animal of another species, images that are so common in pre-scientific cultures, are in a sense anticipations of the Darwinian hypothesis. They are arrived at by different mental processes, and they are expressed in the dream-like imagery of myth instead of the logical syntax of science. But they do postulate a common ancestry for humans and the other animals, especially when they represent royal families or gods, because royal families and gods are themselves the parents of their people. And it is highly probable, in my view, that the tumultuous, world-wide resistance to Darwin at the time, together with the manifest difficulty that many scientists experience, to this day, in bringing their behaviour towards animals of other species into accordance with belief in the Darwinian hypothesis, even though they think they accept that hypothesis intellectually—it seems to me probable that both these phenomena reflect a violent reaction to the emotional content of the imagery concerned and also reflect the fact that humans have so recently, and after such a struggle with ourselves, replaced pre-scientific thought with scientific that we are still scared to acknowledge the cases where, albeit only in outline and virtually by accident, the pre-scientific thinking was scientifically right.

—Thank you, doctor. Your views have been noted and will be included in the record, which I hope will reassure you about the security of your reputation. I wish now to ask you a simple question, which will not draw upon your evident talent for metaphysics. You tell me that you have been Squinch's psychiatrist—I am sorry, psycho-therapist—for four years. On the basis of the considerable knowledge of him you must have gained, how far do you think him responsible for his actions?

—I do not want to retreat into metaphysics or to provoke your hostility by seeming to fence with the question. But I

156

can't answer the question, because I do not know the extent to which any of us is responsible for his actions.

—I see that my question was so large as to invite evasion. I shall therefore abandon it and put to you, instead, a highly specific question. You have agreed that, in the matter of getting the firearm into Ceremony Square without being detected, Squinch displayed a degree of cunning. On the basis of the evidence given by other witnesses, would you agree that, as regards escaping detection *after* he had committed the crime, he displayed no cunning whatever, even of the most elementary and childish kind?

—I think so, yes. I would prefer to know what you are leading up to before I answer definitely.

—I am leading up to nothing more devious than to ask you, as a doctor, how you account for the contrast between his behaviour before and his behaviour after the crime.

—I don't see it as a very marked contrast. I don't see his behaviour before the shooting as very cunning, so I don't see any very strong difference from his behaviour afterwards. I don't think it crossed his mind to run away afterwards, because I don't think it crossed his mind that he had done anything wrong. He didn't regard shooting the Archduke as a crime, any more than he thought (though in this case society agreed with him) that shooting pigeons was a crime. I notice *you* refer to what he did as a crime. It may be such objectively. I am sure, however, he didn't think it was—and as a matter of fact I had always understood that even the law didn't hold a deed to be a crime unless it was first established that the person who committed it had the intention of doing something he knew to be wrong.

—I see there was a loss to my own profession when you took up psychiatry. As a matter of fact, you somewhat over-simplify the conditions the law requires to be fulfilled before it recognises an act as criminal. However, I do not propose to detain you with the niceties of legal theory. I shall merely point out that, if you are right and he did not,

157

after doing it, consider shooting the Archduke to be a crime, then his state of mind had undergone a remarkable reversal remarkably quickly. Before the shooting, he plainly did consider what he contemplated doing to be a crime, since he was at pains to hide the firearm by wrapping it up.

—Before the shooting he considered that the radio waves might detect the idea in his mind and stop him. After it he thought he had stopped the radio waves.

—That is your hypothesis to account for the discrepancy between his conduct before and his conduct after?

—If one is needed, yes, it is.

—I note that your hypothesis involves postulating the hypothesis of his delusions. I am sure, doctor, that you are acquainted with the scientific dictum that, of two plausible hypotheses, the less extravagant is to be preferred? I therefore propose to put to you an alternative hypothesis, which does not require us to postulate delusions or anything except a little cold, commonsensical thought on Squinch's part. I put it to you that, after the shooting, Squinch felt no need to run away because he was confident that any treatment meted out to him in consequence of his deed would be, in your own words, only preventative, not punitive. And I put it to you that the reason he felt such confidence was that he knew, whatever tribunal he might be summoned before, that you would appear before that tribunal and certify that he was an unfortunate deluded creature, no more to be held responsible for his deeds than a child is. I am asking you: is that a tenable hypothesis?

—I think you have forgotten two things. Preventative custody may be less awful than punitive, but it is still not something a sane person would court. Indeed, it is, in one respect, a *more* awful prospect, if one is sane. One doesn't know when it will end, or if it will ever end. The other thing you forget is that to many people, sane and insane—and Petrus is one of those people—to be publicly pronounced mad is a more terrible fate than to be pronounced wicked.

158

—You have produced two very effective smokescreens, doctor. But it does not escape my notice that you have not told me whether you find my alternative hypothesis tenable and, if not, why not.

—I must spell out what your hypothesis implies. You are postulating, first, that Petrus, by deliberate play-acting, deceived his mother into thinking him in need of medical treatment of some sort. She took him to the family physician and eventually, through a series of referrals, he was referred to the Clinic. There, by continuing to play-act, he deceived myself and other experienced doctors. He kept up the deception, consistently, over a period of four years. He conceived this plan some four or five years in advance, in order to provide himself with a background from which he could with comparative safety—at the risk, that is, only of his liberty, not of his material comfort as well—commit a crime which, at the time he embarked on the plan, he had no means of knowing he would ever have the opportunity to commit and which, if he was not really deluded but was only play-acting, he never at any time had any motive to commit. That is the hypothesis you put to me. My answer to your question is that no, I do not find it tenable. If it is correct, Petrus must be even more unfathomably insane than I postulate him to be.

—Thank you, doctor. I am beholden for the time you have given to this enquiry. I hope I shall not have occasion to call on you again.

*   *   *

The governing body of the Communist Party of Evarchia was, according to the Party's written constitution, called the Supreme Praesidium. But the pretentiousness of the name provoked satire from opponents, particularly from Trotskyite opponents, so most members of the Supreme Praesidium spoke of it simply as the council.

159

The members numbered seventy-five. That provoked satire from bourgeois opponents: Skimplepex had once written that there must be more members of the council than there were card-carrying Party members in Evarchia at large whom the council was supposed to represent and instruct.

If he had been better informed, he might without exaggeration have directed his satire against the true fact that the huge and heterogeneous council took so long to conduct its deliberations on any given theme that it never arrived at any decision.

The size of the council was unavoidable, because the Party in Evarchia was organised on a double system, once according to locality (to facilitate meetings of members) and once according to trade or profession (to facilitate infiltration of the trade unions).

A member who defected to the Trotskyites afterwards claimed that the double organisational structure caused the Party 'to exaggerate its own membership count by a factor of two', since a member was liable to be card-indexed under both his job and his neighbourhood: 'I don't allege dishonesty, Comrades, merely incompetence—and I hope you are not so far corrupted by bourgeois liberalism as to suppose that that is the lesser charge'.

Whether or not the dual structure increased the notional membership count, it certainly increased the number of very real presences on the council, because each cell could claim some sort of representation there, with the result that any cell that became exceptionally important, numerically or politically (by, for example, succeeding in taking power in a trade union), claimed that in fairness it should have *two* members on the council.

The growing unwieldiness of the council was less hindrance than help to the Chairman of the Party. He simply conducted all major business through the inner council, which consisted of the Chairman and Deputy Chairman ex officio, plus three council members elected by the council, and which met on the

160

second Tuesday of every month.

This device functioned to the Chairman's liking (or, as he put it to himself, efficiently) until just before Christmas, when his chief opponent on the council became Deputy Chairman of the Party and thus entitled for the first time to a seat on the inner council.

The Chairman had long suspected the new Deputy Chairman of Trotskyite inclinations. Recently his suspicions had sharpened and changed focus. What he suspected now was an inclination or more than an inclination towards so-called Euro-Communism or 'democratic' Communism. He also suspected another member of the inner council of an inclination to ally himself with the Deputy Chairman.

There were still, however, two inner council members the Chairman believed he could rely on, and that, with his own vote, seemed to assure him of a majority.

On the second Tuesday in January (the first Tuesday after the royal assassination), the Chairman therefore sat down at the inner council table with confidence and even, behind his confidence, the exciting nucleus of an expectation that he was about to engineer a coup that would dispose of the Deputy Chairman for good.

Hiding his excitement, he said in his usual flat tone that, as soon as the routine business had been dealt with, he would, with the inner council's leave, raise a matter of urgency which there had not been time to put on the Agenda.

He had expected some procedural obstruction from the Deputy. Instead—and the Chairman read it as a good omen, perhaps even a first symptom that his opponent was becoming tamed—the Deputy said that, in the light of recent events, he considered that a very proper procedure.

While he conducted the inner council through the routine business, the Chairman took occasion to whisper personal remarks, which he intended to be good-humoured and friendly, to both the inner council members whom he believed to be his supporters.

161

One was a garrulous and repetitive Party veteran whom the council regularly re-elected to the inner council in gratitude for his past service to the Party and because it was believed, wrongly, that he was still a power to reckon with in the northern provinces.

The other was a large muscular woman named Magda Lupova, who usually left inner council meetings early. She represented the tram drivers of Asty. (It was one of the idiosyncracies of Asty that the job of driving its trams had always been open to women equally with men—well, not always, but ever since the service had suffered a shortage of male manpower in 1916.) She was an accomplished and inspiring public speaker. Indeed, she had the power to bring tears to the eyes of an audience, particularly an out-of-doors audience, by her mere powerful presence on a platform. Her body seemed to incarnate the heroic and mythical qualities which ought to reside in monumental sculpture designed to be seen out-of-doors but which social-realist sculptors so regularly failed to capture.

The Chairman believed that Magda Lupova disliked him personally but agreed with him politically. Perhaps he was projecting onto her his own personal dislike of her. She was a much better-known public figure than he was; but what probably provoked his dislike and mistrust was that she was a much more dramatic one.

Lupova had several times tried to get the Chairman to alter the date of inner council meetings. He always cut across her request by asking sympathetically if she found it difficult to get leave of absence from the tram depot on the second Tuesday of the month. She would reply that, such was her position these days with the employers, she could have got leave on any day of any month. Before she could continue, the Chairman always interposed that the high esteem in which she was held was itself a triumph for the cause and, forgetting the request she had begun to make, went on to other matters.

The truth, which the Chairman never gave her time to tell

162

him, was that Lupova was subject to a slightly long and slightly irregular menstrual cycle, whose irregularities almost regularly brought it into coincidence with the calendar month. On the second Tuesday of the month she was almost always handicapped not only by a heavy flow of menstrual blood but by active pains in both head and belly that so reduced her ability to concentrate that she could only withdraw herself as useless from the inner council's deliberations.

As soon as the Chairman, having dealt with the matters arising from them, had signed the minutes of the previous meeting, he gave notice of the matter he wanted to raise urgently, namely the royal assassination.

Lupova rose from the table, excused herself and left.

She had gone at an earlier stage of the meeting than usual, but as he gave her leave to withdraw the only comment the Chairman was aware of his own mind making was of regret that she would not witness his victory.

'Now, Comrades', he said to the remaining members. 'The question in my mind is whether action has been taken without consultation and without authorisation.'

'Precisely', the Deputy Chairman said, facing him directly across the table, 'so. That is my question to you, Comrade. And at the same time there is another, no doubt related question. I have had preliminary consultations in private with my Comrades on the inner council, and we are united in requiring an account from you of the discussions you have been regularly holding with the so-called Cultural Attaché at the Bulgarian Embassy.'

It took the Chairman a moment to abandon the mental posture of accuser and recognise that he was suddenly the accused.

When he did recognise it, his thoughts began to run exceptionally fast.

He quickly worked out that, even if the Deputy had, as the Chairman had long thought he might, succeeded in bugging the Embassy building, he obviously could have no knowledge

163

of the content of the Chairman's conversations with the Cultural Attaché, which had wisely been held outside the building.

At this point it even crossed the Chairman's mind to make the flippant reply that what he discussed with the Bulgarian Cultural Attaché was opera.

However, he rapidly saw that the Deputy's ignorance was of no help to him. Out of his ignorance the Deputy had evidently fabricated the entirely absurd and monstrous fantasy that he, the Chairman, was, presumably on orders from Bulgaria, responsible for the assassination.

'Well now, Comrade', the Chairman eventually said, trying to sound bluff but sounding, as always, flat, 'it seems a remarkable piece of procedure for a Deputy Chairman to "require" an account from a Chairman. Are you by any chance, at your very first inner council meeting, attempting a coup d'état against the Chair?'

'The question is, Comrade, whether you were attempting a coup d'état in the state and seeking to usurp the right of the Communist Party of Evarchia to decide what form Socialism shall take in our country.'

When the Chairman considered the absolute absurdity of his being held responsible for the assassination, he found himself forced to wonder if he had been equally absurd in intending, when he began the meeting, to bring the same accusation against the Deputy.

He could not remember whether he had seriously thought it likely that the Deputy had engineered the shooting or whether he had thought only that he could make it look sufficiently likely for it to be used to lever the Deputy out of power. Perhaps he had never made up his mind whether he thought the accusation correct. He scarcely needed to, since it could be used, he had supposed, to the same effect whether it was true or false.

And now that the accusation had suddenly reversed its direction, the Chairman could not tell whether the Deputy

164

really believed it or was merely using it to try to depose him, the Chairman.

The Chairman quickly recognised that he must exert all the numen that emanated from his office and thereby prevent the present meeting from making a decision; he must hang on until the next meeting, or even summon an extraordinary meeting, when Lupova would be present to support him.

He slightly hoped that the Deputy genuinely believed in the accusation. In that case, so fantastic was it, the Chairman might hope to refute it. But if the Deputy was only feigning belief, no refutation would deter him, provided only that the accusation could be made to look sound enough for the conduct of the members of the inner council to appear, when the minutes were read afterwards, to be in good faith.

But their conduct in the present tense was surprising the Chairman. The questions, which were intensifying into an interrogation, came from the Deputy. But he spoke increasingly on behalf of the whole inner council. Nobody denied his claim to do so. Nobody put forward a countermove or even a diversion. The veteran Party member, when the Chairman sought his gaze, looked away.

The Chairman regretted his bluff mention of a coup against the Chair. He instructed himself to look as though he believed his tenure of the Chair to be so safe that no thought of being unseated could lodge in his mind. Though tempted to do so, he forbade himself to question the Deputy's entitlement to speak for his colleagues, because that might lead to a vote. Indeed, he must not say anything that could be held to invite a vote of confidence, because, he was now aware, he would surely, at this meeting, lose it. He must not let the possibility of his resignation become a prize the meeting could play for. He must keep the concept of resignation out of his words and, preferably, lest anyone could read them from his behaviour, out of his very thoughts.

Presently the Chairman found his thoughts assuring him that his accusers were very provincial and inept people. No one with a knowledge of the world or a sense of justice or an awareness of true political realities could either credit an accusation so far-fetched or pretend to credit it through a procedural cloak so crass. Before any politically and procedurally mature tribunal, the Chairman would, he was certain, be vindicated in a trice.

He asked himself (a question he wished a moment later he had kept from himself) where he supposed such a mature tribunal was to be found. He discovered to his shame he was thinking of official tribunals of justice in Evarchia. He cursed the unwariness with which his thoughts had fled from a discomfiting present into utopia. Hastily, like a superstitious person snatching himself back from an unlucky act, he shifted the whereabouts of utopia: it was, of course, in the Soviet Union that a man like himself could expect to be judged correctly, not only on the facts but on the political value, appreciated in an international context, of what he had done and not done.

For a moment he rested in memories of his sojourn, decades before, in Moscow. He remembered the feel of Red Square and the feel of the street where he had lodged, with, on the corner, the restaurant where he usually ate.

He realised he could not remember at all how those two patches of the city were topographically connected.

He turned his attention back to his accusers, informing himself they were parochial hobbledehoys playing at being a Supreme Praesidium.

And yet he felt trapped enough, in the real and non-utopian circumstances, to begin mentally addressing his thoughts to himself, in the form of admonitions, couched in explicit words, naming himself as 'you'.

'You must hang on', his self-instructions said. 'Hold out till the next meeting. You must not hint at offering to resign. You must not offer to resign.'

It occurred to him that Lupova had perhaps left this month's meeting so abnormally early through foreknowledge,

166

by collusion with the Deputy, as the equivalent of an abstention on a vote.

'Since my personal integrity is in doubt, I am of course willing', the Chairman found himself saying (even while his thoughts screamed to him 'Don't resign'), 'to offer the inner council my resignation.'

'We accept it, Comrade', the Deputy said.

*   *   *

After closing her window on the birds, the queen took down her Thucydides from the bookcase, sat at her study table and opened the book to the place where, at the end of her last lesson, she had pencilled an *x* beside a full stop in the Greek text.

It was a mark she had made while her third son was still alive.

There was a knock at her study door and Missy Six came in, more darkly made up than usual to hide the signs of tears and sleeplessness in her complexion.

The words which it came into the queen's mind to say to greet her were 'I hop'd thou shouldst have been my Hamlet's wife'. But as the queen of Denmark did not address them to Ophelia until Ophelia was dead, the queen of Evarchia, with the thought 'absit omen', suppressed them and instead gave Missy Six a silent smile which, against her will, turned into a sigh.

Summer Palace

Chapter Five

'Meet me by the mauve agricultural collective. Will you? At noon?'

'I remember her from last year. The girl with the hibiscus.'

'Noon will be too hot.'

'. . . on the ferry to Clove Island.'

'An Islander? Or a tourist?'

'I wish the hotels would *sort out* the minibuses.'

'I think she's got engaged. At least, I saw her wearing a sapphire ring on her engagement toe.'

*   *   *

Caspar Gregorian (the writer the queen considered the best novelist in Evarchia) declared, in one of his essays, that the history of the Islands was to be apprehended by nose.

Mainland noses, butting and crowding down gangways (from boat or 'plane), were seldom concerned with history—or were concerned only in the episodic and out-of-order mode in which history presents itself to people who go on conducted tours.

At least, however, they would not have disputed that the genius loci was immediately introduced to the visitor in the form of a distinctive—and attractive—smell.

Most often it was a chance smell that provoked resentment in citizens pent for the summer on the mainland: the skeleton staff of a transport system, a Ministerium or a public service, kept back solely, it appeared to them, to transport, administer or publicly serve one another's skeleton staffs.

Amongst themselves the components of the skeleton exchanged the truism that heat in a town, and particularly in Asty, was much less tolerable than what the impartial (or insensitive) thermometer pronounced to be exactly the same degree of heat in the Islands.

Perhaps the true difference was that the Islands were tuned to holiday, Asty to work—even when there was no work to do and the skeletons occupied their empty timetables by writing letters, which were conveyed (slowly, by the skeletal post service) to colleagues and kin on the Islands and eventually replied to on picture postcards whose colour flouted verisimilitude and whose repertory left out many of the most interesting of the monuments on the Islands while including a few that no visitor had ever tracked down.

Even the unevocative colour could sometimes conjure a memory, in the nerve ends, of the Island smell.

Realistic visitors ascribed the smell either to the type of tobacco in the brands of cigarette preferred by the Islanders or to the freesias that grew wild (and innocent of colour) all over the Islands, bunches of which were thrust into the (always, in the heat, open) windows of tourists' cars by wayside Islander children.

Karyl Frumgeour ascribed it to the much washed but usually more or less naked feet of those children, a fancy typical of him in being both cynical and sentimental.

Perhaps it was typical of *him* that Caspar Gregorian (whose essay, reprinted in booklet form by the Tourist Section of the Department of the Interior, was distributed via the pocket on the back of the seat-in-front in all the aircraft that plied to the Islands) identified the scents as those of the spices that had once made the Islands prosperous and desirable to possess—and that had left the imprint of their importance in the nomenclature of the lesser Islands, though the trade in

172

spices had long lost its savour and the Islands' natural harbours had lost their strategic convenience when merchants ceased to seek quick means of dispersing parcels bought at the termini of the caravan routes.

By religious profession, the Islands were, of course, Catholic and Pre-Canonical. Indeed, repeated opinion polls had shewn that the Islanders were more pious, in both belief and observance, than modern mainlanders. And yet there was (so Caspar Gregorian's essay continued), about both the Islanders' religious practice and their everyday life, something undeniably, if not quite definably, Muslim.

You had only (the essay pursued) to study the Island churches to see that, for centuries past, if you commissioned an Island architect (or even a mainland one, imported into and naturalised in the aromatic Island airs) to build you a clock tower, what he would run you up would be, in essence, a minaret. Ask for a baptistery, and his mind would set about placing a circle on top of an octagon.

As for the secular buildings, the most notable was, of course, the Summer Palace—and that was not a palace at all, in the western sense, but an archipelago of small kiosks dotted about a garden, as though in mimicry of the Islands' own disposition in the sea. Were it not for its slightly smaller extent, you could transport the whole thing to Istanbul and put it down in place of Topkapı, and people would scarcely notice the difference. (Gregorian had failed to persuade the printer to print the last letter in 'Topkapı' correctly, as an i without a dot.)

No less tellingly, every public building, sacred or secular, in the Islands was prefaced by a courtyard or a walled garden that contained running water. It was natural enough, in a hot climate, to provide water and shade. But the water that spurted up from basins in the middle of Island gardens or tumbled from bosses in Island garden walls (piped there, incidentally, by systems always kept in working order, though the wall itself might decay and the garden run to sub-tropical riot) was intended not for drinking or for ornament but for washing the feet.

Go, for instance, to the Town Hall on Macranese, the Great Island, on a night when the municipality was promoting a dance. After buying your ticket, you would be ushered into a garden, where you might think yourself outside a Mosque—but for the giggles and but for the inclusion of females in the custom (or the rite). There would be separate fountains (the separateness not always rigidly observed) for boys, girls, men and women. Visitors from the mainland, though in no way segregated, would in fact be distinguished by the pale white shyness with which their feet emerged from their socks and the woodenness with which their enlarged joints and pads of compacted, flaking skin were thrust beneath the gushing water, whereas brown Islander arches and slim, almost dexterous Islander toes met the water as if in conversation, having had to shed, at the most, the flat base of a sandal or a pierced and lacy covering that was no more than a veil—though they would also, of course, have to put aside for the moment any jewellery they might be wearing, or, perhaps, a flower head or a seashell, held, for the occasion of the dance, in the prehensile inlet between the big toe and its neighbour.

This passage about the importance of feet on the Islands won the approval of Karyl Frumgeour (though he dismissed Gregorian's identification of the Island scents with spices as a rather thin literary extravaganza).

Feet, Frumgeour considered, were a characteristic part of the Island fauna, like some particularly attractive, ubiquitous but never still enough to be studied prosaically species of lizard.

Indeed, the prominence given, on the Islands, to a part of the human body that on the mainland was usually kept covered and more or less disregarded (which put it in a piquant opposition to those parts of the body that were kept covered but were highly regarded) could wreak paradoxes in a visiting mainlander's personal tastes. In Asty, Frumgeour

174

often judged a youth handsome without seeing or even bothering to visualise his feet. But on the Islands, though he often tired of the uniform charm of those clipped, rounded, downy and brownish heads, and though the characteristic thickened lips sometimes came near to offending his taste by their too displayed promise of sensuality, he had many times been led on to adventures almost against the grain of his own hedonism by the expressive flexing of a narrow instep or by the polished texture of an ankle inside a bracelet, like a mahogany chair leg with ormolu ornaments.

It was in the eight hundreds that the Islands, then an enviable possession, came under the de facto suzerainty of the Evarchian crown. The change was bloodless, at least by the standards of the time. The inhabitants had asked for protection against pirates.

Technically, it was possession of the Islands that enlarged Evarchia from a kingdom into an empire, incidentally promoting its monarch from a mere to a Most Serene majesty (a point nowadays insisted on only in the most formal documents) and making his sons not only princes but archdukes.

So, at least, the present generation of Archdukes (and the Archduchess) had been informed at the start of one of the summers in the middle period of their childhoods, the one characterised, in their memories, by the attachment to it (at the instigation of the High Chamberlain) of a Protocol Tutor.

By custom, the royal children were loosed on the Islands first, the date of their arrival, published in *The Times of Asty*, being generally taken as the date when the summer holiday was licensed to begin. The arrival on the Islands of their Most Serene majesties, together with the formal removal of the Court to the Summer Palace, was held back for several weeks more: until the heat in Asty was truly unbearable and until Parliament had been (perhaps by the heat) dissolved.

Even so, the High Chamberlain regularly retarded their departure for as long as he could, because the construction of the Summer Palace in the form of a mere group of pavilions inside

175

a garden wall made it impossible to protect with what he considered proper security.

The children (to whom that same pavilion structure gave promise of independence and privacy before they had earned them by growing adult) travelled in the forward cabin of the bumping two-propellor 'plane. (Even now, even Macranese could not afford space for a runway long enough to land a jet.) They were separated from the fashionable rabble of early beginners on holiday by a beige curtain on which the royal arms were embroidered in metallic thread, and their quarters were distinguished by the luxury of two tables fixed to the cabin floor, in place of the pull-down or slot-in ledges from which their unseen fellow passengers took their meals.

At one of the tables, Sempronius, whose voice was then just breaking, Heather, who had not yet made manifest her height to be, and whichever number of Missy it was that year were playing liar dice.

Round the other table sat the other brothers and the Protocol Tutor.

He, the Tutor, was looking out of the window, for want of rapport with his pupils.

The 'plane had already descended from its cruising height. With a couple of internal thumps, it lowered and locked its undercarriage. It had only to pass over the tip of the last of the lesser Islands before turning, over open sea, onto its run-in for Macranese.

It dipped its left wing.

Three dice slid across the table from behind the protective wall of Heather's hand, disclosing that her offer of three kings to Sempronius had been untruthful, and, on the other side of the aisle, the Protocol Tutor, catching a glimpse through his tilted window of the ruins of Pirate Castle on the coast of Clove Island before it veered away into invisibility, was prompted to tell his charges that they owed their archducal status to the Islands they were flying over.

'You say "technically" that's why', Urban took up politely;

'but who devised the technical categories?'

'What a silly question. It's always been so', the Protocol Tutor replied. 'Or at least what I mean is I daresay it's all in the Almanach de Gotha, in the early editions, that is.'

In an attempt to retrieve his position (such as that was), the Protocol Tutor began to narrate some facts that he *did* know, such as that the Evarchian claim to the Islands had been legitimised or at least ratified in 1123, with the marriage of the king-emperor to the daughter of an indigenous family that had had some sort of title to overlordship of the Islands, though scholars nowadays thought it had probably been no more than the richest of the merchant families.

He was still talking or, rather, shouting above the noise of the engines, when the 'plane was trundling along the runway at Macranese.

'Yes', Heather said as she unbuckled her seat belt, politely responding to what she had managed to catch, over distance and din, of the Protocol Tutor's drift, 'the Duchess of Coriander Bay is descended from that family. She has a sort of standing tease of Papa, that, if Salic law applied (or didn't apply—I can never remember which way round it is), she and not he might be monarch of the Islands.'

Accidentally informed that the facts he had been shouting at his pupils were already known to even the youngest of them, the Protocol Tutor sulked.

The children lodged no complaint. But when the Court eventually joined them on the Islands, the queen suggested gently that, if her children's holiday were to be dogged by tuition, it would profit them more to learn Greek; the king roundly told the High Chamberlain that whatever his children needed to know on the silly and snobbish subject of protocol would reach them by osmosis, by virtue of their being *his* children; and the appointment of Protocol Tutor was allowed to drift away into the heat haze and vanish.

Perhaps some long-distance and fragmentary osmosis had conveyed to the Communist Party of Evarchia the notion of a

177

causal connexion between the title 'Imperial Highness' and sovereignty over the Islands. From time to time it called the relation of the mainland to the Islands 'imperialism'. Most people read this, however, as name-calling rather than description, since in modern political fact the Islands were integrated with the mainland, and were equally represented in Parliament, a little more than equally in the cabinet, where there was a portfolio of Island affairs, and a great deal more than equally in the division of public funds.

Caspar Gregorian's essay mentioned the political integration of the Islands in a rather clumsy bridge passage between his evocation of the Island ambience and a dissertation on the difference between Island and mainland idiom.

Although much attention had been paid to the Island pronunciation of Evarchian (and indeed, as Gregorian remarked, one mainlander in two believed himself competent to give, facetiously, an imitation of it), Gregorian argued that there had been a neglect of the characteristic way the Islanders put Evarchian words together to form sentences.

Evarchian was, of course, distantly derived from ancient Greek. ('*Very* distantly', the queen commented when she read Gregorian's essay; 'alas.') As a modern language, Evarchian naturally possessed both a definite and an indefinite article. However, in its phraseology and sentence structure it was possible to discern distinct traces of the fact that Greek, its ancestor, possessed a definite article but did without an indefinite one.

Yet this situation was reversed, Gregorian maintained, if you paid close attention to the phraseology and sentence structure of Evarchian as those were manipulated by Islanders. In the Island turns of phrase, which sounded invariably wayward and often charming to a mainland ear, it was the indefinite article that was used naturally and with point, and the definite article that was either dragged in arbitrarily or simply omitted.

From this Gregorian concluded that the Islanders, though

178

long naturalised in the use of Evarchian, had preserved a tradition of using it according to the sentence and idiom structure of another language: a non-Greek-derived language—in fact probably, Gregorian declared, Turkish—whose properties were the opposite of those of Greek inasmuch as it did possess an indefinite article and did not possess a definite one.

Gregorian's 'probably Turkish' was obviously meant to reinforce his earlier claim to perceive a Muslim or near-eastern strand in Island culture. Yet he was backed up (or, at least, not undermined) by the sober facts that Turkish did indeed have an indefinite but not a definite article, and that Arabic, which on the face of it you might guess to have been a greater influence on the mongrel Islands, possessed a prominent definite article and therefore could not be parent to the many Islander idioms which left it out.

Even so, Gregorian could not resist introducing a point that weakened his diagnosis of Island idiom as a Turkish turn of phrase imposed on a Greek derivative. That diagnosis depended, of course, on there being a great difference, in sentence structure and indeed in syntax itself, between Turkish and Greek. Yet he went on to remark that those two languages were not so totally dissimilar as professors of comparative language studies would have you believe. Gregorian could not conceive that it was by pure coincidence that both exhibited a peculiarity unique, so far as he knew, among languages: in Greek a (grammatically) neuter plural subject and in Turkish a (semantically) inanimate plural subject both took a singular verb.

Karyl Frumgeour judged that, some time before it reached that point, Gregorian's essay had become irretrievably dull.

The author of the essay would have agreed not that it became dull but that its texture became much more dense when it entered the discussion of language. For that the chief reason was that it was precisely the language section that most interested Gregorian himself. He was not distanced enough from his material to dramatise its presentation: he was hacking

179

away at the naked coal face of thoughts that he (or, so far as he knew, anyone else) had never mined before.

However, he was guilty of a technical error. He had left himself too small a proportion of his allotted space (five thousand words) for dealing with the most novel part of his subject-matter, with the result that his expression of it became condensed at the very point where it needed an elastic and colloquial tone to make the reader feel at ease with unfamiliar concepts.

Gregorian would have admitted, too, that his hit at professors of comparative languages was an act of revenge. One of his daughters had brought home a casual acquaintance, a young man who was a lecturer, at her university, in philology. In the essay, Gregorian had, as well as generalising him, promoted him to professor, out of pique. The pique was not, however, oedipal. It was obvious to Gregorian, from the moment he first saw them together, that his daughter and the lecturer took no sexual interest in each other. Indeed, there seemed to be little interest of any kind. His daughter left it largely to Gregorian to sustain conversation at dinner, and in doing so he mentioned his discovery of the plural subject with singular verb that was shared by Turkish and ancient Greek. He found himself snubbed by his junior in the abrupt way that children had sometimes been snubbed, in Gregorian's childhood, by their seniors. He was simply slapped as if by a rule book: by, in fact, an axiom which the lecturer evidently admitted no possibility of questioning. Turkish and Greek, the lecturer pronounced, belonged to utterly different linguistic families, Turkish being an agglutinative language whereas Greek was inflective. Amateurs, the lecturer added, were easily misled by apparently shared peculiarities, just as someone with no knowledge of biology might suppose a bat to be close kin to a bird.

Gregorian had complained afterwards to his daughter that, where language was concerned, he was not an amateur: he made his living from it in a more practical sense than her

180

lecturer friend did. His daughter merely denied that the lecturer was in any serious sense a friend of hers and, by refusing to defend him, frustrated Gregorian's attack on him, which was diverted into the essay instead.

One further trouble beset Caspar Gregorian during the composition of the essay. When it encountered the inherent and technical problems of the concluding section, his mind detached itself a little way from the material and became a self-conscious and commenting agency, looking over his shoulder as he wrote. What it commented on was the circumstance of the commission. Gregorian was asked to write the essay, for a large fee, by a glossy and highly (though, even so, not economically) priced periodical that was jointly published, at irregular intervals, by the Evarchian government (Tourist Section) and a multinational firm of speculative builders which planned to 'develop' parts of the Islands for the international tourist trade.

In this, and particularly in the fact that he was being paid far more than usual, Gregorian read both the opposing dangers to which modern writers were subject: bribery by the state (to write propaganda) and bribery by international capitalism (to write pap).

His method of denoting himself unbuyable was to retreat as far as could be conceived alike from the broad strokes of social realism and from the slick ones of advertising copy—into sheer Gregorianism, at its most personal and its least accessible to an audience.

None of the author's explanations (or excuses) would have budged Frumgeour, had he known of them, from his verdict.

He declined the airline's invitation, printed on the front, to take the booklet away with him when he left the aircraft. He not only put the booklet back into the flap pocket in front of him but pushed its top edge down so that nothing shewed to tempt future travellers to waste time on it.

The state had retained (in view of the large fee paid) the right to reprint Gregorian's essay. But the periodical in which it originally appeared ceased publication almost immediately afterwards, and (as Frumgeour well knew) the plan to attract foreign (as distinct from mainland Evarchian) tourists to the Islands had failed, leaving behind it nothing but a couple of hotels of 'international standard' half-built on the Islands' coasts.

It was Frumgeour who had disclosed (to Skimplepex, who disclosed to the nation) the 'scandal' whereby the failed attempt had swallowed into nothing a great quantity of both public and private capital. Some of the private capital had been Frumgeour's. He discovered its disappearance by exercising a shareholder's right to examine the accounts. He had been annoyed that Skimplepex had devoted the greater part of the fuss he made to the disappearance of the state's money. (Skimplepex had offered the explanation: 'More of my readers are taxpayers than are investors.')

The best part of Gregorian's essay, to Frumgeour's mind, was that it disposed of the 'imperialist' slander, more truthfully than Frumgeour would have expected of a half-communist of Gregorian's pale-washed disposition though less cogently than Frumgeour thought it deserved.

To Frumgeour the Islands were a lair of pirates still, their shores littered with sacked enterprises, despoiled reserves, shipwrecked and plundered merchandise.

Almost every village contained some recently built but already tumbledown structure, its grandiose nameplate surviving intact, as if to exacerbate the sore, though its roof had probably fallen in and its walls had succumbed to an invasion of bougainvillea and wild hydrangeas, that had been set up, on mainland capital and initiative, as a co-operative, intended to provide the Islanders with employment and incentive, and that had failed.

And if the aeroplane were to yaw a little in settling onto the glide-path to Macranese, its mainland passengers would find themselves inspecting through their windows, as it stuck up unsightly through the waves, what the waves had left of a

182

derrick or exploration platform. It marked a costly hope of offshore oil. No oil had been found, of course; and the Evarchian government was unable, and everyone else unwilling, to find the capital to redeem what had already been spent by exploring further.

Frumgeour experienced the expensive incapacities of the Islands quite personally, as though the Islands had been a dependent relative who kept needing costly medical treatment. Frumgeour believed that it was the compounding demands of the Island economy that forced the government of Evarchia to impose higher and higher rates of tax on unearned income, with the result that, of Frumgeour's own inherited income, less and less trickled, each year, through to him.

This year the effect had come near to preventing him from visiting the supposed cause. Frumgeour had seriously asked himself whether he could afford to spend the summer in even the second ranked hotel on Macranese and had seriously considered remaining in Asty.

He reflected not only on how much money he would save, which he worked out, in round figures, with pencil and calculator, but also on the consideration that, if money needed to be saved, this was the year to do it. The Islands' summer social life was expected not to be itself this year, because of the gloom cast on its social centre, the king, by the assassination of his son. No date had been announced yet for the king's arrival, and many predicted he would not come at all.

It was at the last moment that Frumgeour yielded, against prudence and almost against his wishes, to his addictions and booked himself onto the flight which, it turned out, also carried the now depleted clutch of royal children.

The passengers in the forward compartment were given priority at disembarkation. Frumgeour stood up and recovered his cane from the rack above his seat. Too impatient to sit down again, he stood, head painfully bent beneath the rack, knees painfully bent between seats, and tapped his cane against an arm rest while he waited.

183

Shepherdessed at last, by an employee of the Airport, towards the Arrivals Lounge, he raised his cane to a sloping port over his left shoulder.

Even through the circumambient fumes of petroleum his nose caught at the scents of the Islands. They reminded him of flute music.

All the same, he mentally accused the sun of grilling down too fiercely on the path, and the path of reflecting it too sizzlingly back. He noted that the unkempt airport grass through which the path led was already dusty, early summer though it yet was. And as he drew near the Arrivals Lounge, which was in the one substantial building the Airport afforded, and saw the great, stained cracks running down its concrete façade, he almost plunged his hand into his pocket and offered to pay out there and then the impost he felt sure the Islands Airport Authority would be demanding the next year.

Inside the building, the usual delay and muddle took place about the luggage, while little Islander boys, wearing chauffeurs' hats, ran among the worried new arrivals soliciting on behalf of hotels.

In the middle of the Lounge, ignoring the plastic-upholstered easy chairs and detracting from the modernity of the décor, a row of bigger Islander boys squatted on their hunkers, their naked slim feet displayed on the floor in front of them like goods set out on a counter for sale.

When he at last recovered his two suitcases, Frumgeour with difficulty fitted his cane into the same handclasp as the handle of one of them and, a suitcase on each side, walked towards the door marked 'Exit to Buses' instead of, as he had done in all previous years, the door of 'Exit to Taxis'.

A boy he thought he knew stood by the Taxis exit.

Frumgeour pushed his suitcases at the Buses door.

'Karyl?'

'O.' Frumgeour put down his suitcases. 'Hullo.'

'You don't recognise me?'

'You've grown taller', Frumgeour said. He raised his cane,

184

like a ceremonial staff, in front of him by way of acknowledgment.

'It's from Asty you've come?'

'Of course.'

'The king's children have already arrived. I saw them pass through the Airport. Do you know when the king will come?'

'The children were on my 'plane, as a matter of fact. No, nothing has been announced yet about the king. Gossip has it nothing has been decided yet. He may not come at all.' Frumgeour's source of gossip in Asty was his young friend who worked in the High Chamberlain's secretariat—and who was, of course, bound in Asty until (if, this year, it ever did) the Court removed. 'Even if he comes, he may not give the Summer Ball this year.'

'That would be a pity', Frumgeour's young Islander friend said. He tossed his head, as if to clear it of distant uncertainties and potential losses in the future, and asked: 'You are alone?'

*   *   *

Whenever there was the least pretext, in the form of one of the easily-exhausted breezes that breathed in from the sea, a faint rattling ran along the inland routes of the Islands. It came from the dry, sharp leaves of the oleanders that bordered most of the roads—an almost metallic ticking or whirring such as you might have expected from the lizards who, in fact, accomplished their sudden accelerations and sudden petrifactions silently, as they moved from sunned stone to sunned stone at the edge of the dusty road.

Everyone except the lizards sought shade.

At the Summer Palace a note was delivered to the Archduchess Heather. On scented paper ('Where does she *find* it these days?' Heather asked Missy Six), in a hand that seemed to mimic, in an unsteady graph, the baritone to falsetto swoops of her aged speaking voice, the Duchess of Coriander Bay

185

implored Heather to disclose any inside information she might possess about the king's plans, because the time was fast approaching when the invitations should go out for (if there was to be one) the Summer Ball.

By tradition, the invitations were in the name of the king and the Duchess, though the Ball was held at the Summer Palace and entirely at the king's expense, the Duchess contributing only her name, her presence and her advice about who should be asked.

'Papa maintains it's very statesmanlike behaviour on his part. He says if the invitations come from the only person who could put up an alternative claim to be monarch of the Islands, and if they go to, amongst others, the officials of the Island sections of the trade unions, then any tendency to separatism in the Islands, from whichever direction, is quelled before it can start.'

'*Is* there a separatist movement?' Missy Six asked.

'None whatever. I suppose Papa claims the credit. Actually, I suppose, having once included the old thing, he can't drop her.' Heather turned over the scented sheet and discovered that the querulous hand had written a postscript on the back.

I address this appeal to you, my dearest girl, rather than to one of your royal Brothers, because I know your Heart will sympathise with a woman's feeling for what is Right in these matters.

'Honestly', Heather said and blew a raspberry. 'She can't expect a proper reply to such twaddle. I'll telephone tonight, when it's cooler, and leave a message.'

At the sunglasses shop, a grotto hung with outlandish frames and petrol-tinted lenses which gaped onto the main square at Macranese, the Archduke Balthasar recognised the Countess Clara Claribond (who had once, Balthasar believed, been his elder brother's mistress) and reintroduced himself to her.

186

She was carrying a lawn tennis racquet, but when Balthasar questioned her about it she told him she was unable to find on the Islands either a court or someone to give her a game. Balthasar replied that there were courts at Nutmeg, which might not be entirely booked up yet, since it was still comparatively early in the season. He undertook to try to secure one and, if he succeeded, to run her over there in a speedboat which an Islander friend gave him the use of. He took down, in a notebook, the address of the boarding house the Countess Clara was staying at, so that he could get in touch with her. Before they parted, he added that he hoped she was prepared for an early start, because the sun made tennis impossible after about half past ten; evenings, which were the obvious alternative, were less suitable, because the courts were more crowded and because games were sometimes disconcertingly guillotined by the sudden, southern way that darkness fell in the Islands. The Countess agreed that a morning would be better and assured him she was inured to early rising: at home she was often up before dawn in order to go out and gather mushrooms.

On the first three evenings when Heather tried to telephone the Duchess of Coriander Bay, she was answered only by the 'not in working order' noise, which meant either that the Island postmistress had deserted her switchboard or that electrical storms out at sea were again interfering with reception.

The Duchess's letter had gone unanswered for almost a week when Heather at last got through to Coriander Bay Castle, in the habitable part of which (a suite of rooms on the third floor) the Duchess lived, with two companions scarcely less aged than herself (the Duchess called them her ladies-in-waiting) and, intermittently, a squirrel, who came in from the branches of a splendid fir that bordered on the drawing-room window, scampered through the rooms, always keeping to the tops of the furniture, as though playing Shipwreck, opened cupboards by turning their knobs with his human little hands, nibbled at food and sometimes woodwork, posed prettily on

187

the backs of chairs, chattered to the Duchess and, after an hour's visit that charmed the Duchess by reminding her of the days of punctilio and formal calls, withdrew, having let fall his neat little droppings onto the carpets, which he evidently equated with the limbo beneath the branches of trees.

It was the deafer of the two 'ladies-in-waiting' who answered the telephone.

Heather had to shout and repeat herself before she was confident of having lodged the message that, no, she had had no private word from the king and did not know, any more than anyone else, when or indeed if he would be arriving.

'How's the squirrel?' she concluded.

'The who, dear?'

'The SQUIRREL.'

'O, very well, dear, in fact marvellous, when you consider. A little arthritic, you know, but that's to be expected, but I must say she still bears herself magnificently, like one of the Old School, which of course she *is*, but she's really very well *in herself*, if you see what I mean, though of course it *is* fretting for her not knowing about his Majesty and the Ball and so forth . . .'

The same uncertainty fretted, though for different reasons, at Frumgeour's holiday.

His young Islander friend seemed to Frumgeour, this year, rather elderly in temperament, which made Frumgeour himself feel old. (Paradoxically, Frumgeour felt less burdened by his own age when there was a greater discrepancy between it and his companion's.) Perhaps because he had some of the exhaustion and inertia of the old, the youth seemed clinging; and he had taken with ease, as a matter of habit, to the little luxuries and delicacies with which Frumgeour thought it proper for the elderly or even the middle aged to cosset themselves along through life but which he had originally offered to the youth only as dazzling occasional treats, to make a bravura beginning to their friendship.

At noon he and the youth sat as usual at one of the tables,

shaded by a gaudy and fringed umbrella, outside the café in the main square.

Frumgeour sipped at an iced lemonade, which he didn't greatly like but had ordered as a good example. The youth drew towards himself the triangular china ashtray that advertised Cinzano, stubbed out in it a gold-tipped cigarette that was only half smoked and then gulped at his cognac and soda.

Frumgeour was confident he could detach the youth by means solely of hints, silences, trumped-up quarrels and lying excuses so blatant that the youth, for all his passivity, could not refuse to challenge them. It was a method that would, however, take time. The alternative method would work at once, but it would take cash.

It was in order to know whether he could afford the time to save money that Frumgeour wished he could judge of the king's intentions. Frumgeour now considered his young friend in the High Chamberlain's secretariat to be the 'serious' friend of his middle life. Yet between the dismissal of his elderly young Islander friend, however engineered, and the arrival of his serious friend from the mainland in the train of the king and the Court, Frumgeour felt he owed himself, for the sake of his mental health, a certain unencumbered interval of pure holiday in what he thought of as a state of bachelorhood.

At the bar inside the café there was a hubbub. Frumgeour recognised, from previous occurrences, that the machine which automatically squeezed the lemons for the lemonade had again broken down and that many Islanders from neighbouring shops had come in to offer advice.

It occurred to Frumgeour that even the method which avoided a cash settlement was not cash-free, since the youth would drink many cognacs before coming to accept his dismissal. Rather than buy him another, Frumgeour decided to make him pay for the one he had just finished in usefulness. He sent him across the square to the camera shop, to see whether Frumgeour's colour prints, which had twice defaulted on their promised delivery date, were ready yet. He bade the youth also ask, at the post office and at the quay, whether any news of the king's intentions had come in with the noon boat from the mainland.

However, the only news from the mainland that day was pretty much what everyone had been expecting for some time. After a lengthy procès, every word of which had been published as it went along, the assessor judges had unanimously found that Petrus Squinch was the assassin of the Archduke Sempronius, though by a majority they found him not responsible, by reason of insanity, for the deed.

★   ★   ★

It was almost high summer, by which time most people on the Islands had despaired of the king, and the Duchess of Coriander Bay was almost resigned to despairing of the Summer Ball, when he came: not, however, in state and only on a 'flying visit' which was not announced to anyone except (by radio) to Macranese Airport and (by telegram) to Crown Prince Ulrich.

Chapter Six

He came into the little room, spread his arms and said, in a quiet, deep voice:

'My son.'

Ulrich had never received that form of address from him before, and was embarrassed by it.

He was embarrassed again, perhaps even less rationally, when he was at last able to withdraw from the sorrowfully slow embrace of the wide arms and saw, at the end of one of them, fluttering in his father's fingers, what he recognised after a moment's blank (although he had made them himself, he had never seen it with creases in it) as his own letter to his father, sent a few days earlier, on paper headed 'Pavilion of the Perfumes, Summer Palace'.

The only room the Airport had been able to set aside for their improvised interview was the sick bay, a cubicle furnished only by the aggressive whiteness of its walls and by a small metal framed bed, severely made up (as if some very thin, very military patient were already lying in it, at attention, his arms to his sides) with blood-coloured blankets.

Ulrich wondered whether the royal interview would be disrupted if one of the passengers in the milling Arrivals Lounge below were to faint in the heat.

'I have never played the authoritarian with you, Ulrich. I have never concealed from you that I have feelings. I can't conceal from you now that when I received this' (he waved

191

Ulrich's letter) 'I received a painful wound.'

Heavily but with dignity, as if indeed wounded in a chivalrous battle, the king sat down on the bed.

He sat in the centre.

Ulrich, left with nowhere where he could with dignity sit, walked the two paces that were needed to the little window, which was double-glazed against the Airport noise and supposedly immunised against the heat by an air conditioning apparatus that hummed through a grill beneath it.

'Naturally, I didn't intend to hurt you, Papa.'

'But you are a man of imagination, Ulrich. How could you fail to see that it must, inevitably, hurt me?'

'I'm afraid, Papa, that I don't, even now, quite see *why*.'

The king sighed. 'Can't you imagine what it feels like? To have laboured to preserve and pass on a heritage—to have tried to share with you its problems and educate you in the expertise needed to deal with them—an expertise no one else could teach you—to bring you up in a knowledge of all the richness and subtlety of certain cherished traditions—and then to find you reject it all.'

'Papa, I reject nothing.'

'Except', the king said, his voice suddenly as brisk as a trumpet, 'your duty.'

'Papa, since I am singularly unfitted for what you consider to be my duty, isn't it more *sensible*—'

'Ulrich, Ulrich, you are trying to rationalise away your own conscience. When I was a young man, we still had conscription in Evarchia. Do you think I *wanted* to serve my two years? I assure you in those days I was much more interested in dancing and chasing the girls. And when the time came, do you suppose I *wanted* to be king?'

'Papa, you have a talent for being king and a talent for being a cavalry officer. Unfortunately, I have inherited neither.'

'Do you imagine one's duty is conditional on one's talents?'

192

'What you call my duty, Papa, is simply a matter of accident. If I had chanced to be born the youngest instead of the eldest of your children, it would never have occurred to you that I have a duty to be king.'

'Ulrich', the king said slowly, in a voice on whose horizon Ulrich could detect tears, as though the subject he was speaking of were very sad, 'we humans do not understand enough of these things to tell what is accident or even what accident is. We are surrounded by mysteries. It may be that what humans, in their arrogance, call accident is God's providence. Is it', he added, his words accelerating, 'a question of the fair Countess Clara? Is your motive, in putting forward this suggestion, that you want to marry her?'

'No', Ulrich said.

'If it is', the king pursued, as though Ulrich had not answered, 'I cannot conceal from you that I should be unhappy. I do not consider her a suitable person to be queen.'

Ulrich witheld the information that Clara agreed with the king on that score.

'All the same', the king continued, 'if your marrying her were, in your view, essential to your doing your duty, I should, though sadly, accommodate myself to it.'

'I suppose it would have made me very happy if you had seen fit to tell me that a year ago.'

'The love that cannot endure testing is not worth having', the king said.

Ulrich was disturbed that he agreed with the dictum, applying it, however, not to Clara's love for him but to his own past love for her. He said, rather doggedly:

'However, that is not my motive.'

'Then what is? Ulrich, I am human, you can explain to me—Why will you make no effort to share your thoughts with me? Is it a matter of principle? Is it political?'

'No', Ulrich said. 'I can see many arguments in favour of constitutional monarchy and many against it. I suppose, on any deep level it doesn't make much difference either way.

193

But what moves me isn't general at all. Whether kings, as such, are right or wrong, it's simply that I can't see, I simply can't visualise, my particular self as king.'

As soon as he had spoken, Ulrich was disconcerted to find that his reason, wrung from him, he had thought, quite freshly by immediate pressure, was in fact an echo of Clara's reason for not marrying him.

'I don't think I can endure any more', the king said. 'Perhaps I have come to the end of my strength, perhaps to the end of my life.' He propped his elbows on his knees and lowered his face into his hands, into which he presently groaned, through his beard:

'Is another of my sons to be taken from me?'

After a moment Ulrich said:

'You are not the only person who was bereaved by Sempronius's death.'

The king sighed into his hands and made no answer.

After a minute Ulrich began to fear that, when the long beautiful fingers removed themselves, they would release tears or even blood.

'I shan't be taken from you', he said, in a tone of conciliation despite itself, still half belligerent. 'I shall still be your son. I shall cease only to be your heir.'

Presently the king took down his hands, and his brimming look sought up towards Ulrich.

'O Ulrich, Ulrich, that it should come to this.'

Ulrich met his look, truculently, he feared, and said nothing.

'Well', the king said, getting to his feet, 'what I must endure I must endure, I suppose. Since you are adamant, we had better set about the things that will need arranging. Now I'm here, it will be more convenient if I stay. I had intended, you realise, to fly back when the aircraft has refuelled. It's a light aircraft, which I chartered specially. But no matter. I'll send for the High Chamberlain. He'll have to draw up some sort of instrument, I suppose, in constitutional form. I'll tell him to announce that the Court is moving to the Islands. And I must let your mother know. No doubt it will inconvenience her considerably. She always seems to have a great many things to see to before moving to the Islands.'

And so that year the king entered his Summer Palace not in the traditional Islands Landau, with his consort beside him, to the cheers of a crowd whose excitement had climbed towards an appointed date, but sitting, in a sorrowful silence, side by side with his eldest son in a taxi which Ulrich, when he finally contrived to find him, persuaded the Airport Manager to summon privately to a side exit because taxis at the public exit were being fought over by the newly disembarked as if they had been made of gold.

The streets the taxi passed through were full only with the normal holidaying crowd. Rumour had run through them of the king's arrival, but people discounted it as a rumour prompted by wish; a few who looked through the taxi window and saw the king persuaded themselves that they had seen only someone with a degree of resemblance to him.

Rumour indeed preceded the taxi to the Summer Palace and was there discounted by the housekeeper, who as a result had presently to bustle round, apologising as she did so, and make the Gilded Kiosk fit for royal habitation even as the king was taking up his habitation in it.

As soon as the rumours were confirmed, the Duchess of Coriander Bay despatched the less elderly of her 'ladies-in-waiting' to deposit at the Palace the Duchess's visiting card with, on its back, a plea that 'dear Sire' should 'speak, and speak *soon*, on the Subject of the Summer Ball'; and at the café on the main square Frumgeour repeatedly rapped his cane across the palm of his left hand, chastising himself for having made so little speed in dismissing his Islander friend that the Court would now be on the Islands before he had enjoyed his bachelor interval.

*   *   *

One of the things the queen saw to before leaving was the care of the pigeons.

In the heat they had an equal or even increased need of water but (since, even in Asty, summer provided them with alternative sources) the queen felt a diminished need to give them food.

Even so, the stout brown paper bags of grain and nuts, which the queen ordered in bulk enough to see the birds through her absence, took up a good fraction of what spare space there was in the suite of small rooms which Nanny Hausmann occupied on the top floor of the Winter Palace.

Nanny Hausmann's bookcase was overcrowded, too, although she was, as she had once mentioned to the queen, 'no great reader'. At the end of every summer the king thanked her for her summer labours by presenting her with a Royal Bible. (The queen's thankyou present occupied no space once it had passed into her bank account.)

Overcrowded though they might be, Nanny Hausmann was much attached to her own quarters and disliked leaving them, especially in hot weather, even to pay a brief visit to the queen's part of the Palace.

The queen had, therefore, to redirect the pigeons' attendance from her own window to one of Nanny Hausmann's higher and more eastward windows. It was this shift that made the queen's preparations for departure long-drawn. With each meal she gave the pigeons, she moved two windows further along the now strangely parched and unpopulated corridors of the Winter Palace, her stops including a transitional stage when she stood tiptoe on a narrow step of a winding staircase and squeezed the food out through a window that was scarcely more than a slit in the wall.

At last the queen was able to lean from Nanny Hausmann's drawing room, calling and holding out palmfuls of nuts, and the pigeons arrived on the sill.

When she had finished feeding them, the queen gave Nanny

Hausmann good wishes and final instructions and then paid a final visit to Caspar Gregorian in his pretty little house in the Palace precinct.

After writing his long essay on the Islands, Gregorian felt that he had used up the stimulus they offered his imagination; and since, in addition, his cat disliked travelling, he had given up holidaying on the Islands, preferring, as his wife did too, to stay at home, particularly since, whatever the rest of Asty did, the Winter Palace remained, through its sheer size, comparatively cool.

At the queen's request (and expense), and with his wife's happy agreement, he usually flew out to Macranese just for the twenty-four hours that encompassed the Summer Ball— because, the queen declared, he was, the king apart, the only dancer skilled enough to partner her without exposing the deficiencies of her dancing in public.

For the rest of the summer, however, he made it his business to take a daily stroll through the cool corridors of the Winter Palace and look in on Nanny Hausmann, who, despite her indifference to books, regarded a visit from Evarchia's best writer as a privilege, and check up on the queen's behalf that all was well with the pigeons.

He promised now that he would telephone (or, if the telephones had broken down again, telegraph) the queen if any mishap should occur to the pigeons, and to come himself, prepared to dance attendance on her, should the king decide on holding the Summer Ball.

The queen smiled and, after giving Gregorian her hand to kiss, which she knew he liked doing, left for the boat train, a method of travel she preferred to flying. (The king, however, annually forgot her preference.)

*   *   *

Leaning into it and thereby imparting to it the power of his wide shoulders and long torso, Balthasar sent down the service with which he had, at various times, aced each of his brothers and even the professional who had once been engaged to coach them all. He aimed at, and struck, the inside of the furthest right angle of the service court, and after its swift landing the ball seemed to skeeter unpredictably and irretrievably off into the tramlines.

Giving a little facetious grunt at being made to stretch, Clara got her racquet to it, returned it (past Balthasar, who was running towards the net) as swiftly as it had come, in parallel with the side lines, into the right angle between the side and base lines, and thereby took the advantage point.

Arguing to himself that Clara's constant victories were matters as much of psychology as of skill (a theory he only half believed), Balthasar promised himself that a single act of successful surprise could see him back at least into the temporary shelter of deuce. Obviously, his strength was of no help to him, because Clara, like someone practised in judo, merely diverted its course and used it against him in her return of service; so this time he sent over the net a rabbit's service, which plopped without purpose into the middle of the service court.

She replied with the orthodox, boring stroke of a well-trained schoolgirl, trained, perhaps, to keep the ball in play, thereby providing exercise for everyone, rather than win.

The ball bounced slowly and undeceitfully at a height that suited Balthasar. He replied at the same pace, with equal orthodoxy, and discovered, as he completed his follow-through, that Clara had revolutionised the pace of the rally and had already killed him from the net.

He said, meeting her in the tramlines as they changed ends:

'You ought to play with someone better. I can't even give you a game. Do you mind?'

'O, no', she said. 'I'm not serious about tennis. Do *you* mind?'

'It's a privilege for me, an education.'

'Actually, I think we ought to stop now. The sun's high, and you look quite pink in the face, BALtasar.'

198

'May I say something to you I've been wanting to say for weeks?'

'Of course. If you wanted to, why didn't you?'

'I didn't want to sound arrogant, as though I thought it a matter of importance. But in fact I'm pronounced BalTHASar.'

'O how dreadful of me to forget', Clara said. 'Of course I knew perfectly well—from Ulrich.'

He gave a serious little nod, signifying his pleasure that she had advanced to the point of speaking to him of Ulrich.

She touched her hand to his elbow and then led the way off the court.

'I would like to know', Balthasar said, 'what went wrong between you and Ulrich, but please don't tell me if you don't want to.'

'I've no objection to your knowing', she replied, 'but I'd rather you asked him. I'm not quite sure *why* I feel that—except that I think he somehow knows more about it than I do. It seemed as if it was my doing, but I think it was really his.'

'I'll ask him, then', Balthasar said, 'if I get a chance.' He directed their steps towards the lemonade vendor who set up his stall, morning and evening, behind the tennis courts.

He had added the proviso not because he expected to find any material difficulty about making a chance to speak privately to Ulrich but because, as soon as Clara put the idea to him, he was aware of an obstruction in his own mind.

This declared itself, when he questioned it, to consist of an embarrassment lest Balthasar, who had agreed, at Ulrich's urging, to take Ulrich's place in the succession to the throne, should seem to be putting himself forward also to usurp Ulrich's place with Clara.

When he recognised the thought, Balthasar felt himself blush even through his tennis player's flush, and he turned his face away, as they walked along, in case Clara should notice.

As they drank their lemonades, he asked:

'Did Ulrich ever beat you at tennis?'

199

'I don't think so. I don't really remember', she said. 'Ulrich and I didn't play as often as you and I.'

Balthasar felt deeply pleased that she should draw a parallel between Ulrich-and-Clara, that acknowledged pair, and Balthasar-and-Clara.

*   *   *

'And I have brought with me', the High Chamberlain said, 'my Constitutional Consultant.'

The royal children looked up and recognised, through the moustache he had grown since those days, their former Protocol Tutor.

The queen gave the newcomer a shy smile, clearly unaccompanied by recognition.

The king lifted one of his beautiful hands but did not look out from the gloomy huddle in which he was sitting at the centre of a low daybed, which was surmounted by a canopy of stuff still brilliant though in places now bald.

The Gilded Kiosk was furnished according to a fantasy on the Turkish mode. In pursuit of the fantasy, the daybed the king had chosen to sit on was raised above the rest of the room on a shallow dais, with the result that, although the décor of the whole Kiosk was meant to be quite informal (so much so that it was easier to lounge than to sit in it), the king—and his gloom—seemed enthroned.

'I must say, High Chamberlain', Balthasar began, as soon as everyone had found a perch on a divan or in a window embrasure on which to seat or re-seat himself, 'I hope this doesn't mean you are contemplating a *committee*.'

'I know your Highness has scant patience with the consultative process. Nevertheless, there are certain vital and urgent problems to resolve. For instance: what style and titles will his Majesty see fit to bestow on his Royal Highness when he ceases to be Crown Prince? Will he, indeed, still *be* a Royal Highness?'

200

'I don't feel in need of any style or title', Ulrich said, 'but I'll take one if it will help to avoid embarrassment.'

'I came across a rather charming title the other day', Heather said, 'in a history book: Duke of the Marches Palatine. I got the impression it was a royal dukedom and it seems the title is now extinct. Shouldn't Papa revive it for Ulrich?'

'It was created', the Protocol-Tutor-Constitutional Consultant said, 'in the twelfth century, for a natural son of the king.'

'In that case', said the High Chamberlain, 'it would be markedly unsuitable. It would inevitably lead to rumours that his Majesty had disinherited the Crown Prince on discovering that he was illegitimate.'

'Good God', said the queen, sotto voce.

'You will observe', the High Chamberlain said to Balthasar, 'that none of these matters is as simple as you think, when you come to look into it. And then there is the problem of where the former Crown Prince is to reside.'

'I'd thought', Ulrich said, 'of somewhere in the neighbourhood of the Grand Museum. There are some handsome old houses round there, now divided into apartments which, I'm told, are not too expensive . . .'

'Does your Highness mean in Asty?'

'Yes, near the Grand Museum, on the—'

'But your Highness must live abroad.'

'Live abroad?' Ulrich asked, and the words seemed to be echoed soundlessly by the queen's lips.

'Of course', the High Chamberlain insisted. 'At least for the time being. For ten years or so. Naturally.'

'But why?' Ulrich demanded.

'For the avoidance of faction, of course.'

'Faction? What sort of faction could conceivably—'

'A faction might very easily form around the notion that your Highness was still the rightful heir to the throne.'

'But it can't', Ulrich protested. He opened a cardboard folder that lay beside him on the divan he was sharing with his silent youngest brother Urban, took out a sheet of paper and tapped one of its typewritten paragraphs. 'My statement, my instrument of renunciation, as you call it, specifically says I am renouncing the succession *voluntarily*. How could any faction conspire to claim the throne for me when I have signed, sealed and delivered a statement that I don't *want* it?'

'Your Highness is naif. People don't always believe that statements which *say* they are voluntary *are* so. The question is simply which foreign country you choose.'

'How can I choose?' Ulrich asked, letting his sheet of typescript lapse back into the cardboard folder. 'I hardly know any foreign countries. I don't suppose the Jugoslav government would have me. Otherwise, I suppose I'm most in sympathy with Sweden. And I believe they generally let people in there. But I don't know anybody in Sweden, I've never been to Sweden, I don't speak a word of Swedish . . .'

A silence settled, which the High Chamberlain seemed to be using as a weapon.

'But I shan't change my mind', Ulrich said, 'if that's what you're hoping.'

There was a further silence.

Suddenly, for the first time, the king spoke.

'I possess a castle in Sweden.'

'Papa', Heather cried, laughing and flinging herself towards the king's knees, 'do you mean a castle in Sweden or a château en Suède? And if it really exists, why didn't you say so before, and will you give it to Ulrich as a farewell present?'

'Yes', the king said sorrowfully, 'if he persists in his resolve, I'll give it to him. It seems the least I can do, since I have failed to make life in Evarchia agreeable for him. It really exists, I had forgotten all about it, I have never seen it, but I think it is probably an exaggeration to call it a castle. We Evarchians tend to grandiose terminology. From what I recall of the description I was given at the time, it is a four-roomed, two-storey, semi-detached house with a pebble-dashed exterior, built about 1937. It was the home of an Evarchian expatriate who made his living as a deputy bank manager in Malmö. I did not know of his existence, but when he died I was informed that he had left the title deeds to me personally, in his will, with an expression of regret for his disloyalty in leaving his native land.'

'Papa!' Heather exclaimed, and laughed. 'O Papa!'

'Thank you', Ulrich gravely said to the king.

'In return', the king said, 'may I ask you all to keep absolute secrecy about what Ulrich has done. His instrument of renunciation shall be signed and lodged in the Royal Archive. But I prefer to reserve to myself the occasion of making a public announcement about a deed that inevitably pains and humiliates me. For the time being, I shall simply announce, during the Summer Ball, that my eldest son is flying off early the next morning to Sweden, where he will spend the rest of the summer on holiday.'

'So there's to *be* a Summer Ball', Heather said. 'Have you told the D of C B?'

The king, however, had resumed his sorrowful silence. It was the High Chamberlain who gave Heather a 'Yes, she knows' as they all filed out of the Gilded Kiosk.

In the garden outside, where he took (rather slowly) the best shaded of the paths back to his own quarters, the High Chamberlain, who was rather clingingly accompanied by the consultant he had chosen to import, found himself purposefully caught up with by Balthasar.

'Don't think', Balthasar said, while the former Protocol Tutor strolled on and waited tactfully beyond earshot, 'that, just because there are plenty of places to sit or at least lie in the Summer Palace, I've forgotten the underfurnished state of the Winter Palace. As soon as we move back in the autumn, I shall make sure of some armchairs. I shan't be fobbed off with a committee. Remember: by then I shall speak with the authority of a crown prince.'

On another path the present Crown Prince heard pursuit, turned and saw Heather.

'You realise Papa thinks you'll tire of life behind a pebble-dashed exterior and come cringing home?'

'I realise it's in that hope he's delaying the announcement.'

'But you won't, will you?'

'No', Ulrich said.

Heather wiped the sweat from her face. 'I think what you're doing is splendid. Remote though I am from the succession, I shall do the same. Can I borrow your document, to make sure I get the wording right?'

Ulrich lent her a carbon copy from his folder.

When at last it was cool enough to walk in the garden for pleasure, members of the Household whose stroll passed near the Pavilion of the Peacocks, which Heather had chosen for her summer home that year, heard erratic, infuriatingly slow and, an auditor could by some means detect, although the mechanical noise was not really capable of expressiveness, infuriated typing.

When Missy Six came home after her evening swim, Heather said:

'I borrowed your typewriter. It seems to have the keys arranged in the most absurdly illogical order.'

'I think the principle is to put the letters that occur most frequently on the keys the fingers can most easily reach. It's helpful to touch-typists.'

'Why don't they sell a machine that's helpful to non-touch-typists, who are the ones that need help? And now' (Heather unrolled the cylinder and took out her Page 2, which she crumpled and threw onto the floor) 'I've copied "I, Ulrich" instead of remembering to substitute "I, Heather". I don't suppose you'd do it for me?'

Missy Six replaced her at the machine.

'It's all secret, by the way', Heather said. 'Ulrich's renunciation is to remain secret until Papa chooses to announce it. Mine—well, I shall force the High Chamberlain to put it in the Archive, just in case, but I don't suppose it will ever be needed.'

*   *   *

In Asty, too, in—as a matter of fact—one of those handsome and inexpensive old flats near the Grand Museum, three fingers were typing, though much more rapidly and confidently than Heather's or even Missy Six's.

The flat was three stuccoed storeys up. The wooden shutters outside its windows (of a kind characteristic of that part of the city, which made some visitors think that Asty resembled Paris and others that it was a sort of smaller Vienna) were unfolded across open windows, their slats in the open position, thus preserving secrecy (which no one had, in fact, ever tried to violate) and what there was of cool.

The flat served as an informal editorial office for *Red Rocket*, the organ of the Communist Party of Evarchia.

The new Chairman read over the typist's shoulder.

He didn't bother to read beyond the heading, 'PARTY CHAIRMAN RESIGNS', before he said:

'Scrap that.'

The typist suspended work. 'Why, Comrade?'

The new Chairman leaned over the typist's shoulder and pulled at the paper in the machine, but since he hadn't pushed the release lever he managed only to scrunch up the paper in situ.

'There's no particular reason to announce it *now*', he said.

'Except that it's happened now', the typist (who was the editor) replied. 'Or, rather, it happened weeks ago, or at least you told me weeks ago (I don't know when it in fact happened), but we haven't got out an issue since, because of the holidays. The readers have got to be told.'

'Yes, but *when* they're told makes no difference to *them*, and to announce it now is no advantage to *us*. When things start to move again, in the autumn or the winter, we may be involved in some ideological controversy, where the resignation might come in handy.'

'That sounds like opportunism, Comrade.'

'And your arguments sound like corruption. It must be the

205

years you spent working for the bourgeois press, Comrade. Perhaps you actually swallowed the hypocrisies—"Our Readers' Right to Know" and all that? What have they a right to know, Comrade? That some film star's having a baby? And they have a right to know it today instead of waiting till tomorrow? Whose political education will that advance, Comrade?'

The editor sat silent, then sighed, and then said:

'All right. You're the Chairman. Though scarcely anyone knows. I was going to lead the paper with it.'

'Nobody reads the summer number anyway', the Chairman replied. 'Everyone's on the Islands.'

'What am I to go with instead?' the editor asked.

'What do we usually do at this time of year?'

' "Imperialism on the Islands" ', the editor said.

'Well, there you are. Surely that satisfies your bourgeois lust to be "topical"? Get over to the Islands and do our usual piece with some up-dated statistics. Don't forget "Privilege and Extravagance at Summer Ball". Incidentally, I had a postcard from the Islands from our tram-driving Comrade. It's time we ran another interview with her.'

'All right', the editor said. He took the crumpled paper out of the machine and wrote 'Magda Lupova' on a blank bit of it that wasn't too creased, tore it off and put the fragment in his pocket.

'I should think you'll be glad to get out of Asty in this heat', the Chairman said.

*　　　*　　　*

One regular reader of *Red Rocket* (or at least regular skimmer through it, since he found its politics reactionary and its arts criticism jejune when it existed at all) already knew the information it had not yet published.

The Bulgarian Cultural Attaché had been told of his resignation by the former Chairman himself.

Although he had duly forwarded to Sofia the spool on

206

which the former Chairman's rather hysterical account of the matter was recorded, the Cultural Attaché had marked it 'Very Low Priority' and he did not expect to receive 'further instructions' from Sofia until the autumn.

Indeed, he did not expect anything to happen in Asty until the autumn—if then. He was therefore taking a 'plane out: initially to Budapest, whence he would go on to a conference of Cultural Attachés from Warsaw Pact countries that was being held on the shores of Lake Balaton; after that he would join an 'Opera-Lovers' Tour' that was visiting Berlin, Dresden and Prague.

*   *   *

A letter for Missy Six was forwarded from the Winter Palace, Asty, to Pavilion of the Peacocks, Summer Palace, Macranese.

'Just guess', Missy Five had written,

where we, I mean the De Rigueurs and me going along with them, are off to for the summer holidays. ENGLAND!! I know I ought to have written ages ago but there hasn't seemed a moment. The De Rs are very nice. The difficulties I told you I was worried about have turned out perfectly all right, because Count De Rigueur's memory is not what it used to be and he is in a bit of a muddle about things in Evarchia, even, never mind England. Anyway, once I've been there I shan't have to worry ever again. Please give my love to Heather and the queen. We are going to stay with a friend of Count De R's who has a castle at Cheam. The weather is beautiful here. I expect it will be cooler in England, though.

Kindest regards—

Missy Five

P.S. I hope England is still worth visiting, people say it has gone downhill a lot!

Urban was more than ever silent that summer, as though he had decided to include speech among the exertions one avoided in the heat; and he was silent with, in particular, Ulrich—because he knew that Ulrich had tried (unsuccessfully) to keep from him those instalments of the procès in the case of Petrus Squinch which emphasised, by introducing time-tables and so forth into the evidence, that Sempronius had been killed in, as it were, the place of Urban.

And Urban had isolated himself more than ever by his choice of pavilion to spend the summer in.

It was called the Lighthouse and looked like one (in most eyes; Caspar Gregorian saw it as a stubby minaret). As a rule it was inhabited only when the Summer Palace had an excess of guests to put up overnight (usually on the occasion of the Summer Ball). Even so, it could accommodate only one of the excess, because it had in effect only one room, consisting of its circular and not very large ground floor. From there, a utilitarian winding staircase led up through the ceiling and on, up through the core of the tower. It led, however, not to any more living space but only to an eventual exit onto a narrow open balcony, which, as you could see from the outside of the building, braceleted the tower a little distance beneath its summit.

Had Urban's siblings thought about where the stairs led, they might have remarked that the Lighthouse, a strange choice in any case, was a doubly strange choice for a prince who suffered from vertigo. However, none of them had the interior of the Lighthouse much in mind. (Urban invited none of them into it.) None of them had climbed its stairs since early and energetic childhood. The Lighthouse stood some way removed from any of the other kiosks, with the result that Urban's siblings thought of the little circular balcony from a distance and from the outside of the structure, to whose phallic silhouette it seemed to add the detail of a foreskin.

Surely the Lighthouse had never been used as a lighthouse?

Granted it was at the edge of the garden nearest to the sea. But that was not very near. If it had ever displayed a light (and there was no trace in the building, inside or out, that it had), and if (which was by no means certain) it had been able to raise that light high enough to be visible to ships, it would surely have done them nothing but the mischief of misleading them as to the sandy whereabouts of the coast?

Urban had selected the Lighthouse because he meant to teach himself to overcome vertigo.

The course he meant to put himself through was easy to plan so long as he was in Asty. Once he was actually at the Lighthouse, he began postponing: he would begin when he had settled down and become used to the heat; the days were too hot for clambering up the stairs; in the evenings there was the danger that darkness would arrive while he was up there . . .

His mental rehearsals began to flutter with hysteria.

His self-tuition was to be conducted in privacy, of course. Above the level of its habitable ground floor, the Lighthouse turned its back blindly on the garden. The exit onto the balcony, which you reached by a railed platform from the head of the internal stairs, was close above the garden wall. Beyond the wall there was only a salty, tufted waste, with nothing to attract tourists, and, beyond that, only the distant, imprecise shimmer of the sea.

Thus much Urban remembered from his childhood (when his affliction must have been less severe) and counted on for his plan.

Yet the very privacy seemed to offer a chance to cheat— perhaps not to do the thing at all.

Day after day, he didn't do it.

He became more intensely silent, his lips visibly pursed, as if in resolve against speech, in fact in the concentration of willing himself to begin.

It was at the hottest hour of an exceptionally hot afternoon that he eventually did mount the stairs.

He arrived deeply breathless from the climb and shallowly, palpitatingly breathless with fear.

He pushed open the door onto the balcony and the heat from outside touched him solidly, all over, like a material thing.

The balcony was so narrow that two paces would bring him to the balustrade, which, pie-frilly though it looked from outside and below, was solidly stone and would reach, if he stood against it, almost to his waist.

He had no intention of standing against it yet. His plan had always been realistic enough to go by easy stages, for the first of which he would be content to place two freestanding feet on the balcony floor.

He put one foot over the threshold. The pores of his skin seemed to suffocate beneath a sweat there was no wiping away. He brought his other foot out.

He was tossed almost off balance.

For an instant he thought a gale was attacking the tower, and he crouched, from which position he recognised, from the nature of the upheaval, and with an almost euphoric sense of irony, that he had chanced to take his first, tentative lesson at the precise moment when the Islands were struck by an earthquake—the earthquake that geologists (and the superstitious) had long considered owed and indeed overdue to the Islands, which, though in a susceptible area, had not been shaken since the medium-sized tremor of 1566 (in which parts of Pirate Castle had fallen down).

Urban grabbed, behind him, for the edge of the door, which undulated beneath his clasp, and heaved himself back over the threshold.

On the platform he went swiftly down on hands and knees and crawled, swaying, to the stairhead. He bundled himself into sitting on the top step, from which he lowered himself, feet first, down the next few.

When the building seemed still again, he stood upright and ran as fast as he could down the rest of the stairs, through his living quarters, out, across the path and through flowerbeds.

A footman was approaching (as Urban was, though by a less orthodox route) the Gilded Kiosk.

Urban shaped the words 'Is anyone hurt?' and tried, painfully, to collect breath to shout them.

But the man's face (which Urban didn't know, presumably because he was local and engaged temporarily for the summer) was smooth with the calm of an undisturbed hot afternoon. His errand was to carry to the Gilded Kiosk a small, round tray of beaten metal, on which stood a glass of iced lemonade, whose surface was scarcely more agitated than its bearer's look.

When he obliged his intellect to believe, though his senses couldn't, that there had been no earthquake, Urban's immediate reflexion was one that he found even more intellectually than sensually frightening: an illusion of such unflawed and thorough-going conviction was no different in kind from the madness of Petrus Squinch.

⋆   ⋆   ⋆

Each of the phrases and clauses, of which there were as a rule, though by no means always, several to a sentence, carried its own logical tendency, and this, like a positive or negative electrical charge, brought it into a distinct logical relationship with the one next it, which might exemplify or amplify the logic of the one that had gone before, or might qualify it with a reservation or might stand in antithesis to it.

As though tracing the attractions and repulsions between atoms in a molecular structure, the queen construed the text.

She sat in an upright canvas chair in an unvisited part of the Palace garden, a line of junipers standing distant sentinel behind her against the sun, which was now low enough in the sky for defence to be possible.

She found and understood the main verb and, putting her

211

index finger beside it as a marker, paused. Her mind considered simultaneously, and in each case almost without imagery, the death of Sempronius, the departure, soon, of Ulrich, and the beauty, which resembled the beauty of great dramatic tragedies, of Thucydides's cynicism.

It was as if his unique power to analyse and to compound the logic of argument and the logic of syntax had carried him uniquely deep into the selfish motives of human idealism.

Yet even while she admired Thucydides the queen wondered why the human idealism she shared, socialism, seldom extended its compassion beyond the human species.

In front of her a clump of brindleberry bushes twitched and bounced, as a flock of little birds, who had hidden from the high heat of the sun all afternoon, hurried through the foliage, snatching at the brindleberries before night should dismiss them to sleep.

They were of the size, but not the elegance of build, of a greenfinch, and their small, yellow, parroty beaks, whose outline described a pair of bulging parabolas, gave their faces a look of comic challenge. Their plumage was Fauve: green on the breast, a streak of scarlet on the spread wings, and for overall impression a blue which on some birds was true and deep and on others was nearer turquoise.

The variety was peculiar to the Islands and the birds were sometimes known as Island finches. (Caspar Gregorian had told the queen that that was a misnomer and that they were not true finches.) Adult Islanders called them gaudybirds and Island children bobbydazzlers.

Since there was no occasion for her to feed them, the queen, following a principle people had discerned in her relation to her children when they were younger, made no attempt to tame them. But they were used to and tolerant of her presence in the early evenings, and sometimes one would jump onto the arm of her chair or even onto the book open on her lap and, when he noticed where he was, feel no more fear than prompted him to give her a direct and accidentally funny

212

stare.

She resumed her Thucydides. Suddenly, however, all the gaudybirds rose noisily from the bushes, some of them shrieking alarm calls, and a shadow not of a juniper fell across her text.

As she turned, she hoped to see one of the gardeners, all of whom were Islanders, most of whom she liked, though she felt shy of them, and from one of whom she had learnt the childish name for the gaudybirds.

But it was the High Chamberlain who rose behind her, like a second and massive back to her chair—a position he did not, despite her requests, relinquish, as though the better to insinuate from there his purpose into her ear.

That turned out (but not quickly) to be that, as soon as 'present problems' had been 'tidied up' (which the queen could understand only as meaning as soon as her eldest son had left for Sweden), she and he, queen and High Chamberlain, should jointly put into operation a programme for solving a further 'problem'.

It took effort from her and many words from him before the queen detected that the new problem was Heather.

She conjectured that sun or an ancient language had dulled her understanding—and counter-conjectured that the High Chamberlain was swaddling his meaning in his sentences through some awe of her rank or respect for her parenthood (towards which, however, he had not shewn much delicacy in his reference to Ulrich's leaving).

The programme, she in the end detected, that was to be applied to the new problem was a matter of 'finish'.

The queen mimed that she was thinking over the proposal the High Chamberlain had put to her. She had small idea what his proposal was, but she politely set her thoughts to move along what she could make out of its lines. She found herself reflecting that there was indeed a tendency in Heather to take up subjects and abandon them before she reached competence, let alone 'finish'. Much of that, however, must be

213

ascribed to the bittiness of her education, for which the responsibility was the queen's.

Mentally the queen itemised: Heather's Greek was still rudimentary; she was musical, but had no intellectual grasp of the subject; her French was sturdy but unpolished.

On the other hand, her English (the queen had it on the authority of Missy Six) was fluent, largely correct and improving.

'It's true', the queen conceded to the High Chamberlain when she emerged from her check-list, 'that her Greek is poor, but the blame must lie with me because I have been absorbing almost all Missy Six's teaching-time.'

The High Chamberlain made no reply.

When he spoke again it was with a paragraph-making tone, as if he were starting a new subject or even a new conversation.

'I had thought', he said, 'that, for Phase One of our Programme, we might begin by engaging the services, on a temporary basis, of an expert in make-up, a corsetière, a deportment teacher, a dancing master and a bridge tutor.'

'Bridge . . . ?'

'Bridge, ma'am. The card game. A necessary social accomplishment.'

'O I see', the queen said. 'I see now what you mean. O dear.'

'Have I your Majesty's approval to put the matter in hand?'

'But have you asked *Heather*?'

'I was hoping that your Majesty's authority . . .'

'O no', the queen said gently.

She felt the High Chamberlain's sigh, cooling, on the top of her head.

She added, in a kindly voice:

'You can always *ask* Heather . . .'

'I don't feel that her Highness herself is likely to prove sympathetic to . . .'

214

The queen wondered whether, were the High Chamberlain to withdraw now, the gaudybirds would return to the brindle-berry bushes or whether there was too short a space of daylight left for it to be worth their while.

'I can't be sure, of course', the queen replied diffidently, 'but I agree she probably won't. You see, she probably has more important things to do.'

*   *   *

In the Pavilion of the Peacocks, at midnight, the earliest hour when it was cool enough for skin to touch skin without sweating, Heather lay naked above Missy Six.

Missy Six silently remarked the paradox, as she had often done before, that Heather's breasts, which looked so disproportionately large and fluid beneath clothes, should, naked, fit so aptly into Missy Six's hands when those were chaliced, above her own breasts, to receive them.

She remarked, with a touch, almost, of ghostly fright, the changes wrought in Heather's known and loved face when moonlight redistributed its modelling.

Even so, it was possible to discern in Heather's features the thinner outline of Sempronius's. Not for the first time Missy Six asked herself if it was some incestuous impulse in herself that she was expressing. But she asked herself also whether she could have given such passion to Sempronius as she did to Heather—a passion into which she was presently swallowed, to the exclusion of thoughts.

Heather's lumpish profile, too, was changed by the glassy light.

So indeed were the profiles of the very peacocks in the mosaic beside the bed, which gave the pavilion its name.

(They were interspersed with tiny, clumsy representations of gaudybirds, which was held to shew that the mosaic was local work, though no one could form a clear guess about its date.)

215

'There was something', Missy Six said affectionately, 'that Missy Five was going to warn me about, about you. Something else interrupted and she never got it said. I wonder now if she was going to warn me that you were in the habit of seducing all your Missys.'

Heather gave her great, happy shouted laugh, and Missy Six felt the flesh quiver round her hips.

'I don't know about *all* of them', Heather said. 'Not *right* the way back to the beginning. After all, when the first Missy came, I was only two.'

Chapter Seven

The king kissed the Duchess of Coriander Bay on the left cheek and then on the right. Then he assumed his flirtatious manner, seemed to inhale behind her right ear, and murmured into it:

'You smell delicious this evening, Duchess.'

'Ah, Sire, Sire,' the Duchess replied, 'we come, you and I, of night-scented stock.'

★   ★   ★

Although he had been marking off the days to it, Ulrich felt overtaken by the date of the Summer Ball. And when the date had arrived, he felt overtaken by the Ball itself.

At first he was standing, embarrassed, in what seemed too much unoccupied space about the buffet tables, whose symmetricality and unspottedness surely couldn't, Ulrich felt, be intended merely to be disarranged and spotted by guests.

Ulrich dared not take refuge from embarrassment between a table and the solid wall lest his low stature vanish behind one of the hyper-eucharistic vessels that rose from the white cloths: mixing bowls whose vast silver bellies gave the impression that they were bulging with the overwrought confections inside; huge carboys of wine, like an old-fashioned school supply of ink; and stack beside stack of plates.

Because the plates were gold-rimmed, the stacks looked,

217

from the side, like golden towers. But the top plate on each disclosed (almost too high for Ulrich to see) that the plates were in fact white, though decorated: by the royal cipher at the edge, and by three butterflies passing across the middle.

Like a pair of the butterflies, strayed, two guests arrived, before time; and then without a moment of transition all were present, together with several uninvited, and almost all were trying to push through the scalloped and lacy entrance of the Gilded Kiosk.

A few were still trying to get in for the first time. Most, already in, were trying now to get out into the garden, there to pursue, across the dusky groves and beneath the long, swimming-stroke flights of the bats, the annual quest for treasure trove, which consisted of trying to divine whereabouts in the garden the workmen had chosen, this year, to pitch the marquee.

★　　　★　　　★

As tradition bade, the king inaugurated the Ball by dancing the first circuit of the floor alone with his partner, the Duchess of Coriander Bay.

The band (again in obedience to tradition) was playing a slow waltz, and the king was dancing one; but the Duchess, rapturous though distant in the king's embrace, her magnificent and slightly military carriage enhanced, perhaps, by arthritis, was doing a slow fox-trot, the 'smart' dance of her youth and the only one whose steps she knew.

On one of the low daybeds that had been placed at the edge of the floor, her two 'ladies-in-waiting' sat waiting, the Duchess's stick placed, for safe keeping, across their four knees.

Chivvied by an emissary of the High Chamberlain, Ulrich reached the marquee just in time to obey tradition and protocol by inviting his mother to dance, thereby adding a second couple to the second circuit of the floor.

It was a duty, as any onlooker could see, that embarrassed

218

them both. But as a matter of fact Ulrich and the queen were seldom so conscious of the tenderness between them as when each felt compassion towards the other's public embarrassments.

The second circuit completed, Ulrich yielded up his mother, by pre-arrangement, into the arms of Caspar Gregorian.

From then on, the floor was open.

*   *   *

Officers . . .

. . . and water ices: scoopfuls of water ice, like half-translucent fruits from not wholly natural trees, borne up by braided arms, swirled between groups and round knots of people, as though themselves taking part in a dance, and sliding a little, as they began to melt, on their tiny sky-blue plates.

*   *   *

As a matter of fact, in the Island Regiment, which was quite heavily represented at the Ball, the walking-out dress of the ordinary soldiers was a much grander affair, in bottle green and frogging, than the smartest (merely khaki, though exceptionally well-pressed) that could be mustered by the officers.

In mainland eyes, however, the soldiers spoiled the effect when they left off their boots.

Unaccustomed mainlanders were afraid to ask the Island girls to dance, suffering beforehand the pang of sympathy and conscience that must reproach them when (which was inevitable on the thronged floor) the bare feet should be stepped on.

But the girls giggled assurances—and made them good by agility.

*   *   *

'. . . of the nectarine and persimmon compote?'

*   *   *

Heaving beneath a dress that might have been the habit of an order vowed to austerity (not only colourless and shapeless but, somehow, textureless), Heather danced without a partner and without restrictions of step or style round the outside of the floor, ungainly but perfectly in time with the music.

Ulrich (while Balthasar partnered Missy Six) had one dance with Clara and felt shocked by his lack of lust or love. Even his thoughts would not fix on Clara but kept addressing the problem that, during the course of the night, his luggage must be conveyed to the Airport. The High Chamberlain had arrogated the responsibility to his Department, but the High Chamberlain was so minimally resigned to Ulrich's leaving at all that Ulrich doubted if, without a reminder, he would discharge his duty of helping the journey forward.

Jogging past, Heather saw the queen sitting alone on a divan (Caspar Gregorian had gone to fetch her a glass of white wine), jogged back against the current of the dancers and plumped down, with purpose, beside her mother.

'The High Chamberlain has been pestering me with a bizarre plan he calls a "programme".'

'I rather thought you would think it so.'

'He keeps speaking of the need to catch the eye of what he calls "young males"—officers, it seems, or, better still, princes or, best of all, millionaires. Is the man blind, deaf and idiotic? Doesn't he *know* I'm homosexual?' And Heather rose and jogged, outraged, away.

Balthasar claimed Clara again, and they joined the dance.

At the edge of the dance floor stood Karyl Frumgeour, pretending to watch the dancers, his cane tucked beneath one arm and protruding over the border. It seemed by a miracle that it had not yet impaled a couple and removed them from the dance.

220

Frumgeour felt full of conscious hate for the heterosexual conventions of the ballroom.

Beside him stood his 'serious' young friend who worked in the High Chamberlain's secretariat, a pearlier grey than ever in the lightweight suit he assumed for posh social occasions in the summer (and as a matter of fact Frumgeour had recently taken to addressing him sometimes as 'Pearl') and more than ever self-effacing, as though by reducing the thickness of his suiting he could reduce the quantity of space he occupied and the claim he made on anyone's attention.

Pearl seemed to be genuinely watching the dancers, and that provoked in Frumgeour a sensation of distrust.

Although he had recently coined for the young man a nickname that was partly an endearment, Frumgeour had in fact lately questioned whether his serious attachment was so serious as he had thought.

That Pearl had a job and a (tiny) salary of his own saved Frumgeour some expense. But it also meant that Pearl's thoughts could not be entirely of Frumgeour. For example, Frumgeour had not been able to bring Pearl to the Summer Ball. Pearl had had duties at the Summer Palace beforehand; Frumgeour had had to meet him there, after the Ball had begun; and even now Pearl was technically on duty.

Heather bounced her way round again to where her mother sat, still unaccompanied, and, plumping down again, demanded:

'By the way: did *you* know?'

'It had crossed my mind.'

'But you try not to let your mind infringe your children's privacy? Anyway: you don't object?'

'What is there to object to?' the queen said.

'Darling Mama.' Heather kissed the queen's forehead and stood up to dance away. 'I'm sure one of the others will provide you with grandchildren.'

'Heather?'

'Mm?'

'I wondered if you would be interested to read the poems of Sappho in Greek?'

'You relentless and wicked old intellectual,' Heather said. 'All right. I'll ask Missy Six to read them with me.'

*   *   *

'Or perhaps just a little more of the brindleberries in gin . . .'

*   *   *

Stickler for the gallantries but confused about which sex and rank the conventions required them to be paid to, the Duchess of Coriander Bay staggered exaltedly from the king's embrace to the divan where her 'ladies-in-waiting' sat, snatched the hand of one of them, raised it and, meantime stiffly clicking her high, gold heels, kissed it.

*   *   *

As if to endorse that Pearl's time was not exclusively at Frumgeour's disposal, the High Chamberlain was suddenly manifest behind Pearl, making the row of standing spectators two deep at that point, and saying into Pearl's ear:

'Prince Ulrich's luggage: have you the matter in hand?'

'I think so,' Pearl replied, barely wondering why the High Chamberlain had spoken of 'Prince Ulrich' rather than 'the Crown Prince' and concentrating on Heather's lumpish fantasy on the theme of dancing which was jerking through his field of vision.

Sound came from the High Chamberlain's feet: perhaps an incipient dance step, perhaps something remembered from the parade ground.

'I'll go and make sure,' Pearl said.

Before leaving he tried to smile a wan self-excusal to Frumgeour, but Frumgeour would scarcely receive it before

222

resuming his pretended interest in the couples.

As he withdrew, Pearl's vision encompassed the queen, sitting on a day bed alone but clearly not disliking her loneliness or even, as she pursued some removed thought, noticing it, and his mind was brushed by a fragment of a daydream in which, by a mechanism undisclosed, he, Pearl, had been placed under the protection not of Frumgeour, but of the queen of Evarchia.

*   *   *

When, however, it came to seating the exhausted Duchess, neither gallantry nor the practised arms of her 'ladies-in-waiting' nor even the stronger arms of Clara and Balthasar could prevail over arthritis. Simply, the seats of all the divans and daybeds mustered in the marquee were too low.

As discreetly as if she were making an enquiry less publicly voiceable, one of the 'ladies-in-waiting' asked Balthasar if there were not, somewhere in the precincts of the Summer Palace, such a thing as a chair of normal height.

It amused Balthasar to raise his voice and cry for the High Chamberlain.

He added in explanation to the Duchess that the High Chamberlain was expert at this very problem.

In the end, footmen had to be sent on an expedition to the gatehouse, which was used as a store, and the Duchess sat (by virtue of a special dispensation which the king visibly disliked giving and she visibly delighted in receiving) on a throne.

*   *   *

Outside in the garden, the fireworks began.

As the first volley of reports filled the sky and penetrated even the music in the marquee, the queen flinched.

*   *   *

Challenged by ten noisy men in dinner jackets (the executive council of the Island trade union of light engineering workers), Heather agreed to do the Island Dance with them.

The band began the rather babyish tripping phrases of the accompaniment (they scarcely constituted a tune) and many mainlanders left the floor.

A few sought the coolness of the garden, but most stayed to watch. The Island Dance was not unspectacular.

It began, boisterously, and like many other folk dances, with an inner and an outer ring circling in opposite directions. It was only as the music accelerated and the participants began more frequently to let loose the traditional falsetto cry of 'Heigh ho' that it declared itself a test of nerve.

Tradition intended it, of course, to be danced only by men. But nowadays girls as well as boys learned it at the Island schools, and there were two other mixed groups, besides Heather's, dancing it at the Summer Ball.

High on her throne, the Duchess of Coriander Bay spread a black fan sprawled with roses and said, behind it, as though behind an arbour, to one of the 'ladies-in-waiting':

'Makes me perspire merely to look at it.'

Tradition had also designed the dance to be performed with bare feet, and thus the other two groups were performing it; but the executive council had debated the matter privately before issuing their invitation to Heather and had decided by a vote of five to three (with two abstentions) that to dance barefoot when one was wearing a dinner jacket would be to risk damaging the public image of the dignity of labour.

Frumgeour noticed, without acknowledgement, that Pearl had come back to his side in the now much thicker lines of onlookers.

Frumgeour's glance explored what he thought of as the hooligan end of the ballroom, the one from which came the least inhibited 'Heigh ho's.'

He expected to see, somewhere in the sweaty confusion, the

224

journalist who he imagined would be, as usual, covering the Summer Ball for *Red Rocket*.

What particularly angered Frumgeour about the Communist Party's annually repeated criticism of the Summer Ball was that he agreed with every word of its attack on the unjustified extravagance.

He stopped looking, however, for the hated journalist, because his eye was arrested by the sight of the Archduchess Heather lying on her side on the dusty floor, being jumped over in turn by ten noisy men, her huge upthrust pelvis setting quite a serious obstacle to any dancer not sure of the spring of his feet.

Heather clambered upright, unscathed but inelegant, and took her turn at jumping over one of the men, whose turn it now was to lie down.

'Why don't they do something about that girl?' Frumgeour muttered to Pearl. 'They'll never get her married.'

Responding to the fact, not the content, of Frumgeour's speech to him, Pearl replied with a smile, which Frumgeour considered insipid in itself and inept in the circumstances; for what Frumgeour had irritably in mind was that, if Heather proved unmarriageable, the cost of supporting her would eventually, by one means or another, be met out of an increased tax on unearned incomes.

Missy Six sat captive on a daybed beside the other 'lady-in-waiting', the deafer, who, inattentive to the dance going on before them, heaped upon Missy Six a conversation of swift, tripping phrases, not unlike the music coming from the band, in which she described the latest visits of the squirrel, who had disclosed a liking for chocolate—'but plain chocolate, always plain; won't touch milk.'

Missy Six watched Heather, whose long hair flapped like a dank curtain with the exertions of the dance and to whose face sweat had added a fiercely drooping moustache—which, as a matter of fact, drew the diffuse planes together and lent them a look of design.

225

Missy Six felt abashed by her lover's public hoydenism but at the same time proud of it, loyal to it and thrilled by it.

The final round of jumps was more unnerving. Now each dancer in turn knelt on the floor and folded his trunk down over his close-folded knees, assuming much the position of a Mohammedan at prayer. (Even Caspar Gregorian, however, had not been frivolous enough to draw a conclusion from it.)

The jumpers, for their part, made it a point of honour not to take the short route, over the waist, but to leap from head to tip—which meant their jumps had to be not only fairly high but pretty long.

When Heather took her turn at being jumped over, squeezing her huge body as tightly as she could over her huge knees and minimising herself, for what that was worth, Missy Six looked away, pretending an intensified interest in the account of the squirrel and wishing the dancers, like the other groups further up the room, unshod.

Yet the corner of her vision remarked and counted ten black, white and red blurrs (the red their faces) leaping in succession; and then it was aware of Heather rising, unscathed again and proven unafraid, and giving a perfunctory shake, a mere twitch of acknowledgement of the disorder of her dress and hair.

Shutting her fan with a sharp flick and employing it as a ruler, the Duchess of Coriander Bay leaned forward from the throne (dangerously, the closer 'lady-in-waiting' must have thought, as she moved to catch her back) and rapped Missy Six's interlocutor on the wrist:

'Used to do this meself when I was younger. Now it makes me perspire just to watch.'

Unable to hear, or misunderstanding, the deaf 'lady-in-waiting' rose and made hobbling haste to the Duchess's side, freeing Missy Six's attention as the last (and largest) of the executive councillors took his place folded on the floor.

. . . seven, eight, nine of his colleagues leapt him successfully.

226

Heather (by the intricate mathematical rules of the dance) was the last to leap.

Missy Six flexed the muscles of her mind against premonitions of a disaster not only to flesh and dignity but perhaps even to certain balances of political power, perhaps to the very compromise between integration and separation.

Gathering a great clumsy bunch of its material in each fist, Heather hauled her long skirt up above her knees, which were revealed, beneath her tights (which were laddered), rounded and dimpling like the face ascribed to the sun in comic drawings, stood well back and, having taken a long, serious run-up, jumped clean over the executive councillor.

The watchers at the edge of the dance floor clapped.

Her dinner-jacketed fellow-dancers, including the one scrambling up from his knees, let fly 'Heigh ho's of triumph; and Heather, catapulted onwards, tumbled up the steps of the throne and (as the fan flew and the 'ladies-in-waiting' nearly did) fell, shouting with laughter, across the Duchess's lap.

*   *   *

The garden was brushed with murmurs from unseen, shifting sources and pierced by scents released from leaves, cigars and spent fireworks.

The warm night lay gently on the limbs of the people who strolled in it, reminding several of them of the languor of having made more love than one could bear.

*   *   *

The miners (who worked a nearly exhausted and already unprofitable seam at Mace Point) made their fire in a hollow behind the Pavilion of the Perfumes.

Balthasar and Clara sat, close to each other, on the ground, being unable to sustain the squat which the miners preferred.

By the firelight and, occasionally, by the green glow in the sky from the fireworks which someone was still, if lazily, setting off in some part of the garden, it must have been apparent to the miners (who seemed, however, neither curious nor disconcerted) that the Archduke and the Countess were holding hands—until, at least, it was time for each person to hold out both his hands and receive, like a brand in his palms, one of the semi-sweet Island potatoes that had been roasted in the fire.

After the meal, the miners sang.

Balthasar, who knew the song, joined in, not displeased that Clara should hear his voice, which was a baritone quite passable in chorus, even to an ear immediately next to him, though not smooth or accomplished enough to justify a solo.

Clara could only join in the concerted clapping which accompanied every other line.

> How do you know a mining man?
> (clapping) Because his face is black.
> I've met a hundred mining men
> (clapping) And all their faces were black.

*   *   *

Ulrich felt as if, although he was not yet anywhere else, he had already left.

Indeed, he had made his goodbyes, and the king had publicly announced his departure.

During the little ceremony, Ulrich stood beside and slightly behind the king, and Balthasar beside and slightly behind Ulrich—an improvised placing that so exactly mimed the transfer of responsibility that Ulrich was amazed that everyone present had not read in it the secret import of his going.

He had then seen his luggage loaded into the small white van with the royal cipher on its hatch door. The man who was to drive it to Macranese Airport had wished him a happy holiday and added an 'au revoir'.

228

It was only through a certain gracelessness in the airline timetables that Ulrich himself remained.

The farewell he hadn't made but wanted to was to Urban.

Urban had not been present during the king's speech and was not to be found at any of the nuclei of the Summer Ball.

In the garden, Ulrich had to approach almost impertinently near to some solitary figures and several couples before he could be sure that none of them was, in the dark, his brother.

He excused himself with social smiles and cheerful, short-term farewells and received back in each case the impression that he had interrupted, momentarily, some exciting, single-minded and half surreptitious quest.

For some, Ulrich surmised, it was a matter of having set foot for the first time inside the precincts of a royal Palace.

Others, without doubt, were in pursuit of love.

Ulrich supposed he owed his own sense of being already absent from the place to the lack of any such single, secret thread drawing him through it.

He began to tramp the length of the garden in the direction of the Lighthouse.

In the distance he heard and recognized the miners' song.

He passed a clump of trees in the middle of which a statue stood on a plinth and a solitary man (who turned out, on Ulrich's scrutiny, not to be Urban) stood, on the ground, in an attitude of flirtation, de bas en haut, with it.

Ulrich recognized the statue as a daft Artemis of the late eighteenth century striding through the woods in a ruched skirt, with one breast bared, and wearing a flat hat not unlike a boater.

The man he recognized (after passing and smiling at him) as Dr Casimir, holidaying on Macranese and invited for the first time to the Summer Ball in recognition of his attendance (in a junior capacity) on the king during his illness and possibly miraculous recovery.

Light flared in a distant section of the sky, a hectic and, where it shone through the dusky foliage, pointedly unnatural

229

green.

It went out, and Ulrich was plunged into stumbling darkness.

The door of the Lighthouse was, as he had half expected, locked.

Presently Ulrich discerned, by virtue of a light patch in the sky that was probably the reflexion, on a white cloud, of an invisible moon, that an envelope was pinned to the door.

The message inside, wishing Ulrich well in Sweden, was short and inexpressive, as though Urban had become as miserly with written as with spoken words. What Ulrich acknowledged, on a page torn from his pocket diary and pushed under the Lighthouse door, was Urban's mute certainty that Ulrich would come to receive it.

Urban had addressed the envelope to 'His Royal and Religious Highness the Crown Prince'—and then, recognizing the new ambiguity of that form of address, had added on another line 'Ulrich'.

As he walked back towards the noises of the Ball, Ulrich realised he had torn out and given away the first two days of his life in Sweden. But he expected them to be blank anyway.

He passed the Artemis again. Dr Casimir had broken off the unequal flirtation and left only the smell of his pipe trapped under the heavy branches.

*   *   *

It turned out that the words—and the hefty, bumping tune—which Balthasar knew were only the chorus.

Verses, which Balthasar had never heard before, suddenly rose, solo, in a high straightened tenor from the most wizened of the miners, and the song, without quite changing tune, changed into a wail. Perhaps it bore out Caspar Gregorian's belief that there was a Muslim strand in the Islands' culture. Perhaps it only seemed to, because the old miner's voice, though true, wavered.

230

One day I met a mining man
Whose face was white. I said:
'O has there been a fall, down the mine,
That brought the dust on your head?'

Thin, the voice seemed to rise straight and then hang, like
the florets of a firework, above the branches. It must be audible, faint but clear, from every part of the garden.

'O, yes, there was a fall, my friend,
From the roof of Gallery Three,
Where the seam runs rich but the props are weak,
And it crushed the life from me.

'So now I stalk the galleries
Of this dirty working place.
Go and tell your friends you've met
The miner with the white, white face.'

After the song was finished, an echo or a memory of it
seemed to lie on the night until it was dispersed by the noise of
an internal collapse in the fading fire.

'Bit of a sad song, I'm afraid, Archduke,' one of the miners
said. He stood up and began to beat out the remaining smoul-
derings. 'But you'll appreciate that mining's a job with a high
rate of mortality.'

'Yes,' Balthasar replied as he helped extinguish the fire.
'Like being an archduke.'

*   *   *

At his own request, Ulrich went alone to the Airport.

As he walked through the garden of the Summer Palace
towards the gatehouse, where a car was to await him, there
were already streaks of queasy light in the sky.

He realised what a long time, in comparison with most people's experience, he had lived before having to consider what he should or could do with his life. Yet he was considering it now, he thought, as though that made up for his tardiness, by his own volition or at least as the result of his own action.

Ahead of him, the distant horizon, which might have been a cloud bank but was in fact the line of Turmeric Cliffs on Nutmeg Island, was a pale and luminous grey. The gatehouse, however, was still in darkness, presenting a mere solid black shape and that a slightly absurd one, as it might be of a ceremonial howdah.

Ulrich stopped and looked back.

The foliage of the garden was emerging from monotone and acquiring a little cool colour. Blue or white blooms in some of the flowering trees were already fully themselves. Not so—not quite—the pavilions that flowered, even more unexpectedly, here and there in the garden. They were more than silhouettes, bulbous here, fretted there, but the unfamiliar light made them look out of joint. The Lighthouse, of which Ulrich could see one side and the frilled top, seemed almost to lean.

One of the deep shadows on the path not far behind him must, Ulrich knew, be the detective to whom the High Chamberlain had given the task of seeing Ulrich safe off Evarchian soil.

As Ulrich watched, a last red rocket rose and exploded distantly into the sky above the Gilded Kiosk, reducing the roof to silhouette again, its skyline a row of boot-scrapers.

The rocket dispersed and Ulrich walked on, presuming that, somewhere behind him, the delicate-minded detective was doing the same.

He approached the band stand, which was deliberately placed on the outskirts of the garden so that, on the three or four evenings each summer when there was a performance by the band of the Island Regiment (bottle green and frogged and, moreover, hugely badged, in brass, with a stylised lyre), the populace outside the precinct, as well as guests inside, could enjoy Johann Strauss the younger, the Island Dance, Irving Berlin, the refrain of the miners' song and a medley of tunes from *The Gondoliers*.

Surmounted by a crown that might have been a handle for picking it up by, roofed (almost thatched) by metal palm leaves that curled like dragons' tongues in Chinese paintings, walled by a few thin rods that bulged outwards like the stays of an over-used corset, it was bound to put spectators in mind of a bird-cage—a cage, however, that mercifully (in Ulrich's opinion) could not confine anyone, not even the plumpest of green bandsmen, and was perhaps suited only to a mechanical bird (whose soullessly mathematical beat the Island's Regimental bandmaster might seem to his audience to imitate).

And indeed as he walked past the band stand, Ulrich heard the early-morning stirrings and the broken conversational chatter of birds waking up. He peered into the shadows of the structure and could just discern the gaudybirds, under and on top of the roof, inside and then outside the inoperative cage. The brilliancy of their plumage looked, in the small cold light, like moving enamel parts in an enormous clockwork jewel.

Chapter Eight

On the day that followed the Summer Ball, the queen experienced a peculiar fatigue.

In previous summers, staying up for the better part of the night had induced in her Family a communal freedom from care, a mixture of heaviness of hand and lightness of head, in which conversations had free-wheeled until they collided, in laughter, with somebody's remembrance of an absurdity from the night before.

Perhaps the only communal awareness that could have been induced this year was of the community's depletion. Perhaps it was in order to avoid it that the Family dispersed.

Urban came early to the Gilded Kiosk, was silent and left.

Heather and Balthasar had left, separately, earlier still, perhaps retreating before the queen's exhaustion, perhaps driven out by the king—who seemed, by contrast, possessed by a preternatural energy, at least of a vicarious kind.

He insisted on supervising the dismantling, by the footmen, of the trestle tables—interrupting himself, however, every now and then, to advance into the garden (where the heat proved, at each visit, to have intensified) and there urging the foreman of the contractor's workforce to finish striking the marquee and its subsidiary encampment before the high heat of the afternoon should render labour impossible.

Long before afternoon, the queen had found no alternative to going upstairs and lying down.

On the High Chamberlain's Department the king imposed (without forewarning, as the High Chamberlain pointed out) the task of tracing and reporting on each stage of Ulrich's journey.

Comparatively early, the detective had telephoned word of a safe landing at Vienna, which was the first stopping point beyond Evarchian soil and the point where the High Chamberlain had supposed his duty discharged.

But the king's energy was not appeased.

The detective had been permitted (indeed, in the High Chamberlain's ignorance of the king's will, ordered) to set off for home. What the king now demanded was the improvisation of an air traffic control system, which was to take over the surveillance of Ulrich's progress, and for operating which the High Chamberlain's secretariat possessed no instrument more delicate or more reliable than the Islands' telephone service.

Upstairs, the queen simply lay, fully (albeit lightly) dressed as she was. She meant to stand up for a moment and try to make herself a little cooler by taking off some of her clothes. Presently she realised she would do well also to close the shutters. But she lacked the power, physical or mental, to execute even such minor intentions.

Having made the social rooms downstairs chiefly into places for reclining in, the designer of the Gilded Kiosk seemed to have run out of fantasy by the time he reached the true bedrooms.

He had squashed the upper storey up against the roof and divided its area into strips, leaving himself the smallest possible surfaces to decorate.

What ideas he had in reserve he applied to the outside of the building, in the fantasticated shapes of dragon-headed water spouts.

They were half-practical in function. They conducted away from the eaves the thunderous rain that, once or twice in the course of each summer, dropped on the Islands. But

235

they conducted it (and in a more than thunderstormy concentration) no further away than onto any royal or royally invited heads that might be seeking shelter beneath. And on the much more numerous summer days when no rain fell they seemed to sharpen the wish for it, stretching out from the façade as if in yearning, as if to catch any single drop that might pass through the air, as though they were prayers wrought in lead to a rain god whose hearing had run dry.

In the queen's squashed-up bedroom the heat accumulated like an inert substance.

And still she could not summon enough force to defend herself against it.

Neither awake nor asleep nor unconscious, she heard without curiosity the sounds of actions below: slow footsteps from footmen deliberately countering the heat; impatient gestures and impatient, indecipherable syllables from the king; and, repeatedly, the High Chamberlain's voice, raised in order (as he believed) to telephone across the underpopulated wastes between, every sentence clear (though the queen paid no attention to its import) throughout the Gilded Kiosk, as he shouted questions, in his Austrian-accented German, to an airline employee at Frankfurt.

At lunch-time the queen conjured all her strength and called a 'No, thank you' through her bedroom door to an enquiring maid.

The afternoon, everyone agreed, was exceptionally hot. People felt as though the heat itself, not the mere oozing of their own sweat, was furrily stroking their limbs.

Maid, footmen, contractor's workforce withdrew for the siesta.

The High Chamberlain himself, though admitting to no such thing, snoozed.

Only the unseen royal will at the heart of the quiet Kiosk held lesser wills, by remote control, to their tasks. It kept Pearl, for instance, upright and alert before the small switchboard that served the Summer Palace. Seeking to exercise not remote control but merely remoter apprehension, he tried repeatedly to catch the wearied attention of the Macranese exchange and persuade it to undertake those further manipulations that would allow the king to follow his son's recession into the European distance.

Upstairs, the queen lay and thought (or, strictly, found her mind occupied by the images) of the mainland, Asty, the Winter Palace, the pigeons.

Pearl sat in a stagnant little room on the ground floor. A great blaze of sun from the window enveloped his body. He dared not escape it by changing position, because he was not competent to move (and then reconnect) the switchboard. He worked in his shirt-sleeves, which were in any case of a pearly transparency and which sweat had now made translucent. He was in a fair way to achieving the ambition his appearance usually sketched, of becoming unnoticeable if not positively insubstantial. When the High Chamberlain looked in for news, he was dazzled by the great blotch of sunlight and withdrew, and indeed resumed his doze, without realising that Pearl was present and on duty.

The queen found in her mind the thought that the pigeons were not only sexually but socially egalitarian. She had never observed any trace in the flock of the sort of hierarchy books described among hens.

She wondered why her thoughts were engaged with the pigeons, who were remote and (as Caspar Gregorian would by now have confirmed, on his return to Asty) safe in the care of Nanny Hausmann, rather than with, say, the gaudybirds present on Macranese.

Her first answer was that the gaudybirds, being more immediately attractive thanks to their bright plumage, could be presumed to have more well-wishers. This she presently refined into the idea, which she acknowledged without grief, that she owed a greater duty to the pigeons for the reason that parents owed a greater duty to their own than to other people's children: they were allowed to do more for them.

237

In the early evening Pearl logged, in the systematic or pedantic way required of him by his immediate employer, the High Chamberlain, the fact that the Prince (and his luggage, by which, Pearl had noticed, the High Chamberlain seemed to set almost equal store as by the Prince's person) had been safely lifted off, after an even longer than scheduled wait there, from Frankfurt Transit.

Pearl also made a note of the warning he had had from the Macranese exchange that communication with the next staging post, Stockholm, might be hard to establish because an electric storm somewhere off the Islands' coast was already crackling on the line to the mainland.

The shift of the sun and the promise of dusk brought relief to Pearl's eyes. But the heat seemed, if that were possible, to increase. Unliquefied by sunlight, it seemed to lie thick in the air, resting a palpable weight on human bodies when they moved through it.

Pearl could hear his ultimate employer, the king, moving, erratically, in another room, and the High Chamberlain's voice trying to curb him.

Pearl knew that Frumgeour, also making impatient gestures, no doubt with his cane, must be waiting for him at the café on the main square. But he dared not occupy that desired rarity, an outside telephone line in working order, by transmitting a message for him, even if it were to be supposed that the café possessed an ascertainable number to transmit it to.

Instead, he managed, by persistence, to raise Stockholm and eventually to hear, through interference both electrical and linguistic, that the Prince had arrived there.

He passed the message to the High Chamberlain. In Pearl's own mind, he had persevered for the sake not of the king but of the queen (whose whereabouts today he didn't know).

He agreed, when the High Chamberlain asked him, to stay on duty until Malmö was reached.

The heat was so still that it seemed to be listening for something.

238

Pearl found that he was himself listening: for a thunderclap that should blot out his telephone conversations more directly than by interference with the medium; or for the first big, slow-splashing drops—which would surely drive Frumgeour, stung, away from his frustrated vigil in the square.

All that reached Pearl, however, were the overheard pacings, between daybeds he was too impatient to sit down on, of the king.

Pearl thought of him as Prospero, contriving magic (a manifestation, perhaps, of his powerful will) by which to ensnare the storm that was causing disturbance somewhere beyond the coast and draw it over the middle of his Island.

But still no storm broke.

It was dark but no cooler by the time Pearl was permitted to leave the Summer Palace, which he did framing perfectly true explanations which he nevertheless did not expect to convince Frumgeour.

Taking the memorandum Pearl had left him, the High Chamberlain advanced into the pacing presence of the king and reported, with (after he had swallowed a yawn) greater solemnity than he usually bothered to adopt, that Prince Ulrich's flight, together with its full complement of passengers' luggage, had safely reached Malmö.

The king (ungratefully, the High Chamberlain thought) fell (by good luck, onto one of the daybeds) in a dead faint.

*   *   *

Summoned back to the Summer Palace sooner than even his most ambitious daydreams had proposed, Dr Casimir arrived at a time when the royal patient had recovered consciousness but not by any means well-being or appetite.

Even on his own junior authority, the doctor did not hesitate to diagnose a recurrence of the king's winter illness.

Immediately, he told Balthasar, there was little he could do for the patient (a form of words that did not expressly claim,

Balthasar noticed, that there would be more later), beyond ordering him bedded down on the daybed where he had fallen and then rested—and, of course, kept cool—as thoroughly as possible.

After advising the High Chamberlain to appoint some of the longer-serving and more responsible of the royal maids to act as extemporary nurses, Dr Casimir (almost as though he were afraid that some of those unintellectual duties might alight, by default, on him) hurried away from the Summer Palace.

'I take it,' the High Chamberlain said to Balthasar, 'you wish me to telegraph Prince Ulrich? And then summon her Majesty, the Archduke Urban and the Archduchess Heather?'

'No,' Balthasar replied.

As he went to bed, he realised he had for the first time taken a pleasure in the exercise of authority.

*   *   *

Further doctors (supported by the silently abetting good opinions of professional nurses) agreed that the illness was the same. (The gradual assembling of colleagues and subalterns seemed, Balthasar observed, to cut short Dr Casimir's haste to quit the bedside.)

What was not the same, what somehow *couldn't* be (for there was a perhaps paradoxical impression that everyone at the Summer Palace was trying to make it so), was the attendant anxiety.

'Since the illness is the same,' Balthasar wrote by ordinary post to Malmö,

> so, presumably, is the cause, and so no doubt, will the outcome be. What I am trying to say is that I don't know, actually, whether the terms of your renunciation leave you free to do so, but in any case I definitely advise you not to come home.

240

In the definiteness of his advice, as in the imposition of his will on the High Chamberlain's, Balthasar took pleasure.

'Am I in danger of becoming authoritarian?' he asked Clara privately.

'No.'

'In danger of becoming selfish, then? Ought I to be here with you at all?'

Each night he punctiliously warned her that he might be unable to keep his appointment the next day. Each next day, seized by the conviction that Clara was the most urgent business of his life, he kept it.

He comforted himself by the abundance of medical expertise that had promptly flown to the Summer Palace and by the fact that the queen, who during the winter illness had sat so constantly at the king's bed, seemed to content herself this time with a brief morning visit, after which she seemed always shut in her room and, presumably, her thoughts.

From Heather's conduct Balthasar drew no arguments. She was perfunctory in her attendance upon the king and spent most days in distant Island expeditions with Missy Six.

'Neither authoritarian nor selfish,' Clara said.

*   *   *

Perhaps because he sensed the lack of anxiety, or perhaps because he missed the devoted presence of his wife, the king asked feebly (but all the more irrefragably for that) that the Cardinal-Patriarch be sent for.

The request gave some trouble (which fell chiefly to the High Chamberlain himself, since Pearl was taking the hours off that were due to him for duty over-fulfilled at the Summer Ball and on the following day), because the Cardinal-Patriarch was passing the summer in a remote mountain range on the mainland, in retreat in a monastery subject to a rule of silence.

                    *   *   *

'Do you think,' Heather conversationally asked Missy Six, 'that immersion in salt water makes pubic hair grow more vigorously?'

The greater part of their Island expeditions was to an unfrequented cove, where they bathed naked (the only method, Heather insisted, of achieving a tolerable temperature this sultry summer) without risk of being seen, 'except just possibly,' Heather conceded, 'if she happened to be looking out of the window at the east side of the Castle, and if old age has made her, as it's often said to do, long- rather than short-sighted, by the Duchess of Coriander Bay.'

'I don't know,' Missy Six replied, in a tone that indicated she was considering the idea, but not with more than medium interest. She took care not to glance either down at her own or across to Heather's pubic hair. Yet her own reticence of the eyes embarrassed her. She feared not so much that Heather might consider her as that she might in reality be a prude.

                    *   *   *

Pearl talked.

It seemed to him he talked continuously through his forty-eight hours off duty, and he felt in his throat that fruity inflammation which sometimes, after parties, he had conventionally attributed to too many cigarettes—a convention dictated, he now realised, by people's preference for admitting to something that could be claimed as a vice rather than to the shaming incontinence of mere garrulity.

He was talking to hold—or to catch back—Frumgeour's attention.

Frumgeour had declared nothing, but Pearl knew that, especially after his vain vigil for Pearl at the café in the square, Frumgeour had it in his mind to dismiss Pearl.

Pearl therefore talked, informing Frumgeour of almost everything Pearl had ever observed or experienced and could now remember.

Against the grain of his conscientiousness, he flung out fragments of information about his job. Against the much deeper inhibitions of his self-erasing personality, he cast up fragments of autobiography, anecdotes about his childhood, a résumé of his family history . . .

Gestures might have served him better than talking. Frumgeour, however, perhaps deliberately but, if so, certainly with rational pretext, contrived that their time together was spent in public, where gestures of the kind that would have served were precluded.

At night Frumgeour (with full reason, given the weather) wanted his hotel room, and his bed, to himself. By day they must, naturally, be out-of-doors, for the sake of what coolness there was; and for most of the day, they were under an umbrella at a table in the square.

Frumgeour's accustomed waiter at the café breathed disapproval of Pearl (perhaps for reasons, unknowable to Pearl, of chauvinism, because Pearl had displaced Frumgeour's Islander friend).

Pearl suspected Frumgeour of choosing the location to punish him for having failed to keep an appointment there. But again it was with a perfect plausibility that Frumgeour claimed that that café, and indeed that particular café table, which was placed in the route of any current that might be drawn down the alley beside the café by the swirling of the traffic in the square, was the coolest place on Macronese.

His forty-eight hours almost up, Pearl had almost despaired of saying, or even, by sticking to lemonade, drinking anything that should placate Frumgeour, when suddenly Frumgeour's attention was caught.

He leaned across the café table and demanded that Pearl scrape his memory for every last recoverable impression of an idle glance taken, while Pearl had been searching, at the High

Chamberlain's bidding, for something else, into a wire tray that had contained, as well as other papers, a document that began 'I, Ulrich.'

Frumgeour rose sharply and plunged away into the indoor section of the café.

In arrears, Pearl followed him, both bewildered and temporarily blinded by the comparative gloom.

When he could see, the first thing he remarked was that the café did possess a telephone (affixed, at mouth height, to the wall opposite the zinc counter that bore the lemon squeezing machine), so that he could after all have sent a message telling Frumgeour not to wait for him.

He forgot that his chief reason for not even trying had been the need to keep the lines from the Summer Palace open.

Frumgeour was now standing in front of the wall and bullying the telephone, stabbing it with a jeton and agitating its receiver rest with the end of his cane, until he forced it first to disclose and then to connect him to the mainland number of *The Times of Asty.*

*   *   *

The queen admitted to herself, though she believed (correctly) she had succeeded in concealing from everyone else, that she was not only exhausted but a little ill, probably, she diagnosed, with a touch of what the Islanders called summer 'flu and mainland visitors called Island Fever.

What strength she had was used up by the time she had dressed and made, with the appearance of normality, her one brief morning visit to the king.

Thereafter, though she accused herself of neglecting him, she could do no more than call occasionally to a passing maid for news of his progress.

She accused herself also of wasting time and took her Thucydides text with her when she lay down again, meaning, although she had for the time being sent word to cancel her

244

lessons with Missy Six, at least to read ahead in preparation for resuming them.

But she was unable to do even so much, often even to open the book.

For the most part she just lay, without thoughts, her mind passively filled by the image of one of the pigeons at the Winter Palace: the probably female one whose speckled head had sometimes reminded the queen of the obsidian Ulrich had polished in his childhood, and who had come to the flock with an injured leg, who had spontaneously (though the queen did not suppose miraculously) recovered, and who still allowed and expected the queen to do more for her than the other birds.

*   *   *

For once ('You must be so bored with beating me') they didn't play tennis but turned, from the jetty, in the opposite direction, strolled through the village, paused, in the widening of the street that served the village by way of a square, to admire the pretty and enviably cool feet of the children under the water that spurted from the wall, and then took, slowly, the long steep path that led away from the village and up onto the cliffs.

It changed from a path into a chalk staircase of perilous roughness and deep treads, which for the time being made any conversation impossible, let alone the serious one Balthasar intended, and which indeed made Balthasar wonder, though he was too out-of-breath to utter the thought, whether he should have imposed such exertion on Clara unshielded from so violent a sun.

No other humans had undertaken the climb. When they had accomplished it, they found the whole strip of cliff-top occupied only by gullybirds, the slightly small, slightly grey Island variety of seagull, and they discovered that up here, high above the sound and the dazzling sight of the sea, there

245

was a just apprehensible breeze.

Clara lay down, face down, on the tufty grass and then reared up her head and shoulders, in the manner of a lizard, extending them almost over and above the very edge of the cliff, and took the breeze deliberately on her warm face and scalp.

Balthasar lay down beside her.

The grass was of the sapless, almost colourless kind that defied the salt in the air. A blue butterfly landed on a stalk of it near Balthasar and presently moved off.

Clara's response to his speech was:

'This may seem a curious response, Balthasar. What worries me—what quite often worries me, so much that I think about it in the night—is that you're so like Ulrich.'

'As a person?' Balthasar asked. 'Or to look at?'

'Both, I suppose. Chiefly, to look at. It's as if your face was a version of his, even though it's so different. It makes me unsure, as if I didn't know who I was talking to, or as if I was committing incest.'

'I don't think incest is the worst thing one can commit.'

'Neither do I,' Clara said. 'It isn't that; it's the uncertainty. It's as if you have his face. Only yours is so much more decisive.'

'As a face?' he patiently asked. 'Or as an index of personality?'

'Well, as a face, yes obviously. Your features are so much more definite: not just bigger, but more definite. But also, I think, as a personality.'

'I think I have recently become a more decisive personality.'

'Yes, you have,' Clara said. 'Decisive, not authoritarian. I wish I had. Can you accept an indecisive answer from me? Would you mind if I spoke about it, first, to Ulrich? It would make me feel less unsure, easier in my self. When's he coming home?'

'He isn't,' Balthasar said. 'We're all vowed to secrecy, but I feel dispensed in your case. He's renounced his claim to the

246

throne.'

A heavy bee flew between the stalks of the grass, towards one of the scrubby, utilitarian flowers that were all that grew on the cliff-top.

Clara asked:

'Who will be king when your father dies?'

'I shall.'

'Balthasar, didn't Ulrich tell you about me and him? Didn't you speak to him about it?'

'I never found the moment. What didn't he tell me?'

'I wouldn't marry him because I couldn't bear to be queen.'

'O God,' Balthasar said. Suddenly he added: 'Did Ulrich renounce the throne in order to be able to marry you?'

'I don't know,' Clara said. 'I told you, it was all very unclear to me at the time. It all still is, including my own feelings.'

'And to me,' Balthasar said, lowering his forehead, in misery, into the tough grass.

*   *   *

'They've forced our hand,' the High Chamberlain said. 'We have no choice but to make an announcement. With your permission, I'll draft a bulletin now.'

'A bulletin?' the king eventually asked, with only a faint stir of interest in his failing voice. 'Surely that won't—be necessary. I'm sure I shall be quite—better soon.'

The High Chamberlain was nonplussed: had the king simply not heard, not listened, while the High Chamberlain had been reading aloud the report in *The Times of Asty*?

He picked up and, as if to recall the king's thoughts to it, rattled the copy of the newspaper lying across his lap as he crouched on the corner of a daybed that he had drawn close to the king's sickbed.

Under the headline 'ULRICH QUITS', the Skimplepex column appeared, as it had never done before, on the front page, where it was enshrined in a large central box, its text topped by an italic '*Our famous columnist Skimplepex writes*' and tailed by the usual cursive Skimplepex signature printed twice as large as normal.

'I *meant*,' the High Chamberlain said reprovingly, 'a bulletin not so much about your Majesty's health as about Prince Ulrich's renunciation.'

'If,' the king murmured, 'it is—made public, he—may feel too—proud to come—home.'

'It *has* been made public,' the High Chamberlain said testily, 'but in inaccurate form. They haven't even got his new title right. All we can do is publish the correct facts.'

The king gave a sigh: of lassitude, of finding the unbroken heat beyond his power to endure.

The High Chamberlain reached out for the fan that lay on the king's pillow, unfurled it with clumsy fingers and gave a couple of little blows, like curt bows, in the direction of the king's face.

'He—does know that—I am ill?' the king asked.

'Indeed he does. The Archduke or, rather, I suppose I must now say, Prince Balthasar did, though not as promptly as I would have wished, inform him. I have now had a letter from him. I believe Prince Balthasar has had one, too. In his letter to me, Prince Ulrich asked me to wish you, on his behalf, a speedy recovery, and to keep him au courant with your progress.'

'It seems he—is set on not—coming home.'

'Then there's nothing to be lost by issuing a bulletin.'

'There is—nothing, indeed, to be—lost.'

'I'll submit the draft to you. Then it might be advisable to have it telephoned through, direct, to the radio station and so forth.'

The king closed his eyes. 'Do as—you think—best.'

*   *   *

Seeking to comfort him, Clara drew Balthasar's attention to the comic behaviour of one of the gullybirds on the edge of the cliff.

After a moment of looking more exactly, she corrected herself.

The bird's staggering absurdity was the result of fearsome injury, to leg, wing and throat.

'O Christ, Balthasar. It will never recover. It won't be able to feed itself. You must kill it.'

'I can't', he replied instantly, and the unbidden thought at once in his mind was of his mother.

'You must. We can't leave it to die of hunger, of thirst.'

'How can I?' he asked.

She chose to answer the practical, not the psychological question. 'It can't fly. It will be easy to catch. I'll drive it towards you . . . You must do it, Balthasar.'

'Yes,' he said.

*   *   *

Suddenly, capriciously, the king was not nearly so uninterested as he had seemed in the bulletin that was to make public the true facts of Ulrich's renunciation.

Indeed, he wanted to hear it broadcast.

The High Chamberlain proffered his opinion, based on experience, that Radio Asty would not be able to get the bulletin on the air so quickly after its telephoning through. But the king, while still beset by the feebleness of an invalid, displayed also some of the impatience of a convalescent, and insisted on making preparations well in advance, just in case Radio Asty should prove more efficient than the High Chamberlain had cause to expect.

In the course of those preparations, which the king feebly set in powerful motion from his sickbed, an order was passed down (through a chain of command in which Pearl, newly restored to duty, was a comparatively high link) that

249

a housemaid be sent to borrow a radio which, originally the property of Missy Four or Five, had been left behind one summer at the Summer Palace and was now, the king was convinced he remembered, stowed somewhere in the queen's bedroom . . . It was the housemaid who discovered (and one of the half dozen doctors clustered within call of the king's sickbed who confirmed) that the queen had died and that what had now to be thought of as her body was lying slantwise across her bed, where she had perhaps been reaching for the unopened volume (Thucydides, Book IV) that lay just beyond her immobile hand.

*   *   *

The king was not accorded, this time, the indulgence of a presumptively miraculous recovery.

By an exercise of collective will without leader, it was simply assumed, throughout the Household, that his lesser affliction would yield before an affliction that had proved mortal or, perhaps, before his grief about it.

And the king complied.

Arisen, clothed, he stood bewildered and non-participant beside the High Chamberlain, from whom a hundred urgent actions now set expandingly out, as, scarcely bothering to seek the king's consent, he issued announcements ('with deep sorrow'), drafted telegrams (including one to Malmö, his act of revenge) and sent forth messengers, of whom Pearl was the chief.

*   *   *

The Times of Asty put out a special late edition, in which the royal death occupied the front page, although there were few facts to give about it (and not many facts, known to the reporters, about the queen herself). Skimplepex's column about Prince Ulrich's renunciation was cut short and shuffled back to Skimplepex's usual place inside the paper.

*　　*　　*

The High Chamberlain picked Pearl simply because he was at hand and, after his period of leave, the High Chamberlain presumed, fresh. Perhaps the High Chamberlain was thinking (with a memory of military usage or simply an undated historicism) of horses. Certainly, he didn't bother to think that the news of which he made Pearl the bearer might pain Pearl himself.

Through air that seemed now almost puckered under the imminence of thunder, Pearl hurried, with a sensation of horror in his throat, to the Pavilion of the Peacocks.

He learned only, from a footman, that the Archduchess and Missy Six had gone, as usual, out. The footman didn't know where their usual destination was.

Pearl went on, towards the extremity of the Palace precinct, learning on his way, from a (better informed) housekeeper, where the Archduke Balthasar was likely to be and whom with.

But Pearl continued, first, to the Lighthouse, where the door was opened to him by the Archduke Urban.

Urban's reception of the news was wordless, but Pearl was prompted to both embarrassment and compassion by the fact that, when he had understood the news, Urban simply doubled up, soundlessly and, because he was still holding the door handle, awkwardly, as though grief had attacked him in the belly.

Pearl excused himself, wretchedly, and in pursuit of Balthasar took the ferry to Nutmeg Island.

*　　*　　*

Even as the panicked bird scurried towards him, limping, lurching, tumbling every now and then sideways onto its broken wing, Balthasar was still entertaining the childish hope that it would prove, when he caught it, to have miraculously nothing wrong with it. Or, his imagination postulated, some wave of a hand more magical than those sweeps of Clara's palms before which it was fleeing would raise it from half-life into life and, as Balthasar reached for it, it would soar and fly away.

All the same, when the bird, with the last of its strength, veered convulsively away from his stretching fingers, darting lop-sided towards the edge of the cliff, Balthasar responded swiftly, the hunting instinct, perhaps, serving the younger purposes of mercy. He grabbed at the bird, meanwhile flinging himself flat on the ground and securing himself by grasping, with his other hand, a little promontory of turfed chalk that stuck out from the border of the cliff and that looked like a piece of a jig-saw puzzle (which had, however, no answering piece to meet its shape on the other side). Under Balthasar's weight, the little promontory broke off, and Balthasar's hand, shoulder and balance dipped suddenly. He scrabbled, and the whole area of cliff-top he was lying on made a pebbly noise and crumbled and then crashed, carrying him with it, down the cliff.

*   *   *

In the Gilded Kiosk, the king from time to time adopted his old invalidish tones to complain about the continuance of the heat, as though he had managed for a moment to forget the new and circumstance-changing event of his wife's death; and then, evidently remembering the great event but unmindful of the minor fact that Pearl, long since sent out, was now far beyond reach, he would urge the High Chamberlain to bid his messenger make haste about assembling his children to comfort him.

*   *   *

Scrambling, sobbing and heedless, down the chalk staircase, hurrying without definition towards habitation, telephones and help, though she had no hope whatever that help could prevail, Clara met Pearl (instructed by the village children in which direction to search), clambering and panting up.

For a little they were at cross purposes, each blocking the other's path, each blurting news of a death, each unable to conceive that the other, too, had a death to give news of.

*   *   *

Some hours after he received the news of his mother's death, Urban was suddenly visited by the most exalted happiness he had experienced since his early childhood.

The oppressive feeling, which had been with him since adolescence, that life was deprived of value by the necessity to wait for it to be taken away, vanished.

He seemed liberated of bonds and inhibitions whose nature, now they were dissolved, he need not bother to determine but whose going left him free to recognise the nature of the temptation that had been teasing him now for so long, the irresistibly more-than-erotic erotic game it was possible to play with the changing states of one's own consciousness.

He walked measuredly up the internal staircase of the Lighthouse, crossed the balcony without fear, hoisted his legs over the parapet and, laughing slightly with excitement and thinking fondly of his mother's affection for birds, jumped

*   *   *

'It's grotesque, grotesque, grotesque,' Heather roared.

She lay sprawled, belly down, on her bed in the Pavilion of the Peacocks—on, Missy Six thought, with an extra agony be-

253

cause she had a conviction it would never be so again, *their* bed.

Missy Six crouched beside her.

Heather's elephantine legs kicked at the bedclothes.

Missy Six's right hand dug, as painfully as it could, at Heather's shoulder. Her left hand, in a fist, was at her own mouth, and she bit it in her own grief.

Abandoning words, Heather simply roared.

She turned her face, unseeing in sorrow, towards Missy Six.

Missy Six observed that Heather shed no tears, but the great mouth, now squared, went on uttering its loud pain.

*   *   *

Plucked by long-range agency (which, set moving so long before, was out-of-date in the information it gave him when it finally reached him) from his silent mountains, the Cardinal-Patriarch arrived the night before—arrived, indeed, just in time to conduct—the funeral.

His flight into Macranese was delayed: by, at last, the storm.

All night, water shot noisily from the dragon heads under the eaves of the Gilded Kiosk.

In the small, flinty cathedral in the subsidiary square that opened out of the main one, three coffins stood, on three biers, in vic formation before the high altar.

Long candles, whose light flickered as draughts from the storm infiltrated the door jamb, and officers, scarcely less slender and upright, of the Island Regiment guarded three royal corpses and the corpse of the gullybird whom Balthasar had mercifully killed in his fall and whose body was inextricably compressed upwards into the heavier, splattered body above it.

In their notices of his death, both *The Times of Asty* and *The Astean Times* spelled Balthasar 'Baltasar'.

The storm was over before morning. But the air had lost

warmth, and the sky above the funeral was tempestuous.

Slow-marching, though leaning on Heather's arm, down the aisle as they followed the coffins, the king whispered to Heather that the place was not really suitable. 'The Islands insisted on having a cathedral, but it wasn't built as one, it's really no more than a village church, a fishermen's church . . .'

Heather didn't know if he meant the place was insufficiently stately for a triple royal funeral or for a funeral conducted by the Cardinal-Patriarch.

When the door was opened, the pall-bearers paused in their ritual stride, because they were struck by a freakish gust of wind, which was for a moment as cold and powerful as the coming autumn gales.

*   *   *

Heather didn't, in fact, weep until it was truly autumn, by which time she, the king and Missy Six had returned to the Winter Palace.

The choir of the Cathedral in Asty proposed to give a concert performance of the Mozart Requiem in memory of the royal dead. It was to be a secular performance in the concert hall, but because the text (and perhaps the executants) were sacred there was to be (as a note in the programme would request) no applause.

His feelings hurt by even so much secularism, the king accepted the memorial dedication of the concert but, when it came to attending it, appointed Heather his representative.

She sat, to outward appearances unmoved (as indeed she had been through the triple funeral) but listening with evident concentration, through the first four numbers. But when the performance reached the *Rex tremendae majestatis*, with its startling initial choral shout of 'Rex!', her shoulders became galvanised into an inward curve and were shaken by disturbances like hiccoughs, tears of the size of thunderous Island raindrops fell down the sides of her nose, which snuffled, and Missy Six, her arm vibrating as it lay round the eruptive back, had to escort her out.

Palace Revolution

Chapter Nine

In much the tone he employed for making easy conversation with interesting people presented to him whom he didn't personally know,

'What news,' the king asked, 'have you from Ulrich?'

'Ulrich's fine,' Heather replied.

She bounced her legs, more than ever pachydermatous in corded grey trousers, against the chair-arm they were slung over.

Bitterly, there was no longer a shortage of places to sit.

'And what is he doing with his life?'

'By day,' Heather said, exaggerating the rhythms of her sentence in order to point out this was not the first time she had spoken it, 'he works at the bank, and—'

'The bank?'

'The bank whose deputy manager left you the house Ulrich is living in. For sentimental reasons or something, they felt obliged to give Ulrich a job, though not the job of deputy manager. I told you last week, Papa. And in the evenings he's taking a course in jewellery-making.'

The king nodded.

Heather was convinced his memory wasn't fading. She wondered if he had hoped, like a police interrogator, to surprise her into a different story the second time.

Uneasy at the thought, she nodded goodbye to the king and wandered away to look for Missy Six.

Under-inhabited, the Winter Palace was, this winter, gaunt. Heather often thought she heard its structure creak in the night.

She passed the High Chamberlain in a corridor and presently, in a small drawing room previously used chiefly by the queen, found Missy Six.

'The High Chamberlain looks old,' Heather said.

'So does your father.'

'It's not,' Heather replied, 'that I'm not sorry for him. I may even love him. But I don't like him, and I daren't make him any concessions, because . . .' She turned her last clause into a shrug.

After a little, Missy Six said:

'I'm not any use to you. I think I'd better go home.'

'Home?'

'England.'

'O,' Heather said. 'Perhaps I'll come with you. I don't know. Anyway, I'd rather you didn't go yet.'

Missy Six promised not to.

They were no longer lovers. Missy Six had never known a love affair end so completely without turmoil or recriminations or leave behind it such a passionate affection as she felt towards Heather.

The drawing-room door was thrust open on them—purposefully; but when the king entered it was at a stroll, with every signal of mere casualness and chance.

Missy Six rose at once. It was some moments before Heather heaved herself up.

'By the way,' the king said. 'Apropos of what we were speaking of, Heather, just now. Do please sit down again, both of you. I'm not planning to stay. I was just wondering, Heather, if you ever have any news of the Countess Clara?'

'What sort of news do you want?' Heather asked.

'Well, has she, for example, recovered—so far as anyone could, so far as any of us ever will—from the appalling shock she must have received?'

'I gather so,' Heather said. 'So far, as you say, as anyone could.'

'And what is *she* doing with her life, these days?'

'Growing mushrooms in her Castle cellar.'

'Indeed? Do you know this, as the lawyers say, of your own knowledge?'

'No, from Ulrich,' Heather replied surlily.

'They are in touch, then?'

'They occasionally make use of the postal service between Evarchia and Sweden.'

'Please don't be so fierce and sarcastic with me, Heather,' the king said in a very gentle voice. 'I wish only to be friends with you.'

Heather made no reply.

Uninvited, the king sat down.

'I realise,' he presently said in a tone he seemed to intend to be comically rueful, 'I shall risk exciting your intolerance of religion if I say this.' He turned for a polite moment to Missy Six and interpolated: 'I understand you are an unbeliever, too.' Turning back to Heather, he resumed: 'However, to a believer, what is so remarkable in life is the fertility of divine providence,—how, in even the most appalling of disasters, it contrives also to bestow blessing.'

Heather kept silence, looking alert and suspicious.

The king went on without conversational help.

'For the Countess Clara I feel respect, even admiration, and much personal interest and concern. I regret only that this otherwise admirable young person took it into her head that she wanted to be queen—formed, indeed, such an obsession on the subject that she tried to achieve her end through *two* of my sons, and, had it not been for the concealed beneficence of pro—'

'You're unspeakable,' Heather said. 'You're the most awful person in the world.'

The king withdrew. As he went he took care that his hurt should shew: not only in his face but in the postures of his

261

body.

On the following day it became clear that what he had withdrawn into was his sickbed and a further recurrence of his illness.

*   *   *

On the Ring Boulevard, inside the pillared and portly building of the Ministerium for Parks, Ponds, Public Monuments and Culture, the news of the king's illness, which no one, after so many repetitions, could receive as very shocking, impelled the PPPA to a much rarer thought: of Ulrich.

After a moment's debate, at the end of which he settled with himself that Ulrich was indeed the one who was still alive, the PPPA took the lift to the top floor and got the filing clerk to look him out the folder on Ulrich which he had compiled at his Minister's insistence.

As later events had made Ulrich irrelevant to whatever might happen should the king die, the PPPA felt vindicated against his Minister.

The irrelevant folder lay unopened on the top of a filing cabinet beside him as the PPPA stood at the small, high-up window. He gazed across the scraped roadway of Ring Boulevard to the stark chestnut trunks on the far side and the curved banks which had been constructed out of the scraped-up snow—and that now looked as permanent, and as grimy, as walls.

He could think of no method of publishing his vindication to the Minister without danger of inconvenience to himself.

Neither could he remember (he never could, from one year to the next) whether it was yet reasonable to expect the snow to begin melting.

Sunlight lay like a coat of paint on the branches and the twigs of the chestnut trees. The PPPA felt an impatience of their black lack of response.

He was tired of the snow, had exhausted its promise of

262

beauty or exhilaration, saw it now only (as anyone might who had to go to and from work by tram, and seek his inbetween meals on foot) as an impediment that restricted and slowed down everything . . . Not that there was, so far as the PPPA knew, any activity he planned to undertake in particular when mobility was restored.

The outside of the folder was labelled 'Crown Prince', which was no longer apt.

The PPPA opened it and turned to the last typewritten page, where he saw that he hadn't, after all, kept the information up-to-date. There was no record of the Prince's renunciation and translation. The PPPA's recollection, which was quite detailed, must have been a recollection only of meaning to enter it.

He made a note at the bottom of the last page with a pencil that proved to be blunt.

He noticed in himself a contradictory mixture of impatience for activity and a laziness so extreme that he could not bring himself to summon a pencil sharpener from the filing clerk.

It occurred to him that he could simply have the folder destroyed, since it no longer served any purpose.

That, however, would be to destroy the evidence of several of his own hours of work. Besides the PPPA suspected his Minister of sometimes spending time with the files without distinct purpose (and therefore, it seemed to the PPPA, dishonourably, if not positively surreptitiously), in which case a gap might come to the Minister's notice and incite him to order the PPPA to compile a replacement.

He decided therefore to complete the folder perfunctorily, which would require of him no more than a look through the back numbers of *The Times of Asty* to find the date on which Ulrich's renunciation had been made known, and then to transfer the folder, under an amended label, from the current to the reserve file.

Although he had made a decision, and although it was one

263

that licensed at least a minor form of the activity he yearned for, the PPPA continued to stand for a while inactive at the window.

Reminding himself to consult *The Times of Asty*, he thought briefly of Skimplepex: if he chanced to meet him, the PPPA might remember to ask if Skimplepex knew of a compelling unpublished motive for the Crown Prince to have renounced an inheritance that the PPPA, had it been his, would never have surrendered.

Even as he shaped the thought, however, the PPPA recognised that, had it really been his, he perhaps *would*. To be born royal, to be a nucleus round which unknown people compiled folders, must be as impeding to adventure as permanent snow.

And yet there was still no adventure, no really active activity, that he could have wanted to undertake.

He had probably, he thought, been beguiled into a false impatience by looking out on the sunshine from the bodily comfort of an artificial spring inside the building—a sensory delusion created by the heating apparatus, whose thermostat, the PPPA now considered, he had probably ordered to be set a degree or two too high.

*   *   *

Since Heather allotted no more of her daily time to the king's sickbed than she had done during his earlier illnesses (when, however, there had been an entire Family at hand), the royal patient was often without companionship.

Even the Cardinal-Patriarch was less anxious to be let in, and prayed less when he was. Perhaps he felt an exorbitance in requesting the same miracle twice.

Occasionally, the king was without, even, an attendant. Rosters were more frequently shuffled at short notice, as though to nurse the king were no longer so urgent or such an honour that people would cast off their private convenience as carelessly as a rescuer his clothes before diving in; and the improvised arrangements seemed more and more subject to misunderstandings, which made them fail to overlap.

Perhaps the doctors, despairing of diagnosis, let alone cure, suffered their attention to slip. Perhaps the High Chamberlain was too old to recall it. Perhaps in the previous illnesses the queen had exercised more supervision than anyone had been able to read through the abstraction of her manner.

In one of his unaccompanied intervals the king, feeling bored, got out of bed.

Because his previous illnesses had been, if not quite feigned or induced by himself, at least consonant with his consent, the king had assumed the same was true this time. He was astounded that the weakness of his limbs was beyond his control. For a second he panicked. Then he was taken by a great fire of anger, which roared with righteous indignation against the monstrously unjustified interference, as he felt it to be, of outside circumstance in his proper relationship to, his intimate mastery over, himself.

At the same time he felt a sharp little regret that Heather was not present to see him vindicated (and to be moved to pity) by his evidently quite real and objective infirmity.

Her absence, everyone's absence, his inability to take even one step towards the door to call someone, all presented themselves as attacks, unprovoked and unmerited efforts to bear him down by draping on him a characterisation that he might choose to assume but that did not belong to him.

He tried to refuse to believe that he was unable to force one bare foot past the other. It was no longer clear to him whether he was trying merely to bring his own feet back under control of his will or whether he was trying to exert his will over the room and its furnishings, over area itself, commanding the very door to move within his reach.

The nurse who came upon him stretched upon the linoleum had to summon the help of another before she could raise him. They tucked a palm apiece beneath his armpits, soft-speaking him, as they hoisted, with the gentle loquacity, like flowing water, which Islanders addressed to frightened animals. The king could tell, from the care they took and from their cheerfulness, that they were themselves alarmed. He felt affronted that they supposed him unable to see through their pretence and irritated because, despite the ostentation of their care, they accidentally hurt his elbow, which they could not know he had chipped in his fall. He began to shiver, at the indignity of his plight, and at the same time, hardly differentiably, to tremble with rage. He died in the middle of the next morning, on the day the snow began to melt.

★   ★   ★

'I *must* make a proclamation,' the High Chamberlain said.

'Then do,' Heather replied, 'so long as it's not of me.'

She pushed past him in the corridor (a thing it was much easier these days to accomplish, thanks to some loss on his part, not really of bulk but of presence) and pursued her way up the stairs to Nanny Hausmann's suite.

There she watched the feeding of the pigeons in the slush on the window ledge and paid Nanny Hausmann for a further instalment of corn, nuts and care.

Shewing her out,

'It's dreadful about the king, dear,' Nanny Hausmann said. 'Dreadful.'

Heather looked at the row of Royal Bibles on Nanny Hausmann's shelf.

'At least you have plenty to remember him by.'

At the bottom of the stairs, in a little widening of the corridor, the High Chamberlain waited.

'Proclaim the Duchess of Coriander Bay,' Heather suggested.

'That document of yours in the Archive,' he pleaded, 'is totally unofficial. It would be in no way unconstitutional if it were simply destroyed. No one even knows it's there.'

'*I* know.'

'After the funeral,' he said. 'After the funeral you'll see it in a different light.'

Shaking her head, Heather pushed past him again.

'And yet,' he persisted, hurrying along behind her, 'we've waited more than long enough already. Don't you see? In the absence of a proclamation, the country *has* no monarch. Indeed, it's even graver than that. The country has no *status*. Is it, indeed, officially, a temporary republic? In fact, it's not even that. Not even a republic has been proclaimed. It's a nothing. An anarchy. In limbo.'

'I don't expect anyone's noticed,' Heather said comfortingly.

*   *   *

From Malmö, where the snow still held, Ulrich wrote to Heather briefly and with inhibition.

He avoided conventional condolences. They would be of no use to Heather, and he was unwilling to burden his own honour with hypocrisy.

Neither did he think it would in any way compensate Heather for the fact that he had done so if he told her at length what really filled his thoughts, namely that he felt guilty for leaving her alone with the king's death.

Yet as a matter of fact it was not so much the king's as Sempronius's death that oppressed him.

It seemed to Ulrich that it was because he was unwilling to see his father die and unwilling to occupy his place that Ulrich, as if skulking, had remained short, with the result that a lunatic in Ceremony Square had assumed, on the strength of a not wholly unrealistic logic, that it must be the taller and more conspicuous brother who was the heir to the throne.

He sealed his letter and put it aside for posting. It occurred to him that Caspar Gregorian could write a paradoxical essay establishing that many of the world's heroes—explorers and

267

adventurers praised for their courage—had in fact been driven abroad by their terror of being at home at the inevitable moment when their fathers should die.

*   *   *

On the day of the king's funeral, the gutters and gutterings of Asty gurgled with melted snow, producing an illusion that the crowds, who were in fact mostly silent, were moaning some primitive, ritualised wail.

The gendarmerie chronicled, and the journalists reported, a couple of 'incidents' in the streets, though nothing had been visible to the participants in the procession. Heather told the High Chamberlain it was unsurprising if the citizens had become restive after being expected to witness so many funerals.

It was on the following morning that anonymous voices on Radio Asty implored the population to remain calm—the first intimation it had received that there was any occasion to do otherwise.

Chapter Ten

One of the few people who noticed the absence of a proclamation was the former Chairman of the Communist Party of Evarchia.

He was, after all, an expert of sorts on the monarchy.

These days he could no longer count on minions to monitor the radio for him. On the other hand, neither had he much to do except listen to it himself. Since the king's death, he had in fact listened so assiduously that he was perhaps the only person in the country who could be quite sure of not having missed some brief announcement of some half-private ceremony.

It was during the night after the funeral, which he spent sleepless, that the ex-Chairman became convinced that there must be a hiatus in the succession.

He began instantly to plan and to long for day, whose arrival could alone make his plan practicable.

His plan, shaped by an urgent sense of duty, consisted of:— putting aside any personal pique he felt and seeking a rapprochement with his former colleagues in the Party; pointing out to them the extreme and unique ripeness of the moment; begging for the formation of a Left Front which, setting aside ideological differences, would make a united appeal to powers elsewhere to take advantage, while there was time to do so, of the opportunity.

The more he planned during the night, the hotter his feet

became inside the bed, as though he had already been walking for hours towards the office of *Red Rocket*, where, he had calculated (since another issue was overdue), he would be most likely to find the most important of his former colleagues assembled first thing in the morning.

It was in fact nearly morning before he remembered that the thaw had arrived and must have raised the temperature. He pushed off some of the bedclothes and at last fell asleep. He awoke late and only after a period of amnesia retrieved his resolve of the night. Hurrying, he failed for the first time for several days to switch on his radio and therefore failed to hear the voices inviting calm. He was making in reality the journey he had made many times in intention during the night (except that he had intended to make part of it by tram, whereas in the morning, for a reason he didn't bother to guess at, no tram came and the ex-Chairman set off on his weary feet) and was walking up the road that led to *Red Rocket* and, beyond that, the Grand Museum, at the time when the subaltern voices on the radio were ousted by a single, authoritative voice.

*　　*　　*

' . . . have become, all too understandably, confused. We have lost our national sense of identity. Where our soul once was, there is now a vacuum; and when there is a vacuum there is always the danger that extraneous forces will move in and occupy the seat of power.

'Have we not all seen great crimes committed, and no one duly punished? Indeed, we have been told to give our sympathy to the criminal, not the victim.

'Have we not seen licence, dereliction of duty, perversion flaunted in high places?

'Have we not seen the old virtues of hard work, thrift, value for money swamped in petty politicking, greedy bargaining, blackmail, bribery?

'Which of us has not seen public money poured away on the

270

pipe dreams of the shiftless?'

The deep, clear, cultivated voice would have been recognised by recent students at the Evarchian Academy of Advanced Military Studies; and indeed some of those former students had since become familiar with it and had been waiting with urgency to hear it not only on Radio Asty but, with specific and private preliminary purpose, over the telephone.

' . . . a time to issue a call to order, a time for a return to the neglected virtue of discipline.'

Ulrich, had he been in Evarchia, would not have recognised the voice, which he had never heard, but he might have remembered the figure whose image was simultaneously being transmitted on television. (Few Evarchians were watching so early in the morning. But no matter; it was all being taped so that it could be repeated frequently over the next few days.) The speaker wore the uniform of an ordinary soldier (a Grenadier, as one could tell from the flash on the upper arm) but with the insignia, on cuff and shoulder, of a major-general.

'I have been called The Silent Soldier. I am proud to be a soldier. I can no longer be silent. The time has come to speak—and to act—on behalf of our country, which has been silent and bewildered too long.'

*   *   *

When the ex-Chairman came in sight of the building where *Red Rocket* was edited, he was surprised to see the backs of a dozen people standing outside it listening to a speech.

Even before he was close enough to recognise the face, he made out from the monumental body and gestures that the speaker was Magda Lupova.

He connected the fact that Magda Lupova was a tram driver with the fact that no trams seemed to be running in Asty that morning, and began to surmise that she had called a strike at short notice. However, he could not run up a wholly

271

tenable hypothesis, because the shabby residential district near the Museum was not a practical place for assembling the tram workers and, as the tiny group of auditors shewed, was not even a sensible place to hold an improvised political meeting.

He added himself to the audience, which was listening attentively enough, but was perhaps too small to make the communal emotional response usually excited by Lupova's out-of-doors oratory.

She seemed to be advising it that this was the last chance the working class of Evarchia would have to defend itself against reaction, a policy line the ex-Chairman considered far too defensive and negative to meet the circumstances.

He recognised no Party members in the audience and no regular attendants at political meetings.

Because he did not want to ruffle his personal dislike of Lupova, which he thought it wise to keep in abeyance since he still intended to plead for a rapprochement, he listened as carelessly as he could; and because his mind was not examining the content of her words it was repeatedly snagged on one of the mannerisms of her diction. Leaving out the definite article where most Asteans would have put it in was, the ex-Chairman knew, common idiom among the Islanders. There was no just cause for annoyance when Lupova spoke of 'policy of Communist Party of Efarchia'. If she was partly Islander by blood (which the ex-Chairman had never suspected before but thought he should have done, from her large, flat, Gauguinesque face and from the sculpted quality of those postures that could be read so clearly over long distances at larger political meetings than this), then it was, he reasoned with himself, neither shame to her nor skin off his nose. This reasoning merely, however, made the mannerism doubly annoying to him, because it made it into something that convicted him of being unreasonable.

*   *   *

Even those citizens who did listen to their radios that morning were mystified.

The General's speech (or 'call to the nation' as the announcers described it at its many repetitions) went into minute and perfectly concrete detail about the type of behaviour he characterised as obstructive, flippant and time-wasting and to which he ascribed the national collapse of morale. It said nothing, however, about such yet more concrete matters as when the trams, trains and telephones would be fully working again, and it left untouched such puzzles as the fact that the gendarmerie seemed as ignorant as the laity, whereas many of their confrères, the police proper, and especially some who picked themselves out by assuming green arm bands, were in busy action, presumably to a pre-arranged plan, in co-operation with the military.

Rumour held that parties of soldiers and police had seized and were now guarding the airport, the stations, the studios and the transmitters of Radio Asty and Evarchian Television, and other installations of the kind.

Rumour was, however, circumscribed, for the most part, by the distance an individual could walk and the number of pairs of ears to which his tongue could recount his tale.

People were uncertain whether this confinement worked towards exaggeration and inflation or whether, on the contrary, it was a guarantee of exactitude, since all testimony was that of (at perhaps a few removes) an eyewitness. When news came only via one's neighbours, one might suddenly begin trying to remember where one's information had come from in normal times and trying to assess how one could judge whether it was reliable.

*   *   *

When a tank came round the corner, the ex-Chairman's immediate response was fury that Magda Lupova (who, because

273

she was facing outwards, was the first to see it) alerted her tiny audience to its presence with the words 'Look! The tank,' when, as her obvious astonishment shewed, she should have said (by which the ex-Chairman's thoughts meant that a native Astean would have said) 'Look! A tank.'

It seemed to him doubly insulting that she misused the definite article after so persistently failing to use it at all.

The little crowd's immediate response, however, was to disperse, in directions away from the approaching tank; and Magda Lupova herself was engulfed into the building where *Red Rocket* had its office.

The former Chairman of the Communist Party of Evarchia stayed where he was on the pavement, scowling towards the tank, whose slow advance was accompanied (as though it needed guarding) by an armed soldier on foot (who had perhaps been assigned the task of making hand signals to the driver to help him manoeuvre the thing round the corner without crushing the kerb or crashing into houses).

As he peered, the ex-Chairman believed he discerned, painted on the flat top of the snout of the tank, which protruded like the jaw of a hippopotamus and seemed to negotiate the street corner quite independently of the main body, a red star.

(It was in fact the universal emblem of the Evarchian army, a 'sun in glory' stylised into, virtually, an asterisk. It was red because red was the distinguishing colour of the division the tank was attached to.)

Concluding that his so often given advice had at last been taken, even without his giving it again on this occasion, the ex-Chairman called out, to the little crowd that had listened to Magda Lupova (though if he had turned to look he would have seen that virtually none of it was still within earshot or sight):

'Comrades, Comrades, they're our friends!'

He began running down the road towards the tank, making backward beckonings with his arms intended to

274

incite the supposed crowd to follow him.

The tank stopped moving, and so did the foot soldier beside it, who unslung his machine pistol and shouted to the ex-Chairman.

'Stop', which he quickly corrected to a more military:

'Halt.'

The ex-Chairman did not hear, because he was shouting himself, loudly, in the hope that the torrent of air past his running body would carry his words back to the people he believed were running close after him:

'Comrades, it's the Red Army! The Red Army has come to the rescue! Welcome to the heroic Red Army!'

As he got close to the tank, he raised his arms, with his fists clenched, in a gesture of salutation, and the foot soldier, bending at the waist and therefore looking as if he was cringing from the responsibility, shot him dead.

*   *   *

It was of course by design that the General's broadcast speech disclosed nothing of his plan.

He thought the moral matters he spoke of much more important.

In addition, he believed that the revelation of any item in the plan or even an explicit admission that there *was* a plan would result in somebody's guessing the whole plan and frustrating it.

He entertained that belief simultaneously with the belief that nobody in Evarchia retained enough moral integrity to conceive or moral authority to execute a counterplan.

And simultaneously with *that* he believed that the whole population was so earnestly desirous of moral regeneration that everybody supported his (the General's) plan—or would have done, had he disclosed that a plan existed.

What he had put into overnight execution was in fact Plan Omega, the second of his strategies and the one he had thought the less likely to be used because it hinged on an element (said to be among the talents of leadership) of luck.

It was by good fortune that the thaw and the funeral had coincided. The 'incidents' which the General had arranged should take place during the funeral had kept within the limits he had ordained and therefore did not suggest to anyone that the army should be brought to readiness. Instead, the arrival of the thaw suggested to the staff officers, as it had done annually since at the least the eighteenth century, that the time had come for the greater part of the troops under arms to move, from their marshalling points in the capital and other parts of the country, to the eastern provinces, there to set in train the field exercises that were the army's traditional salute to the spring.

As a result, those units (the majority) of whose commanders' complicity the General was not assured, were safely out of the capital and concentrated in a remote district virtually incommunicado.

Indeed, many of the troops were engaged in an exercise, designed to sharpen their initiative, of which the whole point was that they should maintain contact only with one another.

When the manoeuvres were finished, a tradition that dated back to the frivolous decades of the nineteenth century decreed that the officers who had taken part in them should immediately (just in time for the most frivolous engagements of the social season in Asty) go on leave. This year the General's plan decreed that they should return from leave reallocated to new units (ones whose loyalties were in the General's control), so that the potential for disloyalty to the General should never be concentrated at gathering points again.

For the present the General was able to deploy without impediment the troops he was sure of, together with his chief allies, the police.

Comparatively, they were few in number. In the early part of the operation, the General had repeatedly had to pull out detachments that had secured one objective and send them, tired though they were, to seize another, leaving behind a mere token, perhaps only one soldier with a firearm, as a garrison effective more through moral than through military menace.

Mentally he conjoined bluff with luck in the list of the virtues of great commanders and took a vow that, when he had achieved his plan, he would never disclose to history with what thin resources he had done it.

He had no fear that anyone else would. He could (thanks to his studies at the Military Academy) put a name to some of his brother officers who were even now stumbling through the spring drizzle in the eastern provinces unaware of momentous events or indeed of anything (except perhaps a misapprehended tincture of corrupt liberal ideas), beyond the five-mile reach of their walkie-talkies, all of whom would afterwards boast to history that they had been with him at Asty when he saved the country.

*   *   *

'They say,' the PPPA informed his Minister, 'that there's an armoured vehicle outside the Interior.'

The Department of the Interior was only three slots up the Ring Boulevard from the building of the Ministerium for Parks, Ponds, Public Monuments and Culture, though admittedly the buildings between were large and separated from each other by little strips of garden.

'They?' The Minister swooped with an air of self-congratulation. 'Who are "they"?'

'Actually and non-idiomatically,' the PPPA replied in a voice he made sound weary, 'a boy who walked past and saw it and then, when he got to us, came in for a while, in case they were intending to proceed further. I went down and interviewed him myself. I'm convinced he was speaking the truth.'

'And have they proceeded further?'

'Not yet.'

'Hm,' the Minister said.

'I thought it safe to let the boy go. Indeed, I thought it best for him to go while the going was good. I told him to go straight home and not to bother with the marrons glacés which, it appears, his father had sent him out to buy.'

'But you think they will be coming on here? The soldiers, I mean?'

'The armoured vehicle is standing facing in this direction. The boy was quite firm on that point.'

'Was he, indeed?' Turning his back on his PPPA, the Minister walked abruptly to the window and peered out, as though he could see to the Department of the Interior, which was impossible, because the Ring Boulevard was curved.

No less abruptly, the Minister faced about, grinned and flung out one of his challenges:

'And what shall you do when they arrive here?'

The PPPA decided that if there was to be a new régime, of a nature he could not yet guess, he might as well make it the occasion to refuse the Minister's challenges once and for all. 'I shall ask my Minister what he advises,' he said.

*　　*　　*

'EX-CHAIRMAN OF C.P. SH'—, the editor of *Red Rocket* typed, and was interrupted, from behind, by the Chairman.

'Not "Ex-Chairman". Chairman.'

'But he had resigned.'

'No one knows that.'

'You wouldn't let me announce it. Now I'll have to get it in, which will be awkward, along with the report of his death.'

'I told you to hold it in reserve until it could be useful to us. And now it is. You can announce at the end of the piece that I am the new Chairman. Our previous Chairman forfeited his office in the most heroic and useful way conceivable, leading members of the Evarchian working class against the armed might of the oppressor.'

278

*   *   *

With so few troops to perform such extensive deeds, the General had had to create a very centralised structure of command, with swift and efficient communications to transmit his orders.

Early in the operation, he linked his own radio communication network to the civilian telephones, which he had taken over, an act that economically procured the two advantages of making his communications more flexible and preventing the relaying of information (or appeals for help against him) through (or out of) Evarchia.

It was by his own plan that all questions of even moderate moment were put immediately to him. Yet it aroused in him a sense of injury, as he sat in the armoured caravan that served him for mobile command post, that, though there were men willing to jump to their feet and move the token flags and counters about on his tabled relief map, all the decisions about when and where they should be moved had to come from him.

Lack of sleep began to smooth out the texture of his consciousness, so that he seemed to travel through all experiences at a uniform, slightly slowed tempo. Slightly slowly, he felt surprise that one man could do so many things. That one man had to do so he received, without surprise, as evidence of the spinelessness that had tainted his compatriots.

He drafted the very wording of the curfew notices that were posted up round the city, pleased, as he did so, that the result, if only temporarily, would be to close down the pornographic cinemas and sexy nightclubs, thereby incidentally minimising the chances that his soldiers would be infected with syphilis.

Personally (on the telephone) he assured a banker that trading on the exchanges would be permitted again as soon as stability (plus, in consequence, favourable exchange rates) was secure.

Personally he instructed the editor of *The Times of Asty*

279

that the coup had been 'bloodless'. He confirmed the rumour the editor had heard that a man had been shot near the Grand Museum, but 'I've had a very full report, and it was a case of mistaken identity. The mistake was not on our part.'

He wrote in his own hand the decree dissolving the constitutional unity of the Islands and the mainland. In a broadcast he explained that this merely granted the independence the Islands had long wanted, that the mainland was not in an economic position to subsidise the Islands further, and that Islanders who had jobs on the mainland should apply to the military authorities for permits to allow them to remain there.

He found making broadcasts more tiring than he had expected it to be, and could not analyse why it should be so since it required almost no physical activity.

Almost as an afterthought he ordered one element of his forces, although it was already depleted by having left watchmen at the central post office, to take control of Parliament and tell it it was suspended indefinitely.

*   *   *

The armoured vehicle still did not proceed to the Ministerium for Parks, Ponds, Public Monuments and Culture.

The Permanent Personal Private Assistant therefore went to it.

He walked round the gentle curve of Ring Boulevard feeling very frightened. But he preferred to induce whatever impended rather than wait for it suffering long-drawn fright, fright being, after all, a form of pain.

Outside the Department of the Interior he found the vehicle parked, just as the marrons-glacés seeker had described. But he was nonplussed because no human beings were in sight.

The Department of the Interior, usually much frequented, stood silent behind its front door.

The Ring Boulevard, so far as the PPPA could see in each

direction, was deserted—which seemed to be the usual condition of most parts of Asty since the coup.

Timidly the PPPA rattled with his knuckles against the shuttered armoured side of the vehicle and tried to judge from the noise whether it was empty.

The fact that there was so little coming and going in Asty set the PPPA to wonder on what occasions people had, before the coup, come and gone so much. He was disconcerted that he could supply no generalised answer and not many particular ones.

Eventually the door of the Department of the Interior opened. A short common soldier with an Islander look came out and asked the PPPA cheerfully if there was anything he wanted.

'When are you going to get to my Ministerium?' the PPPA said. 'It's only three doors on from here.'

'Give us time,' the soldier, a Grenadier, replied roundly. 'Rome wasn't built in a day. We've got a big job on, controlling corruption, forestalling subversion. We have to have priorities, you realise.'

'Yes, of course,' the PPPA said. 'So long as you will be coming, some time.'

The Grenadier grinned. 'What Ministerium is it, then?'

'Parks, Ponds, Public Monuments and Culture.'

'I'll see what I can do about it.' The Grenadier began to return to the building he had come from.

The PPPA called after him as he mounted the steps:

'It's quite an important Ministerium.'

The Grenadier waved, without looking back.

*   *   *

Summoned to what had been the central offices of the trade union movement but was now, as a green strip hung from its upper storey said, 'Temporary HQ, National Military Government,' Caspar Gregorian set out from his home in the

281

Winter Palace precinct on foot (some trams were now running, but they were sparse) and wondered, in the course of his journey, whether he would have to seek refuge in a café or on a park bench to calm the trembling of his legs.

His terror was provoked only, he realised, by the extreme of what confronted every modern writer, under every régime. He had always known that such an ordeal might be a natural item in his destiny and had always known that he would respond with terror.

He had decided not to tell his wife, who was out when it arrived, of the summons.

He now thought that had been the wrong decision. His sharp, immediate fear for himself sounded inside his soul against an accompaniment of the more diffused agony of uncertainty, which he compulsively and repetitively imagined, that his wife must suffer when he merely and without explanation failed to come home and the cat, to whom one could not explain even that the thing was inexplicable, waited for him at the door . . .

He comforted himself by a plan for instant surrender, though he feared that a surrender offered before resistance had been tested would be simply disbelieved and would be tested the more.

He told himself it would be only a heightened, dramatised version of familiar experience: of, for instance, the vulnerability, nakedness, indecent complicity and humiliation that one felt on being examined by the doctor—to whom also one had tacitly to confess that one could not endure being hurt.

*   *   *

Red Rocket's account of the ex-Chairman's death was typed but never reached the printer, let alone distribution.

Two men wearing on the sleeves of their civilian coats green armbands that perhaps negated the civilianness climbed the

282

shabby stairs in the stuccoed house near the Grand Museum, confiscated typescripts, typewriter and files and arrested everyone they found in the flat that served as an office.

The editor protested that there was no law in Evarchia against the publication of political views.

'There is now,' one of the arm-banded men replied, while the other simultaneously said:

'There'd be no laws at all if you had your way.'

★ ★ ★

At a personal interview, conducted face to face and knee to lap in his mobile command post (which was now almost permanently parked in the grounds of the some time trade union offices), the General made arrangements for the Cardinal-Patriarch to conduct in Asty Cathedral, 'a service of national re-dedication.'

★ ★ ★

Outside the stuccoed house, the prisoners were handed over to soldiers, who had brought a windowless van in which they drove them away.

The two quasi-civilians watched from the steps.

'It's typical of the inefficiency with which this country was being run that we hadn't got this address on our files. We had to ask for it from the CIA.'

His companion grunted, contemplated the empty street for a moment and then went back to the top step and made sure the front door was shut. He disliked not only subversives but untidiness and burglars too.

★ ★ ★

The General was pretty sure that there were now decisions taken, certainly by policemen and probably by bankers, on

283

which he was not consulted.

Contradictorily, he felt as a result not less but more ill used than at the time when all decisions had been presented to him for taking.

One of the things he believed he had to endure, but endured with resentment, was his near-certainty that he benefited from decisions taken elsewhere. The very secrecy of them contributed to a certain clandestine cowedness in the population. That in turn compensated for a disadvantage in the General's very luck. He was proud of the bloodlessness of the coup, but he was also aware that had he had to act on Plan Alpha instead of Omega, there would have been fighting, and his enemies, having suffered casualties, would have been the more pressingly afraid.

He did not follow in detail, no doubt because its expression was deliberately opaque, the reasoning in the memorandum that accompanied it, but he contentedly signed the document someone had on his own initiative drawn up and presented for signature, declaring that the former Cultural Attaché from Bulgaria was no longer persona grata.

An enemy excluded was not, the General knew, the less virulent, but the danger from him was a little distanced, in time as well as place.

At home, the General calculated, where dangers were immediate, it was necessary to increase the fear in which he was held.

Yet even as he planned methods of increasing it, his motive, as he believed, for doing so consisted in a permanent image of himself as endangered, impugned, betrayed, imposed on, exhausted by the demands on his strength, talents and patience: a victim.

It was with the sweet sigh of a martyr that the General raised wearied eyes to Caspar Gregorian, who was ushered stumbling, all but collapsed, up the three awkward metal steps that led to the mobile armoured caravan.

Surprised that his interrogation was to be by the General

himself, Gregorian was yet more surprised by the first question:

'Do you like *Il Trovatore?*'

There was a gap before Gregorian could find voice enough to reply, tremolo:

'No.'

'I consider it about the only reasonable opera that exists,' the General said, his tone accusing Gregorian of wounding him by disagreeing with his taste. 'I want it put on in Asty.'

Gregorian could think of no answer to make, since it would plainly be impolite to question how *Il Trovatore* could be called 'reasonable'.

'I suppose I'll have to deal with that aspect myself,' the General said. 'I was asking too much in expecting a man of letters to be knowledgeable about opera. But it isn't only opera I'm concerned with. Of course, the Royal Opera is the most conspicuous instance. These perpetual strikes, perpetual schedules not kept, programmes not fulfilled . . . We must be a laughing-stock throughout Europe. But in fact there is a scarcely lesser degeneration in our national cultural life as a whole. We need a cultural renaissance. I'm thinking in terms of a discriminating eye, a firm control . . . We need to be firm about what gets into print, what gets exhibited in our galleries and museums, what facets of our national culture we display for outsiders to judge us by . . .'

The General paused.

Gregorian shifted a little.

'A director of national culture,' the General said abruptly, 'I need one. Do you want the job?'

'No,' Gregorian replied and immediately added: 'I suppose it would have been prudent to ask first what the penalties are for refusing.'

'I shouldn't think there are any, unless you do something silly,' the General said, his thoughts obviously moving already to some other task or appointment ahead. 'I'll let you leave the country, if you like.'

285

'I can't. I'm a writer. I'd lose my language.'

'There must be translators, surely? There must be people in other countries who understand Evarchian? If not, it's a national disgrace. I'd better see about Evarchian studies abroad . . .'

'I meant I'd lose touch with my language, my idiom.'

'I don't care much for idiomatic writing, personally,' the General said. 'A lot of modern writers don't bother to express themselves in proper terms. They use slang and all sorts of things. In print. Do you live in Asty?'

'Yes. In the Winter Palace.'

'O yes, the Winter Palace,' the General said, evidently reminded of something. 'I don't think a writer ought to live in town. I daresay that's what makes so many modern writers use slang. If I were a writer, I'd want to be inspired by Nature. I'd live somewhere quiet and clean.'

When he had negotiated the caravan steps going down, Gregorian found his legs still trembling; his knees seemed crazy now with relief and a bodily manifestation of either indignation or laughter.

Inside the caravan, the General made notes to remind himself of two further tasks. One note consisted of 'Winter Palace'. The other read:

Organise R Opera military-style.
Fatigue parties to shift scenery?
Chorus (non-singing): soldiers?
Trov. (Shd be permanently in repertoire.)

He had a telephone call put through to Karyl Frumgeour, whom he invited to become director of national culture. Frumgeour accepted.

*　　　*　　　*

At last the armoured caravan drove across Ceremony Square

286

and into the forecourt, whose gates hastened to open to it, of the Winter Palace.

The caravan stopped in the forecourt but remained closed.

A little snow fell. As the sun continued to shine in a bright sky, many people in Asty mistook the snow for petals blown from cherry trees, though as a matter of fact few trees of any kind were yet in blossom.

The snowflakes melted as soon as they touched the ground. The fall stopped after a few minutes leaving the pavements glistening rather than wet.

The General got out of the caravan and entered the Winter Palace.

Heather received him alone, in the room her father had used as his study.

She had turned aside Missy Six's strong attempt to insist on being present, and likewise an attempt by the High Chamberlain which, Heather suspected, had a different motive, namely his wish to meet the General.

'There are psychological advantages,' the General said, 'in having a monarch who's a woman. I won't pretend you are the woman I would have picked for the part. However, I daresay if we work at it . . .'

'Do you mean,' Heather asked, 'you have a programme in mind for me?'

'Yes.' He was at first surprised she should have penetrated his intention. Then he realised that everybody must by now have noticed that he had a programme for everything.

'Before you waste time describing how you want me improved,' Heather said. 'I must tell you I am not the monarch. Like my brother, I renounced the succession months ago.'

'In that case,' the General began, giving a shrug that he broke off to ask sharply:

'If you're not, who *is*?'

'I'm not sure. You'd have to ask the High Chamberlain or a constitutional expert. Quite probably the Duchess of

Coriander Bay is.'

'She's not suitable,' the General said. 'We'd be better off with a republic.'

'Is it beyond even you to devise a programme for her?'

'If you've no claim to the throne, you've no claim to this Palace.'

'None.'

'The Airport is open again.'

'I've had my things packed for days.'

As Heather's suitcases, together with Missy Six's, were loaded into a car at a side door, the gravel of the forecourt smelled fresh from the snow, reminding the nose of the blossom that was not yet open, and the General summoned his entourage, through the main entrance, into the Palace.

Briskly he explained to them that he had only once before visited the interior of the Winter Palace (for an investiture), though army service had made him acquainted with the guarding of its perimeter. They took this latter to be a reference to the still secret but already legendary period when he, though the holder of a high rank, had chosen to serve as a common soldier—an act which no doubt had practical justification, as he prepared his plans, but which now seemed the numinous, voluntary, preliminary ordeal of a hero.

Briskly he led the little posse of uniformed men on an informal march through the rooms, while he assessed the suitability of the Winter Palace to take the place permanently of the temporary headquarters of the National Military Government.

He judged its furnishing shabby, though grand in design, and impractical for his purposes, since it seemed shaped to a sedentary (and therefore, he pronounced, unhealthy) way of life.

He peered from an upper window, which he remarked had not been cleaned recently, into an internal courtyard. He pointed out to his entourage that the drainpipes were old and very likely for that reason unhygienic.

288

The more perceptive of the officers with him added the instance to the mental dossier they had begun to keep on his preoccupation, evident both in practical life and in his political metaphors, with infection, as though he were a beleaguered city that must inevitably expect an outbreak of plague.

He marched on and, in a corridor, suddenly halted and opened a window—to freshen, the officers assumed, the air in the Palace.

A cloud of pigeons rose, startled and creaking, from the surrounding ledges and sills.

Their suddenness gave him a fright.

He thrust the window shut against such notoriously infested carriers of disease.

'Have them shot,' he ordered the officers.

Chapter Eleven

For some time after take-off Heather was silent. Missy Six, conscious that Heather was leaving native land and language, could think of no consolation to offer.

'Ironic that we all always *wanted* it to be a republic,' Heather presently said. 'Being royal must have misled us into thinking more about the form than the politics. I suppose it's cowardly of me to be getting out.'

Missy Six denied it. 'Anyway you hadn't much choice.'

'Many people have no choice about staying.'

In the end, it was Heather who tried to console them both. She ordered ('No, save your money,' Missy Six whispered, to which Heather replied aloud 'I haven't enough to save') a half-bottle of champagne. The air hostess replied that she could supply it only in fifths of a bottle. 'How peculiar,' Heather said. 'Do the English always drink it in fifths?' 'No,' Missy Six said.

The hostess poured the contents of two stunted bottles into plastic glasses.

The liquid tasted dull and yet fizzed more than it should, like, Missy Six thought, the animation of the hostess's manner.

'I never,' Heather told Missy Six, 'let myself be beguiled by the attractiveness of air hostesses. They are invariably heterosexual.'

*　　　*　　　*

At Gatwick, a manner no less artificially animated but more hurried shewed them into a little oatmeal-coloured room and begged them to wait there for the man from the Foreign Office, who had telephoned his apologies for being delayed in the traffic.

Eventually he came scrambling in, tall, a not quite middle-aged boy, and ran up to Missy Six.

'I must apologise, your Majesty. I was unavoidably delayed.'

By a slight inclination and twist of the upper part of her body, Missy Six passed him on to Heather.

'O Lord,' he said. 'What a boner. Irretrievable. Of course, *you're* her Majesty. Of *course.*'

Missy Six deduced he had been furnished with a description of Heather.

'There's no need to call me "Majesty",' Heather said. 'I'm not queen.'

'In cases like this,' he replied, '—shouldn't we all sit down?—in cases like this, we fully countenance the use of the title, though purely, of course, as a matter of courtesy. It implies no recognition, de facto or de jure, of the status quo ante, on the part of HMG. I am instructed, by the way—let me get this in right at the start, so there's no misunderstanding—that no recognition nor any other help, even on a personal basis, is to be expected from our own royals, either.'

'You don't understand,' Heather said. 'I never was queen Not even in the status quo ante.'

'Really?'

'Really. I resigned the job before it was offered.'

'You mean you're not prosecuting your claim to the throne?'

'I have no claim to prosecute.'

'O,' he said. 'Well, this puts matters in a very different light. I think, in that case, none of my instructions apply to

291

you.'

'No.'

'Whom, then, *do* they apply to?'

'It's a tricky question,' Heather said. 'There is an elderly lady who has a claim, by descent, to be queen of the Islands. But the General has dissolved the union between the Islands and Evarchia. If the dissolution is constitutionally valid, then her claim, even if it were established, would presumably be only to the monarchy of the Islands, not to the whole of the kingdom and empire.'

The man from the Foreign Office made his eyes wander round the little room, in order to demonstrate to his interlocutors that his mind could not focus on such minute and local particulars as Heather was speaking of.

When she finished, he said:

'Still. You're quite clear, at least, that it isn't *you?*'

'Quite clear.'

'Well, then,' he said, and stood up.

Heather gave him her hand.

Yet he seemed to feel, in a surplus, perhaps, of unused energy or charity, that it would be churlish of him to walk abruptly out leaving them in a little room at Gatwick.

He stood, awkwardly tall, in the middle of the room, the edge of a coffee table encroaching on his calves.

'How are you provided? For money, I mean?'

'Wretchedly,' Heather said. 'I shall have to take a job.'

'What did you have in mind?'

'What can I do? I could teach Evarchian, I suppose.'

'I'm afraid the demand is small. And over-filled already, by compatriots of yours who got out from the new régime before you did.'

'Then perhaps, after I have seen England, I shall join my brother in Sweden, though I speak no Swedish.'

'I think that would be much the wisest course,' he said, ridding himself happily of the responsibility, 'much the wisest. I'm told it's not a difficult language to pick up.'

292

'No doubt.'

'Look,' he said cheerfully, seeming to feel another access of energy to spare since so unexpectedly little had been required of him, 'have you somewhere to stay tonight? Why don't I phone through and book you into an hotel? In London? Not too expensive. I can't drive you myself, I have another engagement, but I could at least lay on a car . . .'

*   *   *

In the back of the car, Heather said:

'There is a red bus with two decks. How moved my mother would have been to see it.'

*   *   *

Missy Six felt a strange burstingness, as though she had eaten too much, which she could attribute only to a violence of emotion in herself and a lack of the means to express it.

Hoping, perhaps, that Heather would read a little of it expressing itself surreptitiously in the form of solicitude, she accompanied Heather upstairs ('It seems quite a nice hotel,' Heather said loudly in the lift, 'and modern. As I have stayed before only in tumbledown places and castles, my standards may be awry') and into her bedroom.

'A television,' Heather remarked. 'It will be nice to see a screen not filled by that fascist General.'

Missy Six rejected, as too menial or too intimate, the idea of unpacking for Heather.

Besides there seemed no point; Heather would have all evening to do it in.

Instead, since it was already growing dark, Missy Six drew the curtains.

The dark seemed to summon her home. Yet again there was no point to hurry towards, no timed train to catch. Missy Six had merely to take the tube to her family's house.

293

Heather, too, evidently felt an awkwardness. She heaved one of her suitcases off the luggage stand and dropped it, heavily, short of the bed.

Missy Six picked it up.

Heather unfastened it and pulled out a hank of clothing.

'I shall take a bath and dress for dinner. I hope you will have a drink with me before you go home? I noticed there is a bar downstairs. Missy Five used to end her "typical day in London": "I dress for dinner".'

'I don't think you need to dress,' Missy Six said.

'I remember. You said Missy Five got everything wrong.' Heather went into the bathroom.

What Missy Six would have liked to be able to express was her own conviction that in Heather's personality there lay, probably unperceived by Heather herself, some just cause for hope. Missy Six took Heather to be in some sense a talisman, of more than personal extension. The very elements in her personality that people most condemned were, Missy Six believed, the sources of a vitality that should surmount both guilt and nostalgia.

Missy Six might have expressed her feeling through an embrace had it not been that she and Heather had once embraced as lovers.

Even drawing the curtains and touching the bed as she put the suitcase on it reminded her of making preparations to make love.

Zipping Heather into her appalling evening dress, Missy Six took care not to touch the flesh (which was giving off warmth and a smell of talcum powder) of the back she had once caressed.

The bar was dark with the tinted dimness of fashionable sunglasses, and its noiseless carpet seemed to warn everyone (except Heather) against speaking too loudly.

'No thank you,' Missy Six said. 'I don't really like Scotch.'

'I feel embarrassed to be speaking English to strangers,' Heather said after ordering. 'My Family always made it seem

294

a sacred language.'

'Yes,' Missy Six said, deciding it would be unfitting for her, since she was English, to assert that it was indeed a sacred language and reflecting that it was the Royal concept of its sacredness that had taken her to Evarchia.

'Another?'

'No, I must go.' Missy Six rose, aware of no reason why she *must*, still unexpressed, go at this moment rather than the next, but realising she must pick on *a* moment.

'I shall have another Scotch,' Heather said.

Missy Six considered that Heather was already, probably thanks to emotion and fatigue, a little blunted by drink.

She promised to telephone Heather the next day.

Taking her second Scotch with her, Heather lurchingly accompanied Missy Six to the door of the bar, where Missy Six spoke a quick, inhibited farewell.

Missy Six took a few steps into the foyer, paused and turned round. She saw that Heather, at the entrance to the bar, had bumped her glass into somebody and had spilled drink onto a blouse she was now clumsily brushing at with one of her heavy hands.

With the other Heather gave a little wave, over the stooped head of her victim.

Missy Six returned the wave, laughing invisibly because, she now noticed, the owner of the dampened blouse was attractive and unaccompanied. Heather's apology was not stopping at what politeness exacted and was probably, Missy Six surmised, even now including an invitation to dine.

Missy Six collected her own suitcases from a counter in the foyer and left the hotel, feeling (among other things) happy. In her parting vision, Heather, huge as a pigeon puffed up to woo, had been chesting the unknown woman back towards the bar; and in the lineaments of Heather's massive (and, Missy Six trusted, irresistible) wooing, Missy Six's memory traced the more svelte image of the unfinished love between Missy Six and Sempronius.

BRIGID BROPHY

Brigid Brophy is a Londoner of Irish descent. She is a vegetarian, and a campaigner for the rights of other-than-human animals, as well as for the rights of writers. In the latter capacity she is a member of the Executive of the Writers' Guild of Great Britain and, with her fellow-writer Maureen Duffy, organizes the campaign for British PLR (Public Lending Right). She is married to Michael Levey, writer, art historian and Director of the National Gallery, and they have a grown-up daughter.